PRAISE FOR JAMES PATTERSON'S ALEX CROSS THRILLERS

CROSS JUSTICE

"AN AMAZING BOOK, FULL OF MYSTERIES, TWISTS AND TURNS, AND FLAT-OUT JAW-DROPPING REVELATIONS...Even if you have never read any books in this series, you need to sink your teeth into *CROSS JUSTICE* now."　—BookReporter.com

HOPE TO DIE

"ACTION APLENTY SENDS ALEX CROSS ON TO THE FINISH, AND JAMES PATTERSON HAS DONE IT AGAIN WITH HIS FANTASTIC STORYTELLING GIFTS. Readers will note that this is very close in action and eeriness to some of the best of the best in the series including *Along Came a Spider* and *Kiss the Girls*."　—*Suspense Magazine*

"*HOPE TO DIE* IS FULL OF SURPRISING REVELATIONS, TWISTS AND TURNS, AS WELL AS HEART-STOPPING SUSPENSE AND SHARP-EDGED VIOLENCE. There is something for nearly everyone here. Those who haven't picked up an Alex Cross book for a while by all means should read *Cross My Heart* and *HOPE TO DIE*, both of which demonstrate that Patterson, notwithstanding his prolific ways, retains the ability to surprise, excite and scare the heck out of you."
　—BookReporter.com

CROSS MY HEART

"Twenty years ago, I wrote, '*Along Came a Spider* is the best thriller I've come across in many a year. It deserves to be this season's #1 bestseller and should instantly make James Patterson a household name.' A household name, indeed. CONGRATULATIONS, JIM, ON TWENTY YEARS OF ALEX CROSS AND ON *CROSS MY HEART*, WHICH I AM LOVING. YOU THE MAN."
—Nelson DeMille

"TWENTY YEARS AFTER THE FIRST ALEX CROSS STORY, HE HAS BECOME ONE OF THE GREATEST FICTIONAL DETECTIVES OF ALL TIME, A CHARACTER FOR THE AGES. *CROSS MY HEART* has got to be the most terrifying and shocking Cross thriller to date, full of unexpected twists, savage turns, and electrifying suspense. This is the page-turner to end all page-turners." —*Douglas Preston & Lincoln Child*

"PATTERSON HAS NEVER SHIED AWAY FROM MAKING DRAMATIC CHANGES IN CROSS'S LIFE, AND FOR THIS TWENTIETH ANNIVERSARY BOOK, HE PULLS OUT ALL THE STOPS EVEN MORE SO THAN USUAL."
—BookReporter.com

"*CROSS MY HEART* IS ONE OF THE BEST BOOKS OF THE SERIES BECAUSE IT IS NAIL-BITING SUSPENSE WITH A SURPRISE TWIST OF AN ENDING…will leave readers wanting more."
—WestOrlandoNews.com

MERRY CHRISTMAS, ALEX CROSS

"*MERRY CHRISTMAS, ALEX CROSS* MAY HAVE A HOLIDAY BACKDROP, BUT IT IS A THRILLER NOVEL FOR ALL SEASONS…ONE OF PATTERSON'S BEST BOOKS TO DATE." —BookReporter.com

"FANS WILL BE ENTHRALLED."
—BookLoons.com

"JAM-PACKED WITH ACTION…WE SEE ALEX BEING PULLED IN ALL DIRECTIONS."
—AlwayswithaBook.blogspot.com

"HIS BRUTAL DESCRIPTION IS SPOT ON AND I CAN HONESTLY SAY HE REALLY MOVED ME IN ONE SCENE…A GREAT ADDITION TO THE SERIES."
—RitualoftheStones.blogspot.com

ALEX CROSS, RUN

"THE MAN IS A MASTER OF THE THRILLER. HE KNOWS HOW TO SELL, WRITE SUSPENSE, AND PLOT HIS TALES WITH PRECISION…*ALEX CROSS, RUN* IS PATTERSON AT THE TOP OF HIS GAME…A HELL OF A READ BY A MASTER STORYTELLER."
—Breitbart.com

"A SHOCKER…PATTERSON SHOWS NO SIGN OF SLOWING DOWN AND GIVES EVERY INDICATION THAT HE HAS NOWHERE NEAR EXHAUSTED HIS SUPPLY OF IDEAS OR, MORE IMPORTANT, UNFORGETTABLE CHARACTERS."
—BookReporter.com

"ENTERTAINING AND EASY TO READ."
—ReadersRefuge.blogspot.com

KILL ALEX CROSS

"A THRILLER WITH FAMILY AT ITS HEART… IT'S PATTERSON AT THE TOP OF HIS GAME."
—Lisa Scottoline, *Washington Post*

"A ROLLER COASTER…CLASSIC PATTERSON."
—*Washington Times*

"NON-STOP ACTION...EXCITING...The ending is a typically great, surprising Patterson ending that you'll want to read more than once to make sure you really got it." —AlwayswithaBook.blogspot.com

"PATTERSON'S NARRATIVE STYLE PROPELS READERS THROUGH THE BOOK LIKE A LOCOMOTIVE THROUGH TISSUE PAPER... PATTERSON SHOWS NO SIGNS OF SLOWING DOWN ON ANY FRONT." —BookReporter.com

CROSS FIRE

"FAST-PACED...THE TWISTS AND TURNS WILL KEEP YOU GUESSING WHAT WILL HAPPEN NEXT AND YOU'LL NEVER BELIEVE HOW IT ALL ENDS...another great and addicting tale of murder and mayhem—Alex Cross style! I was hard-pressed to put it down!" —BibliophilicBookBlog.com

"YOU DON'T WANT TO MISS THIS LIFE-CHANGING BOOK...WILL LEAVE YOU TURNING PAGE AFTER PAGE WITH ENDLESS SUSPENSE." —BeyondtheBookshelf.com

I, ALEX CROSS

"THE STAKES ARE HIGHER THAN EVER BEFORE...MORE THAN A CRIME THRILLER, IT'S AN ABSORBING FAMILY DRAMA." —NightsandWeekends.com

"A RAW, ENGROSSING THRILLER THAT WILL KEEP YOU CHURNING PAGES LONG INTO THE NIGHT." —FictionAddict.com

ALEX CROSS'S TRIAL

CROSS COUNTRY

DOUBLE CROSS

"AS WITH THE BEST OF PATTERSON'S WORK, IT IS IMPOSSIBLE TO STOP READING THIS BOOK ONCE STARTED."   —BookReporter.com

THE BIG BAD WOLF

"THE BIGGEST, BADDEST ALEX CROSS NOVEL IN YEARS."   —*Library Journal*

"VASTLY ENTERTAINING...THE FINEST CROSS IN YEARS."   —*Publishers Weekly* (starred review)

"POWERFUL...YOUR HEART WILL RACE."
         —*Orlando Sentinel*

FOUR BLIND MICE

"THE PACE IS RAPID...ACTION-PACKED."
         —*People*

"CHILLING."   —*New York Times*

"BRISK...SATISFYING."   —*San Francisco Chronicle*

VIOLETS ARE BLUE

"PARTICULARLY JUICY...ENJOYABLY SPOOKY... BOTTOM LINE: BLOODY GOOD CREEPFEST."
         —*People*

"AS ADDICTIVE AS ALL OF PATTERSON'S BOOKS...YOU HAVE NO CHOICE: YOU MUST READ IT."   —*Denver Rocky Mountain News*

ROSES ARE RED

"THRILLING...SWIFT...A PAGE-TURNER."
         —*People*

CROSS JUSTICE

JAMES PATTERSON

VISION

NEW YORK BOSTON

Copyright © 2015 by James Patterson
Cover design by Mario Pulice
Cover copyright © 2016 by Hachette Book Group, Inc.

Vision
Hachette Book Group
1290 Avenue of the Americas
New York, NY 10104
grandcentralpublishing.com
twitter.com/grandcentralpub

Originally published in hardcover by Hachette Book Group

ALEX CROSS is a trademark of JBP Business, LLC.

Vision is an imprint of Grand Central Publishing.
The Vision name and logo are trademarks of Hachette Book Group, Inc.

The Hachette Speakers Bureau provides a wide range of authors for speaking events. To find out more, go to www.hachettespeakersbureau.com or call (866) 376-6591.

The publisher is not responsible for websites (or their content) that are not owned by the publisher.

First international mass market edition: February 2016
First oversize mass market edition: September 2016

ISBN: 978-1-4555-8513-7 (oversize mm)

Printed in the United States of America

10 9 8 7 6 5 4 3 2 1
OPM

PROLOGUE

I FEEL PRETTY...

One

LEAVING THE BODY SUBMERGED in the bathtub, Coco entered the enormous walk-in closet wearing black silk panties, elbow-length black gloves, and nothing else. Trained eyes flickered past the casual wear, all fine clothing, to be sure, but not what Coco desired.

Couture gowns. Sleek evening wear. The drama and seductiveness of elegant pieces pulled Coco like a magnet draws iron. Expert eyes and clever gloved fingers examined a mouse-gray, off-the-shoulder dress by Christian Dior and then a white Gucci gown with a plunging back.

Coco thought the designs were brilliant, but the workmanship was not as precise, the execution not as taut, as one would expect for dresses with price tags of ten thousand dollars and up. Even at the high end of luxury, the craft of dressmaking was suffering these days, the old skills all but forgotten. A pity. A shame. An outrage, as Coco's long-departed mother would have said.

Still, both dresses went into a garment bag for future use.

Coco pushed more gowns aside, looking for the one dress that jumped out, the one that stirred deep emotion, the one that made you say, "Ahhh, yes. That's my dream. My fantasy. That's who I'll be tonight!"

A cocktail dress by Elie Saab finally ended the search. Size 6. Perfect. Deep indigo, silk, sleeveless, with a plunging neckline and a diamond cutout in the back, it was spectacularly retro—late fifties, early sixties, right out of wardrobe for *Mad Men*.

Calling Mr. Draper; you may drool now.

Coco giggled, but there was nothing funny about this dress. It was a frock of legend, the kind that could silence all conversation in a three-star Michelin restaurant or a ballroom packed with the rich, the powerful, and the celebrated, the rare type of dress that seemed to have its own gravitational field and was able to draw lust from every male and envy from every woman within a hundred yards.

Coco pulled it off the rack, went to the full-length mirrors at the far end of the walk-in closet, and paused there for a bit of self-appraisal. Tall, lean, with a cover girl's face and a dancer's regal stance, Coco noted the oval hazel eyes and the flawless skin. Add to that the barest suggestion of breasts and the slim boyish hips, and if the world weren't so cruel, this sultry creature would have been the toast of runways from Paris to Milan.

Coco stared for a moment in frustration at the only thing that had blocked a dream life as a glamorous supermodel. Despite the tape strapped beneath the black panties, there was still little doubt that Coco was a man.

Two

CAREFUL NOT TO SMUDGE his makeup, Coco tugged the Elie Saab over his smooth, bald head and feminine shoulders, praying that the flow of the dress would hide any outward evidence of his masculinity.

His prayers were answered. When Coco smoothed the fabric so it clung to his hips and upper thighs, even with the bald head, he was, to all appearances, a stunning woman.

Coco found sheer black thigh-high stockings and slid them on carefully, sensually, before proceeding to the racks of shoes by the mirrors. He stopped counting at two hundred pairs.

What was Lisa, the reincarnation of Imelda Marcos?

He laughed and chose a pair of black stiletto heels by Sergio Rossi. The fit in the closed toe was a bit tight, but a girl had to do what a girl had to do when it came to fashion.

After tightening the gladiator straps and getting his balance, Coco exited the walk-in closet and entered the gigantic master suite. He ignored the exquisite decor and went straight to a large jewelry box on the vanity.

After rejecting several items, he found a set of Tahitian pearl earrings and a matching necklace from Cartier that complemented but in no way overpowered the dress. As his mother used to say: *Know your focus, then accessorize around it.*

He put the pearls on and picked up the Fendi shopping bag he'd set down by the vanity earlier. He pushed aside tissue paper, ignoring the folded polo shirt, the jeans, and the docksiders, and drew out an oval box.

Coco removed the lid, revealing a wig. It was more than fifty years old but had been maintained in flawless condition. The hair was lush, human, and not dyed, an ash shade of blond. Every strand retained its natural shine, bounce, and texture.

He sat down at the vanity, reached back into the shopping bag, and found a short strip of rug tape. With scissors from the vanity drawer, he snipped the tape into four pieces, each about an inch long. His teeth tugged off one of the long black gloves.

He stripped off the backing of each piece of tape and dropped the papers into the Fendi bag. Then he fixed the pieces of tape to his scalp, one at the crown, another three inches forward of center, and one above each ear.

After putting the glove back on, Coco removed the wig from the box, looked in the mirror, and eased it onto his head and into position on the tape, just so. He sighed with pleasure.

To Coco's eye, the wig looked every bit as dramatic as it had the first time he'd seen it, decades before. It had been styled by a master in Paris who had parted the hair down the middle, cut the back high, and then tapered the length so the forward locks on both sides were longest. The hair framed Coco's face in a teardrop that ended just below the jawline and just above the pearl necklace.

Highly pleased with his ensemble, Coco touched up his lipstick and smiled seductively at the woman staring back at him.

"You are gorgeous tonight, my dear," he said, delighted. "A work of art."

With a wink at his reflection, Coco stood up from the vanity and started to sing. "'I feel pretty, oh so pretty. I feel pretty and witty and...'"

As he sang, his practiced eye returned to the jewelry box, and he plucked out several promising pieces that featured large emeralds. He put them in the Fendi bag and returned to the closet. There he pushed aside a rack of men's starched shirts to reveal a safe with a digital keypad.

Coco typed in the code from memory and opened the safe, happy to find ten four-inch stacks of fifty-dollar bills. He loaded them all into the Fendi bag and closed the safe, then he stuffed the bag and its contents into the bottom of the garment bag, zipped it up, and tossed it over his shoulder.

On the way out of the closet, Coco picked up a set of keys. He spotted a geometric, black-and-gold Badgley Mischka Alba clutch purse and snatched it off the shelf. *What luck!*

He put the keys inside.

Out in the suite, he hesitated, then went back into the bathroom, which was the size of a small house, calling, "Lisa, dear, I'm afraid it's time I go."

Coco tilted his head toward his left shoulder, gazing in interest and sadness at the brunette woman in the tub. Lisa's dead turquoise eyes were bugged out, and her collagen-injected lips stretched wide, as if her jaw had been fused open when the plugged-in Bose acoustic radio had hit the bathwater. Amazing in this day and age—what with sophisticated technology and circuit breakers and all—that home electricity and bathwater still created enough of a jolt to stop a heart.

"I must say, girlfriend, you had much better taste

than I ever gave you credit for," Coco said to the corpse. "When it came right down to it, after a brief inventory of your wardrobe, I see you had the money and you spent it reasonably well. And from the bottom of my heart? You are beautiful even in death. Brava, my dear. Brava."

He blew her a kiss, turned, and left the room.

Coco moved with purpose through the mansion, padding down the spiral staircase into the foyer. It was late in the day, almost dusk, and the setting Florida sun threw a golden glow through the windows, illuminating an oil painting on the far wall.

Coco thought the artist had rendered Lisa in all her glory, capturing her at the height of her feminine power, elegance, and ripeness. No one could change that. Ever. From this day forth, Lisa would be the woman in the painting, not that lifeless husk upstairs.

He exited through the front doors and stepped out onto a circular driveway. It was late June and insufferably hot inland. But here, so close to the ocean, a breeze blew, making the air quite pleasant.

Coco walked down the drive, past Lisa's perfectly tended gardens, lush with tropical color and scented with orchids blooming. Wild parrots cackled from their roosts in the palm trees when he pushed a button on the gate and it swung open.

He walked for a block past well-manicured lawns and handsome homes, reveling in the clicking noise the stilettos made on the sidewalk and in the feel of the silk dress swishing against his silk-clad thighs.

A rare old sports car, a dark green Aston Martin DB5 convertible, was parked ahead. The Aston had seen better days and was in need of repair, but Coco still loved the car the way an insecure child will love and worry a favorite blanket until it simply falls apart.

He climbed inside, set the garment bag in the passenger seat, and put the key in the ignition of the roadster. It roared to life. After lowering the convertible top, he put the Aston in gear and pulled out into light evening traffic.

I am beautiful tonight, Coco thought. *And it's a spectacular evening in my paradise, Palm Beach. Romance and opportunity lie just ahead. I can feel them coming to me already.*

Like my mother always told me, if a girl has fashion, romance, and a little opportunity in her life, nothing else really matters.

PART ONE

STARKSVILLE

CHAPTER
1

WHEN I SAW THE ROAD sign that said we were ten miles from Starksville, North Carolina, my breath turned shallow, my heartbeat sped up, and an irrationally dark and oppressive feeling came over me.

My wife, Bree, was sitting in the passenger seat of our Ford Explorer and must have noticed. "You okay, Alex?" she asked.

I tried to shrug the sensations off, said, "A great novelist of North Carolina, Thomas Wolfe, wrote that you can't go home again. I'm just wondering if it's true."

"Why can't we go home again, Dad?" Ali, my soon-to-be-seven-year-old son, asked from the backseat.

"It's just an expression," I said. "If you grow up in a small town and then move away to a big city, things are never the same when you go back. That's all."

"Oh," Ali said, and he returned to the game he was playing on his iPad.

My fifteen-year-old daughter, Jannie, who'd been sullen most of the long drive down from DC, said, "You've never been back here, Dad? Not once?"

"Nope," I replied, glancing in the rearview mirror. "Not in…how long, Nana?"

"Thirty-five years," said my tiny ninety-something grandmother, Regina Cross. She sat in the backseat between my two kids, straining to look outside. "We've kept in touch with the extended family, but things just never worked out to come back down."

"Until now," Bree said, and I could feel her gaze on me.

My wife and I are both detectives with the DC Metro Police, and I knew I was being scrutinized by a pro.

Really not wanting to reopen the "discussion" we'd been having the past few days, I said firmly, "The captain ordered us to take time off and get away, and blood *is* thicker than water."

"We could have gone to the beach." Bree sighed. "Jamaica again."

"I like Jamaica," Ali said.

"Instead, we're going to the mountains," I said.

"How long will we have to be here?" Jannie groaned.

"As long as my cousin's trial lasts," I said.

"That could be, like, a month!" she cried.

"Probably not," I said. "But maybe."

"God, Dad, how am I going to stay in any kind of shape for the fall season?"

My daughter, a gifted track athlete, had become obsessive about her workouts since winning a major race earlier in the summer.

"You're getting to work out twice a week with an AAU-sanctioned team out of Raleigh," I said. "They come right to the high school track here to train at altitude. Your coach even said it would be good for you to run at altitude, so please, no more about your training. We've got it covered."

"How much attitude is Starksville?" Ali asked.

"Altitude," corrected Nana Mama, a former English teacher and high school vice principal. "It means the height of something above the sea."

"We'll be at least two thousand feet above sea level," I said, and then I pointed up the road toward the vague silhouettes of mountains. "Higher up there behind those ridges."

Jannie stayed quiet several moments, then said, "Is Stefan innocent?"

I thought about the charges. Stefan Tate was a gym teacher accused of torturing and killing a thirteen-year-old boy named Rashawn Turnbull. He was also the son of my late mother's sister and—

"Dad?" Ali said. "Is he innocent?"

"Scootchie thinks so," I replied.

"I like Scootchie," Jannie said.

"I do too," I replied, glancing at Bree. "So when she calls, I come."

Naomi "Scootchie" Cross is the daughter of my late brother Aaron. Years ago, when Naomi was in law school at Duke University, she was kidnapped by a murderer and sadist who called himself Casanova. I'd been blessed enough to find and rescue her, and the ordeal forged a bond between us that continues to this day.

We passed a narrow field heavy with corn on our right, and a mature pine plantation on our left.

Deep in my memory, I recognized the place and felt queasy because I knew that at the far end of the cornfield there would be a sign welcoming me back to a town that had torn my heart out, a place I'd spent a lifetime trying to forget.

CHAPTER
2

I REMEMBERED THE SIGN that marked the boundary of my troubled childhood as being wooden, faded, and choked by kudzu. But now the sign was embossed metal, fairly new, and free of strangling weeds.

WELCOME TO STARKSVILLE, NC
POPULATION 21,010

Beyond the sign we passed two long-abandoned, brick-walled factories. Windowless and falling into ruin, the crumbling structures were surrounded by chain-link fences with notices of condemnation hanging off them. In the recesses of my brain, I remembered that shoes had once been produced in the first factory, and bedsheets in the other. I knew that because my mother had worked in the sheet mill when I was a little boy, before she succumbed to cigarettes, booze, drugs, and, ultimately, lung cancer.

I glanced in the rearview mirror and saw from my grandmother's pinched face that she too was being haunted by memories of my mother, her daughter-in-law, and probably also of her son, my late father. We drove by a seedy strip mall that I didn't remember and then by the shell of a Piggly Wiggly grocery store that I distinctly recalled.

"Whenever my mom gave me a nickel, I'd go in there and buy candy or a Mr. Pibb," I said, gesturing to the store.

"A nickel?" Ali said. "You could buy candy for a nickel?"

"In my day, it was a penny, young man," Nana Mama said.

"What's a Mr. Pibb?" asked Bree, who'd grown up in Chicago.

"A soda," I said. "I think it's carbonated prune juice."

"That's disgusting," Jannie said.

"No, it's actually good," I said. "Kind of like Dr Pepper. My mom liked it. So did my dad. Remember, Nana?"

"How could I forget?" My grandmother sighed.

"Did you notice neither of you ever uses their names?" Bree said.

"Christina and Jason," Nana Mama said quietly, and I glanced in the mirror again, saw how sad she was all of a sudden.

"What were they like?" Ali asked, still looking at his iPad.

For the first time in decades, I felt grief and sadness about the loss of my mom and dad. I didn't say a word.

But my grandmother said, "They were both beautiful, troubled souls, Ali."

"Train coming, Alex," Bree said.

I took my eyes off the rearview and saw lights blinking and safety gates lowering. We slowed to a stop two cars and a panel van from the gates and watched the slow-moving freight cars rumble by.

I flashed on images of myself—eight? nine?—running along these same tracks where they passed through woods near our home. It was a rainy night, and I was very scared for some reason. *Why was that?*

"Look at those guys up on the train!" Ali said, breaking into my thoughts.

There *were* two people up on one of the boxcars, one African American, one Caucasian, both in their late teens, early twenties. As they went through the crossing, they sat down, legs hanging off the front of the container car, as if settling in for a long trip.

"We used to call men who rode the trains like that hoboes," Nana Mama said.

"Kind of well dressed for hoboes," Bree said.

As the car the young men were on rolled through the crossing, I saw what Bree was talking about. They wore baseball hats turned backward, sunglasses, headphones, baggy shorts, black T-shirts, and shiny high-top sneakers. They seemed to recognize someone in the car ahead of us, and each of them gave a wave with three fingers held high. An arm came out the driver-side window of that car and returned the salute.

And then they were gone, and the caboose of the train soon after that, heading north. The gates lifted. The lights stopped blinking. We drove on across the tracks. The two cars went right, and I had to slow to let the van take a left at a sign that said CAINE FERTILIZER CO.

"Eeeuw," Ali said. "What's that smell?"

I caught it too, said, "Urea."

"You mean like in pee?" Jannie asked, disgusted.

"Animal pee," I said. "And probably animal poop too."

"God, what are we doing here?" she said with a groan.

"Where are we staying?" Ali asked.

"Naomi made the arrangements," Bree said. "I just pray there's air-conditioning. It's gotta be ninety, and if we're downwind of that smell…"

"It's eighty," I said, looking at the dash. "We're up higher now."

I drove on by instinct, remembering none of the street names but somehow knowing the way to downtown Starksville as if I'd been there the day before and not three and a half decades ago.

The town center had been laid out in the early 1800s around a rectangular common that now featured a statue of Colonel Francis Stark, a local hero of the Confederacy and the son of the town's founder and namesake. Starksville should have been a place you'd describe as quaint. Many of the buildings were older, some antebellum, some brick-faced like the factories at the edge of town.

But hard economic times had hit Starksville. For every business open that Thursday—a clothing emporium, a bookstore, a pawnbroker, a gun shop, and two liquor stores—there were two more that stood empty with their front windows soaped over. For Sale signs hung everywhere.

"I can remember when Starksville was not a bad place to live even *with* the Jim Crow laws," Nana Mama said wistfully.

"What are Crow laws?" Ali asked, scrunching his nose.

"They were laws against people like us," she said, and then she pointed a bony finger at a defunct pharmacy and soda fountain called Lords. "Right there, I remember there were signs that said 'No Coloreds Allowed.'"

"Did Dr. King take those down?" my son asked.

"He was responsible, ultimately," I said. "But to my knowledge, he never actually came to—"

Jannie cried, "Hey, there's Scootchie!"

CHAPTER
3

MY NIECE WAS ON the sidewalk in front of the county courthouse arguing with an earnest-looking African American man in a well-cut gray suit. Naomi wore a navy blue skirt and blazer and clutched a brown legal-size accordion file to her chest, and she was shaking her head firmly.

I pulled over and parked, said, "She looks busy. Why doesn't everyone wait here? I'll get directions to where we're staying."

I climbed out into what was, by Washington, DC, standards, a banner summer day. The humidity was surprisingly low and there was a breeze blowing that carried with it the sound of my niece's voice.

"Matt, are you going to fight every one of my motions?" Naomi demanded.

"Course I am," he said. "It's my job, remember?"

"Your job should be to find the truth," she shot back.

"I think we all know the truth," he replied, and then he looked over her shoulder at me.

"Naomi?" I called.

She turned and saw me, and her posture relaxed. "Alex!"

Grinning, she trotted over, threw her arms around me, and said quietly, "Thank God you're here. This town is enough to drive me mad."

"I came as soon as I could," I said. "Where's Stefan?"

"Still in jail," she said. "Judge's refusing to set any kind of bail."

Matt was studying us—or, rather, me—intently.

"Is your friend the DA?" I asked quietly.

"Let me introduce you," she said, "rattle his chain."

"Rattle away," I said.

Naomi walked me over to him, said, "Assistant district attorney Matthew Brady, this is my uncle and Stefan's cousin Dr. Alex Cross, formerly of the FBI's Behavioral Science Unit and currently a special investigator with the Washington, DC, Metro Police."

If Brady was impressed, he didn't show it, and he shook my hand with little enthusiasm. "You're here why, exactly?"

"My family and I have been through a rough time lately, so we're on a little R and R to visit my roots and provide my cousin with some moral support," I said.

"Well." He sniffed and looked at Naomi. "I think you should be thinking plea bargain if you want to give Mr. Tate moral support."

Naomi smiled. "You can stick that idea where the sun don't shine."

Brady grinned pleasantly and held up his hands, palms out. "Your call, but the way I see it, Naomi, you plead, and your client lives a life behind bars. You go to trial, and he most certainly gets the death penalty."

"Good-bye," she said sweetly as she took my arm. "We've got to be going."

"Nice meeting you," I said.

"Likewise, Dr. Cross," he said and walked away.

"Kind of a cold fish," I said when he was out of earshot and we were heading back to my car.

"He's gotten that way since law school," she said.

"So you've got history?"

"Just old classmates," Naomi said, then broke into a squeal of delight when Jannie opened the Explorer's door and climbed out.

In a few moments everyone was out on the sidewalk hugging Naomi, who couldn't get over how tall and strong Jannie had become and got tears in her eyes when my grandmother kissed her.

"You don't age, Nana," Naomi said in wonder. "Is there a painting in an attic somewhere that shows your real age?"

"The Picture of Regina Cross." Nana Mama chortled.

"It's just so good to see you all," Naomi said, and then her face fell slightly. "I just wish it were under different circumstances."

My wife said, "We'll figure out the real story, get Stefan released, and have a nice vacation."

Naomi's face fell a little further. "That's easier said than done, Bree. But I know the aunties are waiting for us. Why don't you follow me?"

"Can I drive with you, Scootchie?" Jannie asked.

"Of course you can," Naomi said, and she pointed across the street. "I'm the little red Chevy there."

We left downtown and entered more residential neighborhoods, which were full of sharp contrasts. The houses were either run-down or freshly painted. The cars were either brand-new or about to fall apart. And the people we saw on the streets were either shabbily dressed or turned out in the latest urban attire.

We drove onto the old arched bridge that spanned the Stark River Gorge. The granite walls of the gorge were six stories high and flanked the river, which was running fast and churning over huge boulders. Ali spotted kayakers down in the whitewater.

"Can I do that?" he cried.

"Not on your life," Nana Mama said firmly.

"Why not?"

"Because that gorge is a deadly place," she said. "There's all sorts of phantom currents, and there're shelves and logs under that water. They'll trap you and never let you out. Growing up, I knew at least five kids who died down there, including my little brother. Their bodies were never found."

"Really?" Ali said.

"Really," Nana Mama said.

Naomi kept on straight across the bridge. We bounced back over the railroad tracks into Birney, a very run-down section of town. The vast majority of the bungalows along the streets of Birney were desperately in need of TLC. Kids played in the red-clay front yards. Hounds bayed at our passing. Chickens and goats scattered off the roads. And the adults sitting on the front stoops looked at us suspiciously, as if they were familiar with everyone who came to the starkest part of Starksville and knew we were strangers.

That oppressive sense I'd suffered when I'd seen the sign to town returned. It became almost overpowering when Naomi turned onto Loupe Street, a cracked and potholed road that ended in a cul-de-sac in front of the only three homes in the neighborhood that seemed well maintained. The three bungalows were identical and the paint looked recent. Each home boasted a low green picket fence around a watered lawn and flowers growing in beds by a screened-in front porch.

I parked behind Naomi and hesitated in my seat when my wife and son got out. Nana Mama wasn't in any hurry either, and I caught the grim expression on her face in the mirror.

"Alex?" Bree said, looking back in the passenger door.

"Coming," I said. I got out and helped my grandmother down.

We went around the car slowly and then stopped, looking at the closest of the bungalows as if it held ghosts, which for us it did.

"You been here before, Dad?" Ali asked.

I let my breath out slow, nodded, and said, "This is the house where Daddy grew up, son."

CHAPTER
4

"LAND SAKES, IS THAT you here already, Aunt Regina?" a woman cried before Ali or any other member of my family could say anything.

I took my eyes off the house where I'd lived as a boy and saw an old locomotive of a woman wearing a red floral-print muumuu and bright green beach sandals charging off the porch next door. She had a toothy smile and was shaking her hands overhead as if she were bound for a revival tent and some of that old-time religion.

"Connie Lou?" Nana Mama cried. "Young lady, I believe you've lost weight since you came to see me summer before last!"

Connie Lou Parks was my mother's brother's widow. Aunt Connie *had* lost weight since we'd last seen her, but she was still built like a linebacker. When she heard my grandmother's praise, however, her ample body trembled with pleasure, and she wrapped Nana Mama in her arms and kissed her noisily on the cheek.

"My God, Connie," Nana Mama said. "There's no need to slobber."

My aunt thought that was hilarious and kissed her again.

My grandmother got her to stop by asking, "How'd you lose the weight?"

"I went on a cavewoman diet and started walking every day," Aunt Connie declared proudly, and she laughed again. "Lost forty-seven pounds, and my diabetes numbers are better. Alex Cross, you come here now! Give me some sugar."

She threw open her arms and bear-hugged me. Then she looked up at me with misted eyes. "Thank you for coming to help Stefan. It means the world to us."

"Of course. I didn't think twice about it," I said.

"Sure you did, and that's understandable," she said matter-of-factly, and then she went to embrace Bree and the children, gushing over each of them in turn. Nana Mama always said my aunt Connie had never met a stranger. My grandmother was right. All my memories of her were filled with smiles and infectious laughter.

When the greetings were done, Aunt Connie looked at me and then nodded at the bungalow. "You okay with staying in there? It's all been redone. You won't recognize a bit of it."

Dubious, I said, "Nobody lives here now?"

"My Karen and her family, but they're down to the Gulf Coast least through the rest of the summer, caring for Pete's mother, who's in an awful poor way. I've talked to them. They want you to stay if you feel comfortable."

I glanced at Bree, who I could tell was weighing weeks of hotel costs against a free place to stay, and said, "I'm comfortable with it."

Aunt Connie smiled and hugged me. "Good; we'll get you moved in soon as we get you fed. Who's hungry?"

"I am," Ali said.

"Hattie's laying out a spread over to her house," Connie Lou said. "Let's get you somewhere you can wash up and we'll have us a grand time and catch up proper-like."

My aunt was such a force of nature that Ali, Jannie, and Naomi fell right in behind her when she rumbled off. Bree held out her hand to help Nana Mama and looked at me expectantly.

"I'll be right along," I said. "I think I need to go in there alone the first time."

I could tell my wife didn't quite understand. Of course, I'd told her very little about my boyhood, because, really, my life began the day Nana Mama took me and my brothers in.

"You do what you have to do," Bree said.

My grandmother gazed at me evenly, said, "You did nothing to cause any of it. You hear? That was out of your control, Alex Cross."

Nana Mama used to talk to me like this all the time in the first few years after I went to live with her, teaching me to divorce myself from the self-destruction of others, showing me there could be a better way forward.

"I know, Nana," I said, and I pushed open the gate.

Walking up to the screened porch, however, I felt as strange and disconnected as I had ever been in my entire life. It was as if I were two people: a man who was a capable detective, a loving husband, and a devoted father who was heading toward a quiet little house in the South, and an unsure and fearful boy of eight trudging toward a home that might be filled with music, love, and joy or, just as easily, screaming, turmoil, and madness.

CHAPTER
5

AUNT CONNIE WAS RIGHT. I didn't recognize the place.

At some point in the past decades, it had been gutted and the configuration of the bungalow totally changed. The porch was the only part I completely recognized. The entryway where we'd leave our shoes was gone. So was a half wall that used to divide the kitchen from the living area, where me and my brothers, Charlie, Blake, and Aaron, used to play and watch television on those occasions when we had one that actually worked.

The new furniture was nice and the flat-screen television large. The kitchen had new cabinets and a new stove, fridge, and dishwasher. There were more windows in there too, and the dim place where we'd eaten our meals at a dreary Formica-top table was now a bright and cheery spot with a built-in breakfast nook.

Standing there, I could almost see my mother on one of her better mornings, dressed in her threadbare robe but glowing like a beauty queen, smoking a filtered Kent cigarette, making us waffles with sunny-side-up eggs on them, and singing along to Sam Cooke on WAAA 980 AM out of Winston-Salem.

…been a long time coming, but I know a change gonna come…

It was her favorite song, and she had an amazing raspy gospel voice developed in her father's Baptist church. Hearing my mom sing in my head while I stood in the kitchen where she used to sing to us, I choked and then broke down crying.

I never expected it.

I suppose I'd put my mother away for so long in one of those boxes I keep locked in my mind that I thought I was long over the tragedy of her life. But obviously I wasn't. She'd been smart, sensitive, and very funny. She'd been gifted with words and music. She could make up songs right off the top of her head, and on those rare occasions when I witnessed her singing in church, I swear to you, it was as if an angel possessed her.

But there were other times, too many times, when demons took her. She saw her own father commit suicide in front of her when she was twelve and she was emotionally crippled by it her entire short life. She found relief in vodka and heroin, and in the last few years of her life, I rarely remember her stone-cold sober.

I said that demons took her, but really, it was the memories festering in her drug-and-booze-addled mind that created the monster that she sometimes was late at night. From our beds, we'd hear her crying for her dead father, or screaming at him. On those nights, she'd get violent, break things, and curse God and all of us too.

All the children in an addict's family play different roles and have different ways of coping. My brothers retreated into themselves when my mother was using and a danger to us. My job was to stop her from hurting herself and, later, to pick her up off the floor and put her to bed. In the language of recovery, I played the roles of hero and caregiver.

Standing there, recalling all those times I'd tried to forget, I suddenly saw plainly that my mother had created me in more ways than the physical. From an early age, I'd dealt with chaos and chaotic people, and to survive, I'd had to swallow my fears and force myself to understand and deal with sick minds. Those hard-won skills had inevitably led to my calling in life, to Johns Hopkins for my doctorate in psychology, and then to police work. And for those reasons and others, I realized that despite all the craziness and the loss, I was grateful to my mother and blessed to be her son.

Wiping my tears away, I left the kitchen and went into the hallway that led to the bedrooms. When I was a boy, there were just two in the house, and we had a single sorry excuse for a bathroom. Recently, another bath had been added. The large room where my brothers and I slept had been split in two. There were bunk beds in both of them now.

Staring into my distant past, oblivious to any noises in the house around me, I remembered my father on one of his better evenings, sober and funny, telling me and my brothers about some trip he was going to take us on to hear jazz on Bourbon Street in New Orleans.

Gotta have dreams, boys, he'd always say before he turned out the lights. *Gotta have dreams and you've got to*—

"Freeze!" a man shouted. "Hands up high where we can see them!"

I startled but raised my hands, looking over my shoulder and back down the hall into the kitchen. Two men in civilian clothes with police badges on lanyards around their necks were aiming pistols at me.

CHAPTER
6

"ON YOUR KNEES," BARKED the taller and younger of the two, a lean, ropy African American in his early thirties.

The other plainclothes cop was Caucasian, fifties, a pasty, pock-faced man with a hank of dyed brown hair and a mopey face.

"What's going on?" I said, not moving. "Detectives?"

"You are breaking and entering a good friend of mine's house," the African American cop said.

"This house belongs to Connie Lou Parks, my aunt, who let me in and who rents it to her daughter, my cousin Karen, and, I would guess, to your friend Pete," I said. "I used to live here when I was a kid, and by the way, I'm a cop too."

"Sure you are," said the older one.

"Can I show you my creds?"

"Careful," he said.

I reached to push back my jacket, revealing the shoulder holster.

"Gun!" the African American officer shouted, and he and his partner dropped into a combat crouch.

I thought for sure they were going to shoot me if I tried to get my ID, so I eased my hand away, saying, "Of course I've got a gun. I am a homicide detective with the Washington, DC, police department. And in fact, I have two guns on me. In addition to the Glock forty, I have a small nine-millimeter Ruger LC9 strapped to my right ankle."

"Name?" the older cop demanded.

"Alex Cross. You?"

"Detectives Frost and Carmichael. I'm Frost," he said as he and his partner straightened up. "So here's what you are going to do, Alex Cross. Strip the jacket, right sleeve first, and toss it here."

There was no sense in arguing, so I did as he asked and threw my light sports jacket down the hallway.

"Cover me, Carmichael," the older cop said, and he crouched so his partner could keep me squarely in his field of fire.

They were conducting themselves by the book. They didn't know me from Adam, and they were handling the situation the way any veteran cop back in DC, including me, would have handled it.

When Frost got to my jacket, I said, "Left breast pocket."

He squinted at me as he backed up a few feet, still in that crouch, and fished out the folder with my badge and ID.

"Drop your gun, Lou," Frost said. "He's who he says he is. Dr. Alex Cross, DC homicide."

Carmichael hesitated, then lowered his weapon slightly and demanded, "You have a license to carry concealed in the state of North Carolina, Dr. Cross?"

"I have a federal carry license," I said. "I used to be FBI. It's in there, behind the ID."

Frost found it and nodded to his partner.

Carmichael looked irritated, but he holstered his weapon. Frost did the same, then picked up my jacket, dusted it off, and handed it to me, along with my credentials.

"Mind telling us what you're doing here?" Carmichael asked.

"I'm looking into Stefan Tate's case. He's my cousin."

Carmichael went stony. Frost looked like some bitterness had crawled up the back of his throat.

Frost said, "Starksville may not be the big city, Detective Cross, but we are well-trained professionals. Your cousin Stefan Tate? That sonofabitch is as guilty as they come."

CHAPTER
7

AS I WALKED ACROSS the cul-de-sac on Loupe Street to the third bungalow, I was mindful of the unmarked police cruiser pulling out behind me, and I wondered about the strength of the case against my young cousin. I'd have to get Naomi to show me the evidence, and—

Aunt Connie's animated voice came through the screen door, followed by the sound of women cackling and men braying over something she'd said. The breeze shifted and carried the mysterious and wonderful odors from the kitchen of my aunt Hattie Parks Tate, my late mother's younger sister. I hadn't smelled those scents in thirty-five years, but they made me flash on boyhood memories: climbing these same front steps, smelling these same smells, and reaching for the screen door, eager to be inside.

This house had been one of my refuges, I thought, remembering how peaceful and orderly it was compared to the routine chaos across the street. Nothing had changed about that, I decided after peering in through the screen and seeing my family sitting around Hattie's spotless house with plates piled high with her remarkable food, contentment on all their faces.

"Knock, knock," I said as I opened the door and stepped in.

"Dad!" Ali shouted from a wicker couch, waving a bone at me. "You gotta try Aunt Hattie's fried rabbit!"

"And her potato salad," Jannie said, rolling her eyes with pleasure.

Hattie Tate bustled out of her kitchen, wiping her hands on her apron and beaming from ear to ear. "Land sakes, Alex, what took you so long to come see me?"

I hadn't seen my mother's sister in nearly ten years, but Aunt Hattie hadn't aged a day. In her early sixties, she was still slender and tall with a beautiful oval face and wide almond-shaped eyes. I'd forgotten how much she looked like my mom. Long-buried grief swirled through me again.

"I'm sorry, Aunt Hattie," I said. "I…"

"It doesn't matter," she said, tearing up. She rushed over and threw her arms around me. "You've given me hope just being here."

"We'll do everything we can for Stefan," I promised.

Hattie beamed through her tears, said, "I knew you'd come. Stefan knew too."

"How is he?"

Before my aunt could answer, a man in his midseventies shuffled into the room with a walker. He was dressed in slippers, brown sweatpants, and a baggy white T-shirt, and he looked around, puzzled, then became agitated.

"Hattie!" he cried. "There's strangers in the house!"

My aunt was off across the room like a shot, saying soothingly, "It's okay, Cliff. It's just family. Alex's family."

"Alex?" he said.

"It's me, Uncle Cliff," I said, going to him. "Alex Cross."

My uncle stared at me blankly for several moments while Hattie held his elbow, rubbed his back, and said,

"Alex, Christina and Jason's boy. You remember, don't you?"

Uncle Cliff blinked as if spotting something bright in the deepest recesses of his failing mind. "Nah," he said. "That Alex just a scared little boy."

I smiled weakly at him, said, "That boy grew up."

Uncle Cliff licked his lips, studied me some more, and said, "You tall like her. But you got his face. Where he got to now, your daddy?"

Hattie's expression tightened painfully. "Jason died a long time ago, Cliff."

"He did?" Cliff said, his eyes watering.

Hattie rested her face against his arm and said, "Cliff loved your father, Alex. Your father was his best friend, isn't that right? Cliff?"

"When he die? Jason?"

"Thirty-five years ago," I said.

My uncle frowned, said, "No, that's…oh… Christina's next to Brock, but Jason, he's…"

My aunt cocked her head. "Cliff?"

Her husband turned puzzled again. "Man, Jason, he liked blues."

"And jazz," Nana Mama said.

"He like blues most," Cliff insisted. "I show you?"

Hattie softened. "You want your guitar, honey?"

"Six-string," he said, and he shuffled on his own to a chair, acting as if no one else were with him.

Aunt Hattie disappeared and soon came back carrying a six-string steel guitar that I vaguely remembered from my childhood. When my uncle took the guitar, fused it to his chest, and began to play some old blues tune by heart and soul, it was as if time had rolled in reverse, and I saw myself as a five- or six-year-old sitting in my dad's lap, listening to Clifford play that same raucous tune.

My mother was in that memory too. She had a drink in her hand and sat with my brothers, hooting and cheering Clifford on. That memory was so real that for a second I could have sworn I smelled both my parents there in the room with me.

My uncle played the entire song, finishing with a flourish that showed just how good he'd once been. When he stopped, everyone clapped. His face lit up at that, and he said, "You like that, you come to the show tonight, hear?"

"What show?" Ali asked.

"Cliff and the Midnights," my uncle said as if Ali should have known. "We're playing down to the…"

His voice trailed off, and that confusion returned. He looked around for his wife, said, "Hattie? Where my gig tonight? You know I can't be late."

"You won't be," she said, taking the guitar from him. "I'll make sure."

My uncle chewed on that a bit before saying, "All aboard now, Hattie."

"All aboard now, Cliff," she said, setting the guitar aside. "Lunch serving in the dining car. You hungry, Cliff?"

"My shift over?" he asked, surprised.

My aunt glanced at me, said, "You have a break coming to you, dear. I'll get you a plate, bring it to you in the dining car. Connie? Can you take him?"

"Where's Pinkie?" Cliff said as Connie Lou bustled over to him.

"You know he's down in Florida," she said. "C'mon, now. And use your walker. Train's an awful place to fall."

"Humph," Cliff said, getting to his feet. "I worked this train twenty-five years and I ain't fallen yet."

"Just the same," Aunt Connie said and followed him as he shuffled back down the hallway.

"I'm sorry about that," Aunt Hattie said to everyone.

"There's nothing to be sorry about," Nana Mama said.

Aunt Hattie wrung her hands and nodded emotionally, and then turned and went off to the kitchen. I stood there feeling guilty that I'd not come back and seen my uncle in better times.

"Alex, you go get some food so Ali and I can have seconds," Bree said.

"Leave some for me," Jannie said.

I followed Aunt Hattie into her kitchen. She was standing at the sink with her hand over her mouth, looking like she was fighting not to break down.

But then she saw me and put on a brave smile. "Help yourself, Alex."

I picked up a plate on the kitchen table and began to load it with fried rabbit, potato salad, a green-bean-and-mushroom dish, and thick slices of homemade bread, the source of one of those delicious odors I'd smelled.

"How long since you knew?" I asked.

"That Cliff was suffering from dementia?" Hattie asked. "Five years since the diagnosis, but more like nine since he started forgetting things."

"You his sole caregiver?"

"Connie Lou helps," she said. "And Stefan, this last year or so he's been home."

"How're you getting by?"

"Cliff's railway pension and the Social Security."

"Enough?"

"We make do."

"Hard on you, though."

"Very," she said, and pushed back at her hair. "And now all this with Stefan…" Hattie stopped, threw up her hands, and choked out, "He's my miracle baby. How could my miracle baby…"

I remembered Nana Mama telling me that the doctors said Hattie and Cliff would never have children, and then, in her thirties, she'd suddenly gotten pregnant with Stefan.

I put my plate down and was about to go over to console her when Ali ran in, said, "Dad! I swear to God, there's like a gazillion lightning bugs outside!"

CHAPTER
8

WHEN I STEPPED OUT onto the front porch, it was long past dark, and through the screen I could see fireflies everywhere, thousands of them, like I hadn't seen since I was a boy. I flashed on images of Uncle Clifford teaching me and my brothers how to catch them with glass jars, remembered how amazed I'd been to see just how much light two or three of them could generate.

As if reading my mind, Aunt Hattie said, "You want me to get him a jar, Alex?"

"That would be fine."

"Got a big Skippy jar in the recycling," she said, and she turned to fetch it.

We all went outside into Aunt Hattie's yard and watched the fireflies dance and blink like so many distant stars. I felt warm seeing Ali learn how to catch them, grounded by something I'd thought I'd lost all those years ago.

Bree hooked her arm through mine, said, "What are you smiling about?"

"Good memories," I said, and I gestured at the fireflies. "They were always here in the summer. It's…I don't know."

"Comforting?" Nana Mama asked.

"More like eternal," I said.

Before my wife could respond, the shouting began down the street.

"You fuck with us, that's what you'll get!"

I turned to a searing image that locked me up tight.

Well down the block, beneath one of the few streetlights on Loupe Street, two African American boys in their teens struggled against wrist bonds that led to a rope line controlled by three older boys dressed hip-hop. The two at the front were white. The one at the back was black. All three seemed to be taking sadistic pleasure in dragging the two younger boys along, taunting them and telling them to move if they knew what was good for them. It smacked of a chain gang and that galled me.

I glanced at Bree, who looked as wronged as I felt.

"Don't you go sticking your nose in there now, Alex," Aunt Connie warned. "That's a hornet's nest, that's what that is. Just ask Stefan."

My instinct was to ignore her, to run down there and stop the barbarism.

"Listen to her," Aunt Hattie said. "They're some kind of local gang, and those younger boys are just getting initiated."

They'd taken a left on Dogwood Road and disappeared by then.

"But they had those boys tied to a rope, Dad," Jannie complained. "Isn't that illegal?"

That was the way I saw it. Those boys could not have been the age of consent. But I swallowed at the acid taste in my mouth and forced myself to stay in my aunt's front yard, surrounded by fireflies and the North Carolina night sounds, the tree frogs, the cicadas, and the hoot owls, all so strangely familiar and menacing.

"You said ask Stefan about the gang," Bree said.

Aunt Connie glanced at Aunt Hattie, who said,

"Don't know the particulars, but I think he had some troubles with them over to the school. So did Patty."

"Who's Patty?" Bree asked.

"Stefan's fiancée," Aunt Hattie said. "And another gym teacher at the school."

"What kind of troubles did Stefan have at the school?" I asked Naomi.

My niece yawned, said, "You'll want to hear it from him in the morning."

Ali was yawning now too. And Nana Mama looked ready to snooze.

"Okay, let's call it a night," I said. "Get moved in."

I hugged Aunt Connie and turned to do the same to Aunt Hattie, who seemed nervous. In a low voice she said, "I want you to be careful, Alex."

I smiled, said, "I'm a big boy now. Even got a badge and a gun."

"I know," she said. "But you've been away an awful long time, and you may have tried to forget, but this town can be a cruel place."

I was aware of old emotions stirring deep in me, like lava starting to swell in a long-dormant volcano.

"I haven't forgotten," I said, and I kissed her cheek. "How could I?"

Aunt Connie and Naomi stayed behind to help Aunt Hattie clean up. I led my family back across the cul-de-sac toward our bungalow and heartache.

"They're nice," Bree said. "Sweet."

"They are that," Nana Mama allowed. "My, isn't the air cool here, though?"

We all agreed the Starksville weather was a far cry from a DC summer.

"Sad about your uncle," Jannie said. "I guess I've never seen someone, you know, not like Nana."

"Not like me?" my grandmother said.

"Sharp, Nana," Jannie said. "You know."

"Still in possession of my faculties?" Nana Mama said. "That can be a blessing and a curse."

"Why a curse?" Ali asked when we reached the car.

"There are some things in a long life that are best put aside, young man, especially at night," she said softly. "Right now, this old, old lady needs a bed."

Jannie took her into the house and I started unloading the car. My daughter came back out to help me while Bree got Ali to sleep.

"Dad, what causes someone to age one way and someone else another?" she asked.

"Lots of things," I said. "Genetics, certainly. And your diet. And whether you're active, physically and mentally."

"Nana is," Jannie said. "She's always reading or doing something to help out, and she takes all those long walks."

"Probably why she'll live to a hundred," I said.

"You think?"

"I'm betting on her," I said, pulling the last heavy bag out of the trunk.

"Then I am too," Jannie said, and she followed me through the screen door onto the porch. "Dad?"

"Yeah?" I said, stopping to look back at her.

"I'm sorry for being such a bitch on the ride down," she said.

"You weren't a bitch. Just a little testy."

She laughed. "You're kind."

"I try," I said.

"What's it like? You know, coming back here after so long?"

I set the suitcase down and looked through the porch screen at the fireflies and the lit windows of my aunts' homes, and I sniffed at some sweet smell in the air.

"In some ways it seems remarkably unchanged, as if I left yesterday," I said. "And in others, it's like there's a whole other life here now, and my memories don't apply at all, like they happened to someone else."

CHAPTER
9

DESPITE THE DRONE OF the ceiling fan over our bed, I stirred every hour or so as trains rumbled through Starksville. Shortly after dawn, I woke for good to the sound of blue jays scolding in the pine trees behind the bungalow.

Lying there by Bree, listening to those shrill calls, I flashed hard on myself when I was very young, no more than four or five. I'd been lying in bed, blankets over my head but awake, while my brothers were sleeping. I remembered the window had been open, and there were birds chattering. I also remembered being scared by the birds, as if their calling was what had made me want to hide beneath those covers.

That sense lingered with me even after Bree rolled over, threw her arm across my chest, and groaned. "Time is it?"

"Almost seven."

"We've got to get earplugs."

"That's high on my list too. Still disappointed not to be in Jamaica?"

"A whole lot," she said, her eyes still closed. "But I like your aunts, and I like you more than a whole lot. And I think it'll do Jannie and Ali some good to be in a small town for a while."

"Damon gets some of that at his school," I said.

She nodded. "I can see that."

My older boy, Damon, had taken a job as a junior counselor at an annual summer basketball camp at Kraft, the prep school in the Berkshires he attends. That same camp had led him to the school and gotten him a scholarship. Damon giving back to the program had been ample reason for him to miss this trip, but I hoped he was going to come down for a weekend visit at least.

"Shower time," I said, throwing back the sheets.

"Hold on there, buster," Bree said.

"Buster?"

"I don't know, it seemed appropriate," she said, smiling.

"What do you have in mind?" I said, snuggling up to her.

"None of that," she protested good-naturedly.

"Busted Buster."

Bree tickled me, laughed. "No, I just wanted you to get a few things straight for me."

"Such as?"

"Family-tree stuff. Did Nana Mama come from Starksville?"

I nodded. "She grew up here. And the Hopes, her family, they go way back. Nana Mama's grandmother was a slave somewhere in the area."

"Okay, so she met her husband here?"

"Reggie Cross. My grandfather was in the merchant marines. They got married young and had my dad. You'd have to ask Nana, but because of all the time he spent at sea, it wasn't a very good marriage. She divorced Reggie when my dad was seven or eight and took him up to Washington. She worked to put herself through Howard University to become a teacher, but the time required cost her with her son. When he was fifteen, he rebelled and came back down to Starksville to live with my grandfather."

"Reggie."

"Correct," I said, looking up at the spinning ceiling fan. "I can't imagine there was much supervision, which led to a lot of my dad's excesses. I think it kills Nana Mama that she never had a good relationship with her son after that. When he died, I think in some ways she was looking to make things right by taking care of me and my brothers."

"She did a fine job," Bree said.

"I like to think so. Any other genealogical mysteries I can help with?"

"Just one. Who's Pinkie?"

I smiled. "Pinkie Parks. Aunt Connie's only son. He lives in Florida and works on offshore oil rigs. Evidently makes a lot of money doing it too."

"That's his real name? Pinkie?"

"No, Brock. Brock Jr.," I said. "Pinkie's just his nickname."

"Why Pinkie?"

"He lost his right one to a car door when he was a kid."

Bree got up on her elbow, stared at me. "So they nicknamed him Pinkie?"

I laughed. "I knew you were going to say that. It's just how small towns work. I remember there was a guy named Barry, a friend of my dad's, who ran the wrong way at some big football game, so everyone called him Bonehead."

"Bonehead Barry?" She snorted.

"Isn't that awful?"

"What'd they call you?"

"Alex."

"Too boring for a small-town nickname?" she said.

"That's me," I said, climbing out of bed. "Boring Alex Cross."

"That'll be the day."

Pausing in the bathroom doorway, I said, "Thanks, I think."

"I'm saying I love you in my own special way."

"I know you are, Beautiful Bree," I said and blew her a kiss.

"Better than Bonehead Bree," she said with a laugh and blew it right back.

It felt good to laugh and kid each other like that again. We'd been through a rough patch in the spring and it had taken time for us to see the humor in anything.

I shaved and showered, feeling cheery that first morning in Starksville, like life was taking a turn for the better for the Cross family. Isn't it funny how just changing your location changes your perspective? The last couple of months in DC had been claustrophobic, but being back on Loupe Street, I felt like I was on the edge of wide-open country, familiar but unexplored.

Then I thought of Stefan Tate, my cousin, and the charges against him. And the way forward suddenly looked dark again.

CHAPTER
10

AN HOUR LATER, I left Bree and Nana Mama putting together our lives in the bungalow and went with Naomi to the jail where Stefan Tate was being held. As we drove, I reviewed the highlights of the eighteen-page grand jury indictment against my cousin.

About a year and a half prior to his arrest, Stefan Tate joined the Starksville School District as a gym teacher at both the middle and high schools. He had a history of drug and alcohol abuse that he did not reveal on his applications. He met a middle-schooler named Rashawn Turnbull and eventually became the boy's mentor. My cousin led a secret life selling drugs, including the heroin that was believed to be responsible for two overdoses before Christmas last year.

Stefan's personal drug use spiraled out of control. He raped one of his older female students and threatened to kill her if she told anyone. Then he made advances toward Rashawn Turnbull and was rejected. In response, my cousin raped, tortured, and killed the boy.

At least, according to the indictment. It took everything in my power to remember that an indictment was not a conviction. It was just the state's version of events, only one side of the story.

Still, when I finished reading it, I looked up at Naomi and said, "They have hard evidence here."

"I know," my niece said.

"Did Stefan do it?"

"He swears he didn't. And I believe him. He's being framed."

"By who?"

"I'm open to suggestions at this point," she said, turning into a public parking lot near the city hall, the county courthouse, and the jail, all of which were brick-faced and in desperate need of repointing.

Across the street, the police and fire stations looked much newer, and I remarked on it as I climbed out.

"They built them with state and federal grants a few years ago," Naomi said. "The Caine family donated the land."

"Caine, as in the fertilizer company?"

"And the maiden name of the boy's mother, Cece Caine Turnbull."

We started toward the jail. "She credible? The mom?"

"She's a piece of work, that one," my niece replied. "Got a sheet going back ten years. Real wild child and definitely the black sheep of the Caines. But on this, she comes across as more than credible. The murder has ravaged her. There's no denying that."

"The dad?"

"In and out of the picture, recently mostly out," Naomi said. "And he's got about as strong an alibi as you can have."

"He was in prison?"

"Jail down in Biloxi. Doing eight weeks for assault."

"So he wasn't a good role model in the boy's life."

"Nope. That was supposed to be Stefan's job."

We arrived at the jail, went inside. A sheriff's deputy looked up from behind a bulletproof window.

"Attorney Naomi Cross and Alex Cross to see Stefan

Tate, please," my niece said, rummaging in her pocketbook for her ID. Mine was already out.

"Not today, I'm afraid," the deputy said.

"What does that mean, not today?" Naomi demanded.

"It means that, from what I was told, your client has been a less than cooperative inmate—downright belligerent, as a matter of fact. So his visitation privileges have been revoked for forty-eight hours."

"Forty-eight hours?" my niece cried. "We go to trial in three days! I *have* to have access to my client."

"Sorry, Counselor," she said. "But I don't make the rules. I just follow them."

"Who made the call?" I asked. "Police chief or district attorney?"

"Neither. Judge Varney made that decision."

CHAPTER
11

WE WAITED TWO HOURS on the second floor of the Starksville courthouse, stewing on a bench outside the chambers of Judge Erasmus P. Varney, before his clerk said he was ready to see us.

Judge Varney looked up at us from behind several stacks of legal files and a pair of horn-rimmed reading glasses. His steel-colored hair was brushed back in a low pompadour, and his steel-colored beard was close cropped. He wore a rep tie and thin leather suspenders over a starched white shirt, and he studied each of us in turn with sharp intelligent eyes.

"Judge Varney, this is Dr. Alex Cross, my uncle and Stefan Tate's cousin," Naomi said, trying to control her fury. "He's helping me with the case."

"A real family affair," Varney remarked before setting down his reading glasses and standing to shake my hand firmly. "Nice to meet you, Dr. Cross. Your reputation precedes you. I read a *Washington Post* story about the terrible ordeal you and your family went through with that maniac Marcus Sunday. Terrible thing. Miracle you all survived."

"It was, sir," I said. "And I thank God for that miracle every day."

"I bet you do," Judge Varney said, holding my gaze.

Then he turned to Naomi. "So, what can I do for *you,* Counselor?"

"Allow me to see my client, sir."

"I'm afraid I can't do that."

"With all due respect, sir," Naomi said, "we are less than seventy-two hours from trial. You can't limit my time like this without jeopardizing his right to a vigorous defense."

The door opened behind us. I looked over to find four people coming in: a burly, sixtyish, fair-skinned man in a blue Starksville Police Department uniform; a lanky guy, also in his sixties, in the khaki uniform of the Stark County Sheriff's Office; a tall, whippet-thin woman in a gray business suit; and Matt Brady, the assistant prosecutor I'd met with Naomi the day before.

"My men have rights too, Judge Varney," said the man in khaki. "Sheriff Nathan Bean," Naomi whispered.

"And Mr. Tate has infringed upon those rights," said the woman, who turned out to be district attorney Delilah Strong. "Assaulting two jailers is not something we want to be rewarding."

"Since when is due process a reward?" Naomi demanded. "It's a right guaranteed every citizen under the Fourth, Fifth, and Fourteenth Amendments."

The blue-uniformed man—"Police chief Randy Sherman," Naomi informed me—said, "Your client put two deputies in the ER."

"So put him in chains," I said. "Put him in solitary, but you're obligated to let him be seen by counsel."

"We know who you are, Dr. Cross," said Strong. "But you have no jurisdiction here."

"No, I don't," I said. "I came down here as a private citizen to lend a family member a hand. But from the day I started as a police officer and through all my years with the FBI's Behavioral Science Unit, I've known that you can't deny someone the right to a fair trial. If you push this, you might as well send this case straight to an appeals court. So put him in chains or in a straitjacket and let us see him, or, as a concerned citizen, I will contact friends of mine at the Bureau who investigate civil rights violations."

Sheriff Bean looked ready to blow a fuse and started to sputter, but Varney cut him off.

"Do it," he said.

"Your Honor," the sheriff said. "This sends a—"

"It sends the right message," the judge said. "Though I didn't see it that way at first, Dr. and Ms. Cross are correct. Mr. Tate's right to a fair trial supersedes your right to maintain a safe jail. Restrain him as you see fit, but I want him made available to counsel within the hour."

"What that sonofabitch did to that boy?" Chief Sherman snarled at me as he left. "You ask me, your cousin lost all his damn rights that night."

CHAPTER
12

THE PRETTY LITTLE four-year-old girl with the golden curls wore a pink princess outfit and knelt on one side of a low table. She picked up a pot.

"Do you want some tea with your cookie?" she sweetly asked the older man sitting cross-legged on the floor across from her.

"How could I say no to such a kind offer from such a darling young lady?" he replied, smiling.

He knew he looked ridiculous in the crown she'd made him wear. But he was so entranced by the girl that he didn't care. Her skin was the color of fresh cream, and her eyes shone like polished sapphires. He watched her pour the tea into his cup so delicately it made him want to cry.

"Sugar?" she asked, setting the pot down.

"Two lumps," he said.

She dropped two cubes in his cup and one in her own.

"Milk?"

"Not today, Lizzie," he said, reaching for his cup.

Lizzie snatched up a pink wand, reached out, and tapped his hand with it. "Wait. I have to make sure there are no evil spirits around."

His brow knit and he drew back his hand. The little

girl closed her eyes, smiled, and waved her wand. His heart melted to see her caught up in fantasy the way only a four-year-old can be.

Lizzie opened her mouth—to deliver a spell, no doubt.

But before she could, there was a knock behind him.

Irritated at the interruption, the man turned, and the crown fell off his head, irritating him further. A muscular bald white guy in his thirties stood in the doorway, fighting not to show his amusement.

"Can this wait, Meeks?" the man asked. "Lizzie and I are having tea."

"I can see that, boss, but you've got a call," Meeks said. "It's urgent."

"Grandfather, you haven't had your tea and cookie," the little girl protested.

"Grandfather will be back as soon as he's done," he said, groaning as he got to his feet.

"When will that be?" she demanded, crossing her arms and pouting.

"Quick as I can," he promised.

Grandfather walked to Meeks, who was still smirking, and said, "Fill in for me."

The smirk disappeared. "What?"

"Sit down, have some tea, and eat a crumpet with my granddaughter. But you can't wear the crown."

"You're kidding, right?"

"Do I look like I'm kidding?"

Acting like he'd rather put a fishhook through his thumb, Meeks nodded and went to the table, where Lizzie was grinning brightly.

"Sit down, Mr. Meeks," she said graciously. "Have some tea while you're waiting for Grandfather to come back."

Lizzie's grandfather grinned for all sorts of reasons as he walked down a long hallway and into a richly furnished library office. He ignored the books that filled the shelves. They were all his wife's idea. He hadn't read a tenth of them, but they looked good when guests came by.

He picked up a cheap cell phone sitting on the desk, said, "Talk."

"We have problems," said a man with a deep, hoarse voice.

"Tell me."

"She's not listening to reason," he said. "She's talking."

Lizzie's grandfather squinted, calculated. "You're sure?"

"Yes."

"How do you want it handled?"

"We'll take care of it."

This surprised him. "Are you sure? There are others we can turn to."

"Our mess. We'll handle it."

Grandfather accepted the decision, set it aside, said, "Other problems?"

"Naomi Cross threw in a wild card. Brought in her uncle. Alex Cross. Google him. Ex–FBI profiler, now a homicide detective in Washington, DC."

"Reputation?"

"Formidable."

Grandfather factored that into his thinking. "We're clean otherwise?"

"As it stands, yes."

"Then we don't have a choice. Take care of that situation as you see fit."

A moment passed before the man on the other end said, "Agreed."

"Talk to me when it's done."

Grandfather hung up and destroyed the phone. Then he left the office and walked back down the hallway, eager for tea with little Lizzie.

PART TWO

A FASHION STATEMENT

CHAPTER
13

Palm Beach, Florida

" '**I FEEL PRETTY,** oh so pretty,'" Coco sang softly as he looked in the mirror, aware of the dead woman in a black nightgown hanging by her neck from the chandelier behind him but much more focused on assessing the new outfit.

The tangerine linen skirt hugged his hips sublimely. The matching jockey coat was snug through the shoulders, but workable. The Dries van Noten high-heeled sling-backs were a bit toe-crunching. The Carolina Herrera silk taffeta blouse was simply remarkable. And the pearl earrings and choker? Just the right air of sophistication.

All he needed now was the right do.

Coco reached into the box and came up with a lush, shoulder-length, radiant amber wig. It was old, early 1970s, if he remembered correctly. His mother would have known the exact date, of course, but no matter. Once settled on the two-sided tape with the last strands of hair combed into place, the wig made Coco look like another person altogether.

Mysterious. Sexy. Alluring. Unreachable.

"I name you Tangerine Dream, Queen of the Garden Party," Coco cooed to the woman staring back at him. "A vision of…"

He turned and looked at the petite dead woman

dangling by a drapery cord from the chandelier. "Ruth? What would you say? I'm thinking a cross between Julianne Moore in *Boogie Nights* and Ginger on *Gilligan's Island*—the haircut, anyway. Am I right, or am I just a foolish little girl?"

Coco giggled ever so softly before picking up the Prada shopping bag and other goodies pilfered from Ruth's collection. He started to leave the master suite, then paused to listen. Though he knew that the staff had been given the day off and that Ruth's husband, Dr. Stanley Abrams, aka "the Boob King of West Palm," was in Zurich attending a medical symposium, it still paid to be careful.

Sure of himself now, Coco pushed on down a gallery rich with artwork, although the only piece he stopped to look at was an oil painting of the deceased. *There you are,* he thought, studying Ruth's beauty. *Caught at the moment of your ripeness, my dear, a gift to the universe.*

Ruth and Stanley's home was enormous and entirely too modern for Coco's taste. But then again, what would you expect from the house that fake tits built? There was a great deal to be said for classic understatement, he believed.

As his mother liked to say: *When it comes to your art, Coco, and fashion is art, take your motif to the limit and then back off several degrees.*

Coco walked through a kitchen big enough to host an episode of *Iron Chef* and went down a hallway to a steel door. He checked the security system, got a white dust cloth from his bag, and covered his fingers with it before punching in the code. Five seconds later, he shut the garage door and waited for the electronic voice to tell him the system was armed.

The garage had four bays. The near one was empty. The second held Ruth's Mercedes, and the third her husband's Maserati. Coco's beloved Aston Martin occupied the fourth bay. But before going to it, he reached into the Mercedes and removed the garage-door remote.

He backed the Aston out onto a colored concrete area, exited the car, pressed the remote, then wiped it down. When the garage door started to lower, he lobbed it inside, satisfied when it skittered to a halt a few feet from the Mercedes.

Someone intent on suicide would not bother to pick that up, would she? Coco was confident this was the case. He drove out through the security gates of Ruth and Stanley Abrams's massive waterfront estate. Then he realized that the ladies of Palm Beach would already be gathering for cocktails. Maybe he'd go stroll by Oli's Fashion Cuisine.

Would anyone recognize him at Oli's? He was thrilled at his audacity, his taste for high-stakes games.

Let's do it, girlfriend. Let's really shake it up.

Ten minutes later, Coco parked the Aston Martin a few blocks away from his target zone. The vintage sports car was a risk, he knew. But he adored it, so it often caused him to act impulsively, demanding his attention when the Lexus would have done just fine.

Next time you'll stay home, Coco thought and put on a pair of retro white-and-oval-framed sunglasses. He set off up the sidewalk, walking the way his mother had taught him, with his shoulders back, his head high, and his hips swaying like a pendulum.

The first man he encountered was a jogger in his fifties. Coco could feel his degenerate eyes looking over the Tangerine Dream. The second man, a Euro in yachting garb, dropped his sunglasses to gape openly.

That's it, girl, Coco thought, putting just a little more sway in the booty for the Euro who'd no doubt turned

to watch after the dream. Ahead, the yellow tables outside Oli's were already filled with a stylish happy-hour
crowd.

He took a breath, thought: *Mysterious, now. Sexy. Alluring. Unobtainable.*

That's it, Coco. You've got it all.

Now flaunt it all.

He made his walk even more provocative, swaying
his hips back and forth.

Coco raised his chin a degree as he passed the restaurant, ignoring the scene but aware of patrons twisting
to look after him. He almost laughed to cause so much
mistaken lust and envy.

CHAPTER
14

Starksville, North Carolina

THOUGH EVERYONE HAD HEARD the judge's order loud and clear, it was well into the afternoon before two deputies brought my cousin, wearing leg shackles and handcuffs locked to a leather belt around his waist, into an interrogation room. Even through the bruises and swelling, I could see Stefan Tate took after our mothers' side of the family. He was in his early thirties, tall and heavy-boned like me and like Damon. And we all had the same jawline.

I flashed on an image of him as a little boy, running around Nana Mama's yard during one of Aunt Hattie's infrequent trips to Washington. He'd had this infectious laugh, and it seemed like he thought everything was a mystery and an adventure.

"Alex," Stefan said thickly as he sat down. "Glad you came."

I nodded, said nothing.

"Leave his wrists cuffed, but release them from the belt," Naomi said. "He may need to use his hands. And turn off all cameras and microphones."

"Already done on the cameras and mikes," an officer said. "But there is zero chance we're letting him use his hands."

Ignoring her protests, they chained Stefan's legs and the belt to a stout eyebolt in the cement floor and left.

Leaning toward us, Stefan said quietly, "I'd sweep the room for bugs."

I wondered if he was serious or just being melodramatic. But Naomi thought enough of the idea to pull out her iPhone and call up a white-noise app that she turned on high.

"That works," Stefan said. "And thank you again, Alex, for coming. You don't know what it means to have you believe that I did not do these things."

"I don't believe one way or the other," I replied evenly, studying him for signs that he was capable of doing the things he'd been accused of.

"I'm being framed," he said.

"Listen carefully," I said. "I am your cousin, but I do not represent you. Ultimately I'm here representing Rashawn Turnbull. I find out anything that says you killed that boy, I will help the prosecution put you in the chair, or whatever they use here."

"Lethal injection," Stefan said. "I will not lie to you. I did not kill Rashawn."

"Why'd you assault the guards?" Naomi asked.

"Other way around, Counselor. They assaulted me."

"We'll get back to that," I said. "You've read the indictment?"

"More times than you can count. Look, I'm telling you. This case? These circumstances? They're manufactured, Alex."

"You didn't do any of it?"

"Some of it," he admitted. "But nothing illegal. They've twisted things, taken them totally out of context."

"Convince me like you've convinced Naomi," I said, crossing my arms. "Start at the beginning."

"'A very good place to start,'" Stefan sang, and he tried to smile.

According to the particulars of the indictment, two months earlier, Rashawn Turnbull had been found dead in an abandoned limestone quarry, a piece of land undergoing annexation by the city of Starksville. The teenager had been drugged and forcibly sodomized, and his neck had been slashed with a saw. Semen and other evidence found at the scene pegged Stefan Tate, Rashawn's eighth-grade gym teacher, as the killer. DNA also linked Stefan to the drugging and rape of seventeen-year-old Sharon Lawrence, a student at Starksville High School, and she had agreed to testify against him.

So I didn't smile when my cousin sang that line from "Do-Re-Mi."

Instead, for the next hour and a half, I listened closely to his side of the terrible crimes described in the indictment, interrupting only to clarify verifiable facts, names, and times. Otherwise, I followed the adage that if you really want to learn about someone, you should just shut up and listen.

CHAPTER
15

"**THE DAY AFTER RASHAWN** was found, they put the handcuffs on me, Alex," my cousin said at the end of his version of events. "Ever since, I've been in here. No bail. Limited visitation, even with Patty and Naomi. I'm telling you, Alex, I'm being railroaded."

I said nothing, still trying to absorb his story in light of the information given in the indictment.

He leaned forward. "You believe me, don't you?"

"A lot of it has to check out."

"I promise you on my mother's Bible, it will."

"So let's say your version of events is true. Who's behind it?"

Stefan hesitated, and then said, "I don't know. I'm hoping you'll figure it out."

"But you've got suspicions?"

"I do, but I'd rather not put them out there."

"Stefan, your life is on the line here," Naomi said. "We need it all."

"What you don't need is conjecture," Stefan said. "That's the word, right?"

"It is, but—"

He gestured at me with his manacled hands. "I'd rather have Alex go into this with no preconceived notions. Let the facts I've given him take him where they take him. That way, when he says he believes me, I'll know he's telling the truth."

"Fair enough," I said, and I checked my watch. It was past six.

Naomi went to the door, knocked twice. The guards came to get Stefan.

He said, "Tell Patty, my mom, and my dad that I love them and that I'm innocent."

"Of course," Naomi said.

"When will I see you again?" he asked us as the guards stood him up and unlocked his chains from the eyebolt on the floor.

"Tomorrow," my niece replied.

"When I've got something to talk to you about," I said.

"Fair enough," my cousin said, and they led him out.

Naomi waited until we were outside the jail and moving toward her car before asking, "What don't you believe?"

"I believe all of it until proven otherwise," I said.

"But you seemed skeptical in there."

"I'm skeptical of everything when the rape, torture, and murder of an innocent kid is involved," I said matter-of-factly.

That seemed to upset her.

"Am I wrong to think this way?" I asked.

"No, it's just that Stefan needs people in his corner," Naomi said. "I need people in Stefan's corner."

"I know, but as I said, I am ultimately in Rashawn Turnbull's corner. It's the only way I work."

CHAPTER
16

IT WAS TWILIGHT WHEN we parked on Dogwood Road in Birney, only three streets east of Loupe. We walked down the block to a two-story duplex in need of attention, paint certainly, but with a lawn that was freshly mowed. The smell of grass was everywhere.

One of the porch lights was blinking when a middle-aged bleached-blond Caucasian woman wearing running shorts and a Charlotte Bobcats T-shirt exited the right door. She gave us the once-over as we came up onto the porch, said, "Friend or foe?"

"Friends," Naomi said. "I'm Stefan's lawyer."

"Sydney Fox," she said, shaking Naomi's hand. "Neighbor and landlord."

I introduced myself and explained the family connection to Stefan.

"Jesus, isn't it awful," Sydney said softly, her face saddening. "I love that guy. I really do. Stefan's got soul and passion, you know? I just pray what they're saying isn't true. Break my heart if it was, and I don't want to think what it would do to Patty. But I'd best be going to take my run. I like it when it's cool like this. Nice meeting you, and anything I can do to help, you just call Sydney. Patty's got the number."

The blinking porch light went dead, casting her side in shadows.

"Shit," Sydney said, and she had to fumble to get her key in the lock before going inside. "I guess my run will have to wait a couple of minutes."

My niece rang the other bell. The curtain drew back a few moments later.

"It's me and my uncle, Patty," Naomi said.

The door opened. We slipped inside into a simple, tidy living area with a futon for a couch, a trunk for a coffee table, and a flat-screen on the wall. The door shut, revealing a fit, attractive blond white woman in her late twenties. She looked exhausted.

She studied me a beat before sticking out her hand. "Patty Converse. I've heard a lot about you, Dr. Cross."

Eyeing the small diamond engagement ring, I said, "And I've heard very little about you other than what Stefan has told me."

Her eyebrows shot up, and her voice turned yearning. "You saw Stefan? They haven't let me see him in days. How is he?"

"Puffy and bruised but okay," Naomi said. "He was attacked—unprovoked—first by inmates and then by guards."

Her concern turned to anger. "There should be security cameras, tapes."

"I'll be going after those," Naomi promised.

I made a note to myself to find out if the fact that Patty and Stefan were a mixed-race couple had anything to do with the case. Patty offered us coffee, which Naomi declined and I accepted. We followed her into a galley kitchen, and she made the coffee in a French press while answering a few of my questions.

"Stefan says you met the first day of school," I said. "New teacher just like him."

"That's right," she said, scooping coffee from a tin.

"Love at first sight?"

Patty blushed. "Well, it was for me. You'd have to ask Stefan."

"It was for him too," Naomi said.

Patty got teary, and her hand trembled as she covered her lips. "He didn't do this. He loved Rashawn. We both did."

"I know," my niece said.

I asked, "How'd you come to take a job in Starksville?"

Patty said she'd been raised in a small town in Kansas and played softball on scholarship at Oklahoma State. She'd majored in exercise science and minored in education. When she graduated, she decided to move to the Raleigh area, where her older sister had settled, and look for a job.

"Closest openings were here," she said. "They needed two gym teachers to cover high school and middle school."

I said, "Seems fated that you and Stefan would take the jobs."

Patty's eyes welled up again, and she whimpered, "I love to think so."

CHAPTER
17

I WAITED UNTIL SHE'D calmed down and then said, "Tell me about Rashawn Turnbull and Stefan."

"They were connected, right from the start," she said as she poured me coffee. "And I admit that it bothered me because our relationship was just blossoming and Stefan seemed to give as much time to Rashawn and the other students he took an interest in as he did to me."

On the third or fourth day of the school year, Patty said, Stefan found Rashawn sitting in the locker room, refusing to change for gym class. The boy was small for his age, and withdrawn. Both the black boys and the whites picked on him because his mother was white and a recovering addict while his father was African American and a crook.

"Rashawn felt alone, like he didn't fit in anywhere," she said. "Stefan said he'd felt similarly when he was young, you know?"

"Sure," I said. "Stefan ever use drugs in your presence?"

"Never. He knew I wouldn't stand for it."

"But you knew about his past?"

She nodded. "He would never deal drugs. He hates what drugs stole from him and feared what it could steal from kids."

"Did you ever find drugs in the house?"

"Never."

"Did Stefan ever just disappear for hours at a time without telling you where he was going?"

She looked at something in her lap, said, "We love each other, but we're not attached at the hip."

"That doesn't answer the question," I said.

"I don't know," she said, agitated. "Yes. Sometimes he'd go off, said he had things to do."

"When Stefan came back, where did he tell you he'd gone?"

She thought about that. "Usually for hikes or runs. There's a path that parallels the train tracks that he likes. Too noisy for me. Other times he was staking out places in town where kids gathered."

"Why would he do that?"

Patty said that toward the end of last year, there'd been a rash of incidents involving heroin and meth at the Starksville high school, including the two overdoses mentioned in the grand jury indictment.

"There was real pressure from the principal and school board to identify the source of the drugs," she went on. "I don't think any teacher took that more seriously than Stefan. He became obsessed with finding the source."

"He says he was out looking for Rashawn the night he was killed."

Patty nodded. "Rashawn's mother, Cece, called us around eight, said he wasn't home and asked if he was here."

Naomi said, "Stefan said he was upset about many things that night, picked up a bottle for the first time in years, went down by the tracks, drank it, and passed out."

My cousin's fiancée nodded, said, "He said he was frustrated that he wasn't finding the source of the drugs and shocked that Rashawn had told him earlier in the day that he didn't want him as a friend anymore. So he got drunk."

"Why didn't Rashawn want to be Stefan's friend anymore?" I asked.

"Rashawn wouldn't say, and Stefan was—"

Somewhere out front I heard a door slam and then a male shout, "Killer-lovin' bitch! Nigger-lovin' bitch. I hope you rot in hell!"

Two shots from a high-powered rifle ripped through the night.

I was up and moving at the first shot, digging out the Glock in my holster. Three more quick shots blew out the living-room windows, showering me with glass.

As tires squealed, I yanked open the front door and went out in a crouch onto the front porch. The car lights were off, but I could tell it was old, a beater Impala, white, with horrible mufflers. A figure in a black hood, coat, and gloves hung out the window, aiming a scoped hunting rifle at me. He fired.

The sixth bullet hit the cedar-shake siding a few feet from me. I tried to get a bead on him, but the car was gone.

Breathing hard from the adrenaline, I began to straighten out of my crouch when I saw a blond figure in running clothes sprawled at the bottom of the porch stairs, blood pouring from a head wound. There was no use even going down to check for a pulse. There was no doubt in my mind that—

"Sydney!" Patty screamed behind me. "No! No!"

She began to collapse. I twisted and grabbed her in my arms.

"Why?" Patty sobbed into my chest. "Why Sydney?"

I didn't have the heart right then to tell her that it looked to me like a case of mistaken identity.

CHAPTER
18

WITHIN FIFTEEN MINUTES, Dogwood Road was blocked off with traffic cones and the duplex was surrounded by yellow tape. Crime scene techs were photographing the body of Sydney Fox. A crowd had gathered. An unmarked cruiser pulled up at the perimeter, and Detectives Frost and Carmichael stepped out.

"Great," Naomi muttered.

"You know them too?"

"Frost and Carmichael," she said. "They led the city's investigation into Rashawn Turnbull's murder."

"Good cops?" I said, putting aside my first impressions of them.

"Reasonably smart, adequately trained small-town detectives," she said. "They say they're by the book, but I suspect they cut corners, play fast and loose with the facts sometimes. And they tend to jump to conclusions."

"I'll keep that in mind," I said, and I waited for them to study the corpse.

Frost scratched at his acne-scarred nose, nodded at Naomi. "Counselor."

"Detective Frost," Naomi said. "This is Alex Cross, my uncle."

"We've met," he said without enthusiasm. He turned to me. "This is my case."

"I'm on vacation," I said.

"I'm saying that you will have nothing to do with this murder except as a witness," the detective insisted. "Are we good on that right from the get-go?"

"Your town, your ball game, Detective Frost."

Carmichael said, "What happened?"

Naomi, Patty, and I gave our accounts of the evening, including the light going out on the porch and the racial slurs we'd all heard just before the gunfire.

Frost's expression soured, and he asked, "Sydney having an interracial relationship too?"

Patty frowned, said, "Not that I know of."

"Then they were trying to kill you and they shot Sydney by mistake," Carmichael said, relieving me of the burden of telling her. "Both of you blondes and all."

Stefan's fiancée took the news hard and looked sick to her stomach. "Oh God. I wish I'd never come to this town."

"In the morning we'll need you at the station to give sworn statements," Frost told us. "In the meantime, you need to leave the premises. We've got more members of the crime scene team on the way."

Patty said, "Can't I stay here? In my house?"

The older detective said, "You won't get much sleep."

I said, "Come over to my aunt Connie's. She's got two extra rooms."

Stefan's fiancée looked too tired to argue. "Let me get a few things."

"You'll put a watch on my aunt's place?" I asked the detectives when Patty and Naomi had gone back inside.

Frost said, "I can ask, but that doesn't mean you'll get it."

"Budget cuts," Carmichael explained.

Which meant Bree and I would have to take shifts watching the cul-de-sac. When Patty had thrown some things in a small bag, we skirted around the body of Sydney Fox. A coroner had a bright light on her, and a tech was taking pictures. It was only then that I realized she'd been hit in the forehead twice, two wounds three inches apart.

I remembered the pace of the shots, how quick and crisp they—

A male voice called out, "Dr. Cross?"

I slowed near Naomi's car and saw a big, athletic guy in jeans and a black hoodie climbing from a gray Dodge pickup. He wore a badge on a chain around his neck, and he jogged over to us.

"Detective Guy Pedelini," he said, smiling and extending his hand. "Stark County Sheriff's Office. An honor to meet you, sir."

"You too, Detective Pedelini," I said, shaking his hand.

"Kind of outside your jurisdiction, aren't you, Guy?" asked Naomi coolly.

Pedelini sobered, said, "Just paying my respects to your famous uncle, Counselor. But now that I'm here, can you tell me what happened?"

"A highly skilled rifleman in an old white Impala killed the wrong woman," I said, and then I described what we'd heard yelled just before the shots.

The sheriff's detective had gone stern, his full attention focused on me.

"Why do you say he's highly skilled?"

"He was using a bolt-action rifle, not a semi or a pump, and he managed to put two rounds into Ms. Fox's forehead before she hit the ground," I said.

"A hunter," Pedelini said.

"Or military trained," I said. "Know any racists that fit the bill and own a beater Impala?"

The detective thought about that before shaking his

head. "There are a couple of avowed racists around who drive beat-up old white cars and a fair number of decent hunters and ex-military types, but no one who's capable of that kind of shooting. I mean, he'd have to have sniper training, wouldn't he?"

"Makes sense," I said.

"Why are you so interested in this, Guy?" Naomi said.

"Someone tries to kill a material witness in a heinous murder case that went down in my jurisdiction, I'm interested, Counselor," Pedelini said.

"Why would you care if I was shot?" Patty Converse said. "I'm a witness for the defense. You think Stefan's guilty."

"I do," Pedelini agreed. "I think he's guilty as sin. But that doesn't stop me from being concerned about the safety of everyone else. See, Ms. Converse, I don't want there to be any doubt about this trial. I want the judge and jury to hear both sides fully and then deliberate and condemn your fiancé, put him in Central Prison over in Raleigh, and get him in line for a lethal injection."

CHAPTER
19

IT WAS PAST ELEVEN when Naomi pulled up and parked in front of Aunt Connie's bungalow. I climbed out, meaning to head for my old house and my family. But I saw that the lights were all out there. Bree opened the front door to my aunt's place.

I'd called Bree within minutes of Sydney Fox's death, but we'd agreed it was better that she stay where she was while I talked to the police.

Bree hugged me, kissed me, and said, "Your aunt figured you'd all be starving, so she's been cooking and consoling."

"Who's she consoling?"

"Ethel Fox," Bree said. "Sydney's mother. She and Connie are friends."

"How's the mom taking it?"

"Disbelief. Devastation. Shock. Sydney was her only daughter. Her husband passed ten years ago, and her son lives out in California. I don't know what she'd do if your aunts weren't here."

I put my arm around her shoulder, and we followed Naomi and Patty up into the house. Aunt Connie kept her home spotless, but it was by no means a cold or sterile place. The furniture was warm and cozy, and there were pictures of her and her friends and her children, Pinkie and Karen, everywhere. I couldn't find one where my aunt wasn't beaming or hugging someone.

Like I said, she never, ever met a stranger.

I could see Aunt Connie in the kitchen, wearing pink bunny slippers and a matching pink bathrobe and whisking eggs in a steel bowl. The air smelled of bacon, garlic, onions, and coffee. Suddenly I was ravenous and very tired. I wanted nothing more than to eat, then go next door and sleep.

Patty, Naomi, Bree, and I all went into the kitchen. Aunt Hattie was there too, sitting at the table and holding the hands of an older white woman with wispy gray hair. Dried streaks of tears showed on her cheeks, and she seemed to be staring off into nothingness, unaware of us.

"Sydney was the sweetest little thing, Connie," Ethel Fox said in a weak voice. "So pleasing when she was a girl."

"I remember," Aunt Connie said, nodding to us.

"She was finding herself, I think, after the divorce," the older woman went on. "So happy, and looking forward."

"You know that's true," Aunt Hattie said. "She was doing good. A daughter to be proud of."

Patty swallowed hard and said, "I'm so sorry for your loss, Mrs. Fox. Sydney was such a fine, fine person, I..."

The dead woman's mother seemed to break from her trance. She turned her head slowly to look at Stefan's fiancée, who was fighting back tears.

"The police said she was shot 'cause of you," Ethel Fox said in a flat, grieving tone.

Patty's hands flew to her mouth and she choked out, "I wish it had been me. I swear to you, I never...I loved your daughter. She was my best friend here. My only friend."

Ethel Fox got up slowly, staring hard at Patty, and for a second I thought she might strike her. Instead, she opened her arms and embraced Stefan's fiancée, who wept on her shoulder.

"I know you loved her too," Ethel Fox said, rubbing Patty's back. "I know you loved her too."

"You don't blame me? And Stefan?"

The old woman pushed away from Patty and shook her head. "Sydney believed he was innocent as much as you do. We talked about it just the other day. She said Stefan didn't have the kind of heart to do something that dark to anyone, much less to a boy he cared so much about."

Aunt Hattie fought not to break down.

Aunt Connie wiped her own tears on her forearm, said, "Ethel, you hear me now. Our nephew Alex here is gonna find Sydney's killer, just like he's gonna find Rashawn's. You mark my words, he's gonna make them pay. Isn't that right, Alex?"

Every eye in the room was on me. In the short space of time I'd been in Starksville, the town had revealed dimensions more ominous than I remembered. Deep inside, I wondered whether I was up to the task of figuring out who killed the Turnbull boy and, now, Sydney Fox. But they were all looking at me with such hope that I said, "I promise you, someone will pay."

Aunt Connie broke into her toothy grin and then poured the beaten eggs into a black frying pan with a hiss. "Sit down now, I'll finish up."

"Sydney was right," Aunt Hattie said. "Whoever killed that boy had a dark heart, and my Stefan does not."

I realized she was directing the comment at me. Had Naomi told her what I'd said earlier in the day, about owing my allegiance to the victims?

Before I could respond delicately, Ethel Fox said, "You ask me, there's only one heart black enough around here to kill a boy like that. You ask me, that Marvin Bell's involved somehow."

The name sounded familiar, but I couldn't place it.

My aunts evidently could, though.

Hattie got a stricken look and turned her head away.

Connie rapped hard on the edge of the skillet with the wooden spoon, glanced at me, saw my confusion, and then looked to Sydney's mother and warned quietly, "Ethel, you know you don't want to be accusing that Marvin Bell of nothing unless you got fifty God-fearing Christians behind you saying they saw it too, in broad daylight and with their own two eyes."

"Who's Marvin Bell?" Bree asked.

My aunts said nothing.

"He's slippery, that one, always in the shadows, never showing hisself," Ethel Fox said. Then she pointed a bony finger at me. "And you know why your aunts ain't saying nothing to you 'bout him?"

My aunts wouldn't look at me. I shook my head.

"Marvin Bell?" Ethel Fox said. "Once upon a time, before he went all proper, he owned your daddy. Your daddy was one of his niggers."

CHAPTER
20

THE WORD SILENCED the room, and Bree's face turned hard. So did Patty's and Naomi's.

You heard the word used every day on the streets of DC, one person of color to another. But hearing it from the lips of an old white Southern woman in reference to my dead father, I felt like she'd slapped me across the face with something unspeakable.

Her daughter was dead. She was distraught. She didn't mean it. Those were my immediate responses. Then I noticed that my aunts weren't as shocked as the rest of us.

"Aunt Hattie?" I said.

Aunt Hattie wouldn't look at me, but she said, "Ethel didn't mean to shame your father's name or yours, Alex. She's just telling it like it was."

Pained, Aunt Connie said, "Back then, your father *was* Marvin Bell's slave. Bell owned him. Your mother too. They'd do anything he asked."

"'Cause of the drugs," Ethel Fox said.

I suddenly felt so hungry, I was light-headed.

"You don't remember Bell coming to your house when you was a boy to bring your mama or papa something?" Aunt Connie asked, spooning the eggs onto a plate. "Tall white guy, sharp face, slippery, like Ethel said?"

Hattie added, "All nice one second, meaner than a crazy dog the next?"

Something blurry, troubling, and long ago flitted through my mind, but I said, "No, I don't remember him."

"What about—" Aunt Hattie began, and then stopped.

Aunt Connie had fetched plates of potato pancakes, crispy maple bacon, and a mound of toast from the warming oven, and she set them and the freshly made scrambled eggs on the table. Naomi and I attacked the food. Stefan's fiancée pushed at her eggs and bacon and worried a piece of toast.

I stayed quiet as I ate. But Bree asked all sorts of questions about Marvin Bell, and by the time I set my fork on my plate, stuffed to the gills and feeling a lot less light-headed and achy, there was a thumbnail biography of him developing slowly in my mind, some of it fact, but most of it opinion, rumor, conjecture, and supposition.

Slippery described Bell perfectly.

No one at that table could peg exactly when Marvin Bell took control of my parents' life. They said he'd slid into Starksville like a silent cancer when my mom turned twenty. He came bearing heroin and cocaine, and he gave out free samples. He got my mother and a dozen young women just like her strung out and desperate. He hooked my father too, but not just on the drugs.

"Your father needed money for you boys," Aunt Connie said. "Selling and moving for Bell made him that money. And like Ethel was saying, Bell had his hooks into them so hard, they were just like his slaves."

Ethel Fox said, "Once, Bell even ran your daddy out of your house, tied him with a rope to the back of his car, and dragged him down the street. No one moved to stop him."

Flashing on that memory of the boys being dragged on a rope line the day before, I gaped at her, horrified.

"You don't remember, Alex?" Aunt Hattie asked softly. "You were there."

"No," I said instantly and unequivocally. "I don't remember that. I'd...remember that."

The very idea of it made my head start to pound, and I just wanted to go somewhere in the darkness and sleep. Both my aunts and Sydney Fox's mother looked at me in concern.

"What?" I said. "I just don't remember it ever getting that bad."

Aunt Connie said sadly, "Alex, it got so bad, the only way your mom and dad could escape was by dying."

Hearing that after so long a day, I hung my head in sorrow.

Bree rubbed my back and neck, said, "Is Bell still a dealer?"

They argued about whether he was. Aunt Hattie said that soon after my father died, Bell took his profits and went twenty miles north, where he built a big house on Pleasant Lake. He bought up local businesses and gave every appearance of a guy who'd straightened out his life.

"I don't believe that for a second," Ethel Fox snapped. "You don't change your spots just like that, not when there's easy money to be made. You ask me, he runs the underworld of this town and the towns all around us. Maybe even over to Raleigh."

I raised my head. "He's never been investigated?"

"Oh, I'm sure someone has investigated him," Connie said.

"But Marvin Bell's never been arrested for anything,

far as I know," Hattie said. "You see him around Starksville from time to time, and it's like he's looking right through you."

"What do you mean by that?" Bree asked.

Hattie shifted in her chair. "He makes you uncomfortable just by being near, like he's an instant threat, even if he's smiling at you."

"So he knows who you are? What you've seen?" Bree asked.

"Oh, I expect he knows," Connie said. "He just don't care. In Bell's kingdom, we're nothing. Just like Alex's parents were nothing to him."

"Any evidence linking Bell to Rashawn Turnbull?" Bree said.

Naomi shook her head.

Patty Converse seemed lost in thought.

I asked her, "Stefan ever mention him?"

My cousin's fiancée startled when she realized I was talking to her, said, "Honest to God, I've never heard of Marvin Bell."

CHAPTER
21

I AWOKE THE NEXT morning to find my daughter, Jannie, at the side of my bed, shaking my shoulder. She had on her blue tracksuit and was carrying a workout bag.

"Six a.m.," she whispered. "We have to go."

I nodded blearily and eased out of bed, not wanting to wake Bree. I grabbed some shorts, running shoes, a Georgetown Hoyas T-shirt, and a Johns Hopkins hoodie, and went into the bathroom.

I splashed cold water on my face and then dressed, willing myself not to think about the day before and Marvin Bell and what my aunts said he'd done to my parents. Did Nana Mama know? I pushed that question and more aside. For a few hours, at least, I wanted to focus on my daughter and her dreams.

Nana Mama was already up. "Coffee with chicory," she said, handing me a go cup and a small soft cooler. "Bananas, water, and her protein shakes are in there. There's some of those poppy-seed muffins you like too."

"Fattening me up?"

"Putting some meat on your bones," she said, and she laughed.

I laughed too, said, "I remember that."

When I was a teenager, about Jannie's age, I'd gotten my height but weighed about one hundred and sixty dripping wet. I had dreams of playing college football and basketball. So for two years, Nana Mama cooked extra for me, putting some meat on my bones. When I graduated high school, I weighed close to two hundred.

"Dad!" Jannie whined.

"Tell Bree we should be back before ten," I said, and I hurried out of the house with my daughter.

Jannie was quiet on the ride over to Starksville High School. It didn't surprise me. She is incredibly competitive and intense when it comes to running. Sometimes she's irritable before facing a challenge on the track. Other times, like that morning, she's quiet, deep inside herself.

"This coach is supposed to be strong," I said.

She nodded. "Duke assistant."

I could see the wheels turning in her head. One of Duke University's assistant track coaches ran the AAU team out of Raleigh during the summer. Some of her athletes would no doubt be on the track. Jannie was out to impress them all.

I pulled into a mostly empty parking lot next to the high school. At a quarter past six on a Saturday morning, there were only a handful of vehicles there, including two white passenger vans. Beyond them and a chain-link fence and bleachers, people were jogging, warming up.

"You're here to train, right?" I said as Jannie unbuckled her seat belt.

She shook her head, smiled, and said, "No, Daddy, I'm here to run."

We went through a gate, under the stands, and over to the track. There were fifteen, maybe twenty athletes there already, some stretching in the cool air, some just starting their warm-up laps.

"Jannie Cross?" A woman wearing shorts, running shoes, and a bright turquoise windbreaker jogged over to us. She carried a clipboard and grinned broadly when she stuck out her hand and said, "Melanie Greene."

"Pleased to meet you, Coach Greene," I said, shaking her hand and sensing her genuine enthusiasm.

"The pleasure is all mine, Dr. Cross," the coach said.

Then she turned the charm on Jannie and said, "And you, young lady, are causing quite the stir."

Jannie smiled and bowed her head. "You saw the tape of the invitational?"

"Along with every other Division One coach in the country," she said. "And here you are, walking onto my track."

"Yes, ma'am," Jannie said.

"Just for the record, you'll only be a sophomore in the fall?"

"Yes, ma'am."

Coach Greene shook her head in disbelief and then handed me the clipboard and said, "I'm going to need you to sign a few forms here, saying we are not in any way, shape, or form considering this a recruitment meeting. This is summer work, and it's all about training. And there's an athletic release form from the Starksville school system at the bottom."

I scanned the documents, started signing.

"Why don't you take a lap and get warmed up," Coach Greene said to Jannie, all business now. "We'll be working two-hundreds this morning."

"Yes, Coach," Jannie said, looking serious as she put her bag on one of the low bleachers and ran out onto the track.

I signed the last of the documents and handed the clipboard back.

"You're here how long?" Coach Greene asked.

"Unclear," I said. "We're down on a family issue."

"Both sorry and glad to hear it," she said, and she shook my hand again before jogging back to several women wearing AAU and Duke warm-up jackets.

There were other girls and boys coming in now, younger than the college bunch already out on the track, some roughly Jannie's age. Three of them wore Starksville Track hoodies. I took a seat in the stands, sipped coffee, and ate poppy-seed muffins while Jannie went through her prep routine: a slow lap and then a series of ballistic stretches and drills, increasing in intensity and designed to get her quick-twitch muscles firing.

The entire time, the other athletes watched her, sizing her up, especially the high school—age girls, especially the ones from Starksville. If Jannie noticed, she wasn't showing it. She had her game face on big-time.

Coach Greene called in the athletes and divided them into training groups. Jannie was put with the local girls. If she cared, she didn't show it. This was all about the clock.

CHAPTER
22

GREENE CALLED FOR 60 percent effort, and the men went first, running the long left-hand turn of the two-hundred and then slowing into a trot back around. Greene sent the next groups in in waves. The seven college girls were serious athletes, strong and fleet. They seemed to dance down the track, barely touching the surface, their legs churning in a quick, powerful cadence.

Jannie watched them intently but showed nothing. When it came time for her group, the high school girls, to run, she went to the outside, letting the others have the favored lanes. Greene said something to her I didn't catch. Jannie nodded and settled in.

They ran the staggers with no blocks, just taking off at Greene's whistle. Some of the other girls, especially the three from Starksville, were surprisingly gutsy and kept abreast of Jannie through the slowdown. But you could see that they didn't have her natural fluidness and stride.

The difference was more readily apparent two intervals later when Greene called for 80 percent effort. At the whistle, Jannie took off in a smooth, chopping motion that quickly gave way to the long, explosive lopes of a quarter-miler as she rounded the turn. She let up with ten yards to go and still beat the high school girls by three body lengths.

"Hey!" one of the local girls said angrily to Jannie, breathing hard. "Eighty percent!"

Jannie smiled and said, "That was seventy."

Her tone was matter-of-fact, but the girl seemed to think Jannie was being condescending. Her face hardened; she turned and went over to her friends.

Coach Greene must have heard Jannie say she was giving only 70 percent, because she jogged over and said something to her. Jannie nodded and ran to catch up with the older girls.

"Drop to groups of four, ladies," Greene shouted after them.

The college girls nodded to Jannie when she jogged up, but these were Division 1 athletes. After that moment of acknowledgment, they put on their game faces.

"Eighty-five to ninety now," Greene called as the girls moved into the stagger.

At fifteen and a half, my daughter was as tall as or taller than most of the girls, but she didn't have their strength or build. She looked slight next to them.

Jannie ran stride for stride with the two strongest girls until they were a hundred and fifty meters in. Then their conditioning and experience showed. They pulled away from her and crossed the slowdown mark a yard ahead.

"Ninety," Greene called, and all the girls in that heat, including Jannie, nodded, their chests heaving.

They ran two more like that, and Jannie finished third both times. Then Greene called for warm-down and stretching. The two fastest college girls went over and talked to Jannie; the local girls tried to ignore her.

Coach Greene came to the fence, and I went down to talk to her.

"Has she run in the two-hundred in competition?"

she asked.

"No," I said. "Quarter-mile only. Why?"

"Those two that beat her, Layla and Nichole, they're pure sprinters. Two-hundred's their race. Layla was runner-up at the Atlantic championships, twelfth at NCAA nationals."

I didn't know what to say. "I think she wants the four-hundred."

"I know," Greene said. "She's raw, but very impressive, Dr. Cross."

"Thank you, I think."

The coach said, "It's a deep compliment. I…" She paused. "Think you might be able to bring her over to Duke next Saturday morning?"

"For?"

"There's a group from Chapel Hill, Duke, and Auburn, all four-hundred girls; they train there. And I'd like my boss in my other life to see Jannie run."

"Thought this wasn't about recruitment."

"Just a friendly suggestion. I think Jannie will get bored running with the girls up here, and there are more suitable training partners an hour away."

"We'll talk about it," I said. "And it will depend on my family situation."

"Just know the door's open for her," the coach said, and she jogged off.

The three Starksville girls were coming across the track, and Greene high-fived them as she went by, told them, "Tuesday afternoon."

The girls shot me hostile glances as they passed and then went on chattering about something. I watched Jannie kick into her rubber sandals and shoulder her bag. Every move she made was efficient and natural; even the way she ambled was fluid, her shoulders, hips, knees, and ankles in perfect, loose sync.

I realize I'm bragging on my own daughter here, but, proud papa aside, I knew enough about athletics to understand that you couldn't teach what Jannie had. It was genetic, a blessing from God, a level of physical awareness so far beyond my comprehension that at that moment, I looked up to the sky and asked for guidance.

Jannie came up beside me, shaded her eyes, and scanned the sky too. "What's up there?"

I put my arm around her and said, "Everything."

CHAPTER
23

WE GOT HOME AT around twenty past eight. Ali was up but still in his pajamas, sitting on the couch and watching a deep-sea-fishing show on the Outdoor Channel, one of the few stations that came in well.

"This is cool, Dad," Ali said. "They hook these huge marlin and they take like hours reeling them in so they can be tagged and tracked."

"That is cool," I said, peering at the turquoise waters. "Where is this?"

"The Canary Islands. Where's that?"

"Off Africa, I think."

Bree and Nana Mama were in the kitchen, making breakfast.

"Why didn't you wake me?" Bree asked as I came in the room. "I wanted to go."

"I'm sorry," I said. "I was trying to let you rest."

"I'll rest when I'm in Jamaica," she said firmly.

I saluted her, said, "Detective Stone."

"At ease," Bree said, breaking into a soft smile. "After you eat, can we drive around? Like, all around?"

"So I can give you the lay of the land?" I said. "Sure, that makes sense."

"Take me too," Nana Mama said. "I'm going stir-crazy sitting in this house when all there is on the television is fishing and hunting shows. And I don't care what Connie Lou says about how much Starksville's changed. When I close my eyes, I see it as it was."

Oddly, I didn't. I realized that I hadn't thought of the bungalow as my childhood home or as my parents' home since that first night in town. The psychologist in me wondered why that was. And what about my aunts insisting I'd witnessed my father being dragged by a rope? Was I blocking it? If yes, why?

"You all right, Alex?" Bree asked, handing me a plate.

"Huh?"

"You're brooding about something," she said.

"Feels like a brooding day." I shrugged, sat down at the table, and began to eat.

Naomi came in, said, "Isn't this where we left off?"

"Nothing wrong with having two breakfasts in eight hours," Nana Mama said. "You want anything, dear?"

"I can barely move from last night's cholesterol bomb," Naomi said, and then she looked at me. "Do you want to see where he was found? Rashawn?"

"Long as we can take in the sights along the way," I said.

An hour later, temperatures were climbing into the eighties and it was growing stickier by the minute. I put the Explorer's AC on arctic blast; Bree rode shotgun, and Naomi and Nana Mama were in the back.

We drove slowly north, zigzagging through Birney, which was still mostly as I remembered it, a few degrees shy of shabby and inhabited by black folks and a smattering of poor whites. On the east end of the neighborhood, Naomi pointed out a sad duplex, said, "Rashawn lived there. That's Cece Caine Turnbull's place."

"When did his mom last see him alive?" Bree asked.

"That morning, when he went off to school," Naomi said. "He was part of an after-school program at the YMCA, so she didn't get alarmed when he wasn't home by six. But at seven, Cece started calling his cell. He didn't answer. His friends said they hadn't seen him. So Cece called Stefan and the police."

"The police look for him?" Bree asked.

"Halfheartedly, at best. They told Cece he was probably off somewhere with a girl or smoking pot."

"At thirteen?" Bree asked.

"It happens around here," my niece said. "Even younger."

I drove north across the tracks and the arched bridge and through the neighborhoods into downtown. We passed a liquor store, and I noticed the name: Bell Beverages. I wondered whether this was one of the supposedly legitimate businesses Marvin Bell had bought with his drug profits.

We drove through the center of the city and into wealthier neighborhoods. It wasn't wealthy in the New York or DC sense of the word, but there was a definite middle class there, with larger houses than the bungalows and duplexes in Birney and bigger and better-kept yards.

"It was just like this when I was a girl," Nana Mama said. "You had the poor blacks in Birney and the whites up north here with all the jobs."

"Who's the big employer now?" Bree asked.

Naomi pointed through the windshield to a grassy hill surrounded by those middle-class neighborhoods and a vast brick-and-wrought-iron wall. Beyond the wall, a long, sloping lawn had been trimmed like a golf course. In the sun, the lawn seemed to pulse green, and it ran up the hill to the only structure in Starksville that you could legitimately call a mansion. A modern interpretation of an antebellum design, the house was brick-faced with lots of white arched windows and a portico. It took up the full crest of the hill and was ringed by low, blooming bushes and fruit trees.

"That's the Caine place," Naomi said. "The family that owns the fertilizer company."

"Rashawn's grandparents?" Bree asked.

"Harold and Virginia Caine," Naomi confirmed.

"Big step down for Cece, then," I said. "Living where she does."

"Her parents say they had to practice tough love because of her drug and alcohol issues," Naomi said.

"So Rashawn was an innocent victim even before he died," Nana Mama said in a fretful tone. "I couldn't stand this place fifty years ago, and I'm getting the feeling nothing's changed. It's why I had to get out after I left Reggie. It was why I wanted to get Jason out of here all along."

I glanced in the rearview mirror and saw my grandmother wringing her hands and staring out the window. *Reggie.* It was one of the few times I'd heard her use my grandfather's name. She rarely brought up her early years, her failed marriage, or my father, for that matter. Her history always seemed to begin when she got to Washington and into Howard. And she avoided talking about my dad, as if he were a scab she didn't want to pick at.

"Take a right," Naomi said.

We went around the hill below the Caines' place and then veered off to the west, where there were fewer houses. The road went past a Catholic church where a groundskeeper was mowing the lawn.

"St. John's," Nana Mama said fondly. "I took my First Communion there."

I glanced in the mirror again and saw she'd relaxed into some better memory of Starksville. Beyond the church, the road wound into woods.

"There's a pull-off ahead, up on the left, beyond the cemetery," Naomi said. "You'll get the bird's-eye view."

CHAPTER
24

WE PASSED THE OPEN gate to St. John's Catholic Cemetery. Up the hill I could see the pull-off.

"It's a beautiful spot," Nana Mama said, and I glanced in the mirror a third time, catching my grandmother looking into the cemetery. "Your uncle Brock's buried there. He could have been at Arlington, but Connie Lou wanted him here with family."

"He died in the Gulf War, right?" Bree asked.

"Green Beret," Naomi confirmed. "Posthumous Silver Star for valor at Fallujah. It's on the shelf in the front room."

"And Connie never remarried?" Bree asked.

"She never saw the need," Nana Mama said. "Brock was her soul mate, and her men friends all paled in comparison."

"Men friends?" I said.

"None of your business."

I knew better than to pursue the subject. Instead, I drove up and into the pull-off. About three hundred yards ahead, the ground gave way to pale white and irregular cliffs. Hardwood trees, maple and hickory, grew above the cliffs on the far rim. But on the near side, the bigger trees had been cut for lumber, the remaining stumps all but swallowed by raspberry brambles and sapling thickets.

Bree, Naomi, and I got out, aware of the building heat and insect whine all around. My grandmother rolled down the window and stayed put. "I'll wait here, thank you," she said. "I've taught too many thirteen-year-old boys; I can't listen to what you all have to say out there."

"We won't be long," Naomi promised, and she said to me: "You might want binoculars if you've got them."

"I do," I said, and from a compartment in the rear of the Explorer I retrieved the Leupold binoculars I'd bought when I was still with the FBI.

Naomi led us forward to a tall guardrail. We looked over into a large, deep, and abandoned limestone quarry that immediately set my heart racing. I once more flashed on myself as a boy running in the rain at night. I didn't know where or why. Or I couldn't remember.

Or wouldn't.

In any case, I forced myself to calm down and really study the quarry even before Naomi spoke. It was eighty, maybe ninety feet deep. In some places, the bottom was choked with brush, and in others it was solid stone. A creek cut through and disappeared through a gap in the wall to our left.

Gang graffiti marred the lower limestone walls. Above, the cliffs were irregular and staggered where miners had cut out huge slabs of stone. In several spots, there were gaping, jagged holes in the rock face—entrances to caves. Water trickled from the caves and ran down the walls into the creek.

Naomi pointed to the largest bare section of the quarry bottom, a pale and sunbaked rubble field that reminded me of pictures I'd seen of Greek ruins. There were chunks of limestone lying everywhere. The squarer pieces were stacked haphazardly, and the broken stuff was strewn all about.

"See the tallest pile?" my niece asked. "Far out, slightly right? Come left of it toward center, that low stack there closest to us."

"I see it," I said as I trained the binoculars on five door-size pieces of cracked stone. The area around that stack was mostly clear of debris. There was a path of sorts leading from it to the gap in the wall to our left.

"That's where Rashawn was found," Naomi said. "I'll show you the crime scene photographs later, but he was facedown on that top slab, jeans around his right ankle, left leg hanging off the side. I don't think you can see the discoloration on the rock from here, but when Pedelini found him, it had been raining less than an hour, and there was a—"

"Wait," I said, lowering the binoculars. "Pedelini? As in the sheriff's detective?"

"Correct," Naomi said. "Pedelini spotted the body from up here. He said that when he got to Rashawn, despite the rain, there was a pink halo of blood all around the body."

"The indictment said the neck had been sawed," I said.

Naomi nodded. "You can read the full autopsy report."

"They have the weapon?" Bree asked.

My niece cleared her throat. "A foldable pruning saw found in the shared basement of the duplex where Stefan, Patty, and Sydney Fox lived."

"Stefan's foldable pruning saw?"

"Yes," Naomi replied. "He said he'd bought it because he was taking up turkey hunting and another teacher at the school who turkey hunted told him it was a good thing to have along."

"His prints on it?" Bree asked.

"And Rashawn's DNA," Naomi said.

Bree looked at us skeptically. "So how does he explain it?"

"He doesn't," Naomi said. "Stefan says he bought the saw, took it out of the packaging at home, and put it in the basement with the rest of the gear he'd bought to go hunting."

"How many ways into that basement?" Bree asked.

"Three," Naomi replied. "From Stefan's place, from Sydney Fox's place, and through a bulkhead door out back. No sign of forced entry there."

I lifted the binoculars and aimed them into the old quarry again, at that spot on the rocks where a thirteen-year-old boy had suffered and died.

"I want to go down there," I said. "See it up close."

"They've got the old road across from the church chained off, and it's a fair walk in," Naomi said. "At least twenty minutes off the main road. You'll want bug spray, long pants, and long sleeves because of the chiggers. There's poison sumac too."

"We can't leave a ninety-year-old in a car that long in this heat," Bree said. "We'll take Nana Mama home, get what we need, and come back."

For the second time that morning, I saluted my wife.

CHAPTER
25

WE REACHED LOUPE STREET fifteen minutes later. Ali was still watching television, an adventure-hunting show featuring a big affable guy in a black cowboy hat.

"You ever heard of Jim Shockey?" Ali asked.

"Can't say that I have."

"He goes to all these, like, uncharted places and he hunts, like, ibex in Turkey and sheep in Outer Mongolia."

"Outer Mongolia?" I said, looking closer at the screen and seeing a line of what I guessed were Mongolians with packs climbing some remote mountain with Shockey, the big guy in the black cowboy hat.

"Yeah, it's dope," Ali said, eyes fixed on the screen. "I didn't know you could do things like this."

"Outer Mongolia interest you?"

"Sure. Why not?"

"That's right, why not?" I said, and I went upstairs to change.

Naomi decided to stay behind and work on her opening statement. Nana Mama was making herself and Ali grilled cheese and green tomato sandwiches when Bree and I left.

We had the crime scene files and photographs with

us as we approached the church again. The grounds-keeper was finished and loading his mower onto a trailer. I looked for the chained-off and overgrown road that Naomi had shown us on the way out.

"Nana Mama's right," Bree said. "That is a beautiful cemetery."

I looked up the rolling hill beyond the church, saw rows of tombstones and monuments. I remembered something my uncle Clifford had said two nights ago and something else my grandmother had said earlier this morning.

I pulled over, threw the Explorer in park, and said, "Wait here a second."

I went to the groundskeeper, introduced myself, and asked him a few questions. His answers gave me chills up and down my spine.

Back in the car, I said, "Short detour before we go to the quarry."

"Where are we going?"

"The cemetery," I said, swallowing my emotions and putting the car in gear. "I think my parents are buried up there."

Bree thought that over quietly for a few beats and then said, "You think?"

"The other night, Hattie's husband said, 'Christina's next to Brock.' Brock's my mom's brother, Aunt Connie's late husband, and Nana Mama said he's buried up there. My mom's got to be buried beside her brother. And the groundskeeper said there's also a Cross family plot up there."

I drove through the gate and up the gently rolling hill, looking for the monuments that the groundskeeper had described.

"Alex," Bree said softly. "You've never been to your parents' graves?"

I shook my head. "People thought I was too young to go to my mother's funeral, and we were sent to Nana Mama's right after my father died. Given all that we'd been through, she wanted to spare us the pain of a funeral."

Bree thought about that, said, "So your parents died close together?"

"Within a year of each other," I said. "After my mother passed, my father was so heartbroken, he started drinking a lot more, using drugs."

"That's horrible, Alex," she said, her brow knitting. "How come you've never told me that?"

I shrugged. "By the time I met you, my past was... my past."

"And who took care of you and your brothers while all this was happening?"

I thought about that, driving slow, still scanning the hillside. "I don't remember," I said. "Probably Aunt Hattie. We always went to her house when things got—"

The monument was gray granite and far down a row of similar tombstones. The name CROSS was carved across the face of it.

I stopped the car, left it running for the air conditioner, and looked at my wife. Her features were full of pain and sympathy.

"You go see," she said softly. "I'll be right here if you need me."

I kissed her before climbing out into the heat and the clamor of insects coming from the woods. I went around the front of the Explorer and down the row of graves, my attention on the one that said Cross.

A general numbness settled in me when I reached the monument, which was barely tended. Grass grew up at the base. I had to crouch and spread it to find three small granite stones carved with initials. Left to right, they read:

A.C. G.C. R.C.

I dug in the grass to the right of R.C. and found nothing but thatch and soil. There was no fourth stone. No J.C.

I stood and went around the back of the monument, finding more on the people buried there. The first name and the particulars startled me.

ALEXANDER CROSS
BLACKSMITH
BORN JANUARY 12, 1890
DIED SEPTEMBER 8, 1947

The second and third inscriptions read:

GLORIA CROSS
MOTHER AND WIFE
BORN JUNE 23, 1897
DIED OCTOBER 12, 1967

REGINALD CROSS
MERCHANT MARINER
BORN NOVEMBER 6, 1919
DIED MARCH 12, 1993

Puzzled, I climbed back into the car.

"What's wrong?" Bree asked.

"My father's not there. Nana Mama's ex-husband, my grandfather, is, and his parents. I must have been named for my great-grandfather Alexander, who was a blacksmith."

"You never knew that?"

I shook my head.

"Maybe there's another Cross plot up here," Bree said.

"Maybe," I said, and I put the car in gear.

Nine rows up I spotted the pale white monument that said PARKS below a carved American flag. It was closer to the cemetery lane, four graves in, and well tended, with fresh flowers in a vase. Like the Cross plot lower on the hill, there were smaller stones, two of them, separated by a gap of several feet. They were inscribed B.W.P. and C.P.C.

Brock William Parks and Christina Parks Cross.

The grief swept over me like a chill fog thick with regret and loss. Tears began to dribble down my cheeks as I whispered, "I'm sorry I've never been here before, Mom. I'm sorry about...everything."

I stood there trying to remember the last time I'd seen my mother, and I couldn't. She'd been dying in the house. I was sure of that because my aunts were there a lot, caring for her. But I couldn't conjure her up.

Disturbed by that, I wiped at my tears, walked around the back, and looked at the inscriptions.

BROCK WILLIAM PARKS
GREEN BERET
HERO TO HIS NATION

CHRISTINA PARKS CROSS
LOVING MOTHER

I was flooded with emotions and images of my mother on her best days, when she was loving, caring, and so much fun to be around. I could have sworn I heard her singing then, and it took everything I had to make it back to the car.

Bree watched me with tear-filled eyes. "She's there?"

I nodded, and then broke down sobbing. "She's been there for all these years, Bree. And I've...never...been here. Not once. In all this time, I never even wondered where she was buried. I mean, my God, who does that? What kind of son am I?"

CHAPTER
26

Palm Beach, Florida

AT NOON THAT SAME Saturday, Palm Beach County Sheriff's Office Detectives Peter Drummond and Richard S. Johnson were dispatched to a mansion on North Ocean Boulevard.

Detective Johnson was in his early thirties, a big athletic guy, ex-Marine, and a recent hire from Dade County. Detective Sergeant Drummond was in his sixties, a big, robust black man with a face almost devoid of expression due to nerve damage associated with a large burn scar that began beneath his right eye and spread over much of his cheek to his jaw.

Johnson knew he was lucky to have Drummond as his partner. The sergeant was a legend in the department, one of those men who had a knack for figuring out how criminals, especially murderers, thought.

Sergeant Drummond took a left off North Ocean Boulevard and pulled through open gates into an Italianate manor's courtyard where two cruisers, a medical examiner's van, and a midnight-blue Rolls-Royce were parked.

"Who the hell can afford to live like this?" Johnson asked.

"Around here," Drummond said, "lots of folks. And definitely Dr. Stanley Abrams. He owns a big plastic-surgery clinic. They call him the Boob King."

They climbed out of the unmarked cruiser into heat that was ungodly despite the proximity to the ocean.

"I thought most of the super-rich along Ocean Boulevard headed north for the summer," the younger detective said.

"Most do," the sergeant replied. "But guys like Abrams stay around no matter how hot it gets."

One of the uniformed deputies showed them into the house—a castle, really, with so many hallways and rooms that Detective Johnson was soon lost. They climbed a grand staircase, passing an oil painting of a pretty woman in a ball gown, and heard the sound of a man crying.

They entered a bedroom suite and found a slight man in a hall off the bedroom sitting on a padded bench, head down.

"Dr. Abrams?" Drummond said.

The plastic surgeon looked up, revealing a smooth-featured face and a full head of hair that spoke to Johnson of multiple procedures, including hair plugs.

Drummond identified himself, told Abrams he was sorry for his loss.

"I don't get it," Abrams said, composing himself. "Ruth was the happiest person I know. Why would she do this to herself?"

"No inkling that she might have been thinking of suicide?" Drummond asked.

"None," the doctor said.

"Nothing that had upset her lately?" Johnson asked.

The plastic surgeon started to shake his head, but then stopped. "Well, Lisa Martin's death last week. They were close, ran in the same circles."

Both detectives nodded. They'd caught that case too. But the death of Lisa Martin, another Ocean Boulevard resident, had been ruled accidental. She'd knocked a plugged-in Bose radio into the tub while she was taking a bath.

"So your wife was sad about Mrs. Martin's death?" Drummond said.

"Yes, sad and upset," Abrams said. "But not enough to…Ruth had everything to live for, and she loved life. My God, she's the only person in this town, including me, who's never been on antidepressants!"

"You found her, sir?" Johnson asked.

The surgeon's eyes watered, and he nodded. "Ruth had given the staff the weekend off. I flew in overnight from Zurich."

"We're going to take a look," Drummond said. "You touch anything?"

"I wanted to cut her down," Abrams said, looking into his hands. "But I didn't. I just…called you."

He sounded lost and alone. Johnson said, "You got family, sir?"

Abrams nodded. "My daughters. Sara's in London, and Judy's in New York. They're going to be…" He sighed and started to cry again.

Drummond went into the bedroom, Johnson trailing him. The detective sergeant stopped, studying the corpse in situ.

Ruth Abrams hung by a drapery cord that was suspended from a chandelier above the bed and cinched tight around her neck. She was a small-framed woman, no more than one hundred and ten pounds, and wore a black nightgown. Her face was swollen and mottled purple. Her legs and feet were a darker maroon because of the blood that had settled.

"You have a time of death?" Drummond asked the medical examiner, a young Asian woman who was making notes.

"Eighteen to twenty hours is the best I can do for

now," the ME said. "The air-conditioning throws things a bit, but it looks straightforward to me. She hung herself."

Drummond nodded without comment, eyes on the body. He walked over to the bed and stopped about a foot away from it. Johnson did the same on the opposite side.

It looked straightforward to Johnson too. She'd apparently put an upside-down wastebasket on the bed to stand on while she got the noose around her neck and then she'd kicked it away. There it was, on the rug to the right of the bed. She'd hung herself. End of story.

But the sergeant had put on reading glasses and was studying the bedspread, which was bunched to the left side of the bed. He peered at the woman's neck, livid and abraded from the cord, and then removed his glasses to study the knots that held the cord to the chandelier.

"Seal the house, Johnson," Drummond said at last. "This was no suicide."

"What?" the young detective said. "How can you tell that?"

The sergeant gestured to the bedspread and around the bed. "This looks like a struggle to me."

"People struggle when they hang themselves."

"True, but the sheets are all dragged to the left, meaning that the body was dragged up the right side, and the wastebasket was then placed on the right to suggest suicide," Drummond said.

Johnson saw what the sergeant was talking about but wasn't convinced. Drummond pointed to her hands.

"Broken and torn fingernails," he said. "There's a chip of the polish in the braids of the drapery cord. That and the vertical scratches above the neck suggests she was tearing at the cord during the initial struggle, which took place at ground level. And see how the livid lines are crisscrossed above and below the cord?"

Johnson frowned. "Yes."

"They shouldn't be there," the sergeant said. "If she'd kicked the wastebasket, the cord would have caught all her weight almost immediately. There'd be one line behind and along the cord, and we might see some evidence of the cord abrading the skin as it slid into position.

"But these two clear lines suggest that the killer flipped the cord over Mrs. Abrams's head from behind and throttled her. She fought, tore at her throat with her fingers, and maybe kicked at her killer. In any case, she created slack in the noose. The cord slipped, and the killer had to set it tight again, here. She was dead before she was hung up there. See the grooves along the cord where it's tied to the chandelier? That's from the killer hauling the body up."

The young detective shook his head in admiration. Drummond's legend was real, and the evidence was so clear once you heard him explain it.

"You want me to call in a full forensics team?" Johnson asked.

"I think that would be a very good idea."

CHAPTER
27

Starksville, North Carolina

THE WOODS ACROSS THE street from the church were thick with mosquitoes and biting flies that swarmed around me and Bree as we made the hike into the old quarry. Though it was muggy and hot, we were glad we'd taken Naomi's advice and put on long pants and long-sleeved shirts and doused ourselves with bug repellent.

We each carried a knapsack, and between the two we had several water bottles, a measuring tape, a camera, zip-lock bags, files with pictures of the crime scene, police diagrams, and copies of the notes Detectives Frost and Carmichael had taken when Rashawn Turnbull's body was found.

The overgrown trail wound through stands of stinging nettles and brush choked with kudzu. There was no wind. The air was oppressively humid, and the whine of insects was enough to drive us crazy by the time we crossed the stream. The path followed the waterway through a shaded, man-made gap in the limestone wall, ten, maybe fifteen feet wide and forty feet high. The creek spilled over its banks passing through the gap, making a large section of the ground mossy and slippery, and we had to support each other until we were out the other side and into the sunbaked quarry.

Bree looked back through the gap. "The killer supposedly brought Rashawn through there, but I can't see him dragging the boy in."

I nodded. "He'd have fallen. They both would have fallen."

"Any notes about that moss and slime in there being torn up?"

"Not that I saw. Then again, it rained late that night. Hard."

"It wouldn't matter," Bree insisted. "I don't think Rashawn was dragged in. He went along, which means he knew his killer."

The police thought so too. It was in the indictment.

"I'll buy it," I said. "What else?"

Bree smiled. "I'll let you know when I see it."

We moved closer to the stack of rock slabs, stopped where we had perspective. I got out the crime scene photographs, glanced at the sky for strength, and then divorced myself from being a father, a husband, a human being. It's the only way I can get beyond the things I have to witness and do my job.

But when I saw the first picture, a shudder went through me. The small, almost naked body lay face-down, straddling the top stone, wrists bound behind his back with a canvas belt. The arms appeared dislocated. His jeans were bunched around his right ankle, and jagged bone stuck out of the skin of the lower left leg. The head was so battered and swollen it was unrecognizable as a boy's.

"God help me," Bree said, and she looked away. "Who does something like this to a poor little guy like that?"

"Someone with a lot of pent-up rage," I said, looking toward the stack of rocks.

"Which the prosecution says was Stefan's reaction to Rashawn rejecting him," Bree said.

"I don't buy that," I said. "This level of viciousness suggests pathological hatred or sadistic insanity, not a fit of revenge."

We stood there forty feet from the stack and forced ourselves to go through the photographs. They ran the gamut from close-ups of various pieces of evidence in the order they were discovered to a dozen photos of Rashawn's brutalized body, including his sawed neck.

In the pictures, the surface of the slab around Rashawn was pale pink, blood diluted by rain. It had spilled down over the other slabs and run out in fingers onto the stone floor. Seven feet from the stack, the blood disappeared into a debris field of baseball- to football-size chunks of limestone that ended at the creek forty-two feet away.

Rashawn's sneakers, torn Duke Blue Devils T-shirt, and underwear were all found within a twenty-five-foot radius of the stack. So was the prosecution's most damning piece of evidence. A photo showed a white card smeared with mud tilted down between chunks of limestone thirteen feet due east of the body; in the next photograph, the same item had been turned faceup, revealing a bloodied Starksville School District ID with a picture of my cousin Stefan Tate.

CHAPTER
28

IN OUR CONVERSATION AT the jail the day before, Stefan had told me that the last time he distinctly remembered having the ID was three days before the killing. He said that while coaching a tenth-grade gym class outside, he'd stuck it in the pocket of a windbreaker that he'd then placed on a bleacher. He forgot he'd put the ID in there until the next day. When he looked, he couldn't find it.

His fiancée, Patty Converse, had been teaching a class at the same time in the same area, so as many as sixty kids had been in the vicinity of the windbreaker and the ID card. The only identifiable fingerprints on the ID, however, belonged to Stefan, who had failed to report the card missing.

My cousin's fingerprints were also on a plastic sandwich bag found in the quarry seventeen feet east of the ID. The sandwich bag was rolled and sealed inside a larger zip-lock bag. That same sandwich bag contained drugs packaged for sale in cellophane wrappers: six grams of black-tar heroin, three grams of cocaine, and nine grams of crushed crystal methamphetamine.

My cousin had no explanation for the prints on the bag; he speculated that someone could have gone into his trash at school and retrieved a bag he'd discarded after lunch one day.

It was entirely possible but a flimsy defense. The preponderance of the evidence said Stefan was there that night.

"Let's get closer and recheck everything," I said. "Position of evidence, measurements, photographic angle, anything we can think of."

"A lot can change in two months, Alex," Bree said doubtfully as we walked up to the stack of rocks where Rashawn Turnbull had been tortured and killed. "There's nothing here that looks remotely like blood. In fact, it's almost like it's been scrubbed."

I could see what she was talking about. There were swirls and shallow gouges on the surface of the top slab and down the side, as if someone had scoured the area with an abrasive cleanser and a steel brush. Looking around, I wondered what else might have been sanitized after the police had gathered their evidence.

To further confuse things, the area was littered with broken beer and whiskey bottles, shotgun shells and .22 rifle casings, fast-food wrappers, broken plastic utensils, and several empty cans of Mountain Dew.

"All this stuff was tossed here after Rashawn's death?" Bree asked.

I shrugged. "We'll have to compare the photographs to what's there now."

"But they didn't photograph every inch beyond the twenty-five-foot perimeter, did they?"

"Not from the looks of it," I said. "We'll have to do the best we can with what we've been given."

I started checking measurements and comparing the pictures to the current situation. The crime scene diagrams showed the entrance gap as sixty-six and a half feet from the stack. I used a small laser range finder and noted it was closer to seventy. That was unimportant in itself, but it suggested that the rest of the forensics work might have been shoddy too.

I used the range finder again to tell me where the ID card and drugs had been found. Compared with the photographic evidence, those locations were also off by a foot or more. And many of the rocks had been over-turned or moved slightly from the positions shown in the pictures.

Still, I noted the trend line created by the rock stack, the ID, and the drugs. The position of the three sug-gested someone leaving the stack and heading due east, toward the creek. This jibed with the police theory that the killer had escaped over the rocks, gone into the wa-ter, and then waded out of the quarry.

I continued along the trend line, noting by the pic-tures that no stone in the twenty-four feet between the drugs and the water had been left unturned. According to the file, police had found no more evidence along the route, but I went all the way to the creek anyway.

Rock-bottomed and algae-bloomed, the stream was no more than eight inches deep and sixteen inches wide. It ran lazily from my left to my right into and under the bramble of brush I'd seen from the lookout earlier that morning.

I got down into the water and walked in the stream, seeing how the willows overhung it. If things hadn't changed considerably in the past months, a man would have had to crawl through there. A woman too.

Why do that? Why use the stream at all? It's the dead of night. Why not just go out the way you came in?

I supposed someone could argue that Stefan would seek the water to keep his trail scent-free. But it had been raining when the killer left. And what had caused the fleeing murderer to drop the ID and the drugs? A pocket torn during the struggle?

I crouched to peer through the limbs and vines and saw where the creek broke free forty feet on, close by the gap in the quarry wall. On the banks, caught up in the roots, there was plenty of trash: beer cans, a plastic milk jug that looked like it had taken a shotgun blast, and a length of faded orange twine twisted through the roots like a game of cat's cradle.

Toward the far end was what looked like a rusted bike handlebar, and—

Behind me, near Bree, a bullet ricocheted off stone a split second before I heard the distant muzzle blast of a high-powered rifle.

CHAPTER
29

I THREW MYSELF BACK and down into the stream, digging for my gun and screaming, "Bree!"

I heard the second round slap limestone before the report, and then she yelled, "I'm okay, Alex! Shooter on the northeast rim, left of the overlook!"

My backup pistol in hand, I raised my head, found the forested northeast rim, and caught something glinting in the trees a second before the third shot. This one was aimed at me.

The bullet blew up a small rock four feet in front of my position, throwing stone and grit in my face before I could duck.

Bree opened up with her nine-millimeter, three quick shots and then two more, all Hail Marys at better than two hundred yards. But the counterattack seemed to make the sniper think better of continuing to shoot at us.

For almost a minute, there was nothing. I put my face in the water, eyes open to wash them out. I raised my head and blinked before hearing the sound of an engine starting and rubber tires spitting gravel.

I stood, looked up blurrily, and saw a white flash as the shooter went past.

"Was that an Impala?" I yelled.

"Couldn't tell!" Bree shouted back. "You okay?"

"Better than I might have been," I said, blinking and wiping at my eyes until I could see reasonably well.

Bree was standing on the opposite side of the rock pile, scanning the rim in case there were others waiting to shoot.

"Where'd the first two rounds hit?" I asked when I reached her side.

"First shot, he had me exposed from the waist up and hit there," she said, pointing to a fresh chip in the limestone four feet to her right. Then she pointed to a second chip on the surface of the top slab, eighteen inches in front of her. "I'd already dropped behind the stack when that one hit."

I shaded my eyes with my hand, peered toward the spot where I'd seen the glint of the sun on a rifle scope. "Has to be better than two hundred and fifty yards," I said. "But there's no wind."

"What are you saying?"

"The guy who shot Sydney Fox was an experienced rifleman at close range," I said. "If this was the same guy, he's military-trained or a practiced hunter, so with the right kind of rest, he should have hit us easily."

Bree said, "Or maybe he's a local hunter who's good in thick cover around here, a quick shooter who falls to pieces at long distances."

"Or the sight was off," I said. "Or he intentionally missed us."

"To scare us?"

"And let us know we're being watched, and probably followed."

Bree looked around, said, "I feel like a sitting duck out here."

I did too, and I couldn't shake the sensation. We decided to leave, call the sheriff's office, and figure out where the shooter had been. But I went through the slippery gap in the wall feeling like there might be other things to be found in that quarry. I vowed to return the next day.

Once I had cell service, I called the only cop I'd met since arriving in Starksville who seemed more than merely competent. Detective Pedelini answered on the second ring. I told him what had happened. Pedelini said he was no more than twenty minutes away and would meet us at the lookout.

"Do not go into those woods without me," Pedelini said.

We didn't. He rolled up in an unmarked white Jeep Cherokee five minutes after we did. We walked him through it, pointing to the positions we'd been in when the shooting started and giving him our rough estimate of where the sniper had been.

Pedelini nodded, said, "Do not get ahead of me."

The detective started hacking his way through kudzu with a machete he'd gotten from a box in the rear of the Cherokee. From our angle, the sniper had appeared to be very close to the rim, but we soon discovered that six or seven feet back from the edge, the ground turned too steep for anyone to walk on safely.

Pedelini stopped where the footing was treacherous, and we all had to hold on to trees for support.

"Here's your shooter," he said, pointing with the machete to scuff marks in the leaves. "There's the legs of his bipod biting in."

I stepped up, saw the two holes in the duff, and showed Bree where ferns had been matted down. "He was sitting, feet propped against those tree roots, and on a steady rest."

Pedelini listened to our theories as to why a good shot on a steady rest would have missed us out there in the open, and he said all of them were reasonable but none conclusive. We searched the area and found no empty cartridges, meaning that the shooter had taken the time to clean up, which suggested he was smart and nothing more.

Pedelini led us out of the woods. We were all drenched in sweat, and we climbed into the detective's air-conditioned car.

"What were y'all doing down there?" Pedelini asked.

"Due diligence," I said. "I like to walk crime scenes if I can."

"Find anything?"

"Some of the measurements on the diagrams are off," I said.

The detective looked disgusted. "Measurements. That's Frost and Carmichael's work. Any other flaws?"

He said this with no defensiveness in his voice, as if he were merely looking for pointers from more experienced investigators.

Bree said, "Looks like someone's been into that rock pile and scoured the slabs with a steel brush and an abrasive cleanser."

Pedelini looked pained. "Cece Turnbull did that 'bout six weeks after Rashawn died. She'd heard that some of the local kids had been going out to see where her boy had been raped and killed. Like a fucking shrine. Can you imagine?"

Pedelini's cheek twitched and his jaw drifted left of center before he said, "Anyway, Cece had gone back to drinking and drugging by then, and she flipped. She brought in a fifth of Jack Daniel's and some meth and went at that slab with a barbecue brush and graffiti remover. I found the poor thing down there the next morning, stone drunk and weeping."

CHAPTER
30

PEDELINI HAD US FOLLOW him down to the sheriff's office to make a statement. By the time we got there, it was past three that Saturday afternoon, and the uniformed officers were changing shifts.

The detective showed us into the detectives' bullpen and pointed us to chairs near his desk, which featured a recent picture of him in a tricked-out bass boat, grinning and fishing with two darling little girls.

"Your daughters?" Bree asked.

The detective smiled, said, "Two of the joys of my life."

"They're beautiful," I said. "When did your wife pass away?"

My wife frowned at me, but Pedelini cocked his head, said, "How did you know?"

"The way you were rubbing the ring finger of your left hand just then. I used to catch myself doing it after my first wife died."

Pedelini looked down at his hand, said, "Remind me not to play poker with you, Dr. Cross. My Ellen died seven years ago this September. Childbirth."

"I'm sorry to hear that, Detective," I said. "That's rough."

"I appreciate that," Pedelini said. "I really do. But the

girls and my job keep me going. Can I get you something to drink? Coffee? Tea? Coca-Cola? Mr. Pibb?"

"I'll take a coffee," Bree said. "Cream, no sugar."

"A Mr. Pibb," I said. "Haven't had one of those in years."

"I'm partial to them myself," Pedelini said, and he disappeared down a hallway.

"I like him," my wife said.

"I do too," I said. "He's solid."

A female deputy came into the room carrying an armful of files and mail that she distributed to the various desks. When she got to Pedelini's, she said, "Guy here?"

"Getting us something to drink," Bree said.

She nodded, put several dusty old files on his desk, said, "Tell him these came over from the clerk. He's been asking after them."

"We'll do that," I promised, and the deputy moved on.

I had a crick in my lower back suddenly, and I stood to stretch. When I did, I happened to look down at the files; I saw the faded labels on the tabs, and felt my head retreat by several degrees.

The label of the file on top read *Cross, Christina.*

The one below it read *Cross, Jason.*

I picked up the file on my mother and was about to flip it open when Bree said in alarm, "Alex, you can't just start going—"

"Oh, Jesus," Pedelini said.

I looked up, saw the detective balancing a coffee mug and two cans of Mr. Pibb on a small tray. His skin had lost three shades of color.

"I am so sorry, Dr. Cross," he said, chagrined. "I…I ran your name through our databases, and those files came up. So I…requested them."

"My name?" I said. "What are these?"

Pedelini swallowed, set the tray down, and said, "Old investigative files."

"On what?" Bree said, standing to look.

The detective hesitated, and then said, "Your mother's murder, Dr. Cross."

At first I thought I'd misheard him. I squinted and said, "You mean my mother's death?"

"I don't think so," Pedelini replied. "They were filed under homicide."

"My mother died of cancer," I said.

The detective looked puzzled. "No, that's not right. The database says murder by asphyxiation, case eventually closed due to the death of chief suspect, who was shot trying to escape the police and fell into the gorge."

In total shock, I said, "Who was the chief suspect?"

"Your father, Dr. Cross. Didn't you know?"

PART THREE

UNDERWORLD

CHAPTER
31

THREE HOURS LATER, Bree drove us back through the streets of Birney. The pain of reading those files was still raw, still searing.

Bree put her hand on mine, said, "I can't imagine what you're going through right now, Alex. But I'm here for you, sugar. Any way you need me, I'm here for you."

"Thank you. I...this just changes everything, you know?"

"I know, baby," Bree said, and she pulled up in front of the bungalow where the files said my dad had smothered my mother with a pillow.

I got out of the car feeling like I'd just been released from the hospital after a life-threatening illness, weak and unsure of my balance. I started toward the front porch with my mind playing tricks on me, seeing flashes of shattered, disjointed memories: my boyhood self running down the train tracks in the rain; watching my father being dragged by a rope; and, finally, staring at my mother's dead body in her bed, looking so frail, and small, and empty.

I don't remember falling, only that I hit the ground hard enough to knock the wind out of me and set my world spinning.

"Alex?" Bree cried, rushing to my side.

"I'm okay." I gasped. "Must have tripped or… Where's Nana?"

"Probably inside," Bree said.

"I need to talk to her," I said.

"I know you do, but—"

"Dad!" Ali cried, pushing open the screen door and jumping off the stoop.

"I'm okay, son," I said, getting to my feet. "Just haven't eaten enough."

The door slammed again. Naomi came out, looking concerned.

"He got a little dizzy," Bree explained.

"Where's Nana?" I asked.

"At Aunt Hattie's," she said. "They're making dinner."

"I think you need to go inside and lie down, Alex," Bree said.

"Not now," I said, and I fixed on my aunt's house like it was a beacon in the night.

I took my tentative first steps still bewildered and seeking solace from my grandmother. But by the time I was on Hattie's porch, I was moving fast, angry and seeking answers.

I stormed inside. Aunt Hattie, Aunt Connie, and Uncle Cliff were in the kitchen. My aunts were dipping tilapia fillets in flour, getting them ready to fry, when I walked in and said, "Where's Nana?"

"Right here," she said.

My grandmother was tucked into a chair on my left, reading a book.

I went to her, loomed over her, my hands balled into fists, and said, "Why'd you lie to me?"

Nana Mama said, "Take a step back there, young man. And what'd I lie to you about?"

"My mother!" I shouted. "My father! All of it!"

My grandmother shrank from me and raised her arm defensively, as if she thought I might hit her. The truth was I'd been on the verge of doing just that.

It rattled me. I stepped back, glanced around the room. My aunts were staring at me in fear, and Bree and Jannie and Ali and Naomi had come in and were looking at me like I had gone mad.

"None of that now," Uncle Cliff roared, standing up with his walker and shaking his finger at me. "No mugging old ladies on my train. You sit your ass down, show me your ticket, or I will throw you off, next stop. You hear?"

Uncle Cliff trembled with force, and I was suddenly a kid again, weak and dizzy. I grabbed a chair and sat, put my head in my hands.

"Alex, what's happened?" Nana Mama demanded.

"Just tell me why you all lied to me," I said with a groan. "That's all I want to know."

CHAPTER
32

"I SWEAR TO YOU, I knew nothing about this!" Nana Mama cried after Bree told her what we'd read in the files. She looked to my aunts, said, "Is this true? Did you know?"

Aunt Hattie and Aunt Connie were holding on to each other in such a way that they didn't have to say a word.

"Why?" Bree asked.

"Because," Aunt Hattie said, her voice shaking. "Those terrible things that went on, they were so traumatic, so horrible, that you, Alex, blocked it all out. It was like you'd never seen what happened to your father. We figured it was nature's way of helping you deal with it and that you'd be better off believing your mom died from the cancer and your dad from the drinking and the drugs."

"But why lie to *me*?" my grandmother demanded, as shaken as I'd been.

"You'd been through so much already and gone so far in life, Regina," Aunt Connie said, choking. "We didn't want to make you suffer any more than you had to. Alcohol and drugs, you could understand. Jason had been headed for that early grave already. But his killing Christina, and then the way he died. We just couldn't tell you. We thought it would break your heart when your heart needed to be strong for Alex and his brothers."

Nana Mama gazed off into a distance, her lower lip quivering, then looked at me and started to weep.

I went to her, got down on my knees, and laid my head in her tiny lap, feeling her anguish as my own, feeling her tears splash on my face as I said, "I'm sorry I called you a liar."

"I'm sorry 'bout everything, Alex," she said, stroking my head the way she used to when I first went to live with her. "I'm sorry about every bit of it."

There was a heaviness in the air when we finally got around to eating. No one said much the rest of the night. Or at least, I don't remember anything specific until I went to my aunts after dessert and forgave them. They cried all over again when we hugged.

Aunt Connie said, "We didn't mean all this to come out."

"I know," I said. "It's okay."

"You sure?" Aunt Hattie asked.

"You were trying to protect me," I said. "I get that."

Aunt Connie said, "But you still don't remember anything?"

"I've been getting flashes," I admitted. "But not much more than that."

Aunt Hattie said, "Maybe that's all God wants you to remember."

I nodded, kissed them both, and went out the door after my family. Jannie was already heading up the porch stoop to our bungalow. Bree was walking along with Ali and Naomi. Ali saw me, turned, and ran back.

I put my arm around my boy's shoulder, said, "See the lightning bugs?"

"Yeah," Ali said, like he didn't care.

"Hey," I said. "What's the matter?"

"Dad?" he said, not looking at me. "Can we go home?"

"What? No."

"But I don't like this place," he said. "I don't have any friends, and I don't like how it hurts you to be here. And how it hurts Nana."

I picked up my youngest and held him tight to me, saying, "I don't like how it hurts either, son. But I promised I'd help Stefan. And in this life, a man is only as good as his word."

CHAPTER
33

AFTER MASS THAT SUNDAY morning, Nana Mama and I dropped Bree and the kids back at the bungalow. I drove us close to the arched bridge and parked. My grandmother took my arm, and we walked slowly out onto the span above the gorge.

The Stark River was roaring down there, throwing up white haystacks, spinning into dark whirlpools, and surging against the walls as far as the eye could see downstream. I remembered my parents were always telling me and my brothers never to go near the bridge or the river.

"Dad used to say there was no worse way to die than drowning," I told Nana Mama. "I honestly think he was scared of the gorge."

"Because I taught him to be scared of it," my grandmother said quietly. "My little brother, Wayne, died down there when he was six. They never found his body."

She said nothing for a few long moments, just stared at the roiling water four stories below us like it held terrible secrets.

Then Nana Mama shook her head. "I can't bear to think of how terrified your father must have been as he fell."

"According to the report, he was probably dead before he hit the water."

"And you don't remember any of it?" she asked.

"I had a nightmare last night. It was raining and there was lightning, and I was running down the tracks and then toward the bridge. I saw flashing lights before I heard gunshots. And then there were men out on the bridge, looking over, just like we are now."

"What a waste," my grandmother said. "Just a wasted, tragic life."

She started to cry again, and I hugged her until she calmed.

Wiping her eyes with a handkerchief, she said, "Do you think that's all there is about what happened? That report?"

"I don't know," I said. "There's a couple of people I'd like to talk to about it."

"You'll let me know?"

"If I find something, you'll know it," I promised.

On the ride back to the bungalow, I drove through the east end of Birney so Nana Mama could see the house she'd been living in when Wayne died. I pulled over next to the ramshackle building. It was just two blocks from the river.

"I'll never forget that day," she said, gesturing at the house. "I was eight and there on that porch playing with one of my friends when my mama came out the house, asked where Wayne had gotten to. I said he'd gone off down the street to see his buddy Leon.

"She went down after him to Leon's house, which was right there on the corner of South Street across from the gorge," she went on. "Mama saw Wayne and Leon over on the rocks above the river. She saw him fall. You could hear her screaming all the way here. She never got over that. The fact that his body was never found just ate her up. Every spring she'd make my dad go downriver with her to where the gorge spills onto the flat so they could see if the floods had swept Wayne's body out. They looked for twenty years."

"I'm beginning to see why you wanted to leave this place," I said.

"Oh, your grandfather saw to that," she said.

"What was he like?" I asked. "Reggie."

"Huh," Nana Mama said, as if she didn't want to talk about him, but then she did. "He was not like anyone I'd ever met before. A charmer, I'll give him that. He could sweet-talk like it was his second language, and the way he told you about his adventures at sea made you want to listen forever. He swept me off my feet with those stories. And he was handsome, and a good dancer, and he made a lot of money, by Starksville standards."

"But?"

Nana Mama sighed. "But he was away five, six months a year. I'm sure he caroused outside our marriage when he was in foreign ports because he wasn't shy about doing it when he came home. Got to the point where all we did was fight. He didn't mind drinking while we fought, and he didn't mind using his fists either. I decided one day that, despite my marriage vows, that wasn't the life I wanted, or deserved. So I divorced Reggie and got enough money out of it to go on up to Washington and start all over. All in all, it was the best move I've ever made."

She fell silent then for a few moments. "You saw Reggie's grave?"

"He's with his parents," I said.

"Always liked Alexander and Gloria. They treated me kind, and they loved your father, especially Alexander."

"I was named after him," I said.

"You were."

"He was a blacksmith."

"The best around these parts. Never wanted for work." She sighed again, said, "I need to take a nap."

"I know the feeling," I said, putting the car in gear.

We rolled back toward Loupe Street and the bungalow with the car windows down. Along the way, we passed Rashawn Turnbull's house. There was a gleaming, cream-colored Cadillac Escalade parked out front.

I spotted three people on the porch. A tall man with iron-gray hair wearing a blue suit and a blond, sharply dressed woman in her fifties were engaged in a furious argument with a sandy-haired younger woman in cut-off shorts and a red T-shirt.

The younger woman sounded drunk when she shrieked: "That's bullshit! You never gave a shit about him alive! Leave my house and stay the hell out of my life!"

CHAPTER
34

BREE AND I WAITED almost an hour, had lunch, and made sure that Nana Mama had gone to take her nap before returning to Rashawn Turnbull's house.

"So that was definitely Cece?" Bree asked when I pulled in where the Escalade had been parked.

"Sure fit the description," I said, getting out.

We went up on the porch. A trash can had been turned over and was surrounded by broken beer bottles and old pizza boxes. Inside, a television blared the music from one of the Star Wars movies, Darth Vader's theme.

I knocked, got no answer. I knocked again, much harder.

"Go the fuck away!" a woman screamed. "I never want to see you again!"

I yelled, "Mrs. Turnbull? Could you come to the door, please?"

Glass smashed inside before the television went quiet. Then the ratty yellow curtain on the near window was pulled aside. Rashawn's mother peered blearily at us through the screen. You could tell at a glance that she'd been beautiful once, but now her hair was the color and consistency of loose straw, her yellowed teeth were ground down, and her skin was sallow.

Her sunken, rheumy hazel eyes drifted when she asked, "Fuck are you?"

"My name's Alex Cross," I said. "This is my wife, Bree."

Cece lifted a cigarette, took a drag with contempt, said, "I don't go for none of that Jehovah's shit, so get your ass off my porch."

Bree said, "We're police detectives."

Rashawn Turnbull's mother squinted at us, said, "I know all the cops in Starksville and for three towns around, and I don't know either of you two."

"We're from Washington, DC," I said. "We work homicide up there, and I used to be with the FBI."

"Then what are you doing here?"

I hesitated, then told her. "We're looking into your son's case."

"What for?"

"Because my cousin is Stefan Tate."

You'd have thought I punched her. Her head snapped back and then shot forward in rage. She hissed, "That evil sonofabitch is gonna die for what he did. And I am going to be there to see it happen. Now get off my porch before I find my granddad's shotgun."

The curtain fluttered shut.

"Mrs. Turnbull!" I yelled. "We do not work for Stefan. If my cousin killed your boy, I'll be sitting right there beside you when they execute him. I told Stefan the same thing. We work for only one person. Your son. Period."

There was no answer, and for a moment I thought she might indeed have gone in search of her granddad's shotgun.

Bree called out, "Cece, will you please talk to us? I promise you we have no ax to grind. We just want to help."

There was no answer for several beats.

Then a pitiful voice said, "There's no helping this, or me, or Rashawn, or Stefan. No one can change any of it."

"No, we can't change what's happened," I said. "But we can make sure the right person suffers for the horrible things that were done to your boy. Please, I promise you we won't take up much of your time."

A few moments later, a bolt was thrown, and the door creaked inward.

CHAPTER
35

IN THE COURSE OF my career, I have entered the homes of many grieving mothers and witnessed my share of shrines erected in mourning for a lost child. But I'd never seen anything quite like this.

Broken furniture. Broken liquor bottles. Shattered plates and mugs. The small living area was a complete shambles except for an oval coffee table that featured a green marble urn surrounded by a collection of framed photographs of Rashawn from infancy on up.

The older pictures all looked like yearly school portraits. In every one, Rashawn was grinning magnetically. Seriously, you did not want to take your eyes off that boy's smile.

Around the entire edge of the table and surrounding the pictures like the spokes on a medicine wheel, there were toys, everything from an air-soft pistol to action figures, stuffed animals, and Matchbox cars. The only things on the table that looked like they hadn't belonged to Rashawn were a half-empty bottle of Smirnoff vodka, two blackened glass pipes, a small butane torch, and a baggie of some white substance.

On the wall hung a sixty-inch flat-screen. It was split horizontally into two feeds. The lower one was playing *The Empire Strikes Back*, the volume turned down low. The upper one showed home videos of Rashawn as a young boy, four, maybe five. He was wearing a cape and jumping around swinging a toy lightsaber.

"He liked Star Wars a lot," Bree said sympathetically.

Cece rubbed at her nose, sniffed, and curled the corners of her lips up in the direction of a smile. "He'd watch those movies over and over again. Like they were new every time. Sometimes we'd watch them together. He knew all the lines. I mean, all of them. Who can do that?"

"A very smart boy," I said.

"He was that," she said, putting out her cigarette. She scratched her arm and looked longingly at the pipes and the drugs.

"Tell us about Stefan Tate," I said.

Cece hardened, said, "He's a sadist and a cold-blooded killer."

"Did you think he was a sadist before Rashawn died?"

"Who broadcasts they're a sadist?" she asked.

"Good point," I said. "But you had no warning?"

"If I'd had a warning, he wouldn't have spent a second with my boy," Cece said, going around the couch and almost reaching for one of the pipes. Then she seemed to realize the drugs were sitting there in the open and pushed the baggie under a teddy bear.

She lit another cigarette. We asked her about Rashawn and Stefan, and she corroborated what my cousin had told us: that they'd met at school and took an instant liking to each other, that Stefan had become a big brother/father figure to the boy, and that something had happened in the days before Rashawn's death that made him want to sever his relationship with my cousin.

"Stefan says he doesn't know what was behind it," I said.

Cece took a drag, nodded to the urn, and said bitterly, "He came on to Rashawn, and Rashawn rejected him."

"Rashawn told you that?" I asked.

"I'm just reading into the way Rashawn acted the last time I saw him."

"Which was like what?" Bree asked.

"Like he'd seen something to be scared about," Cece said, looking at the screen where Luke Skywalker was preparing to fight his father. "I've asked myself a million times since why I didn't push Rashawn to tell me that morning. But I was late for an AA meeting. And trying to stay sober. And trying to do the right thing."

She paused, and then a shudder went through her, and she choked and wept. "My last memory of my little boy is him staring into his cereal bowl like he was seeing things in the milk. Oh God!"

Cece snatched up the pipe, dug out the baggie, and with shaking hands tried to load whatever it was she meant to smoke. Bree came around to her and put her hand on her arm. She said in a soothing tone, "That's not gonna help."

Rashawn's mother yanked her arm away, turned her back on Bree, protecting the pipe, and sneered, "It's the only thing that does."

I said, "Are you planning to go to the courthouse tomorrow?"

Cece snatched up the small butane torch and backed away to the other side of the table, glaring at us.

"You not going to start in on that, are you?" she demanded. "I already heard an earful on that today."

She lit the torch and stared greedily at the pipe bowl as she sucked and laid the flame. She took a whole lungful, held it, then rocked her head back and exhaled long and slow. I thought she was going to black out, but she just blinked stupidly at us a few times and then set the pipe down.

"Someone talked to you about being in court tomorrow?" I asked quietly.

The anger had left her, replaced by scorn.

"Harold and Virginia, dear Moms and Pops," she said, plopping into a chair with a broken seat. She began doing imitations of a proper Southern belle and a deep-voiced man. "'Straighten up for the trial, Cece. You wouldn't want to be seen like this.' 'You've got to do it in honor of your dear Rashawn, Cynthia Claire.'"

She leaned over, grabbed the vodka bottle, took a belt, and went off on a tirade. "The fucking hypocrites. All caring and such, now that he's dead. Alive, they were ashamed of his blood!"

Cece hugged her knees and shook her head violently. "They still don't give a shit. Only things those two are concerned about is their money and their precious image in the community."

Deepening her voice, she said, "'Don't want to have Cece do any more damage than has already been done. We must do everything we can to minimize our association with the little dead mulatto. With God's blessing, none of our posh friends down on Hilton Head will hear a word of it.'"

She took another swig of vodka and stewed there as if she were alone for almost a minute before hanging her head and saying, "I don't go to court tomorrow, it's like *I'm* ashamed of him, ashamed to be his mother, isn't it?"

Bree said, "If you don't go, you're saying you've given up on him, that he doesn't matter to you anymore."

"But he does matter." Cece sobbed. "Rashawn was everything to me. The one good and decent thing I ever did in my whole life. And look what happened to him! My God, look what happened to him!"

Bree went over and put her arms around the woman's heaving shoulders. "I know it seems impossible, but you've got to be strong now."

"I don't have that kind of strength." Cece moaned. "I never have. It's the story of my life."

"Until today," Bree said, rubbing her back. "The new story of your life is that you hit rock bottom today, Cece. You hit rock bottom, and from the depths of your despair, you asked for help. And when you did, Rashawn's spirit reached out, took your hand, and gave you the strength to go into that courtroom tomorrow morning clear-eyed and sober, because only you can be his representative at the trial. Only his mother can stand there for him and make sure justice prevails."

Head still down, straw hair still hanging, Cece tensed up as if to fight again. Then she shuddered long and slow. And as it died out, something seemed to fall away inside the dead boy's mother. Cece sagged against Bree, and slept.

Bree glanced over, whispered, "I'll stay with her. All night if I have to."

Raw emotion welled in my throat.

"You okay with it?" she asked.

I smiled, said hoarsely, "More than okay."

"Then why are you upset?"

"I'm not. What you did there with her was…just…"

"What?"

"I have never been more proud to call you my wife, Bree Stone."

CHAPTER
36

Palm Beach, Florida

THE MANSION HAD BEEN modeled after a villa on the Amalfi Coast and it had once been a grand place. Now it was showing its age. The grounds weren't as well tended as they had been. The front gate and door needed paint. Much of the brickwork required pointing. And who knew when the windows had last gotten a proper cleaning?

Coco knew all about the house's many deficiencies and needs. He just had to look around the bedroom he was in to get upset. The silk wallpaper was separated at the seams in many places and curling back yellow. Scratches and dings showed on almost all the furniture. And the Oriental rugs were starting to look dingy.

Coco refused to dwell on any of it. He chose to ignore what had to be done to the house, just as he had chosen to ignore the *Palm Beach Post*'s story on Ruth Abrams's death.

Instead, he accessorized the three outfits laid out on a king-size bed. He loved to accessorize. It calmed him as much as cross-dressing did.

For the past hour, ever since he'd read that the police were calling Ruth's death a homicide, Coco had been adjusting the look of each ensemble using items from a large box of estate jewelry.

Wasn't it fascinating, how the effect changed so radically with such small modifications? *Mother always said image is in the detail, and she was right—*

The house phone rang.

Coco ignored it. People were always calling, always hounding, wanting this and that, and he just needed a break from reality for a little while longer.

Is that too much to ask? No. Not at all.

Coco had narrowed the three outfits down to two when the doorbell rang.

They're coming to my front door now?

He forced himself to swallow his outrage. Nothing was going to interrupt his interlude. Not today. Let them all wait. A party isn't a party until the life of it arrives. *Am I right, Mother?*

Coco decided on an ensemble composed of a black taffeta skirt from Argentina, a lavender chiffon blouse with a daring neckline, sheer black hose, and black pumps. He went to a closet door, fished a key off the top of the jamb, and turned the dead bolt.

He pulled open the door. Several bathrobes and kimonos on hooks on the inner side of it fluttered and settled. The walk-in closet was huge and filled with all manner of women's high fashion beneath clear plastic covers. Much of it went back decades, and he had to go well beyond the vanity and makeup mirror to find space for these new additions.

He hung the Tangerine Dream outfit first, and then the indigo Elie Saab dress. Both of them were definite repeats at some point down the road, he was sure. He placed the gladiator-strap stilettos and the orange slingback heels on the floor beneath the ensembles and then retrieved the jewelry box.

Coco set it on a shelf beside the vanity and got to work. He taped his gender back, laid on Lancôme foundation, and glued his fake lashes into place. Feeling slightly breathless as he always did when the transformation was fully under way, he set his makeup aside for the moment.

He found a pair of naughty black thong panties left over from a trip to Paris a few years back and slipped them on. Then he put on the garter belt and hose, loving the thick black stripe up the back.

How pulpy!

Now Coco knew who he'd be for the evening, and he looked to a higher shelf filled with old wig boxes. His attention went to a blue one and he retrieved it. He wouldn't tape the wig in place until he was almost fully clothed, but he couldn't resist trying it on.

The hair was jet black and pulled back severely into a tight bun. Coco set it on his smooth head, adjusted it, and then eased into the black pumps.

He stepped in front of the mirror and pursed his lips in satisfaction.

Tonight you shall be the Black Dahlia, Coco thought. *A sultry Latina with a hint of dominatrix and—*

He heard a gasp. His wigged head whipped left.

A chunky, middle-aged black woman in jeans, a dark hoodie, and yellow rubber dishwashing gloves stood in the closet doorway, gaping at him.

"Oh, Jesus, no!" she whispered in a thick accent.

Then she turned and ran.

CHAPTER
37

COCO KICKED OFF THE pumps, tore off the wig, and bolted after her.

The woman wasn't in shape or athletic, and he caught up to her before she reached the bedroom door. Coco grabbed her by the shoulder, spun the woman around, and pushed her up against the wall.

"What the hell are you doing in my house, Francie?" he demanded.

"I...I forget something important, Mr. Mize," she said, terrified. "I no know you're here."

"Obviously," Mize said. "What could be so important that you broke into my house wearing rubber gloves, Francie?"

She began to cry. "I was looking for...my bank card. The ATM."

"You figured out you were missing your bank card three months after I fired you?"

Francie nodded wildly. "Yes. Just yesterday. I look everywhere. I say, this one must to be at the Jeffrey Mize's house. So I come. I call you from outside. I ring doorbell."

"To make sure I wasn't home," Mize said.

"No! You no answer. You no hear?"

"I was busy."

His former maid's gaze flickered down to his black

panties, garter belt, and hose, and then back to the eye-lashes and makeup.

"I so sorry," she blubbered. "I see this now."

"My secret life?" he said. "My closet?"

"I no mean to! I just looking for—"

"Something to steal, isn't that right?"

"No, Mr. Mize," the maid said, and she made the sign of the cross.

Mize's mind turned to Coco's unique perspective again, and he said, "I was wondering why I'd been missing some of Mother's lesser jewelry. Never suspected you, Francie, but that's my naturally trusting personality."

The maid got more frightened. "No, that's not—"

"Sure it is," Mize said. "You're dirt-poor, Francie. So you steal. It's what you do. It's what I would do if I were you."

She clamped her jaw shut and tried to struggle away, but he threw her back against the wall. "Please, Mr. Mize," she whimpered. "Don't call police. I do anything, but not that!"

Mize thought, said, "You can keep a secret, can't you, Francie?"

She seemed not to understand for a moment, but then her head bobbled like a toy. "Of course, I no tell anyone you like dress lady-boy, Mr. Mize."

He laughed. "Lady-boy? Is that what they'd call me in Haiti?"

Francie's eyes darted around, but her head started bobbling again. "I sorry, Mr. Mize. Is a bad thing? Lady-boy?"

"You tell me."

"No, Mr. Mize," she babbled, "I no care your lady-boy secrets."

"Then I don't care you're a thief, Francie."

She didn't know what to say, but she nodded in resignation. "*Merci,* Mr. Mize. Please, I so sorry."

"How'd you get in?" Mize asked.

Francie looked down.

"If we're going to share secrets, we better start by being honest, don't you think?" Mize said in a more pleasant tone.

Tears dripping down her cheeks, Francie nodded. "I make key last year."

"Show me?"

The maid pulled off one of her rubber gloves, dug in her back pocket, and came up with the key.

He took it, said, "The alarm code?"

Francie blinked. "You give it to me, Mr. Mize. You no remember?"

That was true. Stupid of me.

"I remember," Mize said.

"What I do for you?" she asked. "Clean house again? It look like no clean for long time, Mr. Mize."

"Maybe I'll take you up on that."

"Yes, yes," Francie said. "Anything, Mr. Mize."

"Who else knew you were coming here to steal?"

"No one! I swear to spirits."

"Better to work that way, I suppose."

She nodded again. "No one knows, is better, I think."

"Makes sense," Mize said. "What have you stolen from me before?"

Francie looked down again. "Something silver from dining room, and maybe bracelets and necklace in other room."

"Thin gold bracelets? Little bangles?"

"I so sorry."

"You were desperate," he said. "I know what that's like."

Francie grabbed his hand and kissed it. "Bless you, Mr. Mize."

Mize smiled. "Well, then, I know your secrets; would you like to see mine?"

The maid looked torn.

"C'mon, if we're sharing secrets, we're friends now," he said. "Let me show you the closet and all its beauty."

Francie licked her lips, and then shrugged. "Okay."

"Real ladies first," Mize said, and gestured with a flourish toward the open closet door.

Uncertain, she moved past him, crossed the room, and stopped in the closet doorway. She looked around and her eyes widened.

"Magnificent, isn't it?" Mize asked.

Francie's voice was filled with genuine wonder. "I never see such things before this now. Maybe in movies."

"My mother started the collection," Mize said, taking a white kimono off the door hook and slipping it over his shoulders. "She loved her clothes, and she taught me to love them too."

The maid's face tightened. "Is good. I think."

"It bonded us," he said. "See the jewelry box on the vanity? It was Mother's. She was a spendthrift with exquisite taste in jewelry. Have a look. She'd want you to see."

Francie glanced at him tying the robe. He stopped, smiling. "Go on."

The maid went to the vanity. The lights around the mirror were glowing. She opened the lid. Her jaw dropped.

"Now, that's what you were hoping you'd find, wasn't it?" Mize asked.

He'd slid in behind Francie. In the mirror, she saw

not Mize, but Coco, the smile gone cold, the eyes gone vacant.

Before the maid could reply or even change her expression, Coco flipped the robe's sash over Francie's head.

He cinched it nice, tight, and brutal around her neck.

CHAPTER
38

Starksville, North Carolina

JUDGING BY THE TURNOUT for her wake that Sunday evening, Sydney Fox had been a well-liked person in Starksville. Nana Mama and I went to pay our respects while Naomi finished working on her opening statement and watched the kids, and Bree supported Cece Turnbull as she lurched toward a semblance of sobriety.

"A terrible thing," Nana Mama said as she held tight to my forearm. "Woman like that, in her prime, gunned down on her own front porch. Bad as it was when I grew up here, there was never violence like that."

"I'll take your word for your era," I said. "And, yes, it's bad, part of a general badness about this town. Do you feel it?"

"Every day since we've been here," Nana Mama said. "I'll be happy to go home when the time comes."

"I'm with you," I said. "And we've only been here since Thursday."

We followed a grief-stricken couple into the mortuary. There were very few dry eyes among the forty, maybe fifty people who had come to pay their respects. We waited in line to offer condolences to Ethel Fox, who wore an old but cared-for black dress she'd bought when her husband passed.

"I only figured to wear it again when I was dead and

gone," Ethel said. "And now, here I am, and there my baby girl is, all sealed up in a box."

She hung her head and cried softly. "Just isn't fair."

Nana Mama patted her on the shoulder, said, "Anything you need, you call Hattie or Connie or me. And I'll see you at the church tomorrow."

Ethel wiped tears with a handkerchief, and nodded. "Ten a.m."

I helped my grandmother into the chapel where Sydney Fox's body lay in a closed simple casket. It was standing room only, with a crowd of genuine mourners, people who had been deeply touched by the deceased at some point, enough to appear in public and freely express their grief.

Nana Mama took a seat saved for her next to my aunts and Uncle Cliff, who clung to Aunt Hattie's hand and looked vaguely frightened. Finding a spot just outside the doorway, I watched a few people go to the casket and pay their respects. Then I followed some others into a room where coffee and platters of Aunt Hattie's cookies and brownies were offered.

Talking with several of the mourners, I learned more about Sydney Fox. How she'd grown up in town. How she'd married her high school sweetheart, who'd turned into a colossal asshole once he found out she couldn't have kids. And how for years she'd endured his abuse while working as a beloved first- and second-grade teacher in the local elementary school. Many of the people I spoke to were parents of children who'd been blessed to have Sydney in their first years of school.

After a while I got angry. I'd shared just a few words with Sydney Fox, and now that seemed another crime, an armed robbery of my chance to know her.

I got a cup of coffee, ate more peanut butter–M&M cookies than I should have, and wandered back to see if Nana Mama was ready to leave. There were more people streaming in. I scanned their faces, looking for something familiar. Had I grown up with any of them? Would I recognize them after all these years?

The answer was no until I retrieved Nana Mama from the chapel and led her back for some cookies. Across the room, I spotted an imposing African American man in a dark suit, drinking coffee and munching on a brownie. He was familiar enough that I studied him.

Big dude like my best friend, John Sampson. Taller than me. Heavier than me. Ten, maybe fifteen years younger. The suit was expensive, but the body beneath it suggested hard labor. Then he changed one rough hand for another holding the coffee cup, and I knew him in a heartbeat.

I made sure my grandmother was good, walked over to him, and said, "How are you, Pinkie? Been a long time."

CHAPTER
39

THE FACE OF MY aunt Connie's only son, Brock "Pinkie" Parks Jr., clouded a bit at my use of his nickname, but then he realized who I was and broke into a grin.

"Alex," he said, grabbing my hand and pumping it. "Last time I saw you, you gave me a piggyback on the sidewalk in front of Nana Mama's place."

I had a vague vision of that and said, "Long time ago. I think you'd break my back if I tried to do that now. I heard life's been good for you."

"Was until I heard Sydney died," Pinkie said, his eyes watering. "Straight up? I loved Sydney. I loved her since I was like eight and she was ten. There was something about her, you know, like things went in orbit when she was around."

"You ever tell her?" I asked.

"Nah, we were friends, and then not so much after she married Finn Davis," he said. "He preferred it that way."

"I heard Finn gave her a rough time," I said.

"I set him straight once, but what was I gonna do? I got a good life working offshore and just couldn't be around to protect her, especially when for a while there she didn't want to protect herself."

"She divorced him."

"She told me," he said, full of regret. "We'd been

sending messages on Facebook and stuff, and I'd been meaning to come up to see her."

"I'm sorry."

"Me too," he said. "Any word on who did it?"

"Looked like a case of mistaken identity to me," I said, then explained about Stefan's fiancée being blond too.

Pinkie looked skeptical. "No one's looked at Finn Davis?"

"We heard racial slurs before the shot," I said. "They were yelling at Patty."

"Maybe," Pinkie said. "But Finn Davis is smart enough to use that as a cover. Then again, he was trained by the best."

"And who would that be?"

"Old friend of your father," Pinkie said grimly. "Marvin Bell."

Before I could say anything to that, Aunt Hattie came in with Uncle Cliff, who was in a wheelchair today. She brightened when she saw us and came over. After greeting her nephew, she excused herself to go talk to Nana Mama and Aunt Connie.

Pinkie knelt down by our uncle, said, "How you doing, Uncle Cliff?"

"Vacation's been good," Uncle Cliff said. "Heading back to work next week. Got the City of New Orleans the whole next month. Gonna meet Jason in the Quarter next week, hear us some bad-ass blues and talk old times."

I said, "My dad died, Cliff."

My uncle frowned, but then looked at my cousin and got anxious. "That right, Pinkie? When Jason die? Why no one told me that?"

"He died a long time ago, Cliff," I said. "When I was a boy. He got shot and fell off the bridge into the gorge."

Clifford got even more anxious. "Pinkie, that ain't right. Jason dead?"

My cousin licked his lips, glanced at me, and then patted Cliff's arm and said, "Just like Alex said. You know that. We all know—"

Shouting erupted outside. It sounded like Ethel Fox.

Pinkie and I both left Uncle Cliff and went out on the front porch of the funeral home. Sydney Fox's tiny mother stood toe to toe arguing with a man a solid foot taller than her. Rangy, with a chiseled, hard face, he was about Sydney's age and dressed for the occasion in a dark gray suit.

"You'll go in there over my dead body," Ethel Fox said.

The man smiled. "She was my wife for years, Ethel. Least you can let me do is pay my respects."

"You never respected her in life, Finn Davis!" Ethel Fox shouted. "Why should you in death?"

Davis leaned over his former mother-in-law, put his finger on her chest, and said in a low, threatening voice, "'Cause it's the right thing to do, Ethel."

Pinkie was off the porch in a shot with me right behind him.

"Back off, Finn," Pinkie barked. "Back off, or I will bust you up fierce!"

All of a sudden, out from the shadows and between the cars, four men appeared. Every one of them had a tough, hard edge.

"Pinkie Parks," Davis said slowly, taking a step back from Ethel Fox with an amused expression. "Figured you might be here, so I brought some friends along just in case. Who's your sidekick?"

"My cousin," Pinkie said. "He's a big-time cop, works with the FBI."

If Davis was impressed or intimidated, he didn't

show it. "Way I heard it, he's down here trying to get your sick-fuck cousin Stefan off for killing that little boy. That the blood that runs through all you inbred cousins down there on Loupe Street? Sick-fuck blood?"

"Keep it up, and you'll find out," I said in a low, level voice.

Davis's smile turned cold. "You keep it up, the whole lot of you gonna be driven from this town."

"Leave," Pinkie said. "You've got no legal right to be here, and you certainly have no moral right. So leave."

Davis hesitated, and then took a step back, hands at his sides, palms exposed. "Have it your way, Ethel," he said to his ex-mother-in-law. "You mourn dear Sydney. You bury dear Sydney. Next week I'll go out to the cemetery, pay my respects, and piss on dear Sydney's grave."

CHAPTER
40

STEFAN TATE'S TRIAL BEGAN in earnest the following morning at eight o'clock sharp. The jury of eight women and four men had been empaneled the week before, and Judge Erasmus P. Varney lived up to his reputation for keeping his courtroom moving at a brisk pace.

The place was packed for the opening arguments. Our family turned out in force. Pinkie was there with his mother. I sat with Aunt Hattie and Patty Converse, directly behind Naomi and Stefan, who came into court acting rattled.

He seemed particularly upset by the people sitting behind the prosecution. Cece Turnbull was there, drawn, weak, and holding on to Bree's hand. Bree had spent the whole night with her and made sure she'd shown up sober.

Chief of police Randy Sherman sat on Cece's other side and kept glancing at Bree, as if he were trying to figure out how she fit into the equation. Behind them were several reporters up from Raleigh and Winston-Salem, and another from the Associated Press.

Harry and Virginia Caine, the well-scrubbed couple I'd seen on Cece's porch the prior day, were on hand in the third row. Her parents were dressed for business and seemed relieved to see their daughter's sober condition.

Stark County Sheriff's Office detective Guy Pedelini came in just as the opening arguments began and sat in the back near city homicide detectives Joe Frost and Lou Carmichael.

District attorney Delilah Strong gave the prosecution's opening argument with Matt Brady as her co-counsel. Strong's presentation of the case against my cousin was clear, concise, and damning.

She depicted Stefan Tate as a troubled individual thrown out of several schools and jobs because of substance abuse, then as a liar who hid his past on his application to teach in the Starksville school system, and then as a teacher who'd relapsed, dealt drugs to his students, and raped a student before sexually assaulting and butchering Rashawn Turnbull after the young boy rejected him.

When Strong was done, the jury members were taking lethal glances at my cousin. Cece Turnbull went berserk, screaming, "You'll go to hell for what you did to my boy, Stefan Tate!"

It took Bree and a bailiff to get the victim's mother out of the courtroom. When they brought Cece past her parents, she was bent over and weeping, and Harry and Virginia Caine looked tortured and lost.

Naomi asked Judge Varney for a recess and to instruct the jury to ignore Cece's outburst. The judge gave the instructions but denied the recess and demanded she make her case.

My niece got uncertainly to her feet, saying, "The district attorney paints Stefan Tate as a drug-fueled homicidal maniac. Nothing could be further from the truth."

Gaining confidence, Naomi depicted my young cousin as a man who'd gotten off track, fought demons, and kept the circumstances of his addictions private on his school application because it was his right under the law. He'd come home to Starksville and found his passion as a teacher, and he cared deeply about his students. She described the drug overdoses at the school and Stefan's efforts to fight and expose the drug dealers.

"Ladies and gentlemen of the jury, it is the defense's contention that Stefan Tate was getting very close to uncovering the presence of a major drug ring operating in and around Starksville," Naomi went on. "For that, my client was framed, as a drug dealer himself, as a rapist, and as the brutal murderer of a boy he loved like a son.

"When you've heard the hard evidence, when you see how manufactured it all looks on close examination, you'll realize without a doubt that Stefan Tate is no drug dealer, no rapist, and most certainly no murderer."

CHAPTER
41

a recess at noon.

My poor aunts and Nana Mama were exhausted. Patty Converse drove them home. After taking Cece Turnbull home, Bree joined Pinkie and me for lunch at the Bench, a barbecue joint that catered to the courthouse crowd.

"You thought any more about Finn Davis?" Pinkie asked after we took a booth and ordered.

"A little," I admitted.

"What about Finn Davis?" Bree asked.

As he had with me the evening before, Pinkie filled Bree in on Sydney Fox's ex. Born and raised in Starksville, Finn Davis had been orphaned when his parents died in a car crash. Marvin Bell, the man who'd hooked my parents on drugs, took Finn Davis in, treated the boy like his son.

"Marvin spoiled Finn, trained Finn, probably abused Finn," Pinkie said. "You ask me, Finn turned out just like his adoptive dad. They can both turn on the charisma, make you forget what they are deep down."

"And what's that?" Bree asked.

Pinkie started to speak, but then stopped and stared over my shoulder. He muttered, "The devil himself just walked in."

A thin, angular man, Marvin Bell put me in mind

of the actor Bruce Dern as he walked up to our booth. Longish steel-gray hair. Gaunt, narrow face. Sharp nose. And opaque green eyes that, as Bree said, roamed all over you.

Marvin Bell ran those weird opaque eyes over me and then Bree, showing no reaction. Then he leveled his gaze at Pinkie.

"My two cents, Parks?" he said. "At funerals, all grudges are off. My boy had every right to grieve for Sydney and pay his respects."

"Unless your boy shot her," my cousin said. "Which, in my mind, goes along with his threat to piss on her grave."

The muscles in Bell's cheeks flickered with tension, but his voice remained calm when he said, "Finn signed the divorce papers. He'd moved on. There is no reason he'd do something like that to his ex-wife."

"Oh, I think a case could be made for obsession," Pinkie said. "But I'm thinking spite. You and your boy have never liked to lose face."

Bell stood there a moment, looking as if it was taking all his control not to smash my cousin in the face. "Finn's no murderer."

Then he walked across the room to another booth.

"Think I'll go introduce myself," I said.

Bree said, "That a good idea?"

"Sometimes, you shake something, it rattles," I said, getting up.

The waitress set a cup of coffee in front of Bell and walked away. I slid in across from him. If I unnerved him at all, he didn't show it. If he'd been shaken by Pinkie's accusations, he didn't show it.

"Didn't know I'd invited you to sit down, stranger," Bell said, tearing open a sugar packet and tapping it into the coffee.

"We've met, Mr. Bell," I said. "A long time ago."

"That right?" he said, stirring the coffee and turning his weird green eyes on me. "I don't recall you."

"Alex Cross," I said. "Jason Cross was my father."

Bell cocked his head in reappraisal, tapped the spoon on the side of the cup, and smiled softly. "There now, I see the resemblance."

"I'm a homicide detective in Washington, DC."

"Long way from home, Detective Cross," he replied, setting the spoon down. "And funny, I don't recollect ever meeting you."

"I was young," I said. "It was about a year after my mother died."

"You mean after she was murdered, don't you?" he said in a straight tone delivered with an expression that revealed nothing.

"I remember that night," I said. "You tied my father to your car with a rope, dragged him through the streets."

Bell sipped his coffee, never taking his eyes off me. "It was another time. It was what you did to a man who'd kill his own wife in cold blood and call it good."

I hadn't expected that and said nothing while Bell talked on.

"I gave your father some of the punishment he deserved. And then I did the right thing and immediately turned him over to the police. Sad what happened next, but probably for the good of all. Even you. Even your brothers."

I hadn't expected that either, and it took a few beats before I could reply.

"You sold my mom and dad drugs," I said. "Got them hooked."

Eyes still, Bell smiled with precision. He altered the position of his cup on the saucer by a quarter turn.

"That statement is not true," he said. "I have never sold drugs or been involved with them. Your mother and father, I actually tried to get them clean, and anyone who says otherwise is lying."

"Never been involved with drugs?" I said.

"I am involved in business," Bell said, sipping the coffee. "I have several enterprises, all successful. Why would I need to pursue something risky like drugs?"

"I don't know," I said. "But every time your name comes up, people tell me that I should be looking at you."

Bell seemed amused. "Looking at me in what way?"

"As some kind of criminal mastermind," I said.

Bell laughed, reached for another sugar, said, "That's a small town with a lot of poor folks for you."

"What does poor have to do with it?"

"Everything," Bell said. "Most poor people think that anyone who becomes successful couldn't have done it legitimately, with initiative, with hard work. It's just not part of the myth most poor people want to believe. So they sit around and invent bullshit stories to explain things when someone makes it in the world."

"So there's nothing to the charge?"

"Zero to the charge," Bell said, holding my gaze. "How'd you come to be back in town, Detective Cross?"

I had the feeling he knew this, but I played along, said Stefan Tate was my cousin.

"Butcher," Bell said, hardening. "Sorry that he's your cousin, but based on what I've read, I hope that boy fries."

"It's a popular sentiment."

"There you go."

"You heard the defense's position?"

"Can't say that I have," Bell said, reaching up to pick a coffee ground off the tip of his tongue.

"Stefan came to believe that there is a large and complex criminal organization operating in Starksville," I said.

"If there is, I haven't heard a thing about it," Bell said.

"They run drugs," I said. "Maybe more."

"Maybe more?" Bell said. "Sounds like maybe more bullshit to me. Sounds like a fantasy designed to muddle the facts, which, as I understand them, are conclusive beyond a reasonable doubt. Your cousin murdered that poor boy, and he's gonna pay for it. I had my way? Someone would rope him up and drag his ass through the streets on the way to the death chamber."

"If you were running a criminal enterprise, I imagine you would," I said.

Bell flicked the coffee ground away, leveled his green eyes at me, and said, "If I were you, Detective Cross, I would not be casting aspersions that are unfounded. It looks bad. It looks like you are desperate. If I were you, I'd face the facts about your cousin, pack your bags, and leave the sonofabitch to his fate."

"That's not happening," I said, standing. "Sorry to have taken your time."

"Anything for the son of an old friend," Bell said. "But you tell your niece there that if she tries to bring my name up in this trial in any way, I will surely sue her ass from here to Raleigh and back."

CHAPTER
42

I REMEMBERED BELL'S WORDS as Judge Varney gaveled the court session to a close at five thirty that Monday after four hours of testimony that made my cousin sound like a monster.

Detective Guy Pedelini had gone on the stand first. He'd testified about discovering the body and identified evidence that the district attorney wanted admitted. Chief among them was the semen sample collected off Rashawn Turnbull's body. It matched Stefan's DNA. The prosecution also introduced blood matching Rashawn's that was found on the pruning saw discovered in my cousin's basement.

Naomi did her best to get the sheriff's detective to say these things could have been planted, but he was skeptical in the extreme, and the jury took note.

Even more damaging to Stefan's case was the testimony given by Sharon Lawrence, a teenager I recognized as one of the Starksville girls Jannie had trained with the prior Saturday. On the stand, she was pretty, articulate, and devastating.

Strong began her examination of Sharon Lawrence by getting her to admit that she was ashamed to be there but determined to tell the truth "for Rashawn's sake."

The jury reacted sympathetically. I reacted sympathetically.

Sharon Lawrence had been in one of Stefan's twelfth-grade gym classes. She said there was something between herself and my cousin right from the start.

"Coach Tate was always looking at me," she said.

"Did you like that?" Strong asked.

Lawrence looked in her lap and nodded.

"Coach Tate make advances toward you?"

The girl nodded again, flushing and kneading her hands. "I knew it was wrong, but he was...I don't know."

"Smart? Good-looking?"

"Yes," she said. "And he seemed to care about everyone."

Stefan glared at a legal pad during this entire exchange, scribbling with a pen and shaking his head.

"He seemed to care about everyone," Strong repeated.

"Yes."

"But especially you?"

Lawrence said, "I guess so. Yes."

"What happened?"

"Nothing for a while. It was just like flirting with each other."

"And then?"

"It went further," she said quietly.

"When was this?"

"Like, a few months after Billy Jameson and Tyler Marin overdosed and died, and a week before Stefan killed Rashawn."

"Objection!" Naomi cried.

"Sustained," Judge Varney said. "The jury will ignore that."

"So tell us what happened," Strong said.

You could see Sharon Lawrence wanted to be anywhere but in the courtroom as she mustered up her energy and said that after the two overdoses, my cousin became obsessed with finding out who the drug dealers were.

"He talked about it in class," she said. "Asking anybody who knew anything to come forward."

"Did they?"

"I don't know. And it didn't matter anyway, it was all a bunch of lies."

"Objection," Naomi said.

"Overruled," Judge Varney said.

Strong said, "Can you tell us why you think they were lies?"

"Because Coach Tate was the one dealing the drugs," Lawrence said.

"Objection!"

"Your Honor, with the court's indulgence, Miss Lawrence will explain the basis of her contention."

"Proceed, but you're on a short leash, Counselor."

"What makes you think Coach Tate was dealing drugs?"

"He told me," Lawrence said. "He showed me."

"Where were you when this happened?"

"At his place."

"How did you come to be at his house?"

"At school that morning, he'd asked me to stop by," Lawrence said. "He said Ms. Converse would be down in Raleigh at a doctor's appointment."

I glanced over at Patty Converse, who looked stricken.

Strong said, "And Coach Tate showed you drugs?"

"Yes."

"Did you do drugs with Coach Tate?"

"Yes."

"What kind of drugs?" Strong asked.

Lawrence bit her lower lip, which was trembling. "I don't know all of it. Cocaine for sure. And, like, maybe some meth. He called it a speedball. But I think he put something in my soda too."

"Why do you think that?"

"I woke up a couple of hours later in his bed," she said, looking at her lap again. "I don't remember how I got there. But I was naked and...sore."

"Sore where?"

"You know," she said, and she started crying.

Strong approached the box, gave her a tissue, said, "You're doing fine."

Lawrence nodded, but she wouldn't look up.

"Was the accused there when you woke up?"

"He came into the room."

"Did he acknowledge having sex with you?"

"Kind of."

"Can you be more specific?"

"He said we shared a little secret now. He said if we didn't keep the secret, I could end up like Billy and Tyler."

"The kids who overdosed?"

Lawrence nodded and broke down again.

After Sharon had composed herself, Strong asked, "Was the sex consensual?"

"No," she said forcefully.

"But you'd gone to Coach Tate's house. You'd done drugs with him. You'd flirted with him. Certainly you must have thought sex might occur."

"Maybe I did. But I was never given the chance to back out or say no."

"He just drugged you."

"Yes," Lawrence said, her shoulders trembling.

"And he raped you?"

"Yes."

"How old were you when this happened?"

"Seventeen."

"You report it?"

She hung her head, said, "Not at first, no."

"How long did you wait until you reported the rape?"

"Like, the day after they arrested Stefan?"

"Seven days," Strong said.

"I wish I had come forward straightaway," Sharon Lawrence said, oozing pain and sincerity. "If I had, maybe that boy would be alive, you know? But I'd seen what Coach Tate was really like, and I was scared for my own life."

CHAPTER
43

THAT EVENING, DINNER AT our house was somber and sub-
dued. We were all there except for Naomi, who was
working on her cross-examination, and Patty Converse,
who'd been so upset by the testimony that she'd gone
home alone.

Aunt Hattie looked equally crushed. She sat quietly
with Uncle Cliff and Ethel Fox, who was exhausted from
a day spent planning her daughter's funeral but who had
insisted on coming over to give her friend moral support.

Aunt Hattie needed it. The Raleigh stations were
reporting on Sharon Lawrence's testimony against her
son, focusing as much on her story as on her panties
from the day of the alleged rape. Lawrence claimed
she hadn't washed them because she'd been debating
whether or not to turn Stefan in.

Naomi had objected to having the panties introduced as evidence, calling them "tainted, at best," but
Varney overruled her after Strong informed the court
that a state DNA analyst would testify that dried semen
and vaginal fluids found on the underwear belonged to
my cousin and Sharon Lawrence.

Things looked bleak for the home team.

"Dad?" Ali asked when I went in to tuck him in for
bed. "Can we go fishing sometime while we're here?"

"Fishing?" I said, flashing on vague recollections of

fishing with my father and my uncle Cliff when I was very young.

Ali nodded. "I've been watching those shows on the Outdoor Channel. And I met a kid today named Tommy. He says he goes up to Stark Lake fishing with his father. He says it's fun. Lots of fish."

"Well," I said. "I don't know a thing about fishing, but if that's what you want to do, we'll figure it out."

Ali brightened. "Tomorrow?"

"Tomorrow could be tough," I admitted. "But let me find out what we'd need and where we'd go."

"You could ask Tom's father," he said, yawning.

"If I see Tom's father, I'll do that," I said, and I tucked the sheets up around his chin. "Love you, buddy. Have a good sleep."

"Love you too, Dad," he said. His eyes were already closed.

When I left the bedroom, Aunt Hattie looked at me and said, "Can you take Cliff over to the house? I'll be right along."

"Oh, sure," I said. "Ready, Uncle Cliff?"

My uncle said nothing, just stared off into space. Bree held the door open for me, and I wheeled him down the short ramp to the sidewalk.

"Need help?" Bree asked.

"I got it," I said. "Be back soon."

Bree blew me a kiss and went inside. I rolled him to the street, saying, "You still like to fish, Uncle Cliff?"

It was like a lightbulb going on. My uncle went from confused to lucid in two seconds flat. "Love to fish," he said.

"I heard it's good up at the lake," I said.

"Early mornings," Uncle Cliff said, nodding. "You want to be by the stream inlet on the west shore. Not far from my cabin. You know it?"

"I seem to remember it," I said. "Where else is the fishing good besides the lake?"

"Those big pools below the gorge are always good for trout early and late."

"What big pools?" I asked.

"You know. Where your father swam."

I stopped and came around the front of the chair. "What do you mean? Where did my dad swim?"

My uncle looked at me in renewed confusion, said, "In those pools. All the time when we was kids. Where is he? Jason?"

Aunt Hattie and Pinkie caught up to us. My cousin was carrying the remnants of a pie, and Hattie had two bags of chicken legs.

"Jason's dead, Clifford," Hattie said.

My uncle's expression twisted into shock. "When did he die?"

Hattie said, "Jason died a long time ago. In the gorge."

Uncle Cliff started to cry. "He was like my brother, Hattie."

"I know, Cliff," Hattie said, patting him on the arm and then looking at me and Pinkie, who was upset by the whole thing. "I don't know what it is. He just gets confused and upset sometimes. I'm so sorry."

"Nothing to be sorry about," I said.

She came around behind the wheelchair, said, "It's probably better if I take him from here. Pinkie, can you bring the leftovers?"

My cousin nodded, and I stood there in the street looking after them until they'd gone inside and the lights flickered on.

Hoping to clear my head, get some perspective on the day, I texted Bree that I was going for a walk. Wandering down Loupe Street, I admitted that the evidence against

Stefan felt overwhelming. My niece must have thought so too. She'd gone straight to confer with Stefan after adjournment. How was Naomi going to explain the semen? How was she going to cross-examine Sharon Lawrence?

Was Marvin Bell right? Was this a lost cause? Or were my aunts and Ethel Fox right? Were Bell and his adopted son, Finn Davis, involved? Had one of them killed Sydney Fox? Were they behind the criminal enterprise that Stefan suspected was ongoing in Starksville? How would I even go about answering any of those questions?

I still had no clear idea by the time I realized I'd walked all the way to the dark, arched bridge that spanned Stark River. Standing there, hearing the water roaring down in the gorge, I flashed on that dream I'd had of my younger self on the night my father died: running along the tracks through the rain, seeing the police cars with their lights flashing, and what I hadn't told Nana Mama, what I hadn't remembered until recently—my father out there on the bridge rail, the gunshot, and my dad falling.

I walked out onto the bridge to roughly where my father had been in my dream and looked down into the blackness, hearing the river at the bottom of the gorge but unable to see it.

A car pulled onto the bridge. The headlights swung over and past me. I ignored them, staring down into the void, and—

The car skidded to a halt right behind me. I pivoted in time to see three men jump out of an old white Impala.

They wore hoods and carried crowbars and a Louisville Slugger.

CHAPTER
44

I HAD NO TIME to go for my backup pistol in the ankle holster. They were on me that fast.

The most important thing you can do in a situation like that is pay attention to the open space rather than to attackers or weapons. The more space you have or can create, the safer you are.

I had the bridge railing at my back and three men closing in on me trying to fan out, trying to limit my space. I moved hard to my right, along the rail and at an angle to one of the guys with a crowbar.

He grunted with laughter, raised his weapon, and made to club me down. I stepped forward off the curb with my right foot and spun my left foot back and behind me so the crowbar was no longer headed for my upper back but my face.

Before it could get there, I threw up my hands, reaching in and under the weapon's arc to grab the guy by the wrist. With my left hand, I twisted the wrist and the crowbar away from me. With the heel of my right hand, I hammered up under the left side of his jaw.

He reeled.

I hit him again, this time with my fist, this time in the throat. There was a crunching noise and he dropped, gagging. I stripped him of the crowbar and took four steps backward, trying to create space again.

One of the other two, the one with the baseball bat, understood what I was trying to do. I looked over and saw there was another guy in the car, behind the wheel of the Impala. The driver threw the car in gear. Tires squealed at me at the same time the guy with the baseball bat jumped forward, the bat raised high over his head like it was an ax.

The Impala was going to mow me down. I jumped onto the oncoming car, rolled up on the hood. The driver hit the brakes. I slammed off the windshield and whipsawed back the other way.

The bat hit me hard in the midback and I was flung off the hood and onto the pavement. The wind was knocked out of me. The headlights blinded me.

But I still held the crowbar, and some deep instinct told me to look away from the headlights and down at the pavement.

"Fucker," a man grunted. I caught a flash of shadow on the road a second before the boot caught me in the ribs.

I felt a cracking and gasped in pain.

"Cave his frickin' skull in and be done with it," snarled a second male voice behind the headlights.

I kept my head down, forcing myself beyond the pain, looking at the street surface. The second I caught a flicker in the shadows, I backhand-slashed out and up with the crowbar.

I felt it connect before I saw the knee buckling in silhouette. I felt the bat glance off the side of my head. It wasn't a direct hit, but it was enough to make me dizzy and uncertain of what was up and what was down.

The guy I hit was yelling and clutching at his knee. He stumbled and fell against the hood of the car, screaming and clawing at his knee now.

Grunting in pain, still fighting for air, I thought: *Two left. Other one with the crowbar. And the driver.*

"Shoot him!"

I twisted my head, saw the driver climbing from the car, saw him holding a scoped hunting rifle. As he turned the gun my way, I flung the crowbar at him. It whipped sideways, end over end, and shattered the driver-side window, spraying the gunman with glass.

The rifle went off; the bullet ricocheted off bridge steel.

I heard tires squealing in the distance. Beneath the Impala, I saw headlights coming onto the bridge.

"We're out of here!" the driver shouted, and he dove into the car.

Fearing he'd run me down as he escaped, I scrambled back toward the sidewalk. The one with the blown knee hopped around the car, jumped into the front seat. The guy with the other crowbar pulled the man I'd dropped into the backseat. I reached the sidewalk, swallowed the pain, and bent my body to get the Ruger from my ankle holster.

Doors slammed. Tires smoked. A pistol came out the window.

I drew mine and fired wildly at the Impala, spiderwebbing the rear passenger window as the car began to accelerate. The guy with the blown knee shot as they passed me. The bullet pinged off steel right by my head.

"Get the fuck out of our town, Cross!" one of them yelled as they sped away. "Or you'll end up just like your cretin cousin."

CHAPTER
45

A BLUE DODGE RAM pickup with Florida plates skidded to a stop beside me.

"Alex!" Pinkie yelled as he jumped from the cab.

"Help me up," I said, gasping. "Get me out of here."

"There were shots!" he said.

"Which is why you need to get me out of here," I said, fighting to get to my feet. "I do not want to talk to the Starksville police."

Powerful hands caught me under the arms. I gritted my teeth at the pain in my ribs and hobbled to the passenger door. Pinkie lifted me into the truck and had us off the bridge before I heard the police sirens.

My cousin flipped off his headlights and turned down a road that paralleled the gorge. We were a quarter of a mile away before I saw distant blue lights go whizzing by, heading toward the bridge.

"Where to?" Pinkie asked.

"Somewhere we can wait them out for a little while," I said. "Then we'll circle back to Birney on the Eighth Street bridge."

My cell phone rang. Bree.

"Where are you?" she asked.

"With Pinkie."

"Did you hear those shots?"

"Yes," I said, and I told her what happened.

"Don't you think you should go to the hospital?" she asked.

"No," I said. "I want to stay under the radar on this."

"Why?"

"I'll explain when I get home," I said. "Give me forty-five minutes."

"You're sure you're okay?"

"I'm fine, and I love you."

"I love you too, Alex."

I hung up.

We'd left the east side of town and were heading down a long, gradual slope on a windy rural road when Pinkie finally turned his headlights back on.

"What the hell were you doing out on the bridge anyway?" he asked.

I started to tell him about my dream but stopped when I realized that wasn't why I'd gone out there.

"It was something Cliff said about my dad."

Pinkie shot me a quick glance. "What about your dad?"

"He said there were deep pools below the gorge, and when I said I didn't know them, he told me my dad used to swim in them."

"Okay..."

"I don't know. The conversation just made me want to go to the bridge and look at the river, you know?"

Pinkie said, "I guess I can see that."

We were almost to the bottom of the hill by then and traveling through deep forest.

"You know where those pools are?" I asked, looking out the side window.

A nearly full moon hung in the sky, throwing the woods into dark blue light.

Pinkie was quiet, but he slowed the truck and said, "Sure."

A minute later, he stopped and gestured at a muddy lane that left the pavement. "That will take you in there."

"Your truck make it?" I asked.

Pinkie hesitated, but then he turned us into a two-track that cut across a wooded pine flat. I could see by the ruts that the road was well used, but the forest pressed in from both sides, and thorny vines and branches scratched at the side of the truck.

Ten minutes later, we pulled into a turnaround. Pinkie stopped the truck, shut off the headlights. Here, where the trees opened up, the moon threw an even brighter light.

"Where are the pools?" I asked.

My cousin pointed at a gravel trail. "They're not far. Lot of people go swimming here."

"Got a flashlight?" I asked.

"What do you think you're looking for, Alex?"

"I don't know. I just want to see the pools."

Pinkie paused before he asked, "You sure you're up to it?"

"You give me a hand over anything rough, I think so."

He sighed, said, "Suit yourself."

My cousin came around to my side, opened the door, and helped me out. He fished in a toolbox in the bed of the truck and came up with a portable spotlight. He flicked it on. The shadows fled.

Moving slowly, guarding my ribs, I followed him down the gravel path to a grassy flat area by the banks of the Stark River. Moonlight bathed the place, which featured two large pools almost bisected by an outcropping of granite that looked like a chess bishop laid on its side.

Pinkie turned off the spotlight after we walked out on the ledge. Where the channel narrowed and flowed around the round knob of the outcropping, the current was swift. But in the pools, it was much stiller, and the moon reflected off them brightly. A quarter mile upriver you could make out the wall of the ridge and hear the roar of the water spilling out the mouth of the gorge.

"You ever hear of anyone falling into the gorge and surviving?" I asked.

Pinkie said nothing for several beats before replying, "They got kayakers in there all the time nowadays."

"I meant a swimmer. Have you ever heard of someone swimming out of the gorge after falling from the arched bridge?"

Pinkie didn't reply for several long moments. I turned and looked at him in the moonlight. He was staring at the water.

"Only one, Alex," he said quietly. "Your dad."

CHAPTER
46

WITH THE PAIN IN my ribs and the shot I'd taken to the head earlier in the night, I was sure I'd misheard him.

"Did you say my dad?"

Pinkie still wouldn't look at me, but he nodded.

My stomach fluttered. I tasted bile. I saw dots glistening in front of my eyes and felt like I was going to pass out. Then an irrational anger seized control of me. I grabbed my cousin by his shirt collar.

"What the hell are you talking about?"

"I'm sorry, Alex," Pinkie said, sounding guilty. "Uncle Cliff swore me to secrecy about it years ago."

I stared at my cousin in disbelief. "You're saying my father didn't die that night? He made it through the gorge?"

"Crawled out somewhere right around here," Pinkie said. "Cliff found him passed out on this ledge long before dawn and long before the police came looking for his body. Your father was seriously busted up.

"Cliff got him out of here, took him to his fishing cabin up on the lake," my cousin went on. "He nursed him back to health."

"And told no one?" I asked incredulously.

"Just me," Pinkie said.

"Why you?"

"Years later, we were up at his cabin. I was probably eighteen. Cliff was away from Aunt Hattie and drinking sour mash. A lot of it. He started getting all sad. And then he started crying, and then he started talking. Once he did, it was like a dam bursting. It all came out."

Uncle Cliff told Pinkie about finding my dad and getting him to the cabin. He told him how my father had decided it was best if no one but Cliff ever knew he was alive. Nana Mama wasn't to know. Me and my brothers weren't to know.

"Why?" I asked, still bewildered and unsure of my emotions, which kept surging all over the place.

"I guess because he did kill your mother," Pinkie said. "It was an act of mercy, but he killed her, suffocated her. No matter how you looked at it, though, in rural North Carolina, all those years ago, your father was facing a murder charge. Once he healed up, he decided to head south, disappear into a whole other life."

"Did he?" I asked.

"Yes," Pinkie replied.

My heart started to hammer in my chest. My father? Alive?

"Where did Uncle Cliff say he went?"

"Florida."

"Where in Florida?"

"All Cliff knew was that he lived somewhere around Belle Glade, that he worked in agriculture, and that he belonged to a church for a while," Pinkie said.

"So you're saying he's alive?" I asked.

Pinkie sighed and shook his head. "I'm not saying that at all. I'm sorry, Alex. From what I understand, he committed suicide two years after he left Starksville."

That hit me harder than the kick I'd taken earlier in the evening. One second I was letting the fantasy of actually finding my father build a strange kind of hope in my heart, and the next second I was a grief-stricken boy all over again.

Suicide?

"Thirty-three years ago?" I said, aware of the bitterness in my voice.

Pinkie nodded. "Uncle Cliff said he got a call one night from a woman. She said she'd found Uncle Cliff's phone number among the effects of a man named Paul Brown who'd committed suicide behind her church. Uncle Cliff said he asked her where she was and she said Belle Glade."

"What was her name?" I asked.

"I don't know," Pinkie said. "I don't know if Uncle Cliff even knew. He was just torn up at your dad killing himself after everything he'd been through."

I suddenly felt weak and reached out for Pinkie. He grabbed me under the arm, said, "You okay?"

"Not really."

"Kind of a lot to absorb," Pinkie said.

"It is," I said.

"Let's get you home, have a look at those ribs."

"Probably a good idea."

But as I followed him off the ledge, I kept pausing to look at the moon shining on the surface of the upstream pool, and I felt hollow and robbed of something I hadn't even known I'd had.

CHAPTER
47

"TIME FOR BATH AND bed, pumpkin," he said, wiping chocolate frosting from the corners of the little girl's mouth.

"Tell me a story, Grandfather?" she asked.

"A good one, Lizzie," he promised. "You go to Grandma and take your bath. After you get in your jammies, Grandfather will tuck you in and tell you the best story you ever heard."

"About magical princesses?" She beamed, clasping her hands. "And fairies?"

"What else?"

She kissed her grandfather on the cheek and scampered out of his office and down the hallway. Was there anything better than these moments? Could there be a stronger bond? He thought not. They were more father and daughter than grandfather and granddaughter. It was like they were emotionally welded together in a way that sometimes shocked him.

A phone rang in one of the drawers, broke into his thoughts.

He retrieved the phone, answered, said, "Wait."

He went to the doorway and heard giggling voices and running water in the bathroom down the hall. Shutting the door, he said, "Talk."

"They had Cross dead to rights, and they let him get away."

Lizzie's grandfather rubbed at his brow, wanted to break something.

"Idiots," he said. "How difficult can it be?"

"He's tough."

"Cross is a goddamned threat to everything we've built."

"Agreed."

He thought several moments, said, "We need to go professional."

"You got a player in mind?"

"Contact that woman we used last year. She'll get it done right."

"She's expensive."

"There's a reason. Let me know."

Lizzie's grandfather broke the burn phone and threw it in the trash. Then he left the office and padded down the hall toward the bathroom. With every step, he turned his thoughts toward magical princesses and fairies.

CHAPTER
48

Belle Glade, Florida

EARLY THE NEXT MORNING, Detective Sergeant Pete Drummond drove an unmarked vehicle to the west side of the county, far from the megamansions and the deep blue sea.

Detective Richard S. Johnson looked out the window as they passed what used to be a hospital, and what used to be a grocery store, and a boarded-up shop that used to sell clothes. Some blocks, there were so many abandoned, windowless buildings pocked with bullet holes, it looked like parts of Afghanistan Johnson had seen serving in the Marine Corps.

They crossed a canal and took the Torry Island Road out into agricultural fields south of Pelican Bay on Lake Okeechobee, cane mostly, and corn, and celery. Johnson could see people out there picking in the infernal heat.

Drummond took a left onto a spur road. A sheriff's cruiser was parked in the turnaround ahead, lights flashing. The county medical examiner's van was parked beyond it. The sergeant climbed out of the rig, and Johnson followed him.

Deputy Gabrielle Holland got out of her cruiser, said, "Got her all taped off for you, Sarge. We're just lucky a gator didn't get to her before I did."

"You identify her?" Drummond asked.

"Francie Letourneau. She's from Belle Glade. Haitian immigrant. You know her?"

Drummond shook his head. "I don't know the Glade like I used to."

"Nice lady, for the most part. Worked over in Palm, cleaning castles."

Johnson said, "You were professionally acquainted with the deceased?"

"We got Francie on drunk-and-disorderly a few times, but really, she was just blowing off steam."

"You got an address for Ms. Francie here?" Drummond asked.

"I can get it," Holland said.

"Please," the sergeant said. "We'll go down and take a look."

"You might want your boots," the deputy said as she climbed into the cruiser.

Drummond went to the rear of the unmarked and got out a pair of knee-high green rubber boots. The sergeant glanced at Johnson's shiny black shoes, said, "You're gonna need a pair of these for working the west side of the county."

"Where do you get them?" Johnson asked.

"Best price is that Cabela's catalog," the sergeant said as he put them on. "But you can pick up something local at the Bass Pro Shops in Dania Beach."

Drummond led the way around the cruiser, behind the coroner's van, and over the bank of an irrigation ditch. Holland had taped off a muddy path that led down to the water.

"That's the blackest mud I've ever seen," Johnson said.

"Some of the richest soil in the world," Drummond told him, skirting the tape through thigh-high swamp grass.

Johnson followed. Three steps in, he sank in the mud and lost his shoe.

"Cabela's," Drummond called over his shoulder.

The young detective cursed, dug out his shoe, and wiped it on the grass before joining the sergeant down by the ditch. Francie Letourneau's body lay faceup in the muck, head at the water's edge, feet oriented uphill. Her eyes were open and bulging. Her face looked particularly swollen. And her feet were bare and muddy.

"Cause of death? Time of death?" Drummond called to the assistant medical examiner, a young guy named Kraft who also wore green rubber boots and stood on a folded blue plastic tarp next to the body.

Kraft pushed back sunglasses, said, "She was strangled thirty-six to forty hours ago. Ligature is deep, and looks like there's fibers in the wound."

"She's been here in this heat the whole time?" Johnson said.

"I don't think so," Kraft replied. "She was killed somewhere else and dropped here, probably last night. A fisherman found her at dawn."

The sergeant nodded. "She got a phone on her?"

"No," the medical examiner said.

Drummond looked around before crouching to study the body from six feet back. Then he walked up the bank along the tape and looked at the path and the marks in the mud and the footprints, most of which were filled with murky water.

The sergeant gestured to shallow grooves in the mud.

"Her heels made those marks," he said. "He drags her downhill, holding her under the armpits. Right there, where the grooves get smaller, her shoes come off. Killer dumps the body and goes back for the shoes. So why doesn't he push the body into the water?"

Johnson said, "Maybe he meant to but something spooked him. A car out on the main road. But why take her shoes? A fetish or something?"

"He didn't take them," Drummond said, gesturing across the ditch. "He tossed them. There's one of them hanging on a branch over there."

Johnson frowned, saw the shoe, and said, "How'd you see that?"

The sergeant said, "I looked, Detective. They taught you how to do that down in Dade, right?"

CHAPTER
49

AN HOUR LATER, DRUMMOND and Johnson were back in Belle Glade and parking in front of the Big O bar, which, according to Deputy Holland, was where Francie Letourneau liked to party.

The Big O was a dive fallen on hard times. The cement floor was cracked and irregular. The blue paint was peeling and chipped. Most of the chairs, barstools, and tables had been carved on. The only part of the place that looked remotely cared for was behind the bar. Hundreds of photographs of happy anglers holding up largemouth bass looked down on the four patrons dressed for fishing and the bartender.

"Cecil," the sergeant said.

The bartender, an older man with a big potbelly, started laughing. "Drummond. You want a drink?"

"I think you enjoy being my temptation."

"Hell, yeah," Cecil said, coming over to shake the sergeant's hand. "Everyone's got a job, right?"

"Amen, brother," Drummond said. "Cecil Jones, meet my partner, Detective Richard Johnson. Miami boy."

The bartender shook Johnson's hand, said, "You coming up in the world."

The young detective smiled, said, "I like to think so."

Jones looked to Drummond and said, "You gonna set him straight?"

"I'm trying," the sergeant said.

"I heard they found a body out on the island," the bartender said.

"Why I'm here," Drummond said. "Francie Letourneau."

Jones's face fell. "Shit. That right? Shit."

"She's a regular, then?"

"Not a full-time subscriber, but often enough."

"She been in recently?"

"Sunday, around noon," he said, glancing up at the clock. "Had herself an eye-opener, Bloody Mary, double vodka, and then another for courage."

"Courage?"

"She was heading over to Palm," Jones said. "Said she had an interview for a new job that was gonna pay her four times what her old one did. I asked her what she needed a job for after hitting the Lotto twice in a month."

"That right?" Drummond asked.

"Five grand on a scratcher, seven on her weekly play," Jones said.

"Twelve K's a lot of money," Johnson said.

"It is," the bartender said. "But she said she still needed the work. She'd lost two or three of her regular clients recently. No fault of her own. One got electrocuted in her bathtub."

Drummond said, "Let me guess: another was murdered."

"Yeah, that's right," Jones said. "Wife of that plastic surgeon you see advertising on television all the time. You know, the Boob King."

Twenty minutes later, they pulled up in front of Francie Letourneau's small apartment with renewed purpose. The now-dead maid had worked for two now-dead wealthy women from Ocean Boulevard.

Ruth Abrams's death was clearly a murder by strangulation. Now Drummond and Johnson were questioning whether Lisa Martin really had accidentally dropped the Bose radio in her bathtub. Had she been killed too?

They got the landlord to open the maid's apartment, stepped inside. Johnson gagged at the smell coming from a makeshift altar in the corner.

A rooster's severed head had been placed upright in the dead center of a tin pie plate. Two inches of chicken blood congealed and rotted around the head. The bird's feet were there too, set with their talons facing a doll made of bound reeds, stuffed burlap, and cornhusks.

A long thorn of some sort jutted out of the doll's groin. There were two more thorns in the heart. A fourth one penetrated the top of the head.

"Santeria." Drummond grunted. "She must not have left it behind in Port-au-Prince."

"Who's the doll supposed to be?" Johnson said.

"Let's figure it out," the sergeant said.

They searched for almost an hour.

In a manila envelope on a small desk, Johnson found receipts from the prior month for a new couch, television, and Cuisinart food processor. In the top drawer, he found the receipt for the Apple MacBook Pro that was still in the box on the floor, next to the filing cabinet. Everything had been bought with cash.

The lower filing cabinet drawer was partially open. One file had been shoved in hastily and it jutted above the rest. Johnson pulled it and saw that the day before Letourneau died, she'd bought a brand-new phone and upgraded her plan through Verizon.

Johnson called the number, heard it go straight to voice mail. He made a note to pull her phone records.

Drummond returned after searching the bedroom.

"Anything?" he asked.

"She spent a lot the past month," Johnson said. "All cash. I figure close to four thousand. I looked at her bank accounts. There's no eight grand, and no record of a safe-deposit box."

"Well, she wasn't keeping it under her mattress," Drummond said. "I've been over every inch of this place, both bedrooms, kitchen, all of it, and—"

Johnson looked at the sergeant. He had stopped talking and was fixated on the altar and the doll.

"Maybe Ms. Francie was craftier than we thought," Drummond said, walking over. "Maybe she left that chicken blood there knowing it would reek and the voodoo stuff knowing it would freak out anyone who might break into her house looking for cash."

He lifted the maroon cloth, revealing the legs of a folding card table, the carpet, and nothing more.

"Good thought, though," Johnson said.

Drummond got down on his knees, reached under the card table, and said, "You give up too easy, Miami."

The sergeant worked his fingers into the carpet and ripped up a one-by-two-foot section that had been held in place with Velcro strips. He got out a jackknife and pried up an edge of the floor.

Drummond reached in, came up with a black leather purse, and eased out from under the voodoo altar. He stood up, brought the purse over to the desk, and opened it.

The sergeant whistled, shook his head, said, "Francie, Francie, what did you get yourself into?"

Johnson peered into the purse. "If those are real, Sarge, there's a lot more than eight grand in there."

CHAPTER
50

Starksville, North Carolina

SHARON LAWRENCE HELD UP well under Naomi's initial cross-examination. She stuck to her story about Stefan drugging and raping her and being so afraid of him she didn't report it until after he was under arrest for Rashawn Turnbull's murder.

"You have a lot of girlfriends, Sharon?" Naomi asked.

The girl nodded. "Enough."

"Best friends forever?"

"A couple. Sure."

"You tell any of them you were going to Coach Tate's house that afternoon you say he raped you?"

"No. It was supposed to be a secret."

"Anyone see you around his house?"

"I don't think so," Lawrence said. "He had me sneak in through the basement from the alley bulkhead door."

Sitting behind Naomi with Bree holding my hand, I tried to stay focused on the testimony and listen for discrepancies, but my ribs hurt and my mind kept drifting to the evening before. Jannie and my grandmother had already gone to bed by the time Pinkie dropped me off.

Bree and I are tight. She knew in an instant that something was wrong with me beyond a couple of cracked ribs. I'd repeated Pinkie's story, and she was as shocked as I was.

"Are you going to tell Nana Mama?" Bree asked.

That question had kept me up most of the night. It was still bothering me in court that next morning. So was the fact that Patty Converse had not shown up, and I think several of the jury members had noticed.

Then Naomi said, "Ms. Lawrence, did you see Rashawn Turnbull at Coach Tate's house that afternoon?"

I forgot about the night before and Stefan's fiancée, and focused. It was the first I'd heard about the victim being at the alleged rape scene. I glanced over at Cece, who was sitting beside a pretty blond woman in her late thirties. Two rows behind Cece sat her parents and a young woman I didn't recognize. But they all seemed as interested as I was.

Lawrence said, "No, I did not see Rashawn there. Why?"

"Because Coach Tate says the only person at his home after school that day was Rashawn Turnbull."

The high school senior looked doubtful. "I don't know anything about that."

"What time did you leave?"

Lawrence shrugged. "I don't know exactly. Four? Maybe five? I was still kind of groggy."

"Went out through the basement to the alley?"

"That's right."

"Strange," Naomi said, looking at a couple of pieces of paper. "I have a sworn statement here from Sydney Fox that says she remembers Rashawn Turnbull knocking on Coach Tate's door around four that afternoon. She remembers Rashawn going inside."

Delilah Strong jumped up. "Objection, Your Honor. Sydney Fox is dead and cannot be questioned. I'd like to move that her statement be inadmissible."

"This goes to the witness's credibility, Judge," Naomi said.

Varney thought about that for a moment and then said, "Overruled."

"Your Honor!" Strong cried.

"I said overruled. Ms. Cross, can you rephrase as a question?"

Naomi nodded, said, "Are you sure you didn't see Rashawn?"

Lawrence frowned, looked around, seemed to seek someone out in the courtroom, and said, "I don't remember. I was groggy. Maybe he was there."

"Or maybe you weren't there at all," Naomi said.

"That's not true! Why would I lie about something like this?"

"That's what I've been trying to figure out," Naomi said. "Your parents here today, Sharon?"

Lawrence looked into the courtroom again, said, "My mom. My father's not around anymore."

The pretty blond woman sitting with Cece Turnbull craned her head to see better.

"And who is your mom?"

"Ann Lawrence."

"What was her maiden name?"

"Objection," Strong said. "Where's the relevance?"

Naomi said, "I'm about to show relevance, Your Honor."

Varney nodded, but I noticed that he had gone pale since he entered the courtroom.

"Your mother's maiden name?"

"King," she said. "Ann King."

"She have a sister?"

Lawrence looked uncomfortable, said, "I don't see…"

"Yes or no."

"Yes, Louise was her sister. She's dead."

"And who was Louise married to at the time of her death?"

The girl's jaw seemed to tense a bit before she said, "Marvin Bell."

That got my attention, and I sat up straighter. So did Bree.

"So Marvin Bell is your uncle?" Naomi asked.

"Yes."

"Has your uncle provided you and your mother with financial support since your father left?" Naomi asked.

"Objection!" the prosecutor cried. "What is the relevance here? Mr. Bell has no connection whatsoever to this case."

"With the court's indulgence, I'm trying to establish that connection," Naomi said.

"You're on a short leash, Counselor," Varney said, sweating now despite the fact that it was quite cool in the courtroom.

Naomi said, "Marvin Bell has been giving your family money, correct?"

She lifted her chin, said, "Yes."

"Be tough without that money, wouldn't it?"

I noticed Sharon's mother had gone very tense; she was sitting forward, holding on to the back of the bench in front of her.

"Yes," Lawrence said quietly.

"Tough enough that you'd lie about a rape if he asked you?"

"No," she said, and then she reached across herself with her left hand to scratch her shoulder, in effect shielding her heart.

"You realize you're under oath," Naomi said. "And you understand the penalty for perjury in a capital crimes case?"

"No…I mean, yes."

"Objection, Your Honor," Strong said. "The defense is badgering the witness."

"Sustained," Varney said, patting his brow with a handkerchief.

Naomi paused, and then said, "Did Coach Tate ever come to you asking about your uncle? Marvin Bell?"

Lawrence looked confused. "If he did, I don't remember."

"Funny," Naomi said, returning to the defense table. "We talked to Lacey Dahl, a good friend of yours, correct?"

"Yes."

"Ms. Dahl will testify that she heard Coach Tate ask you about Marvin Bell a few days before you claim the rape occurred," Naomi said. "She heard it outside the women's locker room at the high school. Do you remember now?"

Lawrence fidgeted. "I don't know. Maybe."

"What did he ask about?"

"I don't remember."

"Did he ask whether your uncle was involved in the drug trade in Starksville?"

"What?" Lawrence said, offended. "No, that never—"

Before she could finish, Judge Varney let out a howl like he'd been stabbed. His contorted face turned beet red, and his entire body went rigid. Then he moaned like a wounded animal and pitched forward onto the bench.

CHAPTER
51

"THREE DAYS?" I SAID later that afternoon, standing outside the track stadium at Starksville High School with Bree. We were talking to Naomi with my cell phone on speaker.

"Maybe five," my niece replied. "Judge Varney's riddled with kidney stones and passing two. Strong says resuming trial Friday is the best we can hope for, but more likely Monday."

"It's probably a blessing," Bree said.

"Why's that?" Naomi asked.

I said, "Unless you and Stefan aren't telling us something, Bree and I have both looked at the evidence, and other than Stefan's suspicions about Marvin Bell, we don't see anything that links him to drug trafficking."

"There's circumstantial evidence," Naomi said.

"That's not good enough," Bree said. "We need to prove it."

I said, "If we can peg Bell as a drug lord threatened with exposure, suddenly his niece Sharon's story feels dubious, and we have a strong motive for his framing Stefan."

"Still leaves the DNA evidence," Bree said.

"I think I've got that covered," Naomi said. "Stefan and Patty used condoms. I've got an expert witness willing to testify that it is entirely possible that the semen found on Rashawn and on those panties was stolen from the trash and then planted."

"Put both those things together and there's your reasonable doubt," I said.

"But we don't have Bell," Bree said. "And Patty Converse a no-show in court today didn't help."

"I'm on my way to her apartment," Naomi said. "She's not answering her phone."

"Let us know," I said, and I hung up.

We went into the stadium and climbed into the stands. Many of the same athletes from the other day were there, including Sharon Lawrence, who shot Bree and me a glare as she jogged past with several of her friends.

Bree said, "The other night Cece Turnbull said Rashawn was very upset about something in the days before he died."

"I remember that," I said.

"Would seeing a rape be upsetting enough?" she asked quietly.

I looked over and saw she was serious.

"It would be upsetting enough," I said.

Was Stefan's version of events all lies? Had Rashawn seen him with Lawrence? Had my cousin assaulted the boy to shut him up?

Jannie was again running with the older girls. Coach Greene had them skipping in two-hundred-meter intervals. I couldn't remember Jannie ever doing that in a training session, and I noticed she was having difficulty staying with the college athletes.

When it was over, Jannie went to her bag, threw on a hoodie, and then came over to the fence with an unhappy expression.

"I suck at skipping," she said. "I don't know why I'm doing it."

"Did you ask?" I said.

Jannie shrugged, said, "It's supposed to help with your explosiveness."

"There you go," Bree said.

"I'm plenty explosive when it counts," Jannie said.

"Couldn't hurt to get more," I said, noticing that Coach Greene was crossing the track toward us, carrying Jannie's gym bag and looking serious.

"Dr. Cross," she said, not looking at Jannie. "We have a problem."

"How's that?" I said, standing.

She held out Jannie's bag by the handles. It was open.

Jannie frowned, tried to see what the coach was talking about as I climbed down. But Greene held it away from her, said, "I want your father to see first."

I stepped up and looked in the bag. There, nestled in a wrinkle of Jannie's sweatpants, was a small glass vial filled with white powder.

CHAPTER
52

"THAT'S NOT MINE!" Jannie protested the second she saw it. "Dad, there is no chance that's mine. You know that, right?"

I nodded. "Someone put that in her bag."

"Who would do that?" Coach Greene asked. "And why?"

I looked over at Sharon Lawrence, who was stretching and talking with her friends, seemingly oblivious to what was happening across the track.

"I can think of someone, but I'll let the police deal with that," I said.

"You want me to call the police?"

"You touch it?"

Greene shook her head.

"Then yes, call the police. It's easily proved whether it's my daughter's or not," I said. "Either her fingerprints are on it or they're not."

The coach looked at Jannie. "Are they?"

"No way," Jannie said.

"Was the bag open?" I asked.

"The bag was open," Jannie said. "I got my hoodie out and came over."

"Was that how you saw it, Coach?" I asked.

"Eliza Foster, one of my athletes at Duke, noticed it and called me over."

"So it was put in there either before practice or right after Jannie put on her hoodie and came over to talk to me," I said.

"Eliza would have no reason to do anything like that," Greene said.

"I want there to be concrete evidence that this was absolutely not my daughter's. Jannie will even provide a blood sample that you can drug-test. Right?"

Jannie nodded. "Anything, Dad."

I got out my wallet, dug out a business card, and handed it to the coach. "Call this guy. Sheriff's Detective Guy Pedelini. He'll handle the situation correctly."

Greene hesitated, but then nodded. She walked away with Jannie's bag, punching in the phone number on her cell phone.

Jannie looked about to cry when she sat down beside me and Bree.

"You'll be fine," I said, hugging her.

"Why would someone put that there?" she asked, looking torn up.

"To get at me and Bree through you," I said. "But it won't work."

Detective Pedelini showed up ten minutes later. I let him speak with Greene first, waiting patiently with Jannie and Bree. He put on gloves and bagged the vial. He nodded to me and then went to talk with Eliza Foster.

When he was done, he came over and shook my hand in the twilight.

"Coach says you want it tested."

"I do."

He looked at Jannie. "You're willing?"

"Yes," Jannie said. "Definitely."

"Any idea who might do this?" Pedelini asked.

"I'd start with Marvin Bell's niece," Bree said. "If

Sharon Lawrence would lie about a rape for him, she'd plant drugs for him."

The sheriff's detective pursed his lips, said, "I'll talk to her. Meantime, take Jannie to the office. I'll call ahead for someone to take the prints and blood."

Pedelini walked off toward the other girls, who were acting annoyed that they weren't being allowed to leave.

"Dad?" Jannie said as we stood up and got ready to leave. "Can you make sure I can still go down to Duke to train for the four-hundred on Saturday?"

"Meet you at the car," I said.

I went over to Coach Greene, asked her. She hesitated.

"She's innocent until proven guilty, Coach."

"You're right and I'm sorry, Dr. Cross," she said. "In all my years coaching, I've never had anything like this happen. Unless those tests say different, Jannie can come run with us on Saturday and any other day she wants."

I turned to leave, started toward the tunnel beneath the stands.

But Marvin Bell and his adopted son, Finn Davis, blocked the way.

"For such a big-time cop, you don't listen so well," Marvin Bell said.

"Yeah?" I said. "What did I miss?"

"Your niece brought up my name in court today," Bell said.

"Your niece was testifying in court today," I said.

"That's bullshit," said Finn Davis.

"It's bullshit that she was testifying or that she's Mr. Bell's niece?"

Bell smiled sourly. "I warned you about besmirching my name in court."

"Besmirching?"

"Slandering, whatever you want to call it," Bell said.

"It's only slander or besmirching if it's not true," I said.

Davis said, "Listen, Detective Asshole. That poor girl was raped by that sick fuck Stefan Tate. It took guts for her to go on that stand and face her rapist."

"No argument there," I said.

"Then quit trying to tear her down," Bell said. "You go on and think anything you want about me, but you leave Sharon out of it. She is a victim in all of this, and I won't have her made into a punching bag."

"And I won't have someone try to frame my daughter in retaliation."

"What the hell are you talking about?"

"Someone just put a vial of white powder in her gym bag," I said. "That's a sheriff's detective out there investigating. I figure Sharon for the job."

"Horseshit," Bell said.

I took a step, got right in their faces, said, "No, gentlemen, horseshit is you trying to kill me and strong-arm my family. You're on notice. I am officially declaring war on the two of you."

CHAPTER
53

BREE DIDN'T SAY MUCH on the ride home after we'd taken Jannie to the sheriff's office, where she'd provided blood and urine for analysis. I asked for and received samples from the same specimens, a precaution.

When we got home and went inside, I put the samples in a brown bag in the fridge. Jannie started telling Nana Mama about everything that had happened. Ali lay on the couch, watching another episode of *Uncharted* with Jim Shockey.

"Where is he now?" I asked. Shockey had traded his cowboy hat for a bandanna and was wading in murky water in a jungle.

"Like, the Congo?"

"That Jim Shockey gets around," I said. "Bree come in?"

"I'm out here," she called from the porch.

I went out, found her sitting in a rocker, looking out through the screen. She wasn't happy.

"We okay?" I asked.

"Not really," she said quietly.

"Why?"

"Did you have to say that to Bell and Davis? That you were declaring war on them?"

"I was speaking from the heart."

"I get that, Alex. But now you're more of a target than you were before."

"Good," I said. "We draw them out, and we shut them down."

She looked up angrily. "Why do you always put yourself in harm's way?"

My chin retreated. "Bree, you of all people should know that it's part of—"

"The job?" she asked. "I don't think so. I don't put myself in harm's way intentionally, and you do all the time. Did you ever stop for a second and think that it's a pretty goddamn selfish habit?"

"Selfish?" I said, bewildered.

"Yes, selfish," Bree said. "You have a family that needs you. You have a wife that needs you. And yet, at the drop of a hat, you're ready to risk our happiness and well-being."

I was speechless for several moments. I'd never heard Bree talk like this before. My late wife and Ali's mother, yes. But Bree, no.

I hung my head and said, "What should I have done?"

"Defuse the situation," she said. "Make them think you're no threat until you've got damning evidence against them. But it's too late, you escalated the threat, Alex, and—"

"Bree," I said, holding up my hands. "I get it, and I'm sorry. In my own defense, because Jannie was being used, I got a little hot under the collar. It won't happen again."

"That's good to hear," she said, getting up from the rocker and going inside. "But you remain a target."

I stood there a moment feeling a weight that hadn't been there ten minutes before. She was right. I'd pushed when I should have been smarter and laid off.

In the kitchen, Jannie was finishing up a dinner of country-style ribs with Nana Mama.

My grandmother studied me, said, "You in hot water?"

"Trying to get out," I said, heaping rice on my plate and then helping myself to the ribs, which were falling off the bone and smelled incredible.

"Thank you, Nana," Jannie said, clearing her plate. "That was great."

"Easy recipe," she said, waving off the compliment. "Orange juice and barbecue sauce. Then slow cook them at two fifty for four hours."

"Still great," I said after taking a bite.

Sitting down, I ate and watched Jannie for any sign that she was anxious about the events of the past couple of hours. But she seemed confident when she left the kitchen.

"Jannie told me," Nana Mama said.

"We took care of it," I said.

"What was bothering *you* this morning?"

Part of me wanted to tell her what my cousin had said, that her son had survived the fall from the bridge and the trip through the gorge and went on to live two years on the run before committing suicide.

Instead, I said, "Just a rough night."

"Uh-huh," my grandmother said, unconvinced, and left me to my dinner, which was remarkably good even by Nana Mama's high standards.

When I was done cleaning my plate, I went to our bedroom and found the door shut. I knocked, and Bree said, "It's open."

I went in, shut the door. Bree sat on the bed, studying her laptop.

In a low voice, I said, "I am sorry."

She looked up and gave me a halfhearted smile. "I know you are."

"There's dinner waiting for you. Outstanding country ribs."

"I'll go eat in a minute," she said.

"I can't tell Nana Mama what Pinkie told me," I said quietly.

"Why not?" she asked.

"I don't…" I began and then rubbed at my temples. "I guess I don't want her to hear any of it unless I can prove it's all true."

"Your uncle Cliff is in no position to corroborate the story," Bree said.

"I know," I said, and then saw how to solve two problems at once. "So I'm getting up early, driving to Raleigh, and catching a plane to Palm Beach."

"Okay," she said, confused. "Why?"

"It's the closest airport to where my father killed himself," I explained. "And it gets me out of Starksville for a day or two, which eliminates me as a target."

"But what about Stefan? Despite what I said at the track practice, he could have been framed. Maybe by Bell."

"Or Finn Davis," I said. "Which is why you're going to be careful while I'm gone, hang to the outside, and learn everything you can from the public record about the two of them."

Bree thought about that, and then nodded. "That I can do."

CHAPTER
54

Palm Beach, Florida

DRIVEN BY A HOT WIND, the flames roared and belched black smoke into the late-morning sky. White egrets circled in the smoke, feasting on clouds of bugs fleeing the fire.

They were harvesting and burning sugarcane on both sides of Florida Route 441 as I headed west toward Lake Okeechobee, and twice I had to slow to a crawl, the smoke was so thick.

Finally I got upwind of the fire and the smoke was gone. I saw the sign welcoming me to Belle Glade. It was where my father had killed himself and as hard luck a place as I'd ever seen. I'd heard about the city, of course. Who in law enforcement hadn't? As a municipality, Belle Glade used to have a murder rate the equivalent of a big metro area like DC or Chicago. After five minutes in Belle Glade, I could see some of the reasons why.

But I wasn't there to diagnose and solve social ills, so I ignored the empty buildings and storefronts pocked with bullet holes and relied on Google Maps to lead me to the various churches around town. I wanted to find out how my father came to kill himself behind one of them.

There were a lot of churches in Belle Glade. At the first two, one for Baptists and another for Adventists,

I got no helpful information. At St. Christopher's Catholic Church, I talked with a priest painting the rectory door. Father Richard Lane was in his fifties and had only recently been transferred to Belle Glade.

"Thirty-three years ago?" he said, squinting at me. "I don't know how you're going to find someone just on a name."

"I believe in miracles, Father," I said.

"Well, I can check and see if a funeral Mass was said for Mr. Brown here, but if the old records are as poorly maintained as the newer ones are, I can't offer you much hope, Detective Cross."

I gave the priest my business card, told him to call if he found anything.

Over the next two hours, I knocked on the doors of every other place of worship in town. Someone answered at every church, but no one knew of a Paul Brown committing suicide there years before.

One evangelical minister recommended I try the churches in nearby towns to the north. Another advised me to do a county records search for death certificates. Both were good ideas, and as I left the second minister, I tried to figure out what to do next and how best to do it.

It was beastly hot and humid, and I was eager to climb into my rental car and cool off in the air-conditioning. But then I noticed a Palm Beach County Sheriff's Office van parked up and across the street next to one of those shabby apartment complexes with two floors and exterior stairs.

I wandered over, looked into the complex, and saw a small crowd of people watching the upper floor where yellow crime tape had been strung up around the door of one of the apartments. A criminalist, a young guy, came down the stairs and started to walk past me.

I held up my badge and identified myself before asking where I'd need to go to get someone with the sheriff's department to pull some documents for me as a professional courtesy.

"I honestly don't know," the tech said. "Sergeant Drummond might."

"Where's Sergeant Drummond?" I asked.

"That's him," the criminalist said, gesturing to two men dressed in suits exiting the apartment. "The one with the face scar."

One of the men was big, African American, older, sixties. The other was in his thirties, dark good looks and, judging from his physique, a power lifter. My bet was on the lifter for the face scar, though I can't tell you why. But when the older detective turned to climb down the stairs, I saw the large patch of ragged skin that began beneath his right eye, ran down seven inches, and then looped back above the jaw toward his ear.

"Sergeant Drummond," I said, holding up my badge. "Detective Alex Cross, with the Washington, DC, Metropolitan Police, homicide division."

Drummond's face was flat as he examined my credentials. "Okay?"

The younger detective grinned and stuck out his hand. "Detective Richard S. Johnson. I know who you are, Dr. Cross. You used to be FBI, right? I saw one of your Quantico lectures on tape. Sergeant? Haven't you heard of Alex Cross?"

Drummond handed me back my badge and said, "I hope it doesn't crush your ego that I haven't."

"Unlikely, Sergeant," I said, smiling. "I have a pretty bombproof ego."

"So how can we help?" Detective Johnson said. "You down here tracking some serial killer or something?"

"No, nothing like that," I said, and I explained that

I was looking for a long-lost relative who'd supposedly died in Belle Glade years before.

"We can do a search for you back at the office," Johnson offered.

"Can we, now?" Sergeant Drummond asked. "Or do we need to figure out who killed Francie Letourneau and two Palm Beach socialites?"

"I don't want to mess up your investigation," I said. "Just point me in the right direction. I'll do the legwork."

Drummond shrugged. "Follow us back to the office; we'll see what we can do."

"And maybe you'd want to take a look at our case?" Johnson said.

"Detective," Drummond growled.

"What, Sarge?" his junior partner shot back. "This guy's the expert's expert. He trains FBI agents, for Christ's sake."

"Used to," I said. "And I'd be glad to help. But if it would crush your ego…"

The sergeant actually smiled, said, "What the hell, Dr. Cross. Maybe you can teach an old dog new tricks."

CHAPTER
55

I FOLLOWED THEM BACK to their offices in West Palm, a typical bullpen with cubicles surrounded by other cubicles that had windows and doors. Those were for the commanding officers, including Drummond.

"Johnson, help him find what he's looking for," Drummond said. "Sorry I can't give you the royal treatment you seem to deserve, Cross, but duty calls. I've got to make some phone calls, and I'll get those murder books for you."

"Thank you, Sergeant," I said. He disappeared into his office and shut the door behind him.

While Johnson went to get us coffee, I sat there listening to the familiar sounds of a homicide unit, detectives on the phone, others in discussion. I hadn't been gone a week and already I missed it.

Johnson returned with two cups of decent coffee. "I can't believe Alex Cross is sitting at my desk."

I stood up. "Sorry."

"What? No, sit down. It's an honor. Now, what or who are we looking for?"

"Male. African American. Died roughly thirty-three years ago."

Johnson turned all business, got another chair, and retrieved his laptop computer. "Name?"

"Paul Brown. Supposedly killed himself behind a church in Belle Glade."

"I'll look at county death records and see if he had a sheet with us."

"You have digital back that far?"

"For all of Florida," Johnson said as he typed. "State paid for it. Prescient, you ask me."

I liked the young detective. He was sharp and full of energy. I didn't know exactly what to think of Drummond other than that he had a dry wit.

"So what's with Drummond's scar?" I asked.

Johnson looked up. "First Gulf War. An oil well he was securing blew. Killed two of his men. Shrapnel laid his cheek open like a flap, burned and chewed it all up. Extensive nerve damage. It's why he hardly ever has any expression. His face just sort of hangs there, right?"

"You like him?"

Johnson smiled. "Like? I don't know yet. But I admire him. Drummond's the real deal in my book."

"Good enough for me," I said.

"Paul Brown?"

"Correct."

"And thirty-three years ago," Johnson said, studying his screen and typing. "We'll go plus or minus a year just to be safe. We have a date of birth?"

I told him my father's birthday.

Johnson hit Enter. Almost immediately, he shook his head. "No match."

"Leave the birthday blank," I said, figuring that my father must have been smart enough to leave everything about his old identity behind.

The detective played with it and hit Enter again. "There you go. Three of them."

"Three?" I said, getting out of my chair to look at the screen.

Sure enough, three men named Paul Brown had died in Florida around thirty-three years ago.

"Can you pull up the death certificates?" I asked.

Just then, Sergeant Drummond exited his office carrying several large black binders. "Any luck?"

"We got three Paul Browns," Johnson said. "Is there a way to access the death certificates from vital statistics, Sarge?"

"Miami, what are you, thirty years younger than me? You're supposed to be the technologically advanced part of the team."

The detective shook his head. "I don't—"

"Try clicking on the name," Drummond said.

"Oh," Johnson said, and he clicked the first one.

The screen jumped to a PDF image of a death certificate for Paul L. Brown of Pensacola, age twenty-two. Cause of death: blunt-force trauma.

"Too young," I said. "Try the next one."

Johnson clicked on it. A new death certificate popped up for Paul Brown of Fort Lauderdale, age seventy-nine. Cause of death: stroke.

"Too old," I said, now desperately wanting to find the answer behind door number three.

The third certificate fit the profile. Paul Brown, of Pahokee, Florida, age thirty-two, indigent. Cause of death: self-inflicted gunshot wound.

"That's him," I said, with a sinking feeling. "Where's Pahokee?"

Drummond said, "Fifteen miles north of Belle Glade."

"It's got to be him, then," I said, studying the certificate, oddly detached. "Which means the church is probably there. Says here the body was released to Belcher Brothers Funeral Home for interment."

"Interment?" Johnson said. "Most indigents are cremated in Florida."

"Not this time, apparently," I said.

The sergeant said, "I know the guys who own that funeral home. The Belchers. They run an ambulance service there too. When I was on patrol in the west part of the county, they'd show up at all the fatalities. I'll make a call."

"I'd appreciate that, Sergeant Drummond."

Drummond nodded, gestured to the books. "There's the murders we're working on. We'd appreciate the third eyeball if you have the time."

The sergeant returned to his office. I started scanning the files on the deaths of the socialites Lisa Martin and Ruth Abrams and their maid Francie Letourneau. Two hours later, I was almost finished and flipping my way through the appendix of reports on the cleaning woman when Drummond returned.

"Took a bit to get in touch with him, but Ramon Belcher is working night duty and he said he'd go through the files for you," the sergeant said.

"Thanks," I said.

Johnson returned to the cubicle with more coffee. I waved it off, said, "Any more of that without something to eat and I'll get an ulcer."

Drummond said, "You find anything in there?"

"I saw a few things."

"What do you like to eat?"

"Anything. Seafood."

The sergeant nodded. "Got just the place down in Lake Worth. Johnson, are you in? We can talk about our case over dinner."

"Absolutely," Johnson said. "My wife's pregnant. Let me just call her."

"Pregnant?" Drummond said. "You didn't tell me that."

"Still early, Sarge," Johnson said, digging out his

phone and walking away. "End of the first trimester. Twins."

The sergeant frowned, looked at me. "I would have liked to have learned that sooner."

"It matter?" I asked.

"Course it matters," Drummond grumbled. "As it stands now, I will do everything I can to keep Detective Johnson from screwing himself into harm's way and depriving those babies of their father."

"You're a man of hidden virtues, Sergeant," I said.

He looked at me with that slack, scarred face, said, "That's not virtue, just common sense. It's just me and my wife, and she's got a good job that pays better than mine. But Johnson's got three people depending on him now. Do the math. Tell me where my priorities should be when the shit hits the fan."

Crusty as he was, Sergeant Drummond was beginning to grow on me.

CHAPTER
56

Pleasant Lake, North Carolina

PINKIE PARKS GESTURED THROUGH the windshield to a gravel lane ahead that cut off the highway and dropped steeply to the lake. "There it is."

Bree pulled the blue Ford Taurus she'd rented that morning over onto the shoulder and put it in park.

"Not much to see from here," Pinkie said. "You'd want to be in the woods."

Bree picked up a pair of binoculars and said, "Then let's go into the woods."

Once Pinkie learned that Alex had gone to Florida and that Bree was focusing on Marvin Bell and Finn Davis, he'd insisted on helping her. But now he raised his eyebrow, said, "You looking to kick a hornet's nest?"

She frowned. "These woods are known for hornets?"

"These woods are known for Marvin Bell and Finn Davis, which is the same thing, way I see it."

"Suit yourself," Bree said, opening the door. "I'll be back."

Pinkie groaned but got out as well. It was hazy, hot, and humid. They waited until traffic died and then cut down the steep embankment and entered a thorny raspberry thicket. Pinkie led the way, clawing through it until they emerged into piney woods where crickets were sawing.

Below them and out several hundred yards, Bree could see the clean waters of Pleasant Lake. She heard outboard motors and kids laughing.

Pinkie went down a game path that led through the trees growing on the slope above the lake's eastern shore. Bree followed, her brain going back to everything they'd learned that morning about Marvin Bell and Finn Davis.

After renting the car, she and Pinkie had gone to the Stark County Recorder's Office and gotten online with the North Carolina secretary of state's office, looking into the two men's business interests. Together and individually, Bell and Davis owned five businesses in and around Starksville: a liquor store, a dry-cleaning shop, two automated car washes, and a pawn-and-loan operation.

Pinkie smartly noted that all five businesses would generate and bring in a lot of cash. Convenient if you're also involved in some sort of illegal cash-intensive business.

But Bree had zero jurisdiction here. She couldn't get to databases that might give her a look at the businesses' bank accounts.

On a whim, Bree accessed public databases in Nevada and Delaware because both states had incorporation and tax laws that made them attractive for people interested in creating shell companies. Though there was nothing in Nevada, she was pleased to find that Marvin Bell and Finn Davis were listed as registered agents of six Delaware companies, three apiece. All six corporations had been organized for the purpose of "real estate acquisition and development."

Which, in a roundabout way, led Bree to look up their real estate holdings in Stark County. To her and Pinkie's surprise, neither man appeared to own any property in the area.

Pinkie said that simply wasn't true, that Bell owned all sorts of property in Stark County, beginning with an estate on Pleasant Lake. When they looked up the lakefront property, they found it was owned by one of Marvin Bell's Delaware companies and carried an assessed value of $3.1 million, which made Bree want to see the place.

Alex had told her to hang back, to stay to the outside, but Bree wasn't planning to climb over the fence Marvin Bell had around his compound. She just wanted to look over it, get a sense of how the man lived.

Pinkie motioned to Bree to stop. She did, next to a young, fat pine tree that smelled of sap and blocked her view of the lake.

Looking over his shoulder, Pinkie whispered, "If you get low, slide around in front of me, and stay in the shadows, you should get a good look at it without being seen."

Bree got down on her hands and knees. Pinkie pressed into the wall of pines there and let her pass. She twisted into a sitting position and used her feet to scoot herself sideways out into a shadowy slot in the trees.

A hundred vertical feet below Bree and one hundred yards closer to the lake was the gravel lane and the gate, which was tall, ten feet, anyway, and the chain-link fence was shrink-wrapped in green vinyl. Bree swept the binoculars along the top of the fence, making out coiled razor wire that had also been shrink-wrapped green.

Tiny cameras were mounted on posts to either side of the gate. There were other cameras on posts every forty yards or so before the fence was swallowed by dense vegetation. She assumed the cameras continued on around the six-acre perimeter and turned her attention to the compound.

Rhododendrons had been planted along the interior of the fence, no doubt to block the view from the gravel lane. But this high above the fence and the bushes, Bree had close to a bird's-eye view of Marvin Bell's domain, which featured a small lagoon at her left and a blunt point of flat land that jutted out into the main lake. Set back from the point on a knoll to the right of the lagoon and facing the lake stood the main house, a ten-thousand-square-foot log mansion with a red steel roof and matching shutters.

A beautiful stone terrace with gardens above the lagoon complemented the house. Three stone walkways flared out from a second terrace in front of the mansion, one going to the point, one to a boathouse to the left of the point, and one to a six-bay dock system to the right with lifts that held a fleet of Sea-Doos, motorboats, canoes, and sailboats. There was a bar and a huge barbecue built right into the dock along with lounge chairs and umbrellas.

Out on the point itself stood a miniature version of the main house from which, Bree imagined, the views must be incredible. She could see through several of the large and dramatic windows into the main building and could tell no expense had been spared on the interior. And there was art everywhere—paintings, sculptures, and mobiles.

The place looked like it was worth $3.1 million, no doubt, which raised her suspicions even further. In Bree's mind, owning some small businesses in Starksville, North Carolina, did not get you a home worth upwards of three million dollars. She supposed Bell could have been successful in the stock market, or maybe one of those Delaware real estate investment companies had gone large.

But if so, why would Marvin Bell stay here? The

property looked like a little piece of heaven, she admitted, but didn't people who hit big money like to show it off in more trendy places?

Maybe Marvin Bell was just a homebody, like Warren Buffett. Or maybe he had a reason to stay here despite the wealth. Maybe he had crucial business to attend to.

Before she could weigh those options, Bree caught motion and swung the binoculars to see Finn Davis exiting the mansion. The rest of the estate was quiet and empty. The only sounds—kids laughing, a distant outboard motor—came from well down the shore.

Wearing dark sunglasses, a dirty ball cap, a green work shirt, jeans, and heavy boots, Finn Davis moved in an easy saunter around the circular driveway to a five-bay log garage. He pressed a remote control. A door raised, revealing an old orange-and-white Ford Bronco.

Where was he going in that heap? Looked totally out of place on…

Bree rolled out of her sitting position, scooted back behind the pines, and jumped up.

"We have to get back to the car," she whispered to Pinkie. "Fast!"

CHAPTER
57

Lake Worth, Florida

DETECTIVE SERGEANT DRUMMOND PARKED outside the Kersmon Caribbean Restaurant, and the three of us went in. Althea, the owner and cook, saw Drummond and rushed out from behind a counter to hug him, laughing.

"You leave your old lady for me yet, Drummond?" Althea asked in a Jamaican accent.

"You know she's one in a million," the sergeant replied.

"I do," Althea said. "Just checking to see if you'd lost your mind since I last saw you."

Drummond introduced us, and she found us a seat in the small restaurant.

"Something to drink?" Althea asked. "Red Stripe?"

Johnson looked at Drummond, who said, "You're off duty. Don't mind me."

"Red Stripe," Johnson said.

"Make it two," I said.

Drummond said, "Don't bother with menus, Althea. Just bring us what you think we should be eating. Some of it should be fish."

That seemed to make her happy, and she went off.

"You'll be ruined for Jamaican food for life," Drummond said. "I'm not kidding. Half the customers are from the Caribbean."

"I won't be able to tell my wife," I said. "She loves Jamaica. Me too."

"Yeah?" Drummond said. "I'm fond of it myself."

I looked at Johnson, wanting to include him. "You ready to be a dad, Detective?"

"I don't know."

"Were you?" Drummond asked me. "Ready?"

"No," I said. "All I knew was I didn't want to be like my father."

"That work out?"

"Pretty much," I said, and turned back to Johnson. "Don't worry. You just sort of grow into the job, day by day."

The beers came. So did small bowls of what Althea called fish tea, which was delicious, along with a basket of fresh zucchini bread, which was also delicious. No way I was telling Bree about this place.

"So, did you see anything we missed, Dr. Cross?" Johnson asked.

"Call me Alex," I said. "And I don't think you missed anything, but there are a few things I'm not clear on and a few things you might consider."

"Okay…" Drummond said.

"Just to make sure we're all on the same page," I said. "You've got Lisa Martin and Ruth Abrams, wealthy socialites killed within a week of each other and made to look like suicides."

"That's right," Johnson said.

"Friends?"

"Apparently so," the sergeant said.

"Beyond that, they shared the same maid, Francie Letourneau, who stole jewelry from both women before being murdered herself."

"Correct," Johnson said. "We got confirmation from the husbands on pictures we showed them of several jewelry pieces found at Francie's apartment."

"Francie told the bar owner in Belle Glade—"

Althea returned with a tray. Fried plantains. Rice and black beans. Oxtail stew. And a whole steamed and spiced grouper. Definitely not telling Bree.

We dug in. The oxtail was simply incredible. So was the grouper. So were the second and third Red Stripes. I'd forgotten how easily they go down.

Once we were into second helpings, I said, "Francie told the bar owner in the Glade she was coming to Palm Beach for a job interview the day she died."

"That's right," Drummond said. "Only we haven't found a damn thing to say she ever made it to Palm. She just disappears."

"No phone calls?"

"Her cell phone's missing, but we found the account," Johnson said. "I made a request yesterday for all calls in the last three months. We'll probably hear tomorrow sometime."

"Other thoughts?" Drummond asked.

"Yes. I think you should focus on the links and chains between the victims, and extrapolate from there."

Johnson looked confused, so I said, "You want to isolate each thing that connects them. So, say, focus first on Francie as the common-denominator link in what we'll call the socialites chain. Under this scenario, the maid could have killed them both to rip off their jewelry and then was killed herself by a third party who got wind of the jewels she was holding."

"I could see that," Drummond said, dishing a third helping of oxtail onto his plate.

"What's the second link?" Johnson asked. "Or chain?"

"The socialite friendship," I said. "Maybe Francie was working for a third socialite, was in the process of robbing her, and someone caught her, killed her, dumped her."

Johnson shook his head. "From the files I went through at her apartment, Francie had been on hard times, lost all of her cleaning jobs."

"Before she hit the Lotto?"

"Correct."

"So maybe there was no Lotto hit," I said. "Maybe the jewels were the explanation behind her newfound money. And maybe she wasn't going to Palm Beach for an interview on the day she died; maybe she was going to kill someone and steal more jewels."

CHAPTER
58

SERGEANT DRUMMOND THOUGHT ABOUT that, said, "We'll call the Lotto."

"I'd be calling past clients too," I said. "See if any of them are missing jewelry. I mean, there were jewelry pieces the Abramses and Martins couldn't identify in your photographs, right?"

"True," Johnson said between mouthfuls.

Drummond's cell phone rang. He pulled it out, looked at it, said, "Sorry, gentlemen, but I have to take this."

He got up, leaving me with Johnson, who said, "There's another possibility, you know."

"Go ahead," I said.

"Maybe Francie was the jewel thief, but she wasn't the killer," the young detective said. "Maybe she went to rob someone and surprised the killer."

"You mean in the act of trying to murder a third socialite?"

"Why not?"

"Any reports of assaulted socialites?"

"Not that I know of," Johnson said.

"Dessert?" Althea came over and said.

"I'm stuffed," I said.

She frowned at me, said, "I make it from scratch."

I held up my hands. "I'll make room."

"Sweet potato pudding," she said, smiling. "Coffee? Tea?"

"I'll take a coffee," I said.

"I will too, Althea," said Drummond, sliding back into his chair.

"I have to be going," Johnson said. "Can we get the check?"

"Don't worry about it," Drummond said. "I've got you both covered."

"Let me take my part of it," I said.

"Visiting dignitary, I don't think so," the sergeant sniffed.

Johnson got up, said, "Again, it was great meeting you, Alex."

"Likewise," I said, getting to my feet and shaking his hand.

"See you in the morning, Sarge."

"Bright and early," Drummond grumbled.

Our coffee and pudding came. I didn't know sweet potato pudding could be decadent, but it was.

The sergeant took a sip of coffee, said, "So all we've been doing is talking about our case. What is someone like you working on these days?"

I hesitated, then started telling him about my cousin Stefan, and Starksville, and all the strange twists the case had taken in the few days we'd been there. Through it all, Drummond listened intently and quietly, sipping his coffee and eating pudding.

It took me the better part of an hour to tell it all, and with the beers in me, I probably said more than I should have. But Drummond was a good listener, and it just seemed natural.

"And that's where we are," I said.

After several beats, the sergeant said, "You like this

guy Marvin Bell for killing that kid, but I don't hear anything that says you got him involved."

"Because we don't have him involved," I said. "Like everyone in Starksville says, he's a slippery guy."

Drummond shifted his jaw left and nodded, lost in thought. Then he said, "I've known my share of slippery guys. Trick is to let them get so slippery they get overconfident and they—"

His cell phone rang. He looked at it, shook his head, said, "Sorry again."

The sergeant got up and walked away, and I finished my coffee, thinking that I'd better find a place to stay the evening. Althea brought the check, which was incredibly reasonable considering the quality of the meal.

"I'll handle the tip," I said when Drummond returned.

The sergeant smiled. "I think you're going to want to handle the whole bill once I tell you about those last two phone calls."

"How's that?" I said.

"The first call was from the Belchers' funeral home," he said. "They handled your Paul Brown's embalming and delivered his body in a pauper's casket to a church that isn't in Pahokee anymore. Closed fifteen years back."

I frowned. "And the second call?"

"From the minister who used to run that church," Drummond said. "The Belchers called her. She evidently knew Paul Brown and says she's willing to meet you out in Pahokee tomorrow around six p.m. to tell you about him."

I grinned and snatched the check off the table.

CHAPTER
59

Starksville, North Carolina

BREE FLIPPED OFF THE headlights and coasted the Taurus to a stop diagonally across the town square from Bell Beverages. The Bronco was parked in front. Finn Davis had gone inside. She was beginning to doubt her instincts.

When she'd seen Finn Davis leave Marvin Bell's place in the slouchy clothes driving the beater four-by-four, she figured it as some kind of disguise, or at least a way of moving under the radar. She and Pinkie had made it to the rental car two minutes before Finn drove out of the compound.

Finn Davis had never seen Bree, to her knowledge. While Pinkie slouched down, she faked a cell phone conversation until Davis had driven by her, heading south toward town. She'd U-turned once he'd rounded a curve and had been following him at a distance ever since.

"Just looks like a man tending business, probably collecting the daily take, which explains the workman's getup," Pinkie said. "He doesn't want attention."

It did look a lot like that. Finn had stopped at the pawnshop, the dry cleaners, and both car washes before heading to the liquor store. Maybe her instincts had been wrong.

Bree checked her watch. Eight thirty. She'd texted Alex to see how his day had gone almost an hour ago but heard nothing back so far. And she was starting to get hungry. Nana Mama said she'd hold dinner for—

"You think Alex will find what he's looking for down there?" Pinkie asked.

Bree glanced at the big man, who seemed sincerely concerned.

"I hope so," she said. "But to be honest, Pinkie, I don't think Alex knows exactly what he's looking for. Closure, I guess."

"Does that happen?" Pinkie asked. "I mean, I never really knew my dad. Died when I was pretty young. Still, I think about him, and there's nothing closed about it."

Sydney Fox's ex came out of the liquor store. Bree started the Taurus. She let Davis get ahead of her in light traffic, then pulled out and followed as he headed south out of Starksville. Two miles beyond the town boundary, the Bronco took a right onto a dirt road that wound up into the forest.

"Takes you up to Stark Lake," Pinkie said. "There won't be much traffic to hide in."

"But there will be people up there?" she asked.

"Sure, summer vacationers and all. Campers at the state park."

"Colored folk?"

"That too."

"Then we'll take our chances," Bree said. She waited until Finn's taillights disappeared into the trees before turning in after him.

Stark Lake did not resemble its name. The forest was lush all around it. Cabins dotted the shore; they were nothing like Marvin Bell's place, but they were nice, well maintained. Bree drove along slowly, as if she were following directions, and peered down every driveway looking for the Bronco.

The road ahead cut hard right into a hairpin around a narrow cove.

"Stop," Pinkie said. "Back up and turn around as if you're lost."

"You see him?" Bree said, braking the car to a stop.

"Turning into a cottage on the other side of that cove," Pinkie said as she threw the car in reverse, U-turned, and drove away around a bend. "Pull in ahead there and kill your lights."

Bree backed into the driveway of a dark cabin. They got out and ran to a stand of trees opposite that hairpin around the narrow cove. The water was no more than forty yards across and she had a good look at the cottage and the Bronco. No movement. No sound.

The cottage was nice, newer and more modern than the other places she'd seen on the lake so far. It wasn't as nice as Marvin Bell's, but it was still a trophy house by most people's standards, certainly Bree's.

A girl of nine, maybe ten, came out onto a wrap-around porch that faced the water. Finn Davis came out on the porch after her. He was followed by a second man that Bree couldn't see well. She raised her binoculars as the man turned to shake Davis's hand, and she recognized him.

"Sonofabitch," Bree whispered.

"What?" Pinkie said.

"Wait," Bree said, staring through the binoculars to be sure it wasn't a trick of the light on the porch.

No trick. That was Detective Guy Pedelini smiling and taking an envelope from Finn Davis. He tucked it nonchalantly in his pants pocket before putting his arm around the girl, whom Bree took to be one of Pedelini's daughters. Davis headed for the Bronco.

Bree kept her attention on Detective Pedelini, saw his smile evaporate the second Finn Davis climbed into his vehicle. The detective and his daughter went back inside the cottage.

"Jesus," Bree said, turning to run back to their car.

"What's going on?" Pinkie demanded, huffing along beside her.

"That expensive cottage belongs to Guy Pedelini, the one man in Starksville that Alex and I thought was straight, and now it looks like he's on the take from Finn Davis and probably Marvin Bell," Bree said. "He's also the cop who found Rashawn Turnbull and the detective investigating the drugs Marvin Bell's niece planted on Jannie."

"Fuck. Some things never change about Starksville." Pinkie panted as headlights flashed back along the cove. "You can't trust anyone but family."

Davis's headlights were coming closer. Bree and Pinkie skidded to a stop behind a big pine tree fifty feet from the rental. Finn Davis drove on by.

They ran to the Taurus, jumped in. Bree fired up the car, kept the headlights off, and drove out of the driveway and after Davis.

They lost the Bronco until it was almost back to the state highway. They spotted taillights down there on the flat, turning back toward town. Bree put on the headlights and sped up. There were more cars on the road. She hung back three cars from the Bronco as it passed the crumbling brick factory where Alex's mother had sewn sheets and pillowcases. She stayed in that position almost to the old Piggly Wiggly store.

Right before the railroad crossing, Finn Davis turned hard left, along the tracks, and disappeared from view.

"Where's that go?" she demanded.

"It's a maintenance road, I think."

Train tracks. Hadn't Stefan Tate said there were strange goings-on along the train tracks that he'd been unable to figure out?

Bree made a split-second decision, pulled into the Piggly Wiggly parking lot, and jumped out of the car. She ran along the sidewalk toward the train tracks. The crossing lights began to flash. Bells rang. The gates lowered and she could hear the rumble of an oncoming train.

Bree scanned the area as the train horn blew. An abandoned building to her left. An empty lot with trees that lined the far side, separating the lot from the tracks. She dashed at an angle across the empty lot into the trees and found herself on a small bluff above the tracks. She pushed vines aside.

The headlights of the train and the Bronco lit up Finn Davis, who stood on the maintenance road a hundred yards away and not ten feet from the tracks. Bree got the binoculars on him. He didn't seem at all concerned about the engine. He was looking at the cars behind it, which were rolling into view from around the bend.

Bree moved the binoculars to the boxcars and spotted the silhouettes of two men on top of one, two more four cars back, and another pair six cars beyond that. As they passed Davis, they raised their hands in some sort of salute that she couldn't make out due to shadows.

But Marvin Bell's adopted son was crisply visible when, in response to their salute, he raised his right hand and held three fingers high.

CHAPTER
60

West Palm Beach, Florida

AN HOUR LATER, in my bed at the Hampton Inn, I came wide awake, sat up, and said into my cell phone: "Those guys riding the train on our way into Starksville that first day, they did that same salute."

"Definitely," Bree said, back in North Carolina.

I shook off the cobwebs in my mind. "How many did you see?"

"Six total."

"Were they on specific cars or random?"

"They were all on freight cars, mixed in with tankers."

"What did Davis do after the train had gone?"

"Got back in the Bronco, turned around, and headed north, probably back to Pleasant Lake," Bree said. "I abandoned the surveillance at that point."

"I'm still surprised about Guy Pedelini. I pegged him as a good guy."

"I did too," Bree said. "But I'm coming over to Pinkie's point of view."

"Which is?"

"Don't trust anyone in Starksville who isn't family."

"Cynical, but probably a good idea for the time being."

"Here I've been hogging the conversation. Any luck down there?"

"Nothing but luck," I said and then filled her in on my day.

"Wow, that was fast," Bree said when I was done. "Who's this minister you're going to see?"

"Her name's Reverend Maya and supposedly she knew Paul Brown. The funeral guys remembered her."

"Well, that's good. You'll be able to talk to someone who knew your dad."

"I think so," I said. "Then I can put this all behind me and come back and hold you, and together we'll figure out that three-finger-salute thing."

"Tomorrow night?"

"More like first thing the following morning." There was a silence between us before I said, "You okay?"

"Just trying to figure out where to go next. Any advice?"

"Try to see Stefan if you can. Find out what specifically made him suspicious of the area around the train tracks. I don't think he mentioned it."

"I already talked to Naomi," Bree said. "She's seeing him in the morning. What are you doing tomorrow until you meet the minister?"

"I told Drummond and Johnson I was free to help them," I said. "Least I could do, considering how much they've helped me."

"I miss you, Alex," she said softly.

"I miss you too," I said. "And thanks."

"For?"

"Sticking your neck out for family."

"I'm Alex Cross's wife," she said teasingly. "What else would I do?"

"Very funny," I said, grinning. "I love you, Bree."

"I love you too, Alex," she said. "Have a good night's sleep."

"You too," I said, and clicked off.

It was nearly eleven by then and I'd been up since five. I should have been turning off the light, trying to get back to sleep. But I felt like I'd had a cup of espresso, jittery, wanting something to do. My focus finally fixed on that stack of three binders that held a copy of the murder book covering the investigations of the socialites and the maid.

Had I missed something on my first trip through them?

Figuring I'd be better off seeking the answer to that question instead of lying awake in the darkness wondering what this Reverend Maya might tell me about my father, I opened the first binder and started to read the records all over again.

Sometime after midnight, exhaustion overtook me, and I slipped off into darkness and dreams that were a mishmash of things I'd seen in Starksville and Palm Beach: Sydney Fox lying dead on her doorstep; the sugarcane burning, throwing smoke and bugs into the sky; Rashawn Turnbull's body in the crime scene photos; and a dark-hooded and cloaked man standing with his back to me on a street in Belle Glade.

He raised his gloved right hand and held three fingers high.

CHAPTER
61

Starksville, North Carolina

DEAR, SWEET LIZZIE, her grandfather thought as he dipped an oar into the calm water. Still dressed in her white nightgown and robe, his precious little girl knelt on the floor of the rowboat, forward of the bow seat, her arms flung over the gunnel, and her sleepy eyes trained on lily pads that glistened in the rising sun.

He pulled gently and rotated the oar handle with finesse, causing the flat-bottom skiff to spin in a slow circle across those lily pads. Lizzie held on tight to the sides of the boat and giggled before she let out a "Whee!"

"I told you it was fun," he said.

"Is that really how you catch them, Grandfather? The fairies?" Lizzie asked as she pushed aside the ringlets of blond hair that fell across her innocent, ever-so-blue eyes.

The old man fell in love all over again and said, "I have it on the highest authority that a fine way to catch fairy princesses is to wait for a nice warm dawn when they will be out sunning on lily pads. You spin over them, confuse them, and then snatch them up."

Lizzie turned wide-eyed. "But why?"

"Because if you catch a fairy princess, she must grant you three wishes."

"Three?" the little girl said in wonder, gazing at the water and the lily pads drifting by. "What's her name? What will I call her?"

"The princess?" He thought fast, said, "Guinevere."

"Princess Guinevere," she said, liking that. She lifted her head and looked back at him with a smile that broke away into fear and confusion.

"Who are they, Grandfather?" Lizzie asked.

He realized she was looking beyond him, back to shore. He looked over his shoulder and saw three men coming over the knoll from the house and down the lawn toward the water.

"Who are those men?" she asked again, agitated.

"Friends, Lizzie," he replied as he turned the boat toward the dock. "Old friends. No one to worry about."

"But what about Princess Guinevere?" she complained.

"She'll be here tomorrow," he said.

He pulled up to the dock and tossed a line to Starksville's chief of police, Randy Sherman. Then he handed his granddaughter up to Stark County sheriff Nathan Bean and climbed onto the dock after her.

"Lizzie, run on up to the house, get you some breakfast," he said.

Lizzie kissed her grandfather and ran barefoot up the lawn, adding in a few precious twirls to enchant him.

"Love that little girl," he said, then he looked to the third man on the dock. "How're the kidney stones treating you, Judge?"

"Shitty," Erasmus Varney said with a pinched expression. "But I'll survive."

"Glad to hear that," he said, "because survival is why I brought you all here this morning."

Chief Sherman and Sheriff Bean studied the old

man. Varney was trying, but the judge looked as if he wanted to pace against the pain.

"Been a good life for all of you, yes?" Lizzie's grandfather asked.

The three men nodded without hesitation.

"Then it's important to you that our good life goes on, yes?"

They nodded their heads vigorously.

"Good to hear," he said, then sobered. "I have begun to fear that the survival of our good life is threatened."

"By who?" Judge Varney asked.

"This Alex Cross and his family. All of them. His wife. His niece the attorney. His aunts and uncles and cousins too."

"What do you want us to do?" Chief Sherman said.

"I have made arrangements through a third party to bring in a lace maker that can never be traced to any of us," he said. "She is to be given every opportunity to succeed as she's passing through Starksville."

"She?" Sheriff Bean said.

"Correct."

"She been through town before?" Chief Sherman asked.

"Once."

"When is her trip scheduled?" Sheriff Bean asked.

"She's arriving today. Problems with any of that?"

Judge Varney said, "It has to be done delicately with someone like Cross. He has a reputation. Friends in high places."

"We're aware of that delicacy, Erasmus," Lizzie's grandfather said. "That's why I've called in a lace maker. She'll sew everything together so their deaths look like tragic twists of fate."

PART FOUR

A COAST OF GOLD

CHAPTER
62

Palm Beach, Florida

"SUCH A TRAGIC WAY to die, Maggie," Coco cooed. "But really, it's acceptable now in our social strata, isn't it? Or at least, it's not the shame it once was."

Dressed in a pair of Stéphanie Coudert white linen pants, a pale tan jersey, and ballet slippers, Jeffrey Mize sat wigless at the foot of the bed. He was lost in his alter ego, Coco, analyzing the fetal position of Maggie's body, noting how the sheets were tucked perfectly under her chin, as if the poor dear had sought out a cozy spot in which to expire.

The spent bottle of Patrón on the night table helped the overdose tableau. So did the empty vials that had once held the deceased's notoriously abused prescriptions for pain, anxiety, and sleep.

One cocktail was all it took, Coco thought with satisfaction as he got up off the bed. Maggie never knew what hit her. Not like Lisa Martin, who'd gone all Frankenstein's bride, bug-eyed and shrieking when the radio hit the bathwater. And very unlike Ruth Abrams, who'd fought the noose with surprising strength.

Coco paused in front of Maggie's mirror and admired the new clothes, the makeup, indeed the whole new look, before turning to the red box. He opened it, lifted out the wig. Copper-blond and shoulder-length, the hair fell easily about his shoulders.

A few adjustments and there was the effect he was going for: Faye Dunaway in *The Thomas Crown Affair,* the casual look, not the one in the chess scenes with Steve McQueen where Faye was sheer elegance and glamour.

At least, that's how Mother had always described this wig. Casual yet intriguing, sporty and strong. A woman who was a match for McQueen.

Coco laughed because he'd seen the movie and Mother was dead-on. Putting on tortoiseshell sunglasses to complete the Dunaway effect, he felt adventurous and naughty and very sexy when he pouted in the mirror. Coco left the mirror at last, took the canvas bag, and sauntered out of the bedroom and through the library. He paused where a portrait hung.

Maggie had been painted sitting barefoot on a sand dune at sunset. She wore jeans and a collared pink blouse, and she looked out to sea in three-quarter profile with windswept hair and an expression that suggested an awareness of her fading beauty. *That's how you'll always be,* he thought. *Sitting on a coast of gold and thinking about loss.*

Coco turned, leaving Maggie behind and yet forever with him in the memory of that painting. Beyond the kitchen, he checked the security system in a little room off the garage and was pleased to see it still down.

What had Maggie said? Something about a fifteen-minute reset?

Much more than I need, Coco thought, and flipped a switch that rebooted the system. Moving quicker, he went out into the garage and opened the door behind his beloved Aston Martin.

Coco got in, tied a blue scarf loosely over the wig, just as Faye had done in the famous dune-buggy scene in *The Thomas Crown Affair* with McQueen driving. He threw the Aston in gear and backed out into the first light of day.

The gate swung open. Coco drove out onto South Ocean Boulevard and headed north with the Aston's top down. Salt spiced the air. The wind caused the scarf to flicker in his peripheral vision. The gathering day. The warming light.

It was like being in a movie, with Coco as the star, channeling Faye Dunaway as he drove past mansion after mansion bathed in the rising sun. He thought dreamily, *You'll all be mine someday. Mother always said so. You just have to dream it, Coco, and the whole world can be yours.*

In town, he stopped for breakfast and played the Coco role to the hilt, feeding on the attention, enjoying how it made him and his audience glow. True glamour was always like that, Mother said. Beauty was a shared experience.

Getting back into the Aston Martin, Coco was confused for a moment, unsure where to go next. Then, like a homing pigeon, he relied on instincts to guide him. He drove for a while, parked the car, then walked to the door of Mize Fine Arts.

He'd spent a full night deep in the trance that was Coco, and it was only in front of the gallery that Mize realized who and where he was. Feeling suddenly weak, he fumbled with the lock before finally getting the shop door open.

Inside, he turned the dead bolt and shut down the alarm. He started through the gallery toward his office but felt so dizzy he had to stop and sit down on a stack of fine Oriental rugs in one of the alcoves. When was the last time he'd slept? A day? A day and a half? Had Coco taken all that time away?

Mize lay down, rolled slowly over onto his side, and passed out.

He had no idea how long he'd been there asleep when the sharp sound of knocking woke him. Mize looked around, dazed, then glanced in a mirror on the wall of the shop and saw the Dunaway look with nary a hair out of place.

More knocking.

Mize's head began to pound, but he got up and walked around a corner to the front door, where a muscular guy in a white button-down shirt and a tie was peering in and pressing a police badge to the window.

CHAPTER
63

PALM BEACH COUNTY SHERIFF'S OFFICE detective Richard S. Johnson saw the woman coming to the door of Mize Fine Arts and stepped back.

The lock was thrown. The door swung open, revealing a stunningly attractive woman with flawless hair that looked copper, strawberry, and blond.

She smiled, said in a soft Southern accent, "Can I help you?"

Detective Johnson had never backed down from a fight in his life. He had been in combat six times in Afghanistan and never flinched. But he had also never done well around women in this class of beauty.

"I'm, uh, Detective Johnson, uh, Palm Beach County Sheriff's Office."

"Yes?" she asked, seeming to sense the effect she was having on him, sliding her hand up the doorjamb like some movie star.

"I'm looking for Jeffrey Mize," Johnson said.

"He's not here. He usually doesn't come in for another hour or so."

"Oh," Johnson said. "I went by his house and he wasn't there either."

"He goes out for breakfast. Come back in an hour and I'm sure he'll see you. Can I tell him what it's about, Detective?"

"Routine, follow-up stuff on a case I'm working. And you are?"

"Coco," she said. "I consult and appraise for Mr. Mize."

"Can I come in and wait, Coco?"

Coco gave him an uncomfortable sigh. "Detective, I'm not an employee. I work for Mr. Mize on contract and I come in early so I can do my job when it's quiet. Could you give me an hour? There's a nice coffee shop down the street."

"I'll see you in an hour," Johnson said.

"Unfortunately, I'll be off by then," Coco cooed. "But thanks, Detective."

"You're welcome, Coco," he said, and walked down the sidewalk feeling like he'd been mildly hypnotized by the woman.

Johnson shook his head as he went to the coffee shop. He'd grown up in a tough part of Miami. He'd joined the Marines and done two tours in Afghanistan, and he still fell apart around certain women. He laughed when he thought of the first time he'd met his wife, Angela, how tongue-tied he'd been.

His phone rang. Detective Sergeant Drummond.

"Anything?" Drummond asked.

"I'm supposed to talk to Mize in an hour," Johnson said. "You?"

"I chatted with Marie Purcell's chief of staff," the sergeant said. "She fired Francie four months ago. Suspicion of stealing rare coins."

"Were we notified?"

"No," Drummond said. "People like the Purcells don't like to get police involved. They have their own security people and take care of things quietly."

"Lot of that up here?" Johnson asked as he stood in line for coffee in a shop that had a nice vibe to it.

"I'd say so."

"You hear from Cross?"

"On my way to pick him up," Drummond said.

Johnson was kind of annoyed. He'd hoped to have more time with Dr. Alex Cross, pick his brain about things.

"Who's next on your list?" the sergeant asked.

Johnson dug in his pocket for a piece of paper, studied the names, and said, "Crawford."

"I'll take Schultz."

Johnson agreed and clicked off. He got an espresso shot and a mug of robust Kenyan coffee black and poured them together over ice. He read the *Palm Beach Post* cover to cover and made calls to the Crawford mansion and several others on the list but got nothing other than the opportunity to leave messages.

Johnson walked up to the gallery fifteen minutes early and rapped on the door. A man soon appeared. Tall, stoop-shouldered, and completely bald, he wore white slippers, baggy black trousers, a loose black shirt, and white cotton gloves.

"Detective Johnson?" he said in a deep voice. "Coco said you'd come by. Please, come in. Sorry I wasn't here earlier, and sorry about the gloves, I've had a nasty allergic reaction to some lacquer remover I was experimenting with the other day."

Johnson walked into the shop, gazed all around, said, "Lot of nice stuff in here. What is it you do, sir?"

"I buy and sell things of beauty," Mize said. "Fine art, jewelry, rugs, and furniture. What can I do for you?"

"I'm here about Francie Letourneau."

He frowned, and Johnson noticed he had no eyebrows. No hair of any kind. What did they call that condition?

"What about Francie?" Mize asked.

"She's dead," Johnson said.

Mize straightened, moved a white-gloved hand toward his slack mouth, said, "Dead?"

"Murdered," Johnson said. "Her body was found out past Belle Glade."

"My God, that's awful," Mize said. "I always liked her. Well, at least until I had to fire her."

"Over?"

"She wasn't showing up on time and she was doing a half-assed job," Mize replied. "And though I could never prove it, I think she was stealing things."

"You think?"

Mize gestured all around. "Keeping track of my inventory is more an art than a science. I can't begin to remember every piece of jewelry, for example."

"That what you think she stole?" Johnson said. "Jewelry?"

"Yes," Mize said. "Several pieces that were my mother's that just weren't anywhere one day."

"How'd you come to hire Francie?"

"Through a service," he sniffed. "I was told she was highly recommended."

"When was the last time you saw her?"

"Saw? I don't know, five months ago, but I heard from her a few days back. She left a message on my machine at home. Can you imagine the gall?"

"What was the message?"

"She said she was sorry about any misunderstanding we'd had and was looking for her job back."

"You return her call?"

"Certainly not, and I erased the message."

"What day was that?"

"Saturday? Sunday?"

"Where were you Sunday?"

Mize thought about that. "Worked here the whole afternoon. Had early sushi with Coco and her sister, went home around eight, watched old movies on Netflix for a bit. *The Thomas Crown Affair,* have you seen it?"

"No."

"You should. It's very good. The original, not the remake. But anyway, after drooling over Faye Dunaway and Steve McQueen, I went to sleep around ten. I like to go to bed early and get up early. You?"

"Same," Johnson said. "Do you know Ruth Abrams or Lisa Martin?"

"After I saw the stories in the paper, I racked my brain. I'm sure I've met them both at one social function or another. Terrible, though."

"Francie Letourneau worked for both women."

"Really? Do you think she was somehow involved in their deaths? And then, what, got killed herself?"

"It's possible," Johnson said, and he felt his cell phone buzz.

It was Drummond again.

"Get your ass to the Crawford place," the sergeant growled. "The missus is dead."

CHAPTER
64

DETECTIVE JOHNSON WAS CLIMBING out of his car when Sergeant Drummond pulled us up beside him and parked on Ocean Boulevard between two patrol cars flashing their blue lights.

The heat had been stupefying when I joined Drummond in the parking lot of the Hampton Inn over in West Palm, but here, so close to the beach and water, there was a beautiful shore breeze. No wonder this had been the winter spot for the super-rich for, what, more than a century? Isn't that what the sergeant had said last night?

Before I could make sure the three beers hadn't addled my memory, Johnson started telling Drummond about his trip to Mize Fine Arts as they walked onto the grounds of the Crawford residence, a rambling white Mediterranean with a red-tile roof. The gardens inside the gate were stunning and gave way to a waterfall in a Zen-like setting.

The house was...well, I'd never been in one like it. Then again, I don't get the chance to roam around in Palm Beach mansions a lot. Let's just say that every room was designed for *Architectural Digest.*

The kitchen was over the top, with Swedish and Finnish appliances that gleamed like they'd been installed the day before and gorgeous Italian tile work.

The library looked stolen from some abbey in southern France. And the bedroom where Maggie Crawford lay was as bright as a Florida day.

I scanned the room, saw the pills, the Patrón bottle, and the tumbler on the bed stand by the blowsy woman tucked under the covers. She must have been stunning once. She could have been sleeping there had her skin not been blue.

"Let's not be touching anything," Drummond said. "This will be a forensics case through and through."

I couldn't argue with him. There was no sign of struggle. It would be up to the lab people to tell us how she died.

A deputy appeared at the door, said, "The deceased's personal assistant is downstairs. She called it in."

We found Candace Layne in a miserable state in that beautiful library.

"This was what everyone feared would happen," Layne said. "It's why John, her soon-to-be ex, left. He couldn't watch her self-destruct anymore."

"Drug and alcohol problems?" I asked.

Layne nodded sadly. "Deep down, despite all the money, all the beauty and good fortune, she was an insecure, anxiety-ridden person."

"When did you last see her?" Johnson asked.

"Yesterday around five thirty," she said.

"Would you have been the last person to see her alive?"

"I would think so," Layne said. "She had no plans for the evening. She was going to read and watch a movie."

Drummond asked Layne if she knew the other three dead women, the two socialites and Francie Letourneau. When Layne responded by asking the sergeant if he thought Maggie Crawford had been murdered, he told her he was just covering all the bases.

Layne said she'd fired Letourneau after Maggie caught her stealing silver. She'd e-mailed the personal assistants of Ruth Abrams and Lisa Martin but never met them.

"Did Mrs. Crawford run in their circle?" Drummond asked.

"Same fund-raisers, that kind of thing," Layne said, nodding.

Even though we had no conclusive evidence that Maggie Crawford had been murdered, in my mind the four killings were linked. Three socialites, all using the same Haitian maid at some point. Three socialites and the maid now dead. This was no coincidence, which meant that there was a missing link, some factor that tied them all together.

"How long have you worked for her?" I asked.

"Five years next month," Layne said sadly.

"Would you know if some of her things were missing?" Johnson said. "Like jewelry? Clothes?"

Layne nodded. "I think so. Do you want me to look?"

"We'll wait until the forensics folks do their thing," Drummond said. "Tell me about her."

"Maggie?" Layne said, then thought. "Most of the time she was the kindest, funniest, most generous person you could ever meet, a real joy to work for. But sometimes, when her mind was altered, she was a tyrant, a little rich girl who wanted what she wanted right now. And even when she was sober, she often had this kind of…I don't know…melancholy or wanting about her. There, you can see it in her expression in that painting over there."

Layne gestured toward an oil painting of Maggie Crawford, barefoot, dressed in jeans and a pink blouse. She was sitting on a sand dune with sea grass around her, caught in three-quarter profile as she looked out toward the ocean. I walked over to study it, saw the expression the personal assistant had been talking about.

"That's a big thing among the super-rich, right?" Johnson said behind me. "You know, getting your portrait painted?"

"I don't know; I suppose so," Layne said.

"Ruth Abrams and Lisa Martin had portraits done of them," Drummond said, coming over to examine the painting. "Coco."

"What?" Johnson said.

"Right here in the corner," the sergeant said. "It's signed *Coco*."

"I have no idea who that is," Layne said.

"Oh, I think I might," Johnson said. "I met a Coco just this morning."

CHAPTER
65

Starksville, North Carolina

AROUND FOUR O'CLOCK THAT afternoon, Bree walked along the railroad tracks where she'd seen Finn Davis give a three-finger salute to six young men riding freight cars on a train heading north.

"What are we looking for?" Naomi said.

"I don't know," Bree said. "And unfortunately, neither did your client."

She and Naomi had come to the tracks in a long roundabout way from the jail, where they'd been able to talk with Stefan Tate for roughly thirty minutes. When she asked him about his suspicions regarding the trains, he said he'd overheard a couple of stoners at the high school talking about drugs and the track. He decided to follow one of them.

"Lester Michaels, a senior, one of those kids who lived to get high. I saw him jump a freight train. He didn't come back to school for two days. When I asked him about the absence, he said he'd been sick, but I talked with his mother. She'd been ready to file a missing-person report on him."

"You ever see any other people riding on the trains?" Bree had asked.

"No," Stefan admitted. "I sat down there a few nights, watching, but trains come through Starksville twenty-four/seven."

"I've been lucky, then," Bree said. "I've seen guys on boxcars twice since I've been here, and both times they gave somebody on the ground a three-finger salute. You know anything about that?"

Stefan thought a moment, then nodded. "I've seen a few kids at the school use something like that, I think."

"Names?" Naomi asked.

"I don't know," Stefan said. "I think they were Patty's students. Where is she? She hasn't come to see me or answered my calls."

Bree said nothing.

Naomi said, "I'm sure she's just under a lot of stress."

"Or bailing on me," Stefan said in a fretful tone.

Bree and Naomi had tried to assure him otherwise. But after they'd left the jail, they'd gone by Patty Converse's place. Her car was gone, but from what they'd been able to see through the window, her stuff was still inside. Naomi had tried Patty's phone number several times, but got voice mail.

So they'd come back to the railroad tracks around four that afternoon.

A train rumbled at them out of the south. Bree and Naomi walked well back from the tracks in order to see the tops of the freight cars. But they were all bare of riders, even the caboose. Another train came a few minutes later out of the north. It too was riderless.

"I'm thinking this is a little bit like the needle in the haystack," Naomi said. "I mean, we can't watch all day."

Bree thought about that, looked around, and then back toward the thicket of trees between the tracks and the Piggly Wiggly parking lot. The trees overlooking the tracks triggered a memory of Ali watching some show on the Outdoor Channel the other day.

"Is there a store here that carries hunting and fishing gear?" Bree asked.

"There's an army-surplus place that does, I think."

They were soon back in the car, driving west of town to P and J's Surplus. They went in and were greeted with several Confederate flags on the wall.

Bree ignored them and found the only salesperson, a heavyset white girl in her midteens named Sandrine. She looked at Bree suspiciously and at Naomi with mild interest.

"I seen you in the papers and on TV," Sandrine said to her. "You're defending that kid killer, right?"

"I'm Mr. Tate's attorney," Naomi said.

"You're following the case?" Bree asked.

She shrugged. "Papa says I shouldn't pay attention to any of it."

"Why's that?"

"Just niggers killing niggers, he says. No offense. I'm just quoting."

Sandrine said this offhandedly. Bree swallowed her reaction by wondering how many people in and around Starksville thought about the case like that.

Naomi managed to stay composed as well, said, "We're here looking for something to buy."

"Yeah?" Sandrine said, perking up. "What're you looking for?"

Bree told her, and the girl came waddling and smiling right out from behind her little counter. "We got it all at P and J's! Got six of them in just the other day. How many you want?"

Bree thought and then said, "We'll start with two."

CHAPTER
66

West Palm Beach, Florida

BURNING CANE FILLED THE air with smoke again as I drove toward Belle Glade, wanting to be there and in Palm Beach and in Starksville all at once.

It was five twenty in the evening. I'd spent the day with Drummond and Johnson, who'd quickly reached staff at both the Abrams and Martin residences and confirmed that Coco had painted the women's portraits. None of the staff knew who Coco was, however, much less where she lived.

Maggie Crawford's estranged husband, John, was fishing in Alaska. The Boob King had been in surgery all day and was unreachable. So was Elliot Martin, Lisa Martin's billionaire husband, who was in Shanghai on business.

They'd left messages with all their aides. On the way to Mize Fine Arts on Worth Avenue, Johnson called up the Internet on his phone and ran a search for a Coco in Palm Beach and the surrounding areas. There was no such listing.

Then we'd found Mize Fine Arts closed during prime shopping hours, and no one answered our knocking.

"I'd like to go in there and look around," Johnson said as we turned away.

"I'm sure you would," Drummond said. "But I don't think a name on three paintings gives us a search warrant. And that looks like a serious alarm system. You wouldn't be able to explain yourself if you were somehow caught inside."

When I looked at Drummond, he winked at me.

We went to Mize's home. It must have been a grand place once, not huge like the megamansions out on Ocean Boulevard, but an impressive structure. The front yard and gardens were nicely maintained. But the manor itself needed painting. And up close, you could see the front door required varnishing, and the stucco siding was in minor disrepair.

Drummond rang the bell. There was no answer. He rang it again.

I wandered around the side and into the shadows between the house and a bamboo hedge that separated it from the place next door. The walkway was busted concrete overgrown with weeds. The backyard was worse, looked like it hadn't been tended in months. A gutter downspout was disconnected halfway down from the roof. The lower part hung by a bracket.

"If he's in there, he's not answering," Drummond said when I returned.

"I'd check the tax rolls on this guy," I said.

"Why's that?"

"He's not taking care of his property, which means he's under financial stress of some sort."

Drummond called in a request for all information on Jeffrey Mize as we returned to the car.

"We'll have to sit on the place," Johnson said.

"And the art gallery," I said. "Sooner or later, Mize or Coco will show up."

Because Johnson was the only one who had seen Coco in person, he went to watch the shop. Drummond and I sat on the house until it was time for me to go learn what had become of my father.

"I hope you find what you're looking for," the sergeant said before I left.

Driving north out of Belle Glade an hour later, there was a bug hatch, and so many insects smashed into the windshield that it stayed smeared no matter how much wiper fluid I used. Near the Pahokee city limits, I stopped to fill up with gas and clean off the windshield, then I drove into town, seeing signs about the high school football team.

Drummond said the high school teams at Pahokee and Belle Glade always ranked among the top teams in the state and together had put almost sixty players in the NFL. Pretty impressive when you consider the economic devastation. There were fewer businesses in Pahokee than there'd been in Belle Glade.

But the Cozy Corner Café on Lake Street was still open. I parked in front. The humidity this close to Lake Okeechobee was stupefying. In the ten steps I took between the rental and the front door of the café, I was drenched, though maybe that also had to do with the sudden nervousness that swept through me. What had happened to my father all those years ago?

There were six customers in the café, though only one was female and alone. She smiled at me, waved me over. A pretty, plump older Latina woman with a beaming smile, she got up out of her booth, pushing back her long ponytail of black hair flecked with gray, and adjusted an attractive purple batik dress. A small, simple wooden cross hung on a chain about her neck.

"Dr. Cross?" she said, smiling as she took my hand in both of hers and peered kindly up at me through wire-rimmed glasses. "I'm Reverend Alicia Maya. I understand you're interested in Paul Brown?"

CHAPTER
67

OVER THE COURSE OF an hour, an iced coffee, and a slice of pineapple pie, Reverend Maya told me what she knew about Paul Brown. She'd met him shortly after she had taken over the small Unitarian Universalist church in Pahokee as a first-time minister.

"I was twenty-five, right out of divinity school and sure I could change the world," Reverend Maya said. "You wouldn't believe it now, but back then, Pahokee was a thriving place. Everyone had jobs. People came here for jobs, including Paul Brown."

Reverend Maya said Brown showed up at one of her evening services. He was weak and limped terribly.

"He stayed after the service," she said. "He said he had no place to go and would be glad to clean the church if I let him sleep there. I was doubtful, but I could see he was a man in pain beyond the mere physical, and I said yes. He ended up living in the church for about eight months, working out in the picking fields in the day, cleaning the church at night."

I held up my hands. "Before we go any further, can you answer a couple of quick questions?"

"I'll try."

"After Brown died, did you call someone named Clifford Tate in Starksville, North Carolina?"

The reverend cocked her head, looked off, and then

said, "Yes. I believe the name and number were in a little book I found with Mr. Brown's things."

The loss of my father felt strangely final then, and it must have shown on my face because Reverend Maya said, "Sergeant Drummond said he was a relative of yours?"

"I believe he was my father," I said.

She blinked, took a big breath, said, "Oh. I didn't know that."

Reverend Maya said Brown seemed to be a tortured man doing his best to atone for past sins, though he was evasive when it came to discussing their nature. He rarely spoke to her, but she often found him kneeling in prayer.

"I'd ask him what he was praying for," the minister said. "All he would say was 'Forgiveness.'"

"He never told you what had happened? What he did?"

The minister looked conflicted and I could tell it had something to do with confidentiality between a minister and a member of the flock, even a dead member of the flock. So I told her about Jason Cross.

Reverend Maya listened raptly as I described my parents' descent into hell. I told her how my mother had died and about my disjointed memories of what I'd believed for three and a half decades was the night my father died.

"Mr. Brown confessed some of that to me, though there were never any names used. He said he'd killed his wife because she was suffering so."

"I think that's true. Did he ever mention us, the children? Or his mother?"

She nodded. "He did. He said his children were living with his mother somewhere up north, and that they were doing much better without him."

Reverend Maya said that one evening several months after Brown had appeared at her church, she'd gone to check on him. Brown wasn't there in the little room where he lived. Then she heard a shot and found him lying dead behind the church. He'd shot himself in the face with a shotgun.

"Can I see where it happened?"

She shook her head. "The church was a termite-ridden building that was torn down about five years after I left to take over a church in West Palm. But I'd be glad to show you his grave, if you'd like."

"His grave. I'd like that very much."

CHAPTER
68

"WE'LL TAKE MY CAR," Reverend Maya said. "Funner."

To my surprise, she led me to an older-model, gleaming, two-door white Mazda Miata convertible roadster.

"Do all Unitarian Universalist ministers drive sports cars?" I asked.

She laughed. "This one does. It's my single vice in life."

The reverend was good at her vice; she drove the Miata on the rural roads beyond the decaying streets of Pahokee as if she'd had race training somewhere. I never got the chance to ask her if she had because she peppered me with questions about my life and my family.

I could tell by the end of the fifteen-minute drive that Reverend Maya was as good at probing for the soul of things as she was at driving.

"You've led an amazing life by any definition," she said as she downshifted and turned through the narrow gate of a small cemetery out in the countryside. "I think Paul, uh, your father would have been very proud of you."

I smiled, choked up, and said, "Thanks."

Biting insects whirled around us the second she

stopped the car. But then she reached into her glove compartment and pulled out two ThermaCell bug repellents. She clipped one to her purse. I put mine on my belt and was glad to see the thing worked.

We walked forward two lanes in the cemetery and took a left toward the chain-link fence and the dense vegetation beyond it. At the end of the row there was a simple reddish granite slab about the size of two bricks set side by side.

PAUL BROWN
DEDICATED SERVANT OF HIS LORD, JESUS CHRIST

I felt my shoulders slump a bit reading those words and then the date of his death below. I thought back through the years, wondered where I'd been when my father killed himself.

I'd been, what, twelve? Thirteen? Did I ever once think of him back then?

I doubted it, and that admission let loose a trickle of raw emotion that had been building since I'd come upon the gravestone of my dad. My head swung slowly back and forth. My lungs fluttered for air.

He'd killed my mother and escaped prosecution only to be consumed by guilt and grief. The dam burst in me then, and I gave in to it all, the tragedy, the loss of my father a second time. Burying my face in the crook of my arm, I broke down sobbing.

I felt Reverend Maya's hand rubbing my back.

"Hard thing," she said. "Hard, hard thing."

It was almost a minute before I could control myself. I sniffed and looked away from her, said, "Sorry."

"Nothing to be sorry about," she said in a soothing tone.

"I feel bad about all of it."

"I think it would be natural. What are you most upset about?"

I thought about that and anger pooled in me. "I didn't have a dad. That's what I'm angriest about. A boy deserves a father."

"He does, and I'm sorry," she said, deep empathy in her expression.

"There's nothing for you to be sorry about," I said in a hoarse voice. "My father made his decision. I'm sure he thought it was the right thing to do."

"But it's still a hard thing."

I nodded. "It was like a door slammed shut on him the night he died. And then, just in the past few days, that door was open, just for a second, and I caught a glimpse of a secret passageway, but it ended at another locked door. One that will stay that way forever."

Reverend Maya seemed to feel my pain as if it were her own, and she didn't speak for a moment. Finally she said, "Do you need more time alone?"

I gazed down at the gravestone feeling wrung out, and then I said to my father's ghost, "I love you, Dad. I forgive you, Dad."

Reverend Maya patted me on the back again as I walked away from the gravestone. We were quiet on the drive back to Pahokee.

"I hope I've helped to give you closure, Dr. Cross," she said after I'd disentangled myself from the Miata.

"I wanted to know my father's whole story, and now I do, and now I'll have to learn to live with it, and so will my grandmother."

Reverend Maya gazed at me for a long moment, and then said, "I have to go home and make dinner for my husband, who should be getting off work about now, but I wish you and your family all of Jesus's blessings."

"Thank you, Reverend," I said, smiling weakly and nodding. "I wish the same for you and your husband. And drive safe."

"Always," she said. Then she put the Miata in gear and sped off into the gathering night.

CHAPTER
69

IT BEGAN TO RAIN as I drove across the bridge around eight thirty that evening. I was debating when to call Bree. A part of me wanted to pick up the phone right then, but I didn't want to churn the emotions all over again while in public and behind the wheel. I'd call when I got back to my room at the Hampton Inn after checking in with Sergeant Drummond.

But neither Drummond nor Johnson answered the phone, and when I drove by Mize Fine Arts, I didn't see any sign that the place was under surveillance. I drove on toward Mize's house, knowing that I was doing what I often did in turbulent times. I was turning my mind to a mystery and an investigation as a way of escaping the rest of my life.

I should have gone somewhere to eat, then returned to my hotel and tried to get an earlier flight back to North Carolina. Instead, I was in front of Mize's house, relieved to see Drummond's vehicle right where I'd left it.

I drove around the corner, parked out of sight, and strolled down the sidewalk as nonchalantly as an African American male can in Palm Beach. Johnson saw me in the passenger-side mirror and unlocked the car.

I climbed in the backseat.

"Success?" Drummond asked, looking at me in the rearview.

"It was a great help. She was a great help."

"Then we're happy."

"Yes, thank you, Sergeant."

"Least we could do."

"Given up watching the store?"

Drummond gestured through the windshield. "Those lights went on about an hour ago. Don't know if it's part of a security system or if Mize is in there."

"How long are you going to sit on him?"

"I don't know. Until I—"

"Sarge," Johnson interrupted. "Garage door's going up. Which car's it gonna be? The Lexus or the…"

The rear end of a dark green convertible backed out of the garage into the turnaround. The top was up, and the car had to have been forty years old. It looked to me like something Sean Connery might have driven in his years as Bond.

"An Aston Martin DB Five convertible," said Johnson appreciatively. "A very rare car. A very fast and nimble car. Roadster."

"We'll stay with it," Drummond said, starting the car.

The roadster pulled out, revealing the silhouette of a tall figure behind the wheel. The car turned away from us, heading north at a rapid but legal clip toward Worth Avenue and Mize's shop.

"You going to pull him over?" Johnson asked.

"I want to see where he goes at night after ignoring our phone calls and door knocks," the sergeant said.

"Maybe he goes to Coco's place," Johnson said.

"You're thinking they're in this together?" Drummond asked.

"Why not? Coco could be turning Mize onto his targets. Or vice versa."

Drummond frowned, glanced in the mirror at me. "A woman serial killer? Isn't that rare?"

"You've got multiple killings here, but it doesn't feel serial to me. In every case, effort was made to cast the deaths as suicides. Most serial killers delight in being blatant about their acts. So a woman could be our killer or an accomplice."

"Motive?"

"Money."

The Aston Martin was two cars and almost a block ahead of us as it rolled to the stop sign. Instead of taking a left toward Mize Fine Arts, the Aston Martin turned right and headed toward the ocean.

Drummond stayed well back now, unwilling to risk being noticed, while Johnson and I craned our necks to see the roadster take a left onto Ocean Boulevard just as the rain came on hard. When we turned after it, less than a minute later, we couldn't see where Mize had gone.

Then Johnson saw brake lights in the shadows beyond a gate set in a wall that surrounded a two-story Mediterranean. The house was mostly shielded from the road by a riot of plants and towering palms. We circled the block to make sure Mize hadn't gone somewhere else and returned feeling that he must have been allowed in by someone who lived or worked there. Edwin and Pauline Striker were listed as owners in the county records Johnson pulled up on his iPad.

"Is Pauline a candidate for Coco?" I said.

Johnson shook his head. "Both owners are in their late sixties. But maybe Coco's a daughter or something."

Drummond parked where we could see the gate and then drummed his fingers on the wheel. Even though his face remained expressionless, I was learning to read his other nonverbal cues. He was frustrated, and I sensed why.

The various links we'd established connecting the victims, Mize, and Coco were weak, at best, and some were unproven. We didn't even know, for example, if the Coco who'd painted the portraits was the same woman who worked for Mize. And the only thing that tied Mize to any of it was the fact that he'd employed Francie Letourneau and had been called by the maid just before she'd been killed.

That certainly wasn't enough to warrant us going into Mize's home or even, for that matter, into the Strikers' place. For all we knew, the Strikers were old and dear friends of the art dealer, and he was over for a late visit.

But what if—

Drummond said, "I'm sitting here wondering if Mize is in there alone with Pauline Striker."

"Or with Coco and Pauline Striker."

"Call the house," I said. "Make it sound as if you're checking in with people who used Francine Letourneau as a maid or a woman named Coco as a portrait painter. See if that flushes him out."

Johnson looked up the number, called it, heard it ring into voice mail. He left a message identifying himself and asking that someone give him a call back on his cell phone regarding an ongoing investigation.

When he hung up, I doubted we'd get a call anytime soon and I yawned, glanced at my watch. It was nearly ten.

Then Johnson's phone rang.

"The Strikers," he said, and he put the phone on speaker and answered.

CHAPTER
70

IN A HALLWAY OFF the master suite upstairs, Jeffrey Mize became Coco. He got control of himself and affected a crotchety voice, saying, "This is Pauline Striker. I am looking for Detective Johnson."

"You got him," Johnson said. "Thanks for the quick callback."

"What's this about?" Coco said.

"An investigation I'm a part of," Johnson said. "I'm trying to find out if you or your friends employed a Francine Letourneau as a maid in the past four or five years."

"The answer for me is no," Coco said. "We've been lucky and haven't had a turnover in staff in ten years. Both our girls are part of the family. As far as the staff at other houses, I couldn't say."

"Right," Johnson said.

"Is that all? My husband and I are entertaining."

"Sorry to interrupt, but just one more question."

"Go ahead."

"Have you ever had a portrait of yourself done by an artist named Coco?"

For a moment, the cloud that was Coco lifted, and Mize felt panic surge through him. But in the next instant, Coco reasserted control and said, "The only formal portraits of me and my family are photographs. What's this about? I have guests to entertain."

"Just running down leads, ma'am," Johnson said. "Again, I'm sorry for interrupting your evening."

The line clicked dead.

Coco set the phone back in the cradle, feeling like an immediate danger had been averted. But he stood there several long beats also feeling like the police were closing in.

The Mize circuitry in his brain broke through: *Johnson has met Coco and me. Johnson was pounding on the front door at the house this afternoon. He'll go back to the shop in the morning. You should run now. Take all you can and run.*

But these days, Coco was dominant. He pushed aside the thought of leaving just as easily as he'd pushed aside what his house looked like and hid every other thing that might mar his appearance to the outside world.

This was all that mattered. Appearance. This night. This moment.

One last time?

Dressed only in La Perla black panties and a gorgeous Chantal Thomass blush-and-black corset, Coco padded back into the master bedroom, where Pauline Striker, naked, was gagged and lashed to a chair, clearly terrified.

"What do you think?" Coco asked, running his fingers down the sides of the corset. "Slimming. And sensual. Why, Pauline, in my wildest moments I didn't imagine you and Edwin as the merry-widow type, but I suppose what happens behind closed doors just happens and evolves. And then one day I'm here playing in your kinky side, and you're...you're there."

Coco was transfixed by Pauline's fear and didn't move for several moments. Then he grabbed a pair of fine black silk hose, fresh from Paris, and sat in a chair at the vanity. He rolled them on over his toes and up his calves and thighs. Coco loved that sensation. It never got old.

"Have you ever had the sense there were two of you living inside your brain?" Coco asked Pauline, and then he gestured to the corset. "Finding this in your drawer tells me you have. So in case you were wondering, that's what we're doing here, exploring our personalities, acting out fantasies, you know?"

Pauline Striker's eyes were glued on Coco.

As Coco went by her, he ran the fingernails of his left hand over her cheek softly, saying, "Tonight there's someone else playing in your head, Pauline. Her name is Miranda. She's a wild child, and I love her."

Pauline's brow was knit with confusion when Coco came around the other side of the chair and faced her.

"Miranda's a wild child, and I love her," he said again and felt himself harden. "But she's also my mother, and I hate her."

Coco slapped Pauline across the face so hard it left a palm print.

Over Pauline's cries and whimpers of pain, Coco said coldly, "Gloves are off, Mummy. No more making things look like suicide for Jeffrey's sake. There's just nothing fulfilling in that anymore."

CHAPTER
71

"I'M TELLING YOU, SARGE, some of the time it sounded like Coco," Johnson said. "She had this distinctive cadence when she talked, and so did that lady."

"Cadence?" Drummond said, skeptical.

"Yeah, like where the word emphasis was," Johnson said. "My wife's a speech pathologist. She knows about this stuff, so I know about this stuff. Did you notice how the voice broke every so often? Old and then kind of younger?"

I'd never heard Coco's voice, so I couldn't say, but there had been something odd about the way Johnson's questions had been answered.

"We can't go in on the basis of you saying one woman sounded like another one on a cell phone," Drummond said.

"But maybe I can," I said.

"What?" the sergeant said, swiveling in his seat to look at me.

"You're on the job," I said. "You're handcuffed by the law, but right here, right now, I have no jurisdiction. I am a private citizen with information that suggests a woman might be in danger in that house. Acting on that suspicion, I go into the compound. I look in a few windows. If there's a party going on with Edwin,

Pauline, Mize, and others, I slip out. If I see probable cause, I call you."

"You could get shot," Drummond said.

"If I do, you'll be the first to know," I said, getting out of the car.

"How're you getting in?" asked Johnson.

"The straightforward way," I said, and I shut the door.

It was pouring when I ran across the boulevard, which was lightly traveled at that hour. There was no one in the western lane at all when I accelerated at the gate and then jumped up like I was going for a rebound.

Both my hands found the top of the gate and hung on. I kicked and shimmied and pulled until I'd gotten my belly over it. I straddled the gate, pivoted, and then hung down off it and let go. I landed and moved fast into the shadows.

The driveway was done in some kind of mosaic tile and was slick and puddled everywhere as I moved past the vegetation that blocked the house from the road. There were lights on in the inner yard, revealing a lawn that looked like a putting green at Augusta; beds of blooming annuals ringed the house.

There were lights on at every corner. Tinier lights lit an arched trellis that framed the main entrance. But unless the Strikers were using blackout curtains, there were no lights on in the lower part of the house.

I could see at least three rooms on the second story that were lit up, however. And the drumming rain made hearing anything impossible. I wondered whether this had been another impetuous act, the kind of all-in move Bree had been concerned about.

But more often than not, I've found it pays to be all-in. I ran across the lawn to the walkway and up under the trellis to the door. For a moment I stood there, trying to hear inside. Figuring my scouting trip was likely about to be over, I nevertheless reached for the door handle, because, well, you never know.

The handle moved down, and the locking mechanism gave. The door swung open. You never know.

I was torn at that point, because even though the door had been left unlocked, I was still breaking and entering. I hesitated, and then decided to just step inside and listen. If I heard nothing of alarm, I'd be gone.

I stepped into a dark, air-conditioned foyer, eased the front door shut behind me, and strained to hear. The distant hum of a refrigerator compressor. The closer ticking of a clock. A drip, drip that I realized was me leaving puddles on the entryway floor.

Then I heard a woman's muffled voice somewhere in the house above me. I couldn't tell what was being said, but I caught the odd rhythm of her speech. Was that what Johnson had been talking about?

A smacking noise. A cry. A whimper.

I locked in on the sounds, not sure what to do. What if Mize or Coco was torturing her? But what if the Strikers and Mize and Coco were into bondage or something, and this was all between consenting adults?

The cop in me told me to get the hell out. But when I heard another smack and more crying, the mystery lover in me drove me toward a spiral staircase that rose off the foyer.

I climbed the stairs quietly, moving as fast as I dared. On the landing, I heard the woman's voice again, clearer but still not intelligible. After kicking off my shoes, I drew the Ruger from my ankle holster and snuck down the hall, where I saw a wafer of light coming through a door at the far end; thankfully, no floorboards creaked or—

"What did you expect, Miranda?" a woman said cruelly. "You dress a little boy in silk and lace all the time, this is what you get."

Smack. A moan.

A moan of pain? Or pleasure?

"You did teach me a classic sense of style, though, I'll give you that," the woman went on in that odd rhythmic voice. "But you denied yourself nothing." There was a pause before she shouted, "Nothing!"

Smack.

"Anything you wanted, when you wanted it, Mother!"

Smack! Smack! Smack!

Each blow sounded louder and more furious than the previous one. If this was some kind of sex act, it was full-on S&M. Whatever it was, home invasion or not, I was going to see who was doing the hitting and who was being hit.

"How will it go for you this time, Miranda? Shall we stick with the tried? The true? The erotic? You know what asphyxia does to your orgasm."

That stopped me right outside the door, and I didn't know what to do. If I burst in and it was something consensual, I could kiss a lot of things good-bye.

The woman said, "Once it's over, I'll put a toy in you, complete your method, your scenario."

Then the whimpering turned to whining amplified by what sounded to me like terror, and I didn't care about anything but stopping it.

Gun up, I pushed the door inward, saw an older woman, naked, bound to a chair and gagged. There was some kind of wide sash or gold cord biting into her neck. Standing up behind her on the bed, straining to tighten the cord, was a very pale, very pretty bald woman wearing makeup and an outfit that would have made a trucker blush.

I panicked and was stepping backward when the naked older woman's bulging eyes caught mine and she nodded wildly.

"Let go!" I yelled, moving deeper into the room, aiming right at the bald woman. "Let go or I will shoot you!"

CHAPTER
72

THE BALD WOMAN STARTED, stepped back, let go of the rope, and stared at me and the gun before raising her trembling hands and saying hoarsely, "What is this?"

I grabbed a robe off a chair, tossed it over the older woman I assumed was Pauline Striker, and came around behind her, still aiming at the bald woman.

"Get down on your knees, Coco, then facedown on the bed, hands behind your head," I said.

She seemed even more frightened now that she realized I knew her name, and she started to lower herself to her knees while I worked the gag off Mrs. Striker. She spit it out, choked, and cried, "He—"

"Are you the police?" Coco asked from one knee.

"The next best thing," I said, pulling out my cell phone. "Just need to know one thing, Mrs. Striker. Was that consensual? Or was your life in danger?"

Before the older woman could speak, Coco said in a deep male voice that startled me, "Of course it was consensual. Pauline, tell him. You can't have our interlude coming out in the *Palm Beach Post.* Not with Edwin's new thing just around the corner. It would be everywhere."

I gaped for a second, realizing that Coco had to be Jeffrey Mize. But even though the person in front of me was bald, my brain was having trouble with the idea that *she* was a *he*. If not for the lack of hair, Mize could have been an aging supermodel.

"Mrs. Striker," I said, feeling unsure now. "Please answer my question."

The older woman seemed less upset than before, and she looked at me, then over at Mize, who was on all fours, gazing at her.

"Tell him, Pauline," Mize said. "Whoever he is."

Mrs. Striker swiveled her head to look at me, choked out, "Who *are* you?"

"A Good Samaritan," I said. "I'm here to help and to contact the police if you need them."

"Wait," Mize said, pushing up into a kneeling position. "You're not a cop?"

"How did you get in here?" Mrs. Striker asked, sounding angry.

"That's not important; what's important is whether this was consensual or not," I said, feeling the situation slipping away from me.

"It was consensual," she said emphatically. "But I most certainly did not consent to having you in my house holding me and my guest at gunpoint. Who are you and what are you after?"

"Who I am doesn't matter," I said, trying to figure out a way to exit gracefully and anonymously. "What matters is that Mr. Mize has been linked to the murders of three Palm Beach socialites."

"That's not true," Mize snapped.

"He painted their portraits. Lisa Martin. Ruth Abrams. Maggie Crawford. Is there a portrait of you here in the house, Pauline? Were you about to become number four?"

Mrs. Striker looked bewildered for a moment and then said, "I don't know anything about that."

"See?" Mize said, smiling and straightening.

It was time to either cut and run or do something audacious. I chose audacious.

"Then I apologize and I'll be going," I said, lowering the gun. "But I'd rather see you free of your bonds before I go."

"That's not necessary," Mize said.

"I insist," I said.

Taking my eyes off Mize, I squeezed my phone, then crouched and set it on the carpet behind the ladderback chair at the foot of the bed. With my left hand, I began working at the knots. My right thumb found the latch on the Ruger and I pressed it before I moved the gun to my left hand.

I made a sound of frustration, set the pistol on the bedspread, and set to work in earnest on the knots. I'd undone two and was stepping around Mrs. Striker when Mize dove on his belly, grabbed the Ruger, and aimed it at me, point-blank.

"I don't know who you are, but I am going to enjoy killing you," Mize said in Coco's voice. "And don't you move now, Pauline. We have unfinished business, you and I."

"No, Jeffrey, I—"

Mize slammed the butt of the gun backward, hitting the side of Mrs. Striker's head and opening up a rectangular cut that bled as she moaned.

"Why'd you do that?" I demanded.

"I needed her out of the way so you and I could have fun," he said, coming off the bed, gun three feet from my chest. "Who are you?"

My mind was on overdrive, spinning through the little pieces of what I knew about Mize and the murders and what I'd heard coming up the stairs.

"Why kill me?" I asked. "I don't fit your pattern. The mommy complex. Did you even have a father?"

"Shut up," Mize said.

"It's not difficult to understand you hating your mother and taking it out on these women," I said. "Miranda, your mother, humiliated you right from the beginning, dressed you up like a girl until age...what?"

Mize glared at me, said nothing.

"I figure it had to be one of the few things that got you attention from her," I said. "Women's fashion and style were what you had in common. Maybe fashion was the only way you could tear Miranda away from all those men."

"You don't know anything about her," Mize snarled.

"I know she spent a lot of money. I figure you barely inherited enough to keep up the house she left you. Or maybe, between your trust and the portrait commissions and your shop, you had enough money for a while. But recently the trust ran out, or the commissions stopped, or your shop began floundering. And it all got to be too much for you, didn't it, Jeffrey?"

Mize seemed to be staring right through me now.

"So you went to the women who knew you, the women you'd painted before, the ones who reminded you of your mother, and you decided to let off a little steam."

"Shut up, I said!" Mize shouted and he shook the gun at me.

"And maybe you stole money, jewels, and clothes from your victims, evened the score a little. All of them except Francie Letourneau; you took care of your maid because she was stealing from you, isn't that right? Or, no, because she discovered your secret life as Coco, and—"

"Enough!" Mize screamed. He took a step closer and aimed the pistol at my face from less than a foot away. "Mother always said to get rid of pests fast!"

CHAPTER
73

I LOOKED DOWN THE barrel of the Ruger, saw Mize's slender feminine hand squeezing on the trigger.

"Freeze, Coco!" Detective Johnson yelled. "Drop the gun or I'll shoot!"

"Don't worry, Detective," I said. "It's not loaded."

Mize's flawless porcelain skin tightened over his exquisite cheekbones, and disbelief gave way to rage. He pulled the trigger. Nothing happened. He tried again—nothing.

He pulled the gun back as if he meant to chop me with it. Before he could, I slapped him silly, dazed him, and knocked him to the ground. Johnson was putting cuffs on him when Sergeant Drummond appeared, gasping for breath.

"Tough trip over the gate?" I asked.

"You have no idea," Drummond said, wheezing. "I'm getting too old for this shit."

"You heard everything?" I asked, going past Mrs. Striker, who was still bleeding and looking confused. I crouched down to the carpet and picked up my cell phone and the magazine from the Ruger.

"Loud and clear," the sergeant said, waving his cell at me. "Enough probable cause in anyone's book."

"This is entrapment," Mize said. "I want a lawyer. I'm being persecuted."

"For what?" Johnson demanded as he hauled him to his feet.

"Cross-dressing," he said. "Getting into a little weird sex. Right, Pauline?"

Mrs. Striker raised her bleeding head and glared at him. "He'd been a friend since he'd painted my portrait, and he just tried to kill me. He put on my lingerie, said I was his mother tonight, and tried to kill me. And I'll testify to it in court, Edwin's new deal be damned."

"Can we call an ambulance for you?" I asked, smiling.

"Please," she said. "And could you get me some clothes? I don't want to be seen this way."

"Tell me what you need," I said as Johnson hauled Mize from the room.

She asked for the clothes Mize had stripped her of and held them and the robe against her when she stood unsteadily and walked to the bathroom. Before she closed the door completely, she peered out at me.

"Who *are* you?" she asked.

Drummond said, "That's Alex Cross, don't you know?"

She shook her head and shut the door.

"That was something," the sergeant said as he scratched at his slack chin.

"We good?" I asked.

"Oh, you and me, we're fine," Drummond said. "Me and my boss and the DA? That may be another story."

"I don't know," I said. "Maybe the way I came in here gets some of it excluded in court. But so what? You know who killed the four now. Just have to rebuild the case based on what you know and prove it outside of here. And I'll testify however I'm allowed."

Drummond thought about that, nodded, said, "I suppose the most important thing was saving Mrs.

Striker and getting a lunatic cross-dresser off the streets of Palm Beach."

"Or out of the bedrooms, anyway."

The sergeant seemed to chew on something, and then he said, "This how a lot of your cases go?"

"Actually, every single one of them is different."

"After you make your statement, you'll go back to North Carolina?"

"Tomorrow sometime, I hope."

"Get that guy Melvin Bell?"

"Marvin Bell. He's one of our suspects, but I haven't excluded anyone."

"Sounds to me like he's your man."

Sirens wailed, coming closer.

"My gut says he is too, but we'll see," I said.

Drummond stuck his hand out, said, "A pleasure to meet you, and thank you for your help here."

I shook it, said, "The feeling's mutual, Sergeant. I hope we see each other again someday."

He smiled that crooked smile of his, said, "I'd like that."

The bathroom door opened. Mrs. Striker came out in a beautiful nightgown and a new robe. She held a washcloth to her head.

"Can you help me downstairs?" she asked weakly. "I don't want to receive visitors in my bedroom."

"Of course," I said, coming over and giving her my elbow.

She held on to it. Drummond stepped aside. We walked slowly out into the hallway. At the far end, beyond the stairs, hung a portrait in oil.

I had to hand it to Mize. As Coco, he had captured Pauline Striker at what must have been the pinnacle of her beauty and charm.

CHAPTER
74

Starksville, North Carolina

IN THE REMODELED KITCHEN of the house where I grew up, Nana Mama stared at me blankly and said quietly, "Your father lived another two years?"

I nodded and gave her the rest of it, including the suicide, including a description of her son's small tombstone.

My grandmother held a trembling fist to her mouth. With her other hand, she plucked off her glasses and wiped at tears.

"Why'd he kill himself?" she asked.

"Guilt? Grief? The aloneness?" I said. "I don't think we'll ever know."

"He must have been the one."

"What one?"

"The caller," Nana Mama said. "For the first year or two that you lived with me, always around a holiday or, come to think of it, one of you boys' birthdays, I'd get a call with no one on the other end. At first I thought it was just a mistake, but I'd hear things in the background, a television or music playing. And then the line would click dead."

"When did that stop?" I asked.

"Around two years after you came to DC?"

The timeline fit, but before I could say so, Jannie

rapped on the frame of the kitchen entrance. "We have to go. I want a chance to warm up on my own."

I checked my watch. We did have to go.

"You all right?" I asked Nana Mama as I stood up from the table.

She hesitated and then said, "I suppose I am. Better than before."

"He was punished for his sins, and then he died," I said.

My grandmother said, "There's balance there. Should we go?"

"You're up to the ride?"

"Wouldn't miss it," she said, and she got to her feet. She put her hand on my arm. "Thank you, Alex."

"For what?"

"Clearing things up."

"Wish it had turned out some other way for him."

"I do too. I always will."

I helped Nana Mama out onto the porch, where Jannie, Bree, Ali, and Pinkie were waiting. We trooped out to the car and my cousin's truck. Ali and Jannie wanted to ride with Pinkie. To my surprise, so did my little grandmother, who looked cute and ridiculous in the front seat of the one-ton pickup.

"I've never ridden in one of these," she called out the window, and she waved with such enthusiasm that Bree and I had to grin.

"She's one of a kind," Bree said, climbing into the Explorer.

"Could you imagine if there were two?" I said, starting the car.

"I don't think the world would be big enough." Bree chuckled, leaned over, and kissed me. "Anyway, I'm glad you're back."

"Me too. And by the way, I loved the welcome-back celebration last night."

She laughed contentedly, said, "Mmm. That was nice, wasn't it?"

We held hands as we followed Pinkie through town. Nearing the railroad tracks, Bree said, "Think we have time to stop?"

"Probably, but I don't know the way. Can we do it coming back?"

Bree looked longingly at the tree line beyond the tracks. "It's funny how you want to check every couple of hours. It's like gambling."

"I can see that," I said, and we drove on.

The road soon became steep and windy, and it dropped off the plateau in a series of lazy S turns. I noticed play in the Explorer's wheel that hadn't been there before. And the brakes were slightly sluggish.

"Remind me to check the fluid levels in Raleigh," I said.

"Didn't we do everything before our drive down here?" Bree asked.

"Yes, but something doesn't feel quite—"

There was a slight clanking noise. The car shuddered.

"That can't be good," Bree said. "You better pull over, take a look."

We were on a 10 percent, maybe 12 percent grade at that point, with low guardrails giving way to sheer banks and trees. Ahead, there was a scenic lookout. I put on my blinker, tapped the brakes. Nothing. I pumped the brakes. The car slowed only slightly, then gave another clank and shudder.

Then the vehicle seemed to break free of all restraint and we went into an accelerating, pell-mell, runaway descent.

CHAPTER
75

WE HURTLED DOWN THE road. Ahead of us, it veered sharply left, and all you could see beyond it was pale blue sky.

"Alex!" Bree screamed as I clawed at the wheel and stomped vainly on the brake pedal.

I grabbed the shifter, tried to slam it into low. The arm wouldn't budge.

"Jesus, Alex, we're—"

With my left foot, I stabbed at the emergency brake pedal but did not put it to the floor for fear we'd be thrown into a spin. There was a screeching noise as the tires caught, leaving smoke rising off the rubber-blackened road.

The Explorer lurched to one side and then another, but I managed to keep it from going sideways and then, just before that hard left turn, I slammed the shifter arm down, and the engine braked us some more.

I spun the wheel hard and got the front end around. The rear quarter panel of the car slammed into the guardrail, which tore off the bumper and flung it into the other lane and behind us.

The rest of the ride down the plateau was marred only by the smell of burning brake pads, the roar of a straining engine, and the sweat pouring off both our foreheads. When we reached flatter land, I threw the

shifter in neutral and turned the car off. We coasted to
a stop on the shoulder, and I put on the hazard lights,
laid my head back.

"You should call Pinkie," I said. "Tell him to make
room in the truck."

"Aren't you going to see what happened?" Bree
asked.

"I'm not a car guy," I said. "We're going to have to
have it towed somewhere and looked at."

"You're going to have to file an accident report," she
said, digging out her phone and punching in Pinkie's
number.

"I'd miss Jannie," I said. "I'll leave a note with my
name and number."

"That's called leaving the scene of—"

"I don't care," I said. "Just call him before he gets too
far down the road."

When they came back, we intentionally understated
the situation, saying only that it seemed something was
wrong with the brakes, but we were fine. I used my
phone to find a towing company that agreed to get the
car and take it to a dealership in Winston-Salem, and
then I sat back, put my arm around Bree, and closed my
eyes.

I fell into one of those strange, buzzing sleeps that
follow stressful experiences. I didn't remember a
minute of the hour-and-a-half drive to Duke.

We blundered around before we found the track.
Even with the close call, we were early enough that Jannie was able to start jogging before any of the other
athletes arrived. They were all there by eleven, however, along with Coach Greene, who smiled as she came
over to me.

"Glad you made it," she said, shaking my and Bree's
hands.

"Jannie was so excited she was up before dawn," I said.

"No way we weren't making it," Bree said.

The coach's grin disappeared. "Just to follow up. Those blood and urine tests?"

"Haven't heard yet," I said. "But again, innocent until…"

"Of course," she said, and then she handed me another waiver and apologized for my having to fill another one out. "This will be interesting, though."

"How's that?" Nana Mama asked.

The coach gestured to three women doing ballistic jumps and skips along the track to warm up. "Alice and Trisha are here at Duke. Dawn's over at Chapel Hill. All three were second-team all-Americans this past season."

"Jannie know that?" Bree asked.

"I kind of hope not," Coach Greene said, and she trotted off.

"What's an all-American?" Ali asked.

"They're among the best in the whole country," I said.

"Is Jannie?"

"Course not," Nana Mama said. "Your sister's only fifteen, but it will be a good experience for her."

As I'd seen her do twice before, Coach Greene led the girls through a series of exercises designed to get their quick-twitch muscles warmed up, loose, and firing. When they were ready, she broke them into squads of five and ran them through an Indian drill, where they ran at 40 percent unless they were at the rear of the pack. Then they had to sprint to the front.

They did this twice at four hundred meters. Jannie seemed to have no problem coming from behind in those long, fluid strides and then taking her place at the lead. After a five-minute break for water and more stretching, Greene made some switches, bringing my daughter over with the all-Americans in their early twenties and another girl who was at least four years older than Jannie.

They were watching my daughter out of the corners of their eyes. As I'd seen again and again since earlier that year, Jannie seemed unfazed by the age and experience differences.

"They gonna race now?" Ali asked, standing on the bleacher next to me.

"It's just practice," Bree said.

"Not for Jannie," I said.

"Let's take it to seventy-five percent, ladies," Greene said when they were lined up shoulder to shoulder. "Three, two, one, go."

The older girls took off in short, choppy strides that soon opened into longer bounds and a less frenzied rhythm. Jannie seemed to come up to speed effortlessly but lagged a few feet behind the nineteen-year-old and was two yards behind the all-American trio entering the backstretch.

Jannie stayed right there until she'd rounded the near turn, picked up her pace slightly coming down the stretch, and finished just off the shoulder of the nineteen-year-old. She was four paces off the older girls, who were breathing hard. Two of them looked at Jannie and nodded.

No smile from my daughter, just a nod back.

The second quarter mile, at 85 percent, finished much the same way. Then Greene called for 90 percent effort.

Something about the way Jannie rolled her shoulders back and down let me know that it had become serious now, and even though there were fewer than fifteen people scattered across the bleachers watching, I couldn't help but stand.

For the first time, Jannie adopted that same chopping fast gait off the line and stayed right with the elite bunch as they rounded the first turn. The older girls picked up the pace down the backstretch. Jannie stayed just off the shoulders of the all-Americans. The nineteen-year-old faded.

My daughter made her move coming into the second turn. She accelerated right by the three and was leading as they entered the stretch.

Even without binoculars, you could see the disbelief on the faces of the older girls, followed by the grit and determination that had gotten them close to the pinnacle of their sport. They poured it on, and two of them ran Jannie down and passed her before the finish. But my girl was a stride behind them and a stride ahead of one of the national-class athletes coming across the line.

CHAPTER
76

"THAT WAS A RACE!" Ali said.

"Jannie made it a race," Pinkie said, smiling. "Oh my God, she's good."

"Dr. Cross?" a man said, coming across the grandstand toward us. Clad in unmarked gray sweats and a blue hoodie, he was in his fifties, a welterweight redhead with a rooster's confident manner. "I'm Ted McDonald. To be honest, I came here to watch one of the other girls, but I'd very much like to talk to you about Jannie."

"What about Jannie?" Nana Mama asked, eyeing him suspiciously.

McDonald glanced at the track where Greene and another, older woman in warm-ups were talking to the girls. "I'm a track coach, and a scout of sorts. I'd like to share something with you and Jannie, but let's do it after Coach Greene and Coach Fall have had a chance to talk with you. Would that work out?"

"Before we leave Durham today, you mean?"

"I know a great place for a lunch that will help Jannie nutritionally recover from that workout," McDonald said. "My treat?"

I glanced at Bree and Nana Mama, shrugged, said, "Sure. Why not."

"Great, I'll find you in the parking lot," he said. He

smiled and handed me a card that read *Ted McDonald, Extreme Performance Systems. Austin, Toronto, Palo Alto.*

McDonald shook my hand, went back up into the bleachers, and put his hood up. I didn't know what to make of it, so I started to Google him and his company. Before I could get the names typed in on my phone, up came Coach Greene and the older woman in sweats, Duke's head coach, Andrea Fall.

After introductions and handshakes, Coach Fall said, "I was skeptical after the invitational and more so after Coach Greene's descriptions of Jannie's running in the two-hundred, but now I'm a believer. How are her grades?"

"Outstanding," Nana Mama said. "She's a worker."

"That makes things a lot easier," Coach Fall said. "I'd like to formally offer your daughter a full-ride scholarship to Duke when she's ready to attend."

"What?" I said, dumbfounded.

"Jannie can't officially answer my offer until February of her senior year, but I wanted it on the table as the first of what I assume will be many offers," Coach Fall said.

"She's that good?" Bree asked in wonder.

"I can count on one hand in thirty years of coaching the number of athletes I've seen who have Jannie's potential," she replied. "Barring injury, the sky is the limit."

"This is just mind-boggling," I said.

"I imagine so," Coach Fall said. "So anytime you or Jannie are confused or want to talk about her training or how things are going, feel free to call me. Whatever she chooses to do and whatever college she chooses in the long run is beside the point. Okay?"

"Okay," I said, and I shook her hand.

"Take care of her," Coach Fall said. "She's a thoroughbred."

"What kind of bread is thor-oh?" Ali asked afterward.

"A thoroughbred is a racehorse," Nana Mama said.

"Jannie's a horse?"

"She runs like one," Bree said, and she squeezed my hand.

I squeezed back, full of pride but also anxiety. I felt like I was in way over my head when it came to making decisions about Jannie's future.

"You going to tell Jannie?" Nana Mama asked. "About the offer?"

"I have to," I said. "But I'll wait for somewhere quieter."

When Jannie came up into the stands smiling, Ali said, "You got an offer."

"What?"

"I'll tell you later," I said, and hugged her. "We're very proud of you."

She beamed, said, "Who knew?"

"God did," Nana Mama said. "You've got something only God can give."

We walked out into the parking lot and found Ted McDonald waiting. He shook Jannie's hand, told her what he'd told me, and led us to a nearby café that offered organic sandwiches and the like.

We ordered, and he asked who would be making decisions about Jannie's future training. I said I hadn't even begun to think about that process.

McDonald said, "Then I'm very glad I happened to be here."

He filled us in on his impressive background, including his PhD in exercise physiology from McGill University and his stints as a top coach with the Canadian and

French national track federations. McDonald currently served as an independent training consultant to athletes at a number of U.S. universities, including Rice, Texas, Texas A&M, UCLA, USC, and Georgetown.

He said, "I'm also a scout for—"

Our lunch arrived. McDonald had ordered a salad for Jannie—vegetables, broiled chicken, and hard-boiled eggs—and a smoothie made from Brazilian acai berries that she said was delicious. I tried a sip and ordered my own.

While we ate, McDonald peppered Jannie with questions. How many pull-ups could she do without stopping? How many push-ups? What was her best standing broad jump? Her vertical leap? Flexibility? Endurance? Her mile time? Fastest recorded quarter?

Jannie didn't know the exact answer to some questions, but others she knew right off the top of her head.

The questions went on. Had she ever long-jumped? High-jumped? Pole-vaulted? Hurdled?

Jannie shook her head.

"No matter," he said. "Tell me what happens when you run. I mean, what's the experience like for you?"

Jannie thought about that, said, "I sort of go off in my own world and everything gets kind of slow."

"Nerves before you race?"

"Not really, no."

"Not even today?"

"No. Why?"

"The girls you finished with in that last run were all-Americans."

"Really?" Jannie said, surprised.

"Really."

She grinned. "I think I could have beat them."

"I bet you could have," he said, then he grabbed a napkin, pulled out a pen, and scribbled for a minute or two.

He pushed the napkin across the table to me and Jannie. It read:

WHPT:
2018—USNC
2020—OGT5
2021—WCPOD
2022—WC
2024—OGGM

"What's it mean?" I asked.

He told me, and it felt like everything in our lives changed.

CHAPTER
77

LATER THAT AFTERNOON, I was still struggling with what Ted McDonald had written on the napkin at lunch.

Was that possible? Should you even begin with that end in mind?

"He said we didn't have to give him an answer right away," Bree said from the driver's seat of a rental car we'd picked up in Winston-Salem.

"I know," I said. "But it's just a lot to take in."

"You don't think she should try?"

"She's only fifteen," I said. "Is this when they start thinking like that?"

"Other kids in other sports sure do," she said as we drove past the Welcome to Starksville sign.

I stared again at the napkin and wrestled with its meaning.

Women's Heptathlon
2018—U.S. National Champion
2020—Olympic Games Top Five
2021—World Championships Podium
2022—World Champion
2024—Olympic Games Gold Medalist

Was any of this possible? McDonald said it was. He said Jannie might win any of the titles he'd listed as a pure runner, but he'd seen such athleticism in my daughter that he thought she'd be better suited to the grueling multi-skill heptathlon event.

"The heptathlon decides the best female athlete in the world," McDonald said. "You interested in being that athlete, Jannie? The one who can do anything? Superwoman?"

You could see it in my daughter's face, how in the very instant he'd thrown out that spark, Jannie had caught fire.

"What would it take?" she asked.

"Your heart, your soul, and years of hard work," he said. "You up to that?"

She'd glanced at me and then back at him, and nodded. I got chills.

McDonald said that if Jannie consented, he'd visit her regularly in Washington, DC, during the year to teach her the various events within the heptathlon. She'd compete as a runner until he was satisfied with her skills. If we were all happy after the first year, he'd arrange a scholarship at a private school in Austin, where she could work with him on a more consistent basis.

"The school's excellent. They'll challenge her academically so she's ready for wherever she decides to go to college," he said.

Bree said, "How much is this going to cost us?"

"Zero," the coach said.

"What?" I said. "How's that possible?"

McDonald said he was funded by several athletic-shoe and -apparel companies and charged with finding and nurturing track talent. If Jannie became the kind of athlete he thought she was, she'd be in line for endorsements that would make her life easier in the long run.

Free education. A career as a professional athlete. Olympic—

"They're heading home, Alex," Bree said, breaking into my thoughts.

Nana Mama, Ali, and Jannie were in Pinkie's pickup in front of us. Pinkie reached his massive four-finger hand out the window crossing the railroad tracks and waved to us.

I waved back as Bree put on the blinker and pulled into the old Piggly Wiggly parking lot. I folded the napkin, put it in my shirt pocket.

"Think she can do it?" Bree asked as we headed toward that line of trees on that short bluff above the tracks.

"I'm beginning to think she's like you," I said. "Capable of anything and everything."

She smiled, poked me in the ribs, said, "When'd you get so sweet?"

"Day I met you."

"Good answer."

"I have my moments."

When we reached the trees, Bree led me to a big beech tree that overlooked the tracks. There were steel steps screwed into the tree. She said bow hunters used them, and she'd bought them at the local army-navy.

She climbed up around ten feet to another recent purchase. The Bushnell night-vision trail camera was designed to take pictures of whatever came by. Hunters used them to pattern deer. There seemed to be a commercial for them every eight minutes on the Outdoor Channel.

"Even Jim Shockey uses them," Bree said. "So I thought, Why not? We'll take pictures of every train that comes through Starksville."

Bree had put up this camera and another one three

hundred yards west. She'd checked the memory cards once after twenty-four hours and found pictures of riders heading north on the train late Thursday afternoon, just about the time we'd seen riders the previous Thursday as we drove into town.

Now she traded memory cards on both cameras and reactivated them. We took the cards back to the rental car and looked at them on her computer. It took us a while to scroll through them, but we saw pictures of more riders taken the night before at ten, roughly the same time Bree saw Finn Davis giving that three-finger salute on Wednesday night.

Davis was not in any of the new photographs, but Bree's patterns had been established. Riders at ten o'clock every other night. Riders at five on alternate afternoons.

It was half past four by then. Someone should ride by within the hour. Despite the heat, we decided to return to the trees to see if the pattern would hold. As we sweated and waited, bugs whined all around us, and I had the creepy feeling there were ticks crawling up my legs.

My phone rang. Naomi.

"Stefan's been beaten again," she said. "Some jail inmates got to him."

I sighed, said, "It's like that in every prison with child killers and abusers."

"Except Stefan didn't do it, Uncle Alex," Naomi said forcefully.

"Right. Where is he?"

"In Starksville Memorial under guard," she said.

The train signal at the crossing to our right a hundred yards ahead started to ring.

"I'll try to stop by to—" I began before noticing a train coming slowly out of the south. Twenty cars back, I could make out a lone rider. "Got to go, Naomi."

"Just one rider," Bree said as I pocketed the phone.

"Better than none," I said.

"How do you want to handle this?" she asked as the train engine groaned by at less than fifteen miles an hour.

"Get the car and parallel me heading north," I said. "I'll call you."

"Where are you going?"

"On that train," I said as the lone rider, a young white guy wearing a baseball cap, sunglasses, and a long black T-shirt, went past. He was sitting with his legs off the front of the freight car, looking straight ahead.

When I turned, Bree was already gone.

I waited until another fifteen cars had gone by before I left the trees, jumped off the bluff, and started to sprint.

CHAPTER
78

CUTTING AT AN ANGLE to the train, I timed it so a steel ladder welded into one of the boxcars was coming right by me before I sped up one last time, stabbed out my hand, and caught one of the rungs at head height. Before it could jerk me off my feet, I jumped and got my shoes on the lowest rung.

I hung there for six or seven breaths, then the dinging of the train-crossing bell reminded me I was about to be seen by all the cars waiting on my side of the tracks. I clambered up.

Car horns honked as my boxcar passed through the crossing. I didn't look over my shoulder and didn't go up on top until we were well beyond it and the train was starting to pick up speed.

I peeked over the edge of the container car to check on the rider, make sure he was still looking forward, before I crawled up onto the roof. I laid flat, holding on to one of the flanges until I had enough breath and strength to get up. James Bond makes it look easy, but standing on top of a slow-moving train is tough. Stalking forward on a jolting, swaying, accelerating train takes superhuman balance that I do not possess. I couldn't stand up straight at all and settled for a wide-footed crouch, taking one tentative step after another.

Jumping to the next car made me nauseated, but I did it and kept on, staring at the rooftop right in front of me, then the rider, then the track far beyond with the irrational fear that I was going to miss an oncoming tunnel and be swatted off the train.

It took a solid fifteen minutes to go eighteen cars forward. I was trying to be ninja-like when I jumped to the nineteenth car, the one right behind the container car upon which the rider was perched.

I must have made some kind of sound, or maybe it was just time for him to look around. When I landed, he was staring right at me.

He swung his right arm from his chest, revealing a pistol equipped with a sound suppressor. I threw myself flat just before he shot. The round pinged off the steel rooftop about two feet to my right.

The rocking of the train had thrown off his aim. Or he was a lousy shot. Or maybe a combination of the two. In any case, I dug down, came up with my little Ruger nine-millimeter just before he pulled the trigger again.

His bullet clanged off a flange six inches from my head. I shot at him and missed. But it was enough to change the dynamics of things. He wasn't holding ground anymore. He was getting out of Dodge, jumping to the next car as I struggled to my feet.

He was leaping to an oval-shaped tanker car when I jumped onto the container car behind him. I landed fine but I didn't see the rider anymore. Then I realized he'd slipped when he'd landed on the tanker and done a face-plant.

He was slow to move, dazed by the hit, and I was able to close much of the gap between us. When he finally regained his feet, I saw he was no longer carrying the suppressed pistol. Had he dropped it?

"Stop!" I yelled. "I just want to talk to you."

But he kept moving forward.

"Stop, or I'll shoot!"

He didn't slow.

I aimed to his left, sent a bullet by his ear. That caused him to cringe and turn toward me with his hands up.

That's better, I thought. *Now we're getting somewhere.*

Ahead, I could see we were approaching a train trestle. I cautiously jumped to the tanker and got another ten feet closer to the rider. We were less than twenty feet apart. He crouched, holding on to a wheel on top of the tanker.

"I just want to talk," I said again.

"'Bout what, man?" he asked, trying to act tough but looking scared.

I held up my hand, showed him the three-finger salute, said, "I want to talk about this. And Finn Davis. And Marvin Bell. And you riding this train."

He looked at me like I'd grown horns and shook his head. "No way, man."

"We know you're protecting something on this train. What is it?"

He looked away from me, shook his head again. "No way. Can't."

"We can protect you."

"No, you can't," he said. "Ain't no one can protect anyone from Grandfather and the company."

"Grandfather and the company?" I said as the train started across the trestle high above a deep, narrow canyon thick with woods. "Who's Grandfather? What's the company?"

Looking at me with a stricken expression, he said, "Death of me."

He let go of the wheel, launched out of the crouch,

and dove off the tanker, off the trestle, screaming and waving his arms and trying to fly as he took the long fall to the treetops, crashed down through them, and vanished.

CHAPTER
79

I COULDN'T BELIEVE IT, and I twisted around, looking back and down into the canyon and the forest that had swallowed that young man whole. The only creatures I could see were crows circling lazily above the canopy, all of which disappeared from my view when the train rounded a curve.

The tunnel on the other side appeared so fast I had to throw myself down on top of the tanker and hold tight until we exited the other side into deep woods. I tried to call Bree but got no signal. There was no chance for me to get off the train for ten miles.

By the time it slowed and then stopped, night had fallen and the moon had risen. I'd come a long ways down in elevation. In the dim light I could see agricultural fields to either side of the tracks. I peered ahead, looking for a road crossing. Why were we stopped? I was about to climb off when—

"Let's do this, man," a male voice called from down the embankment.

I startled and then realized he was talking to me.

"What are we doing?" I asked.

"Shit, man, don't be fucking around," he said, nervous, and I made out the silhouette of him below me. "Gimme the order. I got the cash."

"Sorry, I'm new," I said, improvising. "How big's that order again?"

"It's on your sheet, man," he said, irritated. "Just open the hatch, get it, and we do business."

I looked around. The wheel the rider had held on to. It controlled a hatch.

I walked to it, knelt, and got hold of the wheel. Turning counterclockwise didn't work. Neither did turning it clockwise. Then I considered that the hatch might be under spring tension. I put my weight on it, felt something depress, and twisted. The wheel turned clockwise.

When I heard a noise like unbuckling, I lifted. Up came the hatch lid, and the air was filled with a pleasant vanilla scent. I cupped the mini-Maglite I always carry, turned it on. Suspended beneath the hatch was an aluminum basket of sorts, about three feet deep and two feet in diameter. The flashlight beam shone through large holes in the walls of the basket, revealing dozens of yellow-paper packages each about the size of a large bar of soap. Some were banded together. Others were single.

"C'mon, man," the guy said. "Train's gonna leave 'fore—"

The train wheels squealed. The tanker lurched. I almost fell. I almost let go of the hatch lid, the basket, and whatever was in it.

"Hey!" he yelled. "Hey, shit, man!"

"Couldn't be helped," I called down. "Something wrong with the mechanism. I'll put your order in for a ten-twenty delivery tomorrow night. You'll get a discount."

A pause. "How much?"

"Ten percent," I yelled as we pulled away.

"Deal, man, that'll work."

I waited until he was far behind me, then sat with

my legs spread against the walls of the hatch. I moved around the basket, inspecting it with the flashlight, and found a hinged door. I opened it, removed three of those yellow-paper packages. Each of them weighed about a pound.

My phone rang then. It was Bree.

"Where are you?" she asked anxiously. "I've been calling you."

"We went off the plateau and there were tunnels, and I have no idea where I am."

"You talk to the rider?"

I told her all that had happened.

"Jesus, he jumped?"

"I couldn't believe it, like it was better to die than talk to me and face this Grandfather's wrath."

"You think Marvin Bell is Grandfather?"

"It seems likely."

"So, drugs in the yellow packages?"

"I'm assuming so," I said. "Ingenious, if you think about it. Using the trains."

"It is. You going to stay on the train and see where it takes you?"

"No, I'm putting the basket back, sealing the hatch, and then getting off at the next stop. We'll let Bell or whoever is behind this think their man bailed with some of their product."

"Makes sense," she said.

"I'll call back soon, give you my location."

Well down the track, I could see streetlights. I'd replaced the basket and hatch cover by the time the train stopped for the second time. On my right, from the brush by the track, I heard a sharp whistle.

Instead of answering it, I crept down a ladder on the opposite side of the tanker and slipped away as the whistle became louder and more insistent.

CHAPTER
80

THE SWEET LITTLE GIRL with sleepy eyes carried a piece of sheepskin about the size and shape of a face towel. Lizzie rubbed it against her porcelain cheek and sucked her thumb as she ambled across the room to her grandfather.

He had terrible things twisting and knotting his mind, but seeing her so precious, so innocent, they all unraveled. He scooped Lizzie up, said, "Time for bed, young lady?"

She nodded, snuggled into his arms, made him feel perfect. She was hardly a weight at all, not a burden, never a burden. Lizzie's grandfather carried her from his office down the hall to her bedroom.

He got her safe and warm under her sheets and blanket. Her eyes fluttered toward sleep, but she said, "Tell me the story. What happens next to the fairy princess? To Guinevere?"

Her grandfather hesitated, and then said, "One day, a dragon came into Princess Guinevere's kingdom."

Lizzie became more alert. "Did the dragon hurt Guinevere?"

"He tried, but Guinevere's grandfather, the fairy king, sent out his best warriors to slay the dragon. Guinevere's older brother tried first but failed to kill the beast that threatened the fairy kingdom. A girl warrior went next."

Lizzie was listening raptly now. She said, "Did she have a bow and arrow?"

He nodded, said, "She shot at the dragon as he flew by and missed him by an inch."

A soft knock came behind him. Meeks stood there, dead serious.

"Someone downstairs needs to see you," Meeks said.

He understood, nodded. "I'll be a minute yet."

"No, Grandfather," Lizzie complained. "What about the dragon?"

"I'll tell you tomorrow night," he said.

"Oooh," she moaned. "I can't wait. Does she get another shot at the dragon? The girl warrior? What's her name?"

He thought, said, "Lace. And, yes, Lace gets another shot at the dragon, but I won't tell you what happens until tomorrow."

Lizzie yawned, said, "Lacey will get the dragon. She'll save Princess Guinevere. I just know it."

As her eyes started to flutter shut, he leaned over and kissed her cheek. He turned the light off but left the door to the hallway open a crack, just the way she liked it. He walked down the hall, thinking how many changes were under way and how many challenges they created.

Downstairs, he walked past oil paintings and sculptures into a library.

Finn Davis was standing there, looking unsure and uncomfortable.

"What is it?" Lizzie's grandfather asked.

"We lost a company man," Davis said. "His deliveries were never made."

"Product?"

"All but three pounds intact."

"Runner, then."

"You want him tracked down?" Davis asked. "Dealt with?"

"Of course, but we have more pressing problems."

"The Crosses?"

Lizzie's grandfather nodded, said, "They survived the lace maker. She'll try again. Meantime, I think you should take another stab at the big bad dragon."

CHAPTER
81

AT EIGHT THIRTY ON Monday morning, Pinkie drove me and Bree to the courthouse, where Stefan's trial was about to resume. Nana Mama was coming later with Aunt Hattie and Aunt Connie. Jannie was taking care of Ali.

I felt raw and irritated. Bree and my cousin looked wrung out. We'd been at this for the past thirty-six hours with very little sleep. And the secrets of Starksville were as murky and shape-shifting as they'd ever been.

We'd cut open one of the yellow-paper packages and found heavy-gauge plastic vacuum-sealed around what looked like loose blocks of shattered topaz-colored glass. The taste and smell had been unremarkable, so I'd called in a few favors from friends at the FBI crime lab at Quantico. They'd be receiving the samples and analyzing them later in the afternoon.

We still had no idea who owned the tanker. The trail camera had taken a good picture of that tanker's right side, revealing a code of fifteen letters and numbers stenciled in black. When we reviewed all the earlier pictures of riders, the majority were sitting one freight car back from similar tankers with similar codes. Pinkie had worked at the codes, trying to track them all Sunday afternoon and evening, but had gotten nowhere.

Bree and I had taken up position in those trees above

the tracks in Starksville around nine the night before and stayed long past eleven. No riders passed us.

In short, we'd had no luck linking Marvin Bell or Finn Davis or anyone else to the so-called Grandfather and the company. We had even begun to speculate that the riders and the drug ring had nothing to do with Starksville, that the operation was organized elsewhere and the shipments just passed through.

"I'm wondering if that rider disappearing triggered some kind of shutdown in the delivery system," Pinkie said, taking a left into the town square.

"Could be," I agreed.

"I think there's a way to see if the riders are from Starksville," Bree said.

"Okay…" I said.

"More trail cameras," she said. "We set them at crossings to the north and south. If the riders are from elsewhere, they'll already be aboard."

Pinkie nodded as he pulled into the courthouse parking lot. "And if they're not, we know this is their origination point."

"And no one around here manufactures vanilla, right?" I asked.

"Not that I know of," Pinkie said, parking.

When we reached the courthouse lobby, reporters, spectators, and witnesses streaming toward the trial venue were abuzz with news of Sheriff Nathan Bean's fatal heart attack at a local breakfast café not an hour before. Sheriff Bean had had a history of heart problems, but it seemed a shock nonetheless.

In the courtroom I heard a reporter ask Starksville police chief Randy Sherman who the likely replacement was.

"Sheriff's voted in," Chief Sherman replied. "But I'd bet Guy Pedelini would be a strong candidate."

I flashed on Bree's description of Finn Davis standing on Pedelini's back porch a few nights before, and for the first time, I felt as if there might really be a puppet master pulling the strings behind the scenes in Starksville. Grandfather? Even without concrete evidence against him, I could plainly see Marvin Bell in that role, hanging back in the shadows, looking legitimate, and using Finn Davis to do his bidding. We figured Bell and Davis were bribing Pedelini. How else did a detective afford a nice house on a lake like that?

A side door opened. A deputy led Stefan into the courtroom. I winced and heard my aunt Hattie cry out. My cousin's left eye was bruised closed, and his jaw was wired shut.

Naomi rushed forward, looking furious as she helped him to his seat.

"Serves him right," I heard a woman whisper, and I looked across the aisle at Ann Lawrence, who was talking to a sober Cece Turnbull. Rashawn's mother didn't reply, but Cece's parents, who were sitting two rows behind, bobbed their heads in agreement.

District attorney Delilah Strong, however, seemed genuinely concerned about my cousin's condition. So did her assistant Matthew Brady, who walked over to say something to Naomi.

She waved him off angrily. Patty Converse came in and sat in the row behind us. It was the first time we'd seen her in five days. She didn't look at any of us, just stared blankly as the clerk and the court reporter took their positions.

The bailiff called out, "All rise. This court is now in session, Judge Erasmus P. Varney presiding."

CHAPTER
82

JUDGE VARNEY WAS WEAKER and sallower than the last time I'd seen him, when he'd been flushed and contorting against the pain of kidney stones as EMTs rolled him from the courtroom. But the judge still had a commanding presence as he took the bench, picked up his gavel, and called his court to order.

"I apologize for my illness," he said. "Ukrainian blood on my mother's side. And I'd like to say how tragic it is that Sheriff Bean passed so suddenly this morning. He was a man of great integrity and honor."

Varney's eyes stayed locked ahead during his introductory remarks, as if he were not addressing the courtroom as a whole but someone in particular sitting in the gallery. Who, I couldn't tell. But maybe it was just my imagination.

Varney picked up a piece of paper on the bench, read it, said, "Ms. Cross, the court has been notified that your cross-examination witness Sharon Lawrence will be unavailable today, as she has taken ill and is in the hospital. Is that correct?"

Ann Lawrence, her mother, stood and said, "Yes, Your Honor. She's on IVs with a hundred and three fever."

"Then I expect you'll want to be at her side," Varney said.

"Yes, Judge, thank you," she said.

The mother of the girl who'd accused my cousin of rape and tried to frame Jannie glanced hurriedly at us and then left.

"She's hiding something," Bree whispered in my ear.

"Big-time," I said, wanting to get up and follow her, ask her more than a few pointed questions.

But then Judge Varney said, "Counselor, when Ms. Lawrence is recovered, you'll be given the opportunity to continue your cross. In the meantime, I'd like to move forward. Unless you have questions or concerns?"

"I have concerns, Your Honor," Naomi said. "With all due respect to the memory of Sheriff Bean, there has been a fundamental breakdown in my client's protection. Sheriff's deputies allowed inmates to beat and kick my client until—"

"Objection!" the prosecutor cried. "There's no evidence that any deputy 'allowed' the altercation."

"Judge, Mr. Tate appears before you with multiple contusions, swelling, a broken jaw, and a probable concussion," Naomi shot back. "At the very least, you can allow a competent neurologist to examine him before we continue with trial."

Strong said, "Mr. Tate was treated by jail doctors, who tell me that he shows no sign of concussion."

"Mr. Tate?" Judge Varney said. "Do you understand what's going on around you? Where you are? What you're doing here?"

Stefan nodded, spoke thickly through the wires on his teeth. "I do, Judge."

Naomi looked exasperated.

The judge said, "Very well, then, the trial will continue, and I am ordering the sheriff's office to double the guards with Mr. Tate at all times. Does that satisfy, Counselor?"

Naomi hesitated, then gave up and said, "It does, Judge."

As far as the defense was concerned, that was the high point of the day. The district attorney called forensics experts who hammered home the damning evidence as it was introduced: Stefan's semen on Rashawn's body, Stefan's semen in Sharon Lawrence's panties, and Rashawn's blood and body tissue on the foldable pruning saw found in my cousin's basement.

Patty Converse turned ashen during this last testimony, especially when a fingerprint expert testified that the only clear prints on the saw were Stefan's.

Naomi tried to damage the evidence of Stefan's DNA in the teenage girl's underwear, asking if, in the days between the time Lawrence claimed my cousin had raped her and Rashawn's death, someone could have planted the semen. The people's expert said it was possible but unlikely, given that Lawrence had thought to put the panties in a zip-lock bag.

"Unless Ms. Lawrence put the semen there herself," Naomi said.

The expert said, "Correct, but we have no evidence of that."

During the lunch recess, the service manager at the dealership where we'd left our Explorer called to tell me it looked like a rock had knocked an already loose hydraulic brake line free of its connection. The fluid ran out. We'd lost the brakes.

"You been driving many dirt roads?" he asked.

"A few, but I don't remember something like a big rock hitting the undercarriage," I said. "You're not seeing signs of sabotage?"

"Like someone wanted your brakes to fail?" he said.

"Like that."

"There's easier ways to make brakes fail than banging a rock on the hydraulic line."

"Unless you want it to look like an accident," I said.

"I guess."

I asked the manager to take pictures of the damage, and we agreed on a price to fix the car and a time for me to pick it up the following morning.

After lunch, the trial got even worse for Stefan and Naomi. Detective Carmichael took the stand and walked the jury through the evidence that had been logged in the old limestone quarry, including Stefan's bloody school ID card.

Naomi tried to get Carmichael to admit the ID could have been planted, but the detective wouldn't bite, said, "Your client was so hopped up on booze and drugs and so deep into his sadistic ways that he wasn't thinking straight."

Detective Frost testified about photographs taken at the scene. I'd seen them all before, but blown up like that, the brutality of what had been done to Rashawn's body was magnified. There were audible gasps in the room, several from the jurors.

"Monster!" Cece Turnbull screamed as she leaped to her feet and stabbed her finger at Stefan. "You butchered him! You butchered him like there was nothing human and good there at all!"

For several beats, Judge Varney hammered his gavel and called for order, and then he instructed the bailiffs to escort Rashawn's mother from the court yet again.

Cece was having none of it and screeched and spit at Stefan before the bailiffs could get hold of her and muscle her out. Cece's mother wept while her father held his wife and stared in loathing at my cousin.

After the session, Naomi emerged from the courthouse and tried to put a positive spin on the day for the reporters gathered out front.

She left them finally and came over to Bree, Pinkie, and me in the parking lot. My aunts and Nana Mama had gone home at lunch.

Naomi said, "I know the judge instructed the jury to ignore Cece's rant, but they'll remember it."

"They couldn't help but remember it," Bree said. "She left me shaking."

Naomi looked away, wiped at her watering eyes. "Me too. I know it's unprofessional of me, but I'm beginning to wonder whether Stefan did those things to Rashawn."

"I am too," said Patty Converse, who walked up to us. "I'm asking myself how I could have missed so much."

"I'm considering whether or not to ask for a plea bargain," Naomi said. "I know Matt Brady. He'll be fair."

"Don't throw in the towel just yet," I said.

"We've got nothing to refute Stefan's being at the crime scene," Naomi said. "They've got his DNA all over the place."

Before I could respond to that, my phone rang, and I turned away. It was Coach Greene calling.

"You don't know how much I hate to say this, Dr. Cross, but I just received a call from Detective Pedelini with the sheriff's office. The blood and urine tests on your daughter both came back positive for cocaine and methamphetamine. I'm afraid Jannie can't continue training with us, and Duke will be withdrawing its offer of a scholarship."

CHAPTER
83

"THIS IS BULLSHIT, COACH," I said, struggling to control my fury. "Those samples had to have been tampered with. Probably by Detective Pedelini."

"Well," she said skeptically, "I don't know how you're—"

"Going to prove it? We have our own samples from that day in a brown paper bag in my refrigerator. I asked for them as a precaution. I'll be sending those samples to an impartial lab. Will Duke take the FBI's word?"

The line fell silent. Then Coach Greene said, "If the FBI says Jannie's clean, then she's clean."

"Thank you, Coach," I said curtly. "I'll be in touch."

I punched the disconnect button, wanting to hurl my cell phone through the windshield of my rental car. But I summoned every reserve of control I had left and told Bree and the others about the lab report.

"There is no way Jannie could have run like she did the other day if she was on coke and speed," Bree said.

"Yeah," Pinkie said. "Can't they see that?"

"Evidently not, until we've got evidence that says otherwise," I said and told them about Greene's agreement to let the FBI's lab be the final word.

"That works," Pinkie said.

It did, and I started to calm down. Then something

about the whole issue of drugs in the bloodstream and in the urine made me ask, "Naomi, has anyone run drug tests on the semen off Rashawn's body and the Lawrence girl's underwear?"

She thought about that, said, "Not that I know of."

"Do you have access to those samples?"

"We received small subsamples that we are free to use to conduct our own tests," she said. "They're at the office."

"Get them and bring them to our house," I said, then I turned to Bree. "Get Jannie's samples from our fridge and what Naomi brings you and pack it all up. Pinkie will take you to the Winston-Salem airport."

"Okay..."

"Buy a round-trip ticket to National Airport," I said. "I'll call my friends at Quantico. Someone will meet you when your plane lands. You'll go home, check on the house, fly back here in the morning."

"You think this drug test might help Stefan?" Pinkie said.

"Depends on the results," I said.

"And what are you going to do while I'm gone?" Bree asked.

"Pay Detective Pedelini a visit, and maybe Marvin Bell too."

CHAPTER
84

BY THE TIME I reached Pedelini's office, the detective had left for the day.

I drove to the lake, following the directions Bree had given me, and found the house where she'd watched Finn Davis deliver a payoff to Pedelini. It was a nice place, gorgeous lot, big house, well cared for, with a swing on the grass and a dock. It faced east, and I thought that the dawns must be special there.

I drove on, parked behind Detective Pedelini's car, and went around and up onto the deck. Inside, the television was playing, a baseball announcer calling a game. Over that there was the louder sound of children giggling, and I smelled baking chicken. I knocked on the screen door.

"Daddy!" a girl called. "There's someone at the door."

I heard him say something that sounded like "I'm busy with the cat. Go see who it is."

A second later, a pretty girl about ten came to the door, said, "Hello?"

"Hello to you," I said. "What's your name?"

"Tessa Pedelini."

"Tessa Pedelini, can you tell your father that Alex Cross is here to see him?"

She nodded and scampered away to relay the message.

There was a pause, and then I heard Pedelini say, "Here, you help her, then. Slow, right?"

"Right," Tessa said.

The detective came to the screen door, hesitated, and then came out onto the porch. He extended his hand to shake mine. I didn't take it.

"I was as surprised as you must have been to see those reports on your daughter," he said, putting his hands in his pockets. "But they're conclusive."

Feeling cold and merciless, I said, "I had you wrong, you know?"

"How's that?" he asked, frowning.

"I've known my share of dirty cops in my time, but you didn't trip my alarms at all when I met you," I said. "You came across as one of the good guys. Bree thought so too."

"I *am* one of the good guys," Pedelini said, looking me in the eye. "The best around here."

"That's not saying much, is it?"

His eyes narrowed. "If I'm out there doing my job, you can jaw all you want at me like that. But here on my own back porch, I won't tolerate it. I'll ask you to leave now before one of us does something stupid."

Pedelini looked at me expectantly.

I stood my ground, said, "My wife saw you accept a payoff from Finn Davis the other night. Right here. And your daughter was there to witness it."

He was rocked by that, took a step back, said, "Wasn't like that."

"What wasn't like that?" I asked. "Payoff's a payoff."

Pedelini's entire body tensed as if he were going to launch himself at me; he rose up on his toes, his fists curling and uncurling, before he said in a thin voice, "You have no idea of the pressures I'm under."

I could see it everywhere about him, then. What

I'd taken for a pre-attack pause was actually his body's tensing under some heavy burden.

"Why don't you tell me?" I said.

"Why would I?"

"I'm a shrink as well as a cop," I said. "I'm offering you a twofer."

Pedelini almost smiled. Then he gazed around as if looking for an escape route.

"Maybe I wasn't wrong," I said, wanting him to open up. "Maybe my initial read of you was the correct one. Maybe you are a good man and I just lack understanding."

"Damn right you do," he said.

"Tell me."

He struggled, finally said, "Come with me."

The detective turned and entered the house. I followed him into a short hallway off a country-style kitchen where a small-screen television was showing the baseball game. A younger girl, eight, maybe nine, was sitting at a round table eating pretzel sticks, transfixed by the game.

"Braves up by two, Daddy," she said.

"There's a God after all, Lassie," Pedelini said.

"When's dinner?" Lassie asked.

He glanced at a timer on the stove, said, "Thirty-two minutes."

Pedelini left the kitchen. His daughter never glanced at me as I followed him into a family room with a large window that overlooked the lake.

"Beautiful place," I said.

"If you think dirty money bought it, you're wrong," Pedelini said. "My late wife inherited it from her father."

He turned into a doorway.

I stepped in after him and found myself in a hospital room.

CHAPTER
85

MEDICAL EQUIPMENT FILLED TWO stainless-steel racks of shelves. An elaborate wheelchair stood empty in the corner. Glowing monitors were mounted on wall brackets above and to the sides of a hospital bed with high railings.

"Cat?" Pedelini said to the girl sitting up in the bed, straining to open her mouth to get the spoonful of food Tessa was offering. "This is Dr. Cross. He wanted to meet you."

The detective's youngest took the spoonful, closed her mouth, and turned her eyes toward me. In a thick, garbled voice, she said, "Another one?"

Catrina Pedelini was her name, and she reminded me of a baby robin I'd seen once when I was walking with my mother to the linen factory. The newly hatched bird, sparse-feathered and bony and broken, had fallen from its nest. Cat Pedelini was all angles with a pigeon chest, a spine that arched to the left, and crippled hands and arms that curled back toward her torso so that she appeared to be holding something dear. Her face was at once disfigured and attractive.

"I'm not a medical doctor," I said. "I'm here to see your father, but I'm very glad to meet you."

"Dad needs a doctor?" she asked, looking to her father.

"He's here about work, sweetheart," Pedelini said, coming over to stroke the wispy silver-blond hair on her head. "You're doing a good job."

"I watch *Criminal Minds* after dinner?" she asked.

Tessa looked at me, said, "That's Cat's favorite show."

"You eat everything on your plate, you can watch one episode before bath time," Pedelini said.

She made a gurgling, pleased sound in her throat and then said, "But I use a bowl."

"Bowl, then," Pedelini said gently and kissed her on the head. "I'll be in soon."

The detective moved by me, back out into the hall, and I followed him to the kitchen, where his middle daughter said, "Braves up by one, Dad. When's dinner?"

"There is a God after all," Pedelini said as he passed. "And twenty-four minutes. Have a pretzel."

"I've eaten almost the whole bag."

"Another of life's tragedies."

He went down a short hall, out the screen door, and onto the deck.

"Tell me about Cat," I said.

Pedelini shrugged, said, "She had a damaged gene to begin with, or so they tell me. But she was further damaged in the labor that took my Ellen. The official diagnosis is cerebral palsy."

"She seems sharp," I said.

"Very. She's quite a girl. A fighter."

The sheriff's detective had tears in his eyes. He wiped at them.

"She why you take money from Finn Davis?" I asked.

"You have any idea what it's taken to get her this far?"

"I can't imagine," I said.

"Every cell, every fiber of my being. I promised my wife when she knew she was dying and had already seen Cat. I promised her I would move heaven and earth for our baby. And I have."

I had been right. Guy Pedelini was a man of conscience and inner goodness. I could almost feel it pulsing out of him at that moment.

"But care like that costs a lot of money," I said, pressing the issue.

"Whole lot," he agreed. He scuffed his shoes, looked at the deck.

"More than your insurance will pay."

"That too," he said, and sniffed.

"So, what, Marvin Bell's money makes up the difference?"

He paused as if disgusted with himself, said, "Almost."

"What's he pay you to do?" I asked.

The detective took a deep breath, went to the railing, and looked out over the lake, where the reflection of the three-quarter moon shimmered on the water.

"To look the other way?" I asked, following him. "When the trains come through Starksville with guys who use a three-finger salute riding on top of freight cars carrying loads of drugs bound for dealers up and down the line? Is that what you do to help Lassie, Tessa, and Cat?"

Pedelini had his back to me. His shoulders trembled slightly, and he started to pivot toward me. We were less than sixteen inches apart. The sheriff's detective had turned nearly ninety degrees to his left and was facing the narrow cove and the shore road beyond it when the rifle shot rang out. I caught the muzzle flash from across the cove a split second before I heard the blast.

Pedelini spun around, sagged on the railing, and then rag-dolled to the deck.

Blood trickled from a head wound.

CHAPTER
86

I DOVE ACROSS THE detective to shield him from a second shot, but it never came. All I heard was the screaming of Pedelini's girls.

"Call 911!" I yelled at Tessa, who'd come to the screen door.

I didn't wait to see if she complied, just turned to her father, whose eyes had rolled up in his head. He was breathing, though. And his pulse was strong.

I didn't want to move him, but I turned his head slightly to look at the wound. The bullet had dug a nasty groove through the scalp and along the surface of his skull, like a wood-carving tool had worked it. But I couldn't see anywhere the bullet had penetrated his cranium.

I heard a car start, wheels squealing. I stood, peered across the cove, and spotted the taillights of a car racing away on the shore road. The car swerved, and I saw an old couple dive out of the way.

The car lost control, hit something hard with a tremendous crash. The brake lights never came on.

I started to run. That was my shooter.

"Wait!" Tessa screamed after me.

"Your dad's going to be all right!" I yelled, jumping off the porch and sprinting to the rental car.

I threw it in reverse, spit gravel onto the road, and

jammed it in gear. I almost lost control going around the hairpin at the back of the cove and slowed at the curve near the spot from where the shooter must have fired. When my headlights came around, I could see an older couple standing, shaken, by the road. But there was no car beyond them.

I roared up to them and they looked frightened.

"I'm a police officer," I said. "Where did that car go?"

The elderly man's hand was trembling. "Up the road. A white Impala. Almost hit us."

A white Impala. I drove away slow, trying not to spin up rocks that might hit the couple, my attention darting off the road to a stripped and gouged stump with bits of steel embedded in it. I figured he'd hit it hard head-on, which meant the radiator might have been damaged, or the front end.

In any case, I couldn't see the car being able to maintain its pace down the winding mountain road from the lake back toward town. The moment I turned off the shore road onto the main route, I sped up again.

Halfway down the mountain, I spotted brake lights ahead of me, and then they were gone around a curve. I caught up on the next bend, my high beams finding the rear of the Impala. Judging from the silhouettes showing through the back window, there were only two inside.

The passenger twisted around as if to look back at me, raised a pistol. I mashed the pedal and rammed the rear bumper before he could shoot. The impact flung the Impala at a steep angle up the road and away from me. My headlights caught the driver clawing at the wheel.

Finn Davis managed to regain control of the car and picked up speed through the next turn. When I came around the curve, a guy was hanging out the passenger window and aiming a shotgun at me left-handed.

CHAPTER
87

HE FIRED JUST AS I hit the brakes.

Double-aught buckshot shattered the right side of the windshield. I hit the gas again when I saw the shooter awkwardly trying to work the pump action. He wasn't a lefty.

I swung into the other lane where he couldn't get an easy shot at me, then caught up and cut the wheel to ram the Impala a second time. My bumper hit the car at a quartering angle. The rear end of the Impala swung hard right. The guy with the shotgun was hurled from the car; he sailed through the air and disappeared into the night.

Finn Davis was in my headlights again, clawing at the wheel.

I didn't give him a second chance, just sped up and rammed the Impala a third time, hitting it almost broadside. My car threatened to spin, and I had to slam the brakes. But Finn's car reached a tipping point on the road shoulder.

It flipped off the embankment.

I skidded to a halt, heard sirens coming, dug out my pistol and flashlight, and ran back up the road. The Impala had turned over at least two times and was wedged at an angle against the trunk of an old pine. One of the headlights was still on, cutting deeper into the forest.

I shone my flashlight down into the gully, tried to find the driver-side door and Davis. He wasn't there.

I flicked the light up to the car's roofline and found him. He was bleeding, leaning out the passenger-side window, and leveling a scoped hunting rifle at me.

We fired at virtually the same time, me from the hip at fifty feet and Davis at that same distance from a dead rest. His scope had to have been off because, as it had with Pedelini, the bullet went left of me by no more than an inch or two.

I clicked off the light, threw myself flat on the shoulder, and listened for the sound of a rifle's action over the hissing of the Impala's radiator and the sirens coming up the mountain. I counted to twenty, stayed belly down, extended my hand to the edge of the gully, and rapidly clicked the light on and off.

Nothing.

I flicked it on again, slid to the side, and looked down into the gully. Finn Davis was rocked back against the tree trunk, blank eyes open and already dulling. A gout of blood showed in the wound at the center of his throat.

CHAPTER
88

"ARE YOU ARRESTING ME?" I asked eight hours later.

"Just trying to get the story straight in our heads," said Detective Frost, rubbing his belly in an interrogation room.

Wearily, I said, "I went to see Detective Pedelini about some lab tests, and someone shot at him while we were talking on his deck. I saw the bullet had hit him hard enough to knock him out, but nothing fatal. So I left, gave chase. Some folks out on the lake, an elderly couple, were almost run down by Davis making his escape. I tried to follow. His accomplice shot at my car. I took defensive action. Davis's car went off the side of the road. He tried to kill me. I killed him in self-defense."

"Why would Finn Davis try to kill Pedelini?" asked Carmichael.

Tired as I was, I decided I couldn't trust the two men interviewing me. I withheld any and all theories spinning in my brain.

"I can't give you a clear motive," I said. "His adoptive father might be able to."

"We put calls in to Marvin's house and cell," Carmichael said. "He isn't answering."

"Go to his place on Pleasant Lake."

"A trooper did about an hour ago. No answer at the

door, so he went inside. There were signs of a struggle. Know anything about that?"

"Nothing," I said. "For all you know, Bell ordered Finn to kill Pedelini and is now running, making his house a mess so you'd think otherwise. But whatever. The fact remains that Finn shot at Pedelini and me. Test his rifle. I guarantee it will match the one that killed Sydney Fox."

"You think Finn killed Sydney?" Frost said.

"I do," I said.

"Why?"

"Spiteful ex-husband. Maybe more."

They fell silent. Carmichael drank from a Diet Coke can. Frost sipped his coffee, said skeptically, "You make yourself out to be an innocent bystander."

"With the attempt on Detective Pedelini's life, most definitely. How is he, by the way?"

"In a medically induced coma," Carmichael said. "Mild brain swelling."

"Someone taking care of his daughters?"

"They're covered," Frost said.

I sat back in my chair confidently, said, "Then I'm not saying anything until Pedelini wakes up. You talk to him. He'll back me up."

The door opened, and Naomi entered, saying, "Not another word, Alex."

"That's already the plan," I said.

"You charging him?" my niece snapped.

"Not at this time," Frost admitted.

"Then I'd appreciate his release," she said. "Dr. Cross is an integral part of my defense. He's not leaving town. You'll find him in Judge Varney's court if you need him."

Ten minutes later we slipped out the back door of the police station to avoid the television news crews and walked down the alley toward the courthouse in the dawn light. Part of me wanted to go home and get some sleep. Instead, I called Nana Mama, told her I was okay and would see her at the trial. I texted Bree to call me as we went to a café for breakfast with Pinkie.

I drank three cups of coffee, ate three eggs sunny-side up, bacon, and hash browns, and related everything that had happened to me during the night.

"Why would Finn Davis want to kill Guy Pedelini?" Naomi asked.

"Maybe Davis saw Pedelini as I do: an essentially good guy corrupted by circumstances," I said. "Under duress, these kinds of people don't hold secrets long before they break, confess, and implicate others."

"So the sheriff, and then Pedelini?" Pinkie said. "You think someone's trying to clean house?"

"If you add in the busted brake line of our car, it sure looks like it."

"Someone's under pressure," Naomi said.

"Someone?" Pinkie said. "Try Marvin Bell."

"Bell's vanished," I said.

"Which means we were getting close, right?" Pinkie said.

"Close to something. But it's still like a jigsaw that won't piece—"

My phone rang. A number I almost recognized but couldn't place.

"Cross," I said.

"Drummond."

I smiled. "How are you, Sergeant?"

"Peachy," he said. "Mize is copping to it all and pleading insanity."

"He might be right."

"Not my call," Drummond said. "Your case? You get that guy Bell?"

"Close," I said. "But he's vanished."

"Runner."

"Looks like it."

"Your nephew's trial?"

"My cousin's trial. And, to be honest, unless we can come up with some counterevidence fast, he's looking at death row."

Drummond didn't reply for several beats, and then said, "You never know when something's going to turn things around."

"True," I said. I heard a clicking, looked at the caller ID, saw it was Bree.

I told the sergeant I had to take another call but would keep him posted, and then I switched lines.

"Hey," I said. "Where are you?"

"At National Airport, about to board a flight back to Winston-Salem," Bree said. "I just got some preliminary results e-mailed to me from the FBI lab."

"And?"

CHAPTER
89

JUDGE VARNEY GAVELED THE court to order at nine o'clock that Tuesday morning.

Before either of the attorneys could speak, the judge pointed his gavel toward the spectators, said, "Cece Turnbull? You in my court?"

Cece's eyes were beet red and rheumy when she stood up and nodded.

"You gonna cause any more trouble?" he demanded.

"No, sir, Judge Varney," she said in a tremulous voice. "I...I apologize. It's just that—"

"Just nothing," the judge said. "Long as you're quiet, you can remain. But the first peep out of you and you're gone for the duration. You understand?"

Cece nodded, sat down. Ann Lawrence leaned forward and patted her on the shoulder comfortingly. Sharon Lawrence sat next to her mother, pale, weak, and looking at her cell phone. Cece's mother and father were behind the Lawrences. Mrs. Caine was staring into her lap while her husband sat ramrod straight in his business suit, arms crossed, focused completely on Judge Varney.

In those same moments, Police Chief Randy Sherman was sending hard glances at me and Nana Mama, who sat beside me, and at Pinkie, Aunt Connie, and Aunt Hattie, who were in the row behind us.

The bailiff led my cousin into the court. Stefan Tate's facial swelling had gone down, but his skin was bruised a livid purple.

Patty Converse came in and took a seat next to Pinkie. I smiled. She nodded but wouldn't meet my gaze.

"Where were we at adjournment?" Judge Varney asked his clerk.

"Detective Frost," the clerk said. "Ms. Strong is still on direct."

The older detective, who looked as tired as I was, took the stand.

Varney said, "I remind you you're under oath."

"Yes, Judge," Frost said.

The district attorney let her assistant Matthew Brady take the lead in questioning the detective. Brady focused on other items gathered at the scene of Rashawn Turnbull's rape and murder. Those pieces of evidence included a broken bottle of Stolichnaya vodka with Stefan Tate's prints on it not ten feet from where the body was found.

During our first talk in the jail, my cousin said the bottle was probably his but that it must have been stolen from his apartment. The excuse was weak.

The weight of evidence against Stefan seemed overwhelming again. You could see it in the faces of many in the jury box. Stefan's semen was at the scene of the crime. His prints were there. He killed that boy, deserved to fry.

"Detective," Matthew Brady said. "You went to talk to the defendant the day Rashawn's body was found."

"That's correct," Frost said. "We found Mr. Tate at his house that morning."

"How would you describe his condition?" Brady asked.

"Hung over. You could smell stale liquor on his breath."

"What did you tell him?"

"That Rashawn's body had been found," Frost said. "And that we found his ID there covered with blood."

"What was his reaction?"

"Went down on his knees and started sobbing."

Frost said they took my cousin in for questioning and sealed the apartment until it could be searched by a forensics team. Before they interrogated Stefan they took his blood alcohol level, which registered as .065. Not legally drunk in North Carolina, but a solid indicator that he'd been drinking hard the night before.

Brady took the detective through the interrogation, in which Stefan steadfastly maintained his innocence. Yes, he'd been drinking the night before. He and his fiancée had had a fight. He'd stormed out, gone for a long walk, and picked up a bottle. He ended up passing out by the railroad tracks.

I glanced back at Patty Converse. She was staring at the floor.

"Did Mr. Tate say why he'd gone down by the tracks?" Brady asked.

"He said for no reason at all, and that made him hysterical," Frost said.

"Did you believe him?"

"The hysteria? The anguish at what he'd done? Yes. That he went down by the tracks and passed out? No, I did not and do not. There was no evidence down there that put him anywhere near where he said he woke up."

Frost went on to describe leaving Stefan in a cell under suicide watch while he and Carmichael searched the duplex where my cousin lived along with Sydney Fox and Patty Converse. The older detective found the pruning saw with Rashawn's blood and flesh in the teeth on a shelf in the common basement along with some turkey-hunting equipment and a vial of methamphetamine.

"Was the saw or the meth vial hidden?" Brady asked.

"Yes. In a pack."

"Odd that he would keep the weapon."

"Mr. Tate's blood alcohol level had to have been sky-high, and the brutality with which Rashawn was attacked suggests a berserk state," Frost said. "Coming out of it, he probably wasn't thinking too straight, dumped the saw where he found it."

"Objection," Naomi said. "The witness is speculating."

"Sustained."

Brady said, "Were Mr. Tate's fingerprints on that saw?"

"Five fingerprints."

"Anyone else's?"

"No."

Brady's questioning went on for another hour. Around ten thirty, the assistant district attorney said, "No further questions."

Judge Varney said, "Ms. Cross, you can choose to proceed with cross-examination of Detective Frost now or finish with Sharon Lawrence."

Sharon Lawrence's mother stabbed at her daughter's thigh with her index finger. Sharon Lawrence jerked, looked up from her cell phone in disgust.

Naomi looked back at me. I nodded.

She said, "The defense will start with Detective Frost."

CHAPTER
90

AS NAOMI CAME OUT from behind the defense table, she glanced at me again, and I shot her an encouraging smile.

"She got something?" Nana Mama whispered to me.

"Maybe," I said, and gave her hand a squeeze.

"Detective Frost," Naomi began. "At what time did you arrive at my client's apartment the morning after the victim's body was discovered?"

"Nine? Nine fifteen?"

"How was Mr. Tate dressed?"

"Gray sweatpants, blue hoodie."

"His hair was wet?"

"Correct," Frost said. "Mr. Tate stated that he'd just gotten out of the shower when we knocked."

"Was the shower drain searched?" Naomi asked.

"It was."

"Any of Rashawn Turnbull's blood found in that drain?"

"No."

"Any blood evidence found in that drain?"

"Mr. Tate's."

"Did Mr. Tate tell you that he has a history of nosebleeds? That they often occur when he's exposed to hot water?"

Frost shifted, said, "He said that."

Naomi returned to the defense table, picked up a document, said, "The defense would like to introduce our exhibit A: medical records dating back to Mr. Tate's childhood that reflect this ongoing problem with nose-bleeds."

Judge Varney took the documents and nodded.

If the fact that my cousin suffered nosebleeds in any way contradicted the people's case, neither Delilah Strong, Matt Brady, nor Detective Frost showed it.

"So you found Mr. Tate's blood in the drain?" Naomi said.

"Correct."

"But not Rashawn Turnbull's?"

"Asked and answered, Counselor," Judge Varney said.

"Don't you find that odd?" my niece said to Frost. "I mean, the prosecution has spun this theory about my client entering a drunken, drug-fueled, berserk state to rape and kill Rashawn Turnbull, slashing at the boy's neck with a pruning saw. And we've seen photos of the blood-spatter patterns at the crime scene. So why no blood in the drain? If your theory is to be believed, the boy's blood should have been all over my client's clothes and body."

"We think Mr. Tate got rid of his clothes and washed off somewhere else."

"But there's no evidence to back that up."

Frost said nothing.

"Do you have my client's clothes with blood on them?"

"No."

"Did you find the victim's blood anywhere in that building other than on the pruning saw in the base-ment?"

Frost shifted uncomfortably, said, "No."

"Did you find illegal drugs anywhere else in the house besides the vial of methamphetamine in the basement?"

"No."

"In Mr. Tate's office at the school?"

"No."

"In his car?"

"No."

"And yet you'd have us believe that Mr. Tate is not only a habitual user of meth but a dealer whose wares may have resulted in two overdoses at the high school."

"Mr. Tate has a history of drug and alcohol abuse," Frost said. "He got thrown out of—"

"Objection, Judge," Naomi said.

"Sustained," Varney said. "The jury will ignore that."

But it had already been said. You couldn't take something like that back and expect the jurors to actually eliminate the information from their brains. Stefan had past issues. That was all they would care about. Naomi looked frustrated but pushed on.

"Was there any sign of methamphetamine in my client's blood the morning of his arrest?"

"Trace levels," Detective Frost said.

"Trace levels? I thought he was in an alcohol-and-drug-fueled rage that night."

"Large amounts of alcohol in the bloodstream can mask the presence of meth in certain tests."

"Really?" Naomi said. "I hadn't heard that. But again, you're no expert."

"Objection," the district attorney said.

"Sustained," Varney said before rapping his gavel. "We'll take a lunch break and resume at one o'clock."

CHAPTER
91

PINKIE SLID INTO THE same booth we'd used before at the Bench, the restaurant by the courthouse. I sat opposite him while Nana Mama and my aunts took a table next to us. I'd tried to invite Patty Converse, but she'd left the courtroom before Varney ended the morning session.

"I thought things went better for Stefan today," Pinkie said.

"I did too," I said. "For the first time since the trial began, I saw some of the jurors really thinking about the evidence against him."

My cell phone buzzed. An e-mail alert. The waitress came over to take our orders. I asked for the patty melt with a salad instead of fries and another cup of coffee. I'd been up for so many hours at that point that I was feeling woozy again.

"If Stefan did it, he would have been covered in Rashawn's blood," Pinkie said.

"Unless Frost is right and he washed off somewhere else and buried his clothes," I said.

"But why not the saw?"

"I know. It's not logical. But sometimes murder and its aftermath are not logical events. It twists people into something unrecognizable."

"You're kind of raining on Naomi's parade."

"Not at all," I replied, happy to see the waitress bringing my coffee. "I think she's going to mount a vigorous defense on Stefan's behalf."

"I can hear a *but* coming."

"But I've worked on enough of these cases to know that when the evidence to convict a child killer is formidable, the defense had better be able to do more than just poke holes in the prosecution's narrative."

"Like what?" Pinkie asked.

"Like find the real killer," I said. "We do that, Stefan walks. If not, even with some of the lab results we got back, he risks conviction."

"I swear on my dead daddy's grave that Finn and Marvin were in on it," Pinkie said.

I glanced over at the booth where I'd spoken with Bell the week before, said, "Well, unless the police find some evidence that links Bell and Davis to the killing, you're swearing in vain."

"Finn tried to kill Pedelini, who all but admitted to you before he was shot that he was looking the other way for payoffs."

"Maybe."

"What do you mean, maybe?"

"I'd have to see the test results on Davis's rifle, but there is the possibility that Davis was shooting at me and hit Pedelini. We were fairly close and it was a long shot across that cove."

The waitress returned with our orders, and we dug in. My head ached, and I had to force the food down.

After we'd finished, I was surprised that Nana Mama wanted to stay for the afternoon session. She'd been taking naps in the afternoon the past few months.

"I feel like something big is going to happen in that courtroom this afternoon," she said, holding my elbow as we walked back to the courthouse. "And I don't want to miss it."

"You having premonitions now?" I asked, amused.

"I'm no swami or seer," she snapped. "I just get feelings sometimes, and this is one of them."

"Okay. This something big you're feeling—is it good or bad for Stefan?"

My grandmother peered up at me with a confused expression on her face, said, "I can't tell you one way or the other."

We were outside the courthouse when my cell phone buzzed again, this time alerting me to a text. I sent Nana Mama in to claim our seats with Pinkie and my aunts, pulled out the cell to see a text from Bree:

Landed; in taxi on way to dealership to pick up car. Plan one stop, and then see you in court in two hours. How are things going?

I texted her back: Better. Naomi cross-examining Frost and scoring points. Drive safe and see you soon. Love you.

A moment later: Love you too.

I was about to stick my cell phone in my pocket when I remembered the e-mail that had come in during lunch. It was from one of my friends at Quantico, a report on the chemical compound that I'd taken from that basket in the tanker.

CHAPTER
92

I RUSHED INTO Judge Varney's rapidly filling courtroom, went to the railing, and waved Naomi over. I said, "Do you have the state's assay report on the meth found in the vial in Stefan's basement?"

She thought about that, nodded, and went to dig through several large, legal-size boxes to retrieve it.

"What's going on?" Naomi asked.

"I don't know yet," I said. "Just a hunch at this point."

"You'll let me know if it gets beyond a hunch?"

"You'll be the first to know."

I took my seat next to Nana Mama, kissed her on the cheek, and started reading through the state's report, a chemical assay that identified the substance found in the vial in Stefan's basement as a very pure designer methamphetamine. They described the chemical structure, but the science went over my head. There was, however, a graphic representation of that structure on the second page.

Then I called up the report I'd just received from my FBI friends and saw the graphs matched. I reread the note attached to the Bureau's study, which stated the substance was "a designer drug created by a gifted chemist."

All sorts of suppositions and assumptions I'd been

playing with now became concrete fact. Someone called Grandfather, probably Marvin Bell, was running a designer-meth distribution operation via the freight-rail system.

Some of that signature meth was found in Stefan's basement. Either my cousin had access to the drug and was holding out on us, or someone involved in the designer-meth distribution system had planted it there.

I got up and gave Naomi a summary of what I'd found before the bailiff called, "All rise."

Judge Varney came in, said, "Carry on, Ms. Cross."

My niece approached the witness box, said, "Just to recap where we were, Detective Frost. The prosecution believes that on the night in question, Mr. Tate went into an alcohol-and-drug-fueled rage and raped and murdered Rashawn Turnbull."

"No doubt in my mind," Frost said.

Naomi let that slide, said, "What's Mr. Tate's motive? Why take his rage out on a boy? A boy who supposedly idolized him?"

"You don't know how many nights I've lain awake thinking about that," Frost said, directing his reply to the jury. "At some level, you can't get your head around the depravity of what was done to Rashawn. The pure hatred behind it.

"But Tate had gone off the wagon in a big way. He was feeding drugs to underage girls, raping them. Sydney Fox said she saw Rashawn going into Tate's place the same day Sharon Lawrence says he drugged and attacked her. If so, I think Rashawn saw the rape. I think Rashawn said he was going to tell the police, and Tate just snapped."

In the silence that followed, four or five jury members stared at Stefan as if he were already heading for death row. The others were watching my niece as if wondering why she hadn't objected to Frost's speculation.

Naomi went to the jury box, got the jury's attention, said, "Detective, how do you explain the fact that Sydney Fox saw Rashawn go into that apartment but Sharon Lawrence testified that she never saw the victim the day she was allegedly attacked?"

I glanced over and saw Sharon Lawrence unglue herself from her cell phone.

Frost said, "She'd been drugged with a date-rape drug."

"Any residue of a date-rape drug in Sharon Lawrence's blood at the time of her reporting the alleged rape?"

Frost said, "She reported the attack a week after it happened."

Naomi went to the defense table, retrieved a file. "The defense would like to introduce sworn testimony by several expert witnesses that all say date-rape drugs can linger in the bloodstream for up to fourteen days."

Varney squinted, took the documents, scanned them, and then handed them to the clerk. He ran his hand back over his pompadour, looking kind of anxious. Another kidney stone coming on?

Naomi said, "So that part of Sharon Lawrence's story is not correct, is it, Detective Frost? She wasn't drugged, was she?"

"You said the drug *can* linger for up to fourteen days," Frost said. "*Up to* means in some people, the drug is gone in a lot less than two weeks."

Naomi paused, seemed to shift gears.

"The semen in her underwear. It was a direct match to my client?"

"DNA doesn't lie," Frost said.

"There's no disputing the DNA test," Naomi agreed.

"When Ms. Lawrence came forward with her rape story, she had my client's DNA in her panties."

"Correct," Frost said.

Naomi said, "Did you also find Ms. Lawrence's DNA in the panties?"

"Yes," Frost said.

Sharon Lawrence was looking at the ceiling above Judge Varney. Her mother held her hand tight.

"So you've got Mr. Tate's semen and Ms. Lawrence's body fluids, and you test them for DNA. What else did you test those substances for?"

The police detective frowned. "I'm not following you."

"Did you have your lab do other tests on the semen and Ms. Lawrence's body fluids? Say, drug tests?"

Frost blinked, said nothing.

"Detective?"

"Uh, no, I don't think so, no."

"We've checked the record and you haven't," Naomi said. "So we had the FBI perform other tests on those samples."

CHAPTER
93

NAOMI HELD UP A document, said, "The defense would like to introduce exhibit—"

"Objection!" Strong said, jumping to her feet. "The prosecution was not made aware of any such tests."

"Because we ordered them last night and they came in this morning."

"That's impossible. The backlog of work at the FBI's lab is—"

"Quantico did a rush job on the tests as a favor to my uncle."

The district attorney looked to Judge Varney.

The judge rotated his head around to ease a cramp in his neck, glanced at me and the others in the cheap seats, said, "The court will admit the FBI's tests."

Naomi beamed. She handed copies to the clerk, the prosecution, and Detective Frost. Interested now, the jurors shifted in their seats, wondering just what the tests said. I tried not to smile, but I was proud of my niece. She had every person in the courtroom in the palm of her hand.

Naomi said, "You'll see the necessary stamps, signatures, and so forth on pages one and two. Turn to page three. You'll see that we submitted Ms. Lawrence's body fluids at the time of the alleged rape for evidence of illicit drugs commonly used during date rapes, like Rohypnol."

She walked over to the witness, said, "Can you read us the results, Detective?"

Frost said, "No drugs or alcohol present."

"No drugs or alcohol present in Ms. Lawrence's sample," Naomi said.

Sharon Lawrence looked ready to be sick. She said something to her mother, who shook her head and held her hand tight.

Strong and Brady, meanwhile, were poring over the pages. So were the judge and the detective on the witness stand. The jurors were transfixed. Police Chief Sherman was leaning over the railing trying unsuccessfully to get the prosecutors' attention.

Naomi said, "Detective Frost, on page four, what are the results of the test on my client's semen at the time of the alleged rape?"

Frost's voice cracked before he cleared his throat and said, "Negative for drugs and alcohol."

"At the time of the alleged rape?"

"Correct."

"No drugs or alcohol at all," she said to the jury. "But that goes completely against the story to which Ms. Lawrence testified under oath. She said they were drinking, doing drugs, carrying on, and having a good old time before Mr. Tate slipped her a date-rape drug and had his way with her. Is that a fair summary of her story, Detective?"

"It is," Frost said.

"Do you now believe my client raped Ms. Lawrence as she described?"

"Objection!" Strong said.

Sharon Lawrence was weeping silently. Her mother looked ready to crawl out of her skin.

Naomi said, "Judge, I'm asking a detective with two and a half decades of experience to evaluate the facts as he knows them now and form an opinion."

Varney hesitated, said, "Overruled, Ms. Strong. Rephrase the question, Ms. Cross."

"Does Ms. Lawrence's story jibe with these FBI tests?"

"No, but she could have just embellished that part of the story," Frost said.

"Or she embellished the entire story, in which case she can be prosecuted for perjury, along with her mother, and for planting false evidence," Naomi said. "They'll both do time."

"No!" Ann Lawrence cried, getting to her feet. "She…we…"

Varney rapped his gavel, said, "Sit down, Mrs. Lawrence."

She sat back down, looking wobbly, next to her daughter, who stared at the floor.

Naomi said, "The defense calls Sharon Lawrence to the stand."

"Are you done with Detective Frost?" Judge Varney asked.

"For the moment, Judge," Naomi said. "But I'd prefer he remain available."

Varney instructed Frost to stay and, along with the rest of the crowded courtroom, watched him pass a pale, nervous Sharon Lawrence heading toward the witness stand.

Ann Lawrence's face had gone flushed, and she sat small in her seat. Cece's mother and father were staring at the woman as if she were some dark mystery.

"Ms. Lawrence," Naomi said. "Did you hear Detective Frost's testimony just now?"

"Yes."

"And the results of the drug tests?"

Sharon Lawrence nodded feebly.

"Did Coach Stefan Tate drug and rape you?"

The girl said nothing for several long moments. Her lips trembled, and she looked out at her mother and then at Stefan Tate.

"No," she whispered as tears poured down her face. "It was all a lie."

PART FIVE

JUSTICE

CHAPTER
94

THE COURTROOM ERUPTED. My cousin put his face in his hands, his shoulders shaking. Judge Varney looked bewildered as he gaveled the court silent. Stefan picked up his head and looked at his mother and then Patty Converse. For the first time in days, I saw hope in Patty's face.

"Ms. Lawrence," the judge said. "You understand you have admitted to committing perjury under oath?"

She nodded, sobbed. "Am I going to jail?"

Varney said nothing. A second went by, and then another.

Naomi said, "Not if you tell the court the truth."

The judge looked annoyed at Naomi, then glanced out into the audience before saying, "Yes, the truth will help."

Naomi got a Kleenex and handed it to Sharon Lawrence, waited for her to regain her composure.

"Why did you lie?" Naomi asked.

Shoulders hunched forward, she replied, "It was like you said. We, my mom and me, we don't have much. Finn said he'd make sure we had enough if I accused Coach Tate of raping me."

"The late Finn Davis?" Naomi asked.

"Yes."

"Adopted son of your uncle Marvin Bell?"

"Yes."

"Knew it," Pinkie whispered behind me.

"How much did Finn Davis offer you and your mother to cry rape?"

Sharon Lawrence glanced at her mother. Ann Lawrence stared at her hands on her lap as if they were deep, dark holes.

"Six thousand dollars a month for the rest of my mom's life," Sharon Lawrence choked. "Don't you see? It saved her. That's why I did it."

Ann Lawrence burst into tears and hid her face in her hands.

"Why did Finn Davis want you to accuse Coach Tate of rape?"

Sharon Lawrence said, "I don't know. He said he wanted to make sure Coach Tate was punished for what he'd done."

"Did Finn Davis provide the semen that went in your panties?"

"Yes," she said, looking disgusted. "I don't know how he got it."

"One last question," Naomi said. "Did Finn Davis ask you to plant drugs in the athletic bag of Jannie Cross?"

"Objection; relevance," Strong said.

Varney again looked caught between a rock and a hard place and finally said, "Sustained."

"He did ask," Sharon said anyway. "Finn. He promised me two thousand a month if I put the drugs in her bag. Are we going to jail? Me and Mom?"

This last question was aimed at Judge Varney, who said, "That's a matter for another time and place, young lady. You're dismissed for the time being."

If it was possible, Sharon Lawrence looked even smaller and weaker when she got up and left the witness stand. She didn't look at Stefan or any of us, just slid in next to her mother, who held her tight, whispered, "It's all right. We're going to be all right."

"Judge," Naomi said. "Based on Ms. Lawrence's recanting of her testimony and the overwhelming physical evidence, the defense moves that the rape charges against my client be dropped."

Varney licked his lips, said, "Ms. Strong?"

The district attorney hesitated, and then said, "The state does not object."

"So ordered," Varney said.

Naomi went over and put her hand on Stefan's shoulder, said, "The defense asks that Detective Frost retake the stand."

Varney looked at his watch and then nodded.

Frost looked rattled when he took his seat.

Naomi took up more documents, said, "The defense wishes to enter the next exhibit, a second series of FBI tests based on evidence found at the murder scene."

Again Strong voiced no objection, just took her copy of the test, as if fearing its contents.

Frost took his copy as Naomi said, "This is a drug test done on semen samples taken off Rashawn Turnbull's body, correct, Detective?"

Frost scanned the document, said, "It is."

"This would be the same semen sample that the state's DNA testing identified as belonging to my client?"

"Uh, correct."

"Please read pages four and five," Naomi said.

Frost flipped the pages and read, and it was like watching a balloon with a slow leak wilt and collapse.

Naomi said, "Detective Frost, can you read aloud the results of the test on my client's semen gathered off Rashawn Turnbull's body?"

Frost chewed the inside of his lip. He said in a defeated voice, "'Negative for drugs and alcohol.'"

"'Negative for drugs and alcohol,'" she repeated to the jury. "The prosecution says my client drank to excess, did copious quantities of drugs, and went into a berserk rage on the night of Rashawn's rape and murder. But the FBI says Stefan Tate was stone-cold sober when that semen was produced."

BREE SLID INTO THE seat in the courtroom I'd been saving for her. Her eyes were shining when she whispered, "I've got something. Something big."

"Hold on," I whispered back. "Naomi's about to destroy the state's case."

My niece said, "Detective Frost? You agree that's what the test indicates?"

"Apparently so," the detective said, looking like he'd gone too many rounds with a heavyweight contender.

"That's strange," Naomi said, strolling over to the jury. "Because the blood sample you took from my client the morning after he allegedly killed Rashawn Turnbull showed he had a blood alcohol level of point zero six five, indicating he'd probably been very drunk the night before. Correct?"

Frost took a big breath, said, "Yes."

"But we now know that's contrary to the FBI's results," Naomi said, hands on the jury box. "Which means that the semen on Rashawn's body and in Sharon Lawrence's panties came from my client, but not on the nights in question. Which means someone, probably Finn Davis, somehow got to one of my client's condoms after he had had intercourse with his fiancée."

I glanced over my shoulder and saw that Patty Converse's face had gone red, but she was nodding in agreement.

"Objection, Judge!" Strong cried. "The defense attorney is drawing conclusions out of thin air."

"These conclusions are not drawn out of thin air!" Naomi insisted. "These are scientific facts, Ms. Strong. Flip to page nine of the FBI's report, third paragraph, reference to a third distinct DNA source in Ms. Lawrence's panties. Initial test indicates the DNA is female and unrelated to Ms. Lawrence. Vaginal secretions of another woman, suggesting, again, a used condom was stolen after use to plant evidence in order to frame my client for a crime he clearly did not commit."

Both the judge and the district attorney were digging through the document, looking for the reference.

Naomi gave them twenty seconds and then said, "These are facts that cannot be spun. All the evidence found at the murder scene has to be considered tainted. The vodka bottle, Mr. Tate's school ID, the meth sample, and the semen must be thrown out."

Strong said, "Judge, the vodka, the meth, and the ID are solid."

"No, they are not," Naomi said. "The placement of those three pieces of evidence is illogical at best, especially since they were left by a so-called berserk killer. My client's semen was clearly planted. So were the vodka, the meth, and the ID."

My niece turned to face the bench. "In short, Judge Varney, the state no longer has a viable case against my client. I move for mistrial and release of Stefan Tate from custody immediately."

The courtroom exploded.

Stefan rocked back in his chair, looking toward the heavens and hugging himself. Aunt Hattie started cheering and clapping. Pinkie, Nana Mama, and I joined her.

Judge Varney looked panicked when he whacked his gavel and called for order in his courtroom.

Bree tapped my elbow and held her iPhone in front of me, showing me riderless boxcars going through one of the railroad crossings south of Starksville. Then she showed me a picture of the same containers going through the crossing on the main Starksville road. Two riders were aboard.

"What—" I began.

Delilah Strong cried, "Judge, there remains other compelling evidence that links Mr. Tate to this murder."

Naomi said, "Judge, it's clear now that someone else killed Rashawn Turnbull and framed my client for the crime."

"The defense offers no evidence of that at all," Strong said. "Who does she think killed that boy?"

"That's really not our concern," Naomi said. "But we have a theory."

"Alex, you have to see this," Bree said, shoving the iPhone in front of me again. I glanced at the screen, saw a satellite view of train tracks by an industrial complex. I held up my index finger and then looked back to Naomi.

My niece glanced at me, and I nodded.

She said, "Judge, we have evidence that the meth planted in Mr. Tate's basement is tied to a drug ring using the trains that pass through Starksville to distribute methamphetamine and other drugs up and down the East Coast. My client had growing suspicions about the freight trains, and we believe the drug traffickers killed Rashawn and framed my client for the murder to keep him from digging further."

"This is ridiculous," Strong said. "The defense has introduced no evidence of any such drug ring. Judge, you can't—"

The rear doors to the courtroom were flung open with a bang.

Strong, Naomi, Judge Varney, the bailiff, the clerk, and many of the jurors gaped in disbelief and fear.

I twisted around in my seat to see what they were gawking at and got the shock of my life.

Palm Beach County's Detective Sergeant Peter Drummond looked like he was out for blood as he pressed the muzzle of a sawed-off pump-action Remington twelve-gauge to the side of Marvin Bell's head.

CHAPTER
96

"NOBODY MOVES OR THIS man dies!" Detective Sergeant Drummond roared, and he jerked at the rope he had tied around Bell's neck and hands, which were horribly swollen and bruised. Several of Bell's fingers pointed in directions they shouldn't.

Spectators began to cry, panic, and push back toward the walls. Nana Mama squealed in fear beside me, and I held up an arm to shield her. Bree started for her backup pistol, but I said, "Don't. I know this guy."

Drummond shouted, "Unload your gun there, Bailiff, and put it on the floor. You. In the witness box. Same."

Frost and the bailiff did as they were told.

Drummond scanned the room for threats, said, "You too, Chief Sherman, and you, Detective Carmichael. Primary weapons and backups on the floor."

Sherman and Carmichael seemed shocked that the madman knew their names, but they did as they were told. Then Drummond marched Bell deeper into the courtroom. Marvin Bell looked more lost than frightened, shuffling forward, staring at his hands and quivering in pain.

As they got close, I stood up, said, "Sergeant, what are you doing?"

Drummond turned his scarred, expressionless face

past Bree and toward me, said, "Something I should have done a long time ago."

"C'mon, Drummond. You don't want to do this."

"You don't understand, Dr. Cross. I have to do this."

The sergeant pushed and dragged Bell into the well of the court. He glanced at Strong and Naomi, said, "Take a seat, Counselors."

Then he motioned for Frost to get down, said, "This man wants to testify."

The detective hesitated, but then climbed from the witness stand. Drummond said, "Sit there on the floor by the jury box."

Frost did as he was told. The sergeant maneuvered Marvin Bell into the chair and got behind him, keeping the gun at his head and dropping the rope so it dangled off the back of the chair.

"Sergeant, whoever you are," Judge Varney began, "and whatever problem you might have with Mr. Bell, this is not the way to address the—"

"With all due respect, Judge," Drummond said, "we are no longer in a court of law. This is truth-seeking where the ends justify the means."

Beside me, Bree typed on her phone and then held it up. I realized she was filming him. I looked over my shoulder and saw that Patty Converse and Pinkie Parks had gone wide-eyed.

What do we do? Pinkie mouthed.

"Not a thing," I whispered, and looked at my aunts, who were sitting forward in their chairs and raptly watching Drummond.

The sergeant peered around the courtroom as if he owned it, then focused on the jury box, said, "Wouldn't you just like to know what happened for once? No BS. The whole thing out in the open for you to judge?"

Despite their collective fear, several jury members nodded.

"I would too," Nana Mama whispered. "You *know* him, Alex?"

"Met him in Florida," I whispered. "He's a cop."

"What happened to his face?"

"First Gulf War."

I knew the source of the scarring, but what had happened to Drummond in the few days since I'd seen him? Why in God's name would he do something this rash? Destroy his career and reputation? His life?

I'd talked to Drummond about Marvin Bell and how frustrated I was at not being able to link him to the web of secrets we'd been uncovering in Starksville. And the sergeant had asked me about Bell several times. He'd done it on the phone that very morning. Drummond had obviously been close by when he called me. And Bell had never left the area. The sergeant had been holding him hostage somewhere, torturing him into a confession.

But why?

"We'll start at the beginning, Marvin, way, way back, more than thirty-five years," Drummond said. "You sold drugs in Starksville then, built a nice little business out of it, didn't you?"

"No," Marvin Bell said, sounding bewildered. "I—"

From out of nowhere, Drummond pulled out a small ball-peen hammer. He snapped it forward with power, speed, and accuracy. The round head of the hammer smashed into Bell's swollen left hand, and he howled in agony.

"Try again, Marvin," Drummond said, waving the hammer in Bell's peripheral vision. "You sold drugs. You built a gang."

"Yes," Marvin Bell whimpered. "I sold drugs. I built a gang."

"Here in Starksville?"

"Yes."

"Name of that gang?"

"The Company."

There it is, I thought. *Bell started the Company. He's Grandfather.*

Drummond said, "You had a ruthless business model, Marvin. Got people addicted on freebies until they were like your slaves. You had people killed. You killed people yourself."

"I never killed anyone," Marvin Bell said, crying. "I keep telling you that and you don't believe me."

"I DON'T BELIEVE YOU," Drummond said, wagging the hammer. "But we'll come back to that. You admit you made a lot of money dealing drugs?"

Marvin Bell looked from his hands to the hammer, and nodded sullenly.

"You laundered that money in legitimate businesses all around Starksville," Drummond went on.

Looking as if his world was ending, Bell said, "Yeah."

"But even after you'd bought the legit businesses, you didn't stay away from the drug trade, did you?"

Bell set his jaw as if he were going to argue, but then he shook his head.

"Course not," the sergeant said. "Moving coke and heroin and meth was just too lucrative. The money was almost too easy if you were smart about it. So one day you noticed the freight trains going back and forth all day and all night through Starksville, and thought, *Why not use them? Why not expand?* Am I summarizing your personal history correctly?"

Bell tried to move his hands and gasped before nodding.

"Yes," Drummond said. "You built a distribution network that stretches from Montreal to Miami?"

Again, Bell said, "Yes."

"And with all that money, you bought yourself an estate up on Pleasant Lake, a gorgeous beachfront place down on Hilton Head, and a condo in Aspen. Trips all over the world. Art collector. Isn't that right?"

He nodded.

"Got your adopted son, Finn Davis, involved too."

Bell swallowed, said, "Finn's part of it."

"Finn kill his ex-wife?" Drummond asked. "Sydney Fox?"

I heard a creak behind me as Pinkie sat forward.

Marvin Bell looked around the room as if desperate for someone to rescue him. Drummond lashed out again with the hammer, hit Bell's right hand. Bell let out a scream that shook everyone in the room except Drummond, who seemed calm, clinical.

"Answer the question, Marvin," the sergeant said. "Did Finn Davis shoot Sydney Fox?"

"Yes." Bell moaned.

"Fucking knew it," Pinkie said, and he smacked his fist in his palm. "That sonofabitch."

"Why did he kill her?" Drummond asked.

"'Cause he hated her, and she needed killing."

"Why did Sydney Fox need killing?"

"Having been married to Finn, she suspected too much," Bell said. "And she was talking to Tate, who was poking around the train tracks. It was all no good, so he killed her."

Drummond asked, "Did Sydney Fox know about your supplier?"

Marvin Bell groaned and shifted in his chair, said, "No."

"Your distribution system got so big you were having trouble getting supply, especially methamphetamine, correct?" Drummond flipped the hammer in the air and caught it.

Marvin Bell flinched, said, "Yes."

"So you found a secret partner right here in Starksville who could manufacture meth for you. In fact, a partner who could provide you with an almost unlimited supply and never get caught. Right?"

A secret partner? I thought.

"I called it," Bree whispered, lowering her iPhone and pumping her fist.

"Called what?" I said.

Before she could answer, Drummond said, "Is that correct, Marvin?"

"Yes. I had a partner."

Judge Varney had broken out in a sweat and looked agitated, and I feared he was about to keel over again from kidney-stone pain.

Drummond said, "You and your partner, you didn't like Stefan Tate sneaking around, looking into things by the tracks, did you?"

"No."

"You and your partner decided that Stefan Tate had to go."

Marvin Bell moved his hands, winced, said, "I agreed Tate had to go. But I had no idea what he had in mind. No idea that he'd do all that to the boy."

"You know for a fact your partner killed Rashawn Turnbull?"

Bell looked out into the spectators and seemed to be speaking directly to Cece Turnbull. "I know for a fact he killed Rashawn and framed Tate. He told me so himself afterward."

"What did your partner say?" Drummond said. "Word for word."

Bell swallowed and replied, "He said he'd gotten rid of two problems at the same time, Stefan Tate and his black bastard grandson."

CHAPTER
98

FOR TWO SECONDS, THE silence in that courtroom was so deep and complete you could have heard a mouse in the walls. I was tired, wrung out. It took me a full two seconds to figure out the killer, and then I twisted around, looking for Harold Caine.

Rashawn's grandfather. Owner of a fertilizer company. Chemist, no doubt. Racist? Grandfather?

Caine's expression seemed electrified by the charge. His body had gone rigid. His lips were peeled back. And he was clinging so hard to the bench in front of him that I thought his fingers might snap like Bell's.

Caine's wife stared at him like he was something unthinkable and cowered from his side.

Caine noticed, turned his head to her, said, "It's not true, Virginia. He's—"

"It is true!" Cece Turnbull screeched.

Caine's daughter had twisted around and was looking past Ann and Sharon Lawrence to face her father two rows back. "You always hated Rashawn! You always hated that a nigger fucked your lily-white Southern daughter and left you with a living, breathing tarnish on the Caine family name!"

"No, that's not true!"

Cece went over the back of her bench then, stepped up next to Ann Lawrence, and launched herself at her father. She crashed into him, slapping and scratching at his face.

"You treated my boy worse than dirt his entire life!" she screamed. "And you stole my Lizzie. Rashawn had as much of your precious blood as my Lizzie, and you cut it out of him with a pruning saw!"

Bree jumped up and went to Cece, who'd broken down sobbing as she feebly tried to continue her assault on her father. Bree pulled Cece off and held her while Caine slumped there, chest heaving, blood oozing from those scratches, looking around like a cornered animal at all the people in the courtroom watching him.

"None of it's true," Caine told them in a hoarse whisper. "None of it!"

"It's all true!" Bell shouted from the witness stand. "You sick fuck. You deserve to burn in hell for what you did."

The courtroom doors were flung open again. Two men and a woman, all wearing business suits, came in carrying pistols and badges.

The woman said, "My name is Carol Wolfe, FBI special agent in charge of the Winston-Salem office. Put the gun down, Sergeant Drummond."

Drummond kept the shotgun to the back of Bell's head, said, "I'm not quite done yet, Agent Wolfe. Mr. Bell here has one more thing to get off his chest."

CHAPTER
99

MARVIN BELL SEEMED GENUINELY puzzled, said, "I told you everything."

"Not all of it," Drummond said. "You said you've never murdered anyone in your life."

"That's a fact," Bell said.

"Never smothered anyone—a woman, maybe?" Drummond said. "Thirty-five years ago?"

"No."

"You were her drug dealer," the sergeant insisted. "She was dying of cancer, and no one was paying you for the heroin her husband was using to ease her pain."

Bell shook his head.

"You got her husband damn-near-overdose high on smack," Drummond said. "And then you smothered her with a pillow while he watched, so numb he couldn't stop you."

Drummond was breathing hard. He said, "Then, for almost a year, you made him work for you, and finally, when he was no use to you anymore, you tied that man to your car with a rope just like the one around your neck here, and you dragged that poor bastard through the streets, called him a wife killer, a mother killer.

"You alerted the police, said he'd murdered his wife, and gave him to the young men who were already in your pocket. Officer Randy Sherman and Deputy

Nathan Bean. You paid them to make it look like he tried to escape. Judge Varney, a young assistant district attorney at the time, was there too. They pushed that man to the railing, and he didn't understand why they went back to the cruisers and then turned and pulled their guns. Then they shot him, and he fell off the bridge and into the gorge. Isn't that the way it happened, Marvin?"

Drummond had dropped the hammer and was holding the shotgun against Bell's head so hard his hands were shaking.

"Yes, yes," Bell whined. "That's what happened."

Judge Varney pounded with his gavel. "That is not true!"

Police Chief Sherman was on his feet, about to protest, but the FBI agent said, "Chief, you're under arrest. And you too, Judge Varney."

I don't remember getting to my feet, only that I was, suddenly, and staring across the courtroom at Drummond as if down a vast tunnel of time.

"Who are you, Sergeant?" I said, realizing that Nana Mama was standing up beside me. "How do you know all these things?"

Tears streamed down Drummond's expressionless face as he withdrew the shotgun barrel from Bell's head and looked toward me and my grandmother.

"I know these things, Alex," he choked out, "because in another lifetime, my name was Jason Cross."

CHAPTER
100

NANA MAMA GASPED, REACHED for her heart, and toppled against me. Her frail ninety-pound body almost bowled me off my own liquid feet. I had to take my eyes off Drummond to regain my balance and hold her up.

"Is it true?" my grandmother whispered into my chest, as if she couldn't bear to look Drummond's way.

"That's impossible," Bell said, craning his neck to look at Drummond. "Jason Cross took a bullet, went into the gorge. He never came out."

"Yes, he did," said Pinkie, who'd also gotten to his feet. "My uncle Clifford found him down on the river that night. Nursed him back to health."

"Is Clifford here in Starksville?" Drummond called to Pinkie. "I would sure like to see the second best friend I've ever had. Maybe take him to Bourbon Street like we always talked about."

"Oh my God." My aunt Hattie gasped.

"It's a miracle," my aunt Connie cried.

I looked down at Nana Mama, saw my grandmother dissolving through sheets of tears.

"It's him," I whispered. "I don't know how, but it's him."

When I looked up, Drummond had left Bell in the witness stand, handed the shotgun to Detective Frost, and was coming toward us with tears streaming down his blank face and his arms cast open.

"You don't know how much I missed the both of you," he said. "You have no idea of the loneliness without you."

I slid into my father's arms and he slid into his mother's as if they were the most natural and familiar acts possible.

We bowed our heads into one another, suddenly apart from everyone else in that courtroom, like a miniature universe unto ourselves. I don't think any of us managed to utter an intelligible word in those first few moments of reunion. But I know we were communicating deeply in a whole other language, like people embraced by holy spirits and speaking in tongues of fire.

CHAPTER
101

TWO WEEKS AND TWO days after we'd arrived in Starksville, on a warm, clear Saturday afternoon, we had ourselves a proper reunion in Aunt Hattie's backyard. Everybody who mattered to me in life was there.

Damon had flown into Winston-Salem the day before to meet his grandfather, which had been as emotional and satisfying as every other moment of my dad's return to my life. Naomi's mother, Cilla, and my brother Charlie had come in the day before that.

At first, Charlie had not believed Nana Mama and me when we'd called him with the news. Then he'd gotten angry and said he wasn't interested in meeting someone who'd cut out on us thirty-five years before. But Cilla and Naomi had insisted, and when Charlie laid eyes on our dad, all had been forgiven. The only thing that would have made it better was having my late brothers Blake and Aaron there too, and we all shed tears over those tragedies.

My best friend, John Sampson, and his wife, Billie, had come in that morning. Sampson and my dad had hit it off immediately, and when Drummond wasn't sitting by my uncle Cliff, he and John were trading cop stories and laughing.

Stefan Tate was there with his fiancée, Patty Converse, the two of them looking as in love as any couple I'd ever seen. Special Agent Wolfe was there as well.

Evidently, the FBI had been looking at Starksville with suspicions of judicial and police misconduct long before my father called Wolfe and told her to come listen to the shocking testimony about to come out in the courtroom of Erasmus P. Varney.

I went over to Agent Wolfe, said, "What do you think my dad's chances are?"

Wolfe said, "Well, he's not going back to his job with the Palm Beach County Sheriff's Office. They've been pretty clear on that, but I don't think he'll end up being prosecuted for taking Bell hostage and marching him into court."

"You don't think?" I asked. "Pretty extreme move."

"It was," she said. "But we arrested the police chief and the presiding judge in Stark County, and the sheriff's been murdered. And Guy Pedelini regained consciousness and spilled everything on all of them. The DA's office is even under investigation. Basically, there's no one left in Starksville to go after your dad, and I don't know what federal statute would apply."

"So he walks free into a new life," I said.

"He walks free into an old life," Bree said, coming up beside me.

"And Marvin Bell and Harold Caine go down for so many things," Wolfe said. "If they're not given the death penalty, which I think is the appropriate punishment, they'll at least never see the outside of a prison."

I thought about Harold Caine, his callous, cruel indifference. We'd gotten more of the story from Cece.

After Rashawn's birth, her parents had all but disowned her. Then Cece got pregnant by a white boyfriend she picked up while Rashawn's father was doing time. Her parents found out, and they also found out that Cece was on drugs while she was with child.

The Caines used the rigged courts of Starksville against Cece and had the baby girl, Lizzie, taken from her mother's arms within minutes of birth. The courts awarded Lizzie's grandparents full custody, and they had greatly limited Cece's involvement in her daughter's life.

Harold Caine had evidently spent years bitter and humiliated about his mixed-race grandson while at the same time doting on his lily-white granddaughter and running a meth business from secret underground labs beneath his fertilizer factory.

The most terrible thing about it all was that the frenzied nature of the wounds Rashawn had suffered before death clearly indicated that Caine had enjoyed killing his grandson. He'd enjoyed murdering his own flesh and blood. When it came right down to it, that poor, innocent boy had been tortured and slain for the color of his skin.

I'd heard too many variations of that story over the years—young black boy killed for his race—but this one was the worst. The cruelest. The most heinous. The most sadistic. The least understandable.

Like Cece Turnbull, I would never get over Rashawn's death.

Caine had lawyered up and wasn't talking. Marvin Bell was talking to prosecutors who were going after Caine for murder, kidnapping, and depraved indifference within the course of a race-based incident. I hoped that whatever the jury decided about Caine, they'd make him suffer.

I spotted a middle-aged woman wearing a Domino's hat coming around the corner carrying two pizzas. Wolfe, Bree, and I immediately went on alert. Varney,

Bell, and Sherman had continued to turn over evidence against Caine, and they'd all stated that he had hired a female assassin known as the lace maker to kill members of my family and make it look like accidents.

She'd missed getting Bree and me with the broken brake line. Now that Caine was behind bars, there was no reason to think the lace maker was still around. But you never knew.

"Can I take those off your hands?" I asked the woman.

"Please," she said as she smiled and handed them to me. "I'm a little late, so it'll be five dollars off."

"Who ordered them?" Bree asked.

"Connie Lou."

"Oh, Edith, there you are," my aunt said, hustling over with the cash.

They hugged, and Bree and I relaxed.

Then I saw something that warmed my heart. Cece Turnbull came into the backyard with a beautiful little girl who was the spitting image of her mother, and Cece looked clean and sober and thrilled to be with her daughter.

Bree went into the house for something to drink. I got in line for food. With my plate loaded with fried rabbit, coleslaw, broccoli salad, and little roasted red potatoes, I spotted Pinkie talking to Bree and started over.

"You didn't eat all the rabbit, did you, Dad?" Jannie asked from a lawn chair between Damon and Ali.

"God, it's really good," Damon said. "There better be seconds."

"I want some more too," Ali said. "But Pinkie said he'd cook the bass I caught yesterday up at the lake."

"I'm sure he hasn't forgotten," I said. "But I'll remind him."

Jannie said, "Coach Greene and Coach Fall said they were going to try to come by later."

"Looking forward to seeing them," I said. "But I want you to keep your options open, young lady. Okay?"

"Yeah, for real, Jannie," Damon said. "If you have Duke already at your door, you know there's going to be a whole lot more."

Jannie nodded, and then sobered. "Sharon and her mom going to jail?"

"They're turning evidence against Marvin Bell, but even if they convince a jury that he forced them into lying about the rape, planting Stefan's DNA, and putting the drugs in your bag, I still think they're both looking at convictions and sentences."

"I don't want it to, like, completely ruin their lives," Jannie said.

"Neither do I," I said. "Have fun."

"Always," Ali said.

I grinned. "You do, don't you?"

"Like Jim Shockey. Life's an adventure."

Feeling like my youngest had an understanding of life far beyond his years, I walked over to Pinkie and Bree.

"Gimme some rabbit so I don't have to stand in line," Bree said, looking hungrily at my plate.

"Not a chance," I said.

"What?" she said, miffed. "After how hard and ingeniously I worked on behalf of your cousin?"

"Okay," I said. "Take the thigh there."

Bree snatched it off the plate.

"What about me?" Pinkie said.

"You're able-bodied enough to work on oil rigs," I said. "Get in line."

My cousin laughed and went off toward the food.

Bree took two bites of the rabbit and looked like she

was in heaven. "I had it figured out, you know. About Caine. Well, everything except Rashawn."

"I believe you."

I did. That satellite photo she'd shown me in court was of Caine Industries, which sat by the tracks between the Starksville Road and the crossing three miles to the south. Bree had figured out from the trail-cam photographs that the riders were boarding between those two crossings.

She'd called up Google Earth, saw the rail-line spur that ran out of Caine's business, and thought, *What a great cover for a meth-manufacturing op.*

Bree said, "If your dad hadn't gone Rambo, I would have pinned Caine to the wall."

"Yes, you would have," I said. "And for that, I think you've earned some downtime in Jamaica."

Bree perked up. "Really?"

"Why not?"

"Just us?"

"Why not?"

"When?"

"Soon as you want."

"God, I love the way you think sometimes," she said, and she kissed me.

"Get a room, you two," Nana Mama cracked as she eased into a lawn chair near us.

"We were talking about doing just that," I said.

"TMI, as Jannie says," my grandmother said, and she waved us off.

"You happy you came back to Starksville, Nana?" Bree asked.

"I'd be some kind of ungrateful wretch if I wasn't," Nana Mama said. "This is like the story of the prodigal son, only I'm living it. Honestly, Bree, I could die right now and it would be perfectly fine by me."

"Not by me," I said.

"And not by me either," my father said, coming up behind her, bending down, and kissing her on the cheek.

Nana Mama usually made a fuss over public displays of affection, but she put her hand on her son's cheek and closed her eyes, and I had a flash of her when she must have been very young and holding her newborn child in her arms.

My dad's cell phone buzzed. He stood up, dug it out, and read a text. He looked at me, and then at my grand-mother.

"I'm afraid I haven't told you all of it," he said. "How I came to be Peter Drummond and all."

That was true. He'd been very evasive about that part of his life.

"You going to tell us?" Nana Mama said.

"In a minute," he said. "First, there's someone I want you all to meet."

CHAPTER
102

MY FATHER CAME BACK holding hands with Reverend Alicia Maya, who looked absolutely radiant in the last full rays of sunshine.

"Alex," my dad said, "Mom. I'd like to introduce you to my best friend, the woman whose love saved me. My wife, Alicia."

For the umpteenth time in the last two weeks I got tears in my eyes.

"I'm so sorry I had to lie to you that day in the cemetery," Reverend Maya said, coming to me and holding my hands. "But your dad thought that things would be better for you if you just went on believing he was dead. He considered his chance to see you a gift from God, and he said that was enough for him. But after you'd left Florida, he realized it wasn't enough. He wanted to know you, to be a part of your life. To do that, he had to come back and face Bell and destroy the life he'd made for himself."

The story came out from the two of them as the day ebbed toward twilight, and everybody at the party stopped to listen.

Reverend Maya found my father just the way she'd told me, weak, homeless, and limping into her church one day. She'd allowed him to sleep there. She'd provided him with counseling and helped him battle his addictions.

"Through Alicia, I found God and have been sober for thirty-four years," my father said. "I was guilty of abandoning you boys, and you, Mom, but I was terrified of what might happen to me and to all of you if I ever returned to Starksville."

Reverend Maya said, "He confessed it all to me one night about a year after he started living in the church. He told me about seeing Marvin Bell kill your mom, about being arrested and shot, surviving the gorge, recovering with the help of his beloved Clifford. I told him I believed that God would forgive him."

"Is that when you fell in love with him?" Nana Mama asked.

"No, love came later, after the war, when I realized how close I'd come to losing him."

The night my father met Alicia Maya, he had fake papers that identified him as Paul Brown. But shortly after he confessed to the reverend his true identity, a tragic miracle occurred.

A nineteen-year-old named Peter Drummond came into the Reverend Maya's church seeking counsel, just as my father had a year before. Drummond told her that he was an orphan and had been out of foster care in Kansas City for less than a year. He'd been homeless, and so, on a whim, he'd enlisted in the Marine Corps.

"He said he'd made a mistake," Reverend Maya said. "That he never should have enlisted and that he knew he was incapable of handling the pressures of war, especially of killing other men."

She paused, and my father put his hand on his second wife's shoulder, said, "You couldn't have known."

"I know." She sighed. "Turns out he was in far deeper psychological and spiritual pain than I'd sensed. I told him to pray about it and trust that God would show him the right…" She choked up.

My father said, "Drummond went out in back of the church and shot himself in the face with a shotgun."

"Jesus," Pinkie said.

"We were the only ones who heard the shot," Reverend Maya said. "I was hysterical when your father and I found him."

"She told me to call the police, and I didn't dare because I was scared," my father said. "Then I started going through his pockets. And there was his ID and his enlistment papers that said he had to be at Camp Lejeune in two days."

"You switched papers," Ali said.

"Very good, young man," my father said. "Alicia wanted no part of it at first, but I showed her that, for me, it could be a total rebirth and a chance to do something hard and good for the first time in my life."

"No one questioned the papers?" Bree asked.

"Both ID photographs weren't the best, and he'd shot himself in the face," Reverend Maya said. "The police in Pahokee never questioned that the dead man was Paul Brown."

"And the Marines were glad to have me," my father said. "I made corporal and went to Kuwait during the Gulf War. I was part of a crew that was supposed to seize and protect the oil wells that the Iraqis set on fire as they retreated. One blew, and I was too close."

Reverend Maya said she and my father had kept in contact, writing letters back and forth before the explosion.

She said, "When I saw him lying there at the VA hospital, I don't know, I just knew that I loved him and couldn't live without him ever again."

"I felt the same way," my dad said. "You don't know what it did to my heart when she came in to see me."

"And then you became a cop," I said.

"I'd been a criminal," he replied. "I figured I'd be good at catching them."

"He's good at it," Reverend Maya said. "But when he found out that you'd gone into the same field, Alex, he was beside himself with pride. He's followed your career every step of the way."

"And you bump into each other in Belle Glade, Florida," Nana Mama said.

"What are the odds of that happening?" Jannie asked.

"Astronomical," Reverend Maya said. "That's why I believe we were guided by a divine hand."

"You believe that?" Nana Mama asked.

"I do," she said.

"I do," my father said.

"I do too," I said.

"How else do you explain it?" Nana Mama said, and she smiled.

We all fell into a reflective quiet that had me wondering about the mystery that had been my life and how perfectly complete I felt at that moment.

"I'd like to make a toast," my dad said. "So everyone get a glass."

By the time we'd all gotten glasses and gathered together again, fireflies were flashing in the pines.

My dad raised his ginger ale and said, "To our extended family and all our friends, living, dead, and now living again: May God bless the Crosses."

"Amen," Nana Mama said, and we all echoed her. "Amen."

ABOUT THE AUTHOR

JAMES PATTERSON has created more enduring fictional characters than any other novelist writing today. He is the author of the Alex Cross novels, the most popular detective series of the past twenty-five years. His other bestselling novels feature the Women's Murder Club, Michael Bennett, Private, and NYPD Red. Since his first novel won the Edgar Award, in 1977, James Patterson's books have sold more than 300 million copies.

James Patterson has also written numerous #1 bestsellers for young readers, including the Maximum Ride, Witch & Wizard, Middle School, and Treasure Hunters series. In 2010, James Patterson was named Author of the Year at the Children's Choice Book Awards.

His lifelong passion for books and reading led James Patterson to create the innovative website ReadKiddoRead.com, giving adults an invaluable tool to find the books that get kids reading for life. He writes full-time and lives in Florida with his family.

BOOKS BY JAMES PATTERSON

FEATURING ALEX CROSS

Cross Justice • *Hope to Die* • *Cross My Heart* • *Alex Cross, Run* • *Merry Christmas, Alex Cross* • *Kill Alex Cross* • *Cross Fire* • *I, Alex Cross* • *Alex Cross's* Trial (with Richard DiLallo) • *Cross Country* • *Double Cross* • *Cross* (also published as *Alex Cross*) • *Mary, Mary* • *London Bridges* • *The Big Bad Wolf* • *Four Blind Mice* • *Violets Are Blue* • *Roses Are Red* • *Pop Goes the Weasel* • *Cat & Mouse* • *Jack & Jill* • *Kiss the Girls* • *Along Came a Spider*

THE WOMEN'S MURDER CLUB

15th Affair (with Maxine Paetro) • *14th Deadly Sin* (with Maxine Paetro) • *Unlucky 13* (with Maxine Paetro) • *12th of Never* (with Maxine Paetro) • *11th Hour* (with Maxine Paetro) • *10th Anniversary* (with Maxine Paetro) • *The 9th Judgment* (with Maxine Paetro) • *The 8th Confession* (with Maxine Paetro) • *7th Heaven* (with Maxine Paetro) • *The 6th Target* (with Maxine Paetro) • *The 5th Horseman* (with Maxine Paetro) • *4th of July* (with Maxine Paetro) • *3rd Degree* (with Andrew Gross) • *2nd Chance* (with Andrew Gross) • *1st to Die*

FEATURING MICHAEL BENNETT

Alert (with Michael Ledwidge) • *Burn* (with Michael Ledwidge) • *Gone* (with Michael Ledwidge) • *I, Michael Bennett* (with Michael Ledwidge) • *Tick Tock* (with Michael Ledwidge) • *Worst Case* (with Michael Ledwidge) • *Run for Your Life* (with Michael Ledwidge) • *Step on a Crack* (with Michael Ledwidge)

THE PRIVATE NOVELS

The Games (with Mark Sullivan) • *Private Paris* (with Mark Sullivan) • *Private Vegas* (with Maxine Paetro) • *Private India: City on Fire* (with Ashwin Sanghi) • *Private Down Under* (with Michael White) • *Private L.A.* (with Mark

Sullivan) • *Private Berlin* (with Mark Sullivan) • *Private London* (with Mark Pearson) • *Private Games* (with Mark Sullivan) • *Private: #1 Suspect* (with Maxine Paetro) • *Private* (with Maxine Paetro)

NYPD RED NOVELS
NYPD Red 4 (with Marshall Karp) • *NYPD Red 3* (with Marshall Karp) • *NYPD Red 2* (with Marshall Karp) • *NYPD Red* (with Marshall Karp)

SUMMER NOVELS
Second Honeymoon (with Howard Roughan) • *Now You See Her* (with Michael Ledwidge) • *Swimsuit* (with Maxine Paetro) • *Sail* (with Howard Roughan) • *Beach Road* (with Peter de Jonge) • *Lifeguard* (with Andrew Gross) • *Honeymoon* (with Howard Roughan) • *The Beach House* (with Peter de Jonge)

STAND-ALONE BOOKS
The Murder House (with David Ellis) • *Truth or Die* (with Howard Roughan) • *Miracle at Augusta* (with Peter de Jonge) • *Invisible* (with David Ellis) • *First Love* (with Emily Raymond) • *Mistress* (with David Ellis) • *Zoo* (with Michael Ledwidge) • *Guilty Wives* (with David Ellis) • *The Christmas Wedding* (with Richard DiLallo) • *Kill Me If You Can* (with Marshall Karp) • *Toys* (with Neil McMahon) • *Don't Blink* (with Howard Roughan) • *The Postcard Killers* (with Liza Marklund) • *The Murder of King Tut* (with Martin Dugard) • *Against Medical Advice* (with Hal Friedman) • *Sundays at Tiffany's* (with Gabrielle Charbonnet) • *You've Been Warned* (with Howard Roughan) • *The Quickie* (with Michael Ledwidge) • *Judge & Jury* (with Andrew Gross) • *Sam's Letters to Jennifer* • *The Lake House* • *The Jester* (with Andrew Gross) • *Suzanne's Diary for Nicholas* • *Cradle and All* • *When the Wind Blows* • *Miracle on the 17th Green* (with Peter de Jonge) • *Hide & Seek* • *The Midnight Club* • *Black Friday* (originally published as *Black Market*) • *See How They Run* • *Season of the Machete* • *The Thomas Berryman Number*

BOOK**SHOTS**

Superhero (with Chris Tebbetts, illustrated by Cory Thomas) • *House of Robots* (with Chris Grabenstein, illustrated by Juliana Neufeld) • *Homeroom Diaries* (with Lisa Papademetriou, illustrated by Keino) • *Med Head* (with Hal Friedman) • *santaKid* (illustrated by Michael Garland)

For previews and information about the author, visit JamesPatterson.com or find him on Facebook or at your app store.

CROSS KILL

CHAPTER
1

A LATE WINTER STORM bore down on Washington, DC, that March morning, and more folks than usual were waiting in the cafeteria of St. Anthony of Padua Catholic School on Monroe Avenue in the northeast quadrant.

"If you need a jolt before you eat, coffee's in those urns over there," I called to the cafeteria line.

From behind a serving counter, my partner, John Sampson, said, "You want pancakes or eggs and sausage, you come see me first. Dry cereal, oatmeal, and toast at the end. Fruit, too."

It was early, a quarter to seven, and we'd already seen twenty-five people come through the kitchen, mostly moms and kids from the surrounding neighborhood. By my count, another forty were waiting in the hallway, with more coming in from outside where the first flakes were falling.

It was all my ninety-something grandmother's idea. She'd hit the DC Lottery Powerball the year before, and wanted to make sure the unfortunate received some of her good fortune. She'd partnered with the church to see the hot-breakfast program started.

"Are there any doughnuts?" asked a little boy, who put me in mind of my younger son, Ali.

He was holding on to his mother, a devastatingly

thin woman with rheumy eyes and a habit of scratching at her neck.

"No doughnuts today," I said.

"What am I gonna eat?" he complained.

"Something that's good for you for once," his mom said. "Eggs, bacon, and toast. Not all that Cocoa Puffs sugar crap."

I nodded. Mom looked like she was high on something, but she did know her nutrition.

"This sucks," her son said. "I want a doughnut. I want two doughnuts!"

"Go on, there," his mom said, and pushed him toward Sampson.

"Kind of overkill for a church cafeteria," said the man who followed her. He was in his late twenties, and dressed in baggy jeans, Timberland boots, and a big gray snorkel jacket.

I realized he was talking to me and looked at him, puzzled.

"Bulletproof vest?" he said.

"Oh," I said, and shrugged at the body armor beneath my shirt.

Sampson and I are major case detectives with the Washington, DC, Metropolitan Police Department. Immediately after our shift in the soup kitchen, we were joining a team taking down a drug gang operating in the streets around St. Anthony's. Members of the gang had been known to take free breakfasts at the school from time to time, so we'd decided to armor up. Just in case.

I wasn't telling him that, though. I couldn't identify him as a known gangster, but he looked the part.

"I'm up for a PT test end of next week," I said. "Got to get used to the weight since I'll be running three miles with it on."

"That vest make you hotter or colder today?"

"Warmer. Always."

"I need one of them," he said, and shivered. "I'm from Miami, you know? I must have been crazy to want to come on up here."

"Why did you come up here?" I asked.

"School. I'm a freshman at Howard."

"You're not on the meal program?"

"Barely making my tuition."

I saw him in a whole new light then, and was about to say so when gunshots rang out and people began to scream.

CHAPTER
2

DRAWING MY SERVICE PISTOL, I pushed against the fleeing crowd, hearing two more shots, and realizing they were coming from inside the kitchen behind Sampson. My partner had figured it out as well.

Sampson spun away from the eggs and bacon, drew his gun as I vaulted over the counter. We split and went to either side of the pair of swinging industrial kitchen doors. There were small portholes in both.

Ignoring the people still bolting from the cafeteria, I leaned forward and took a quick peek. Mixing bowls had spilled off the stainless-steel counters, throwing flour and eggs across the cement floor. Nothing moved, and I could detect no one inside.

Sampson took a longer look from the opposite angle. His face almost immediately screwed up.

"Two wounded," he hissed. "The cook, Theresa, and a nun I've never seen before."

"How bad?"

"There's blood all over Theresa's white apron. Looks like the nun's hit in the leg. She's sitting up against the stove with a big pool below her."

"Femoral?"

Sampson took another look and said, "It's a lot of blood."

"Cover me," I said. "I'm going in low to get them."

Sampson nodded. I squatted down and threw my shoulder into the door, which swung away. Half expecting some unseen gunman to open fire, I rolled inside. I slid through the slurry of two dozen eggs, and came to a stop on the floor between two prep counters.

Sampson came in with his weapon high, searching for a target.

But no one shot. No one moved. And there was no sound except the labored breathing of the cook and the nun who were to our left, on the other side of a counter, by a big industrial stove.

The nun's eyes were open and bewildered. The cook's head slumped but she was breathing.

I scrambled under the prep counter to the women, and started tugging off my belt. The nun shrank from me when I reached for her.

"I'm a cop, Sister," I said. "My name is Alex Cross. I need to put a tourniquet on your leg or you could die."

She blinked, but then nodded.

"John?" I said, observing a serious gunshot wound to her lower thigh. A needle-thin jet of blood erupted with every heartbeat.

"Right here," Sampson said behind me. "Just seeing what's what."

"Call it in," I said, as I wrapped the belt around her upper thigh, cinching it tight. "We need two ambulances. Fast."

The blood stopped squirting. I could hear my partner making the radio call.

The nun's eyes fluttered and drifted toward shut.

"Sister," I said. "What happened? Who shot you?"

Her eyes blinked open. She gaped at me, disoriented for a moment, before her attention strayed past me. Her eyes widened, and the skin of her cheek went taut with terror.

I snatched up my gun and spun around, raising the pistol. I saw Sampson with his back to me, radio to his ear, gun lowered, and then a door at the back of the kitchen. It had swung open, revealing a large pantry.

A man crouched in a fighting stance in the pantry doorway.

In his crossed arms he held two nickel-plated pistols, one aimed at Sampson and the other at me.

With all the training I've been lucky enough to receive over the years, you'd think I would have done the instinctual thing for a veteran cop facing an armed assailant, that I would have registered *Man with gun!* in my brain, and I would have shot him immediately.

But for a split second I didn't listen to *Man with a gun!* because I was too stunned by the fact that I knew him, and that he was long, long dead.

CHAPTER
3

IN THAT SAME INSTANT, he fired both pistols. Traveling less than thirty feet, the bullet hit me so hard it slammed me backward. My head cracked off the concrete and everything went just this side of midnight, like I was swirling and draining down a black pipe, before I heard a third shot and then a fourth.

Something crashed close to me, and I fought my way toward the sound, toward consciousness, seeing the blackness give way, disjointed and incomplete, like a jigsaw puzzle with missing pieces.

Five, maybe six seconds passed before I found more pieces, and I knew who I was and what had happened. Two more seconds passed before I realized I'd taken the bullet square in the Kevlar that covered my chest. It felt like I'd taken a sledgehammer to my ribs, and a swift kick to my head.

In the next instant, I grabbed my gun and looked for...

John Sampson sprawled on the floor by the sinks, his massive frame looking crumpled until he started twitching electrically, and I saw the head wound.

"No," I shouted, becoming fully alert, and stumbling over to his side.

Sampson's eyes were rolled up in his head and quivering. I grabbed the radio on the floor beyond him, hit the transmitter, and said, "This is Detective Alex Cross. Ten-Zero-Zero. Repeat. Officer down. Monroe Avenue and 12th, Northeast. St. Anthony's Catholic School kitchen. Multiple shots fired. Ten-Fifty-Twos needed immediately. Repeat. Multiple ambulances needed, and a Life Flight for officer with head wound!"

"We have ambulances and patrols on their way, Detective," the dispatcher came back. "ETA twenty seconds. I'll call Life Flight. Do you have the shooter?"

"No, damn it. Make the Life Flight call."

The line went dead. I lowered the radio. Only then did I look back at the best friend I've ever had, the first kid I met after Nana Mama brought me up from South Carolina, the man I'd grown up with, the partner I'd relied on more times than I could count. The spasms subsided and Sampson's eyes glazed over and he gasped.

"John," I said, kneeling beside him and taking his hand. "Hold on now. Cavalry's coming."

He seemed not to hear, just stared vacantly past me toward the wall.

I started to cry. I couldn't stop. I shook from head to toe, and then I wanted to shoot the man who'd done this. I wanted to shoot him twenty times, completely destroy the creature that had risen from the dead.

Sirens closed in on the school from six directions. I wiped at my tears, and then squeezed Sampson's hand, before forcing myself to my feet and back out into the cafeteria, where the first patrol officers were charging in, followed by a pair of EMTs whose shoulders were flecked with melting snowflakes.

They got Sampson's head immobilized, then put him on a board and then a gurney. He was under blankets and moving in less than six minutes. It was snowing hard outside. They waited inside the front door to the school for the helicopter to come, and put IV lines into his wrists.

Sampson went into another convulsion. The parish priest, Father Fred Close, came and gave my partner the last rites.

But my man was still hanging on when the helicopter came. In a daze I followed them out into a driving snowstorm. We had to shield our eyes to duck under the blinding propeller wash and get Sampson aboard.

"We'll take it from here!" one EMT shouted at me.

"There's not a chance I'm leaving his side," I said, climbed in beside the pilot, and pulled on the extra helmet. "Let's go."

The pilot waited until they had the rear doors shut and the gurney strapped down before throttling up the helicopter. We began to rise, and it was only then that I saw through the swirling snow that crowds were forming beyond the barricades set up in a perimeter around the school and church complex.

We pivoted in the air and flew back up over 12th Street, rising above the crowd. I looked down through the spiraling snow and saw everyone ducking their heads from the helicopter wash. Everyone except for a single male face looking directly up at the Life Flight, not caring about the battering, stinging snow.

"That's him!" I said.

"Detective?" the pilot said, his voice crackling over the radio in my helmet.

I tugged down the microphone, and said, "How do I talk to dispatch?"

The pilot leaned over, and flipped a switch.

"This is Detective Alex Cross," I said. "Who's the supervising detective heading to St. Anthony's?"

"Your wife. Chief Stone."

"Patch me through to her."

Five seconds passed as we built speed and hurtled toward the hospital.

"Alex?" Bree said. "What's happened?"

"John's hit bad, Bree," I said. "I'm with him. Close off that school from four blocks in every direction. Order a door-to-door search. I just saw the shooter on 12th, a block west of the school."

"Description?"

"It's Gary Soneji, Bree," I said. "Get his picture off Google and send it to every cop in the area."

There was silence on the line before Bree said sympathetically, "Alex, are *you* okay? Gary Soneji's been dead for years."

"If he's dead, then I just saw a ghost."

CHAPTER
4

WE WERE BUFFETED BY winds and faced near-whiteout conditions trying to land on the helipad atop George Washington Medical Center. In the end we put down in the parking lot by the ER entrance, where a team of nurses and doctors met us.

They hustled Sampson inside and got him attached to monitors while Dr. Christopher Kalhorn, a neurosurgeon, swabbed aside some of the blood and examined the head wounds.

The bullet had entered Sampson's skull at a shallow angle about two inches above the bridge of his nose. It exited forward of his left temple. That second wound was about the size of a marble, but gaping and ragged, as if the bullet had been a hollow point that broke up and shattered going through bone.

"Let's get him intubated, on Propofol, and into an ice bath and cooling helmet," Kalhorn said. "Take his temp down to ninety-two, get him into a CT scanner, and then the OR. I'll have a team waiting for him."

The ER doctors and nurses sprang into action. In short order, they had a breathing tube down Sampson's throat and were racing him away. Kalhorn turned to leave. I showed my badge and stopped him.

"That's my brother," I said. "What do I tell his wife?"

Dr. Kalhorn turned grim. "You tell her we'll do everything possible to save him. And you tell her to pray. You, too, Detective."

"What are his chances?"

"Pray," he said, took off in a trot, and disappeared.

I was left standing in an empty treatment slot in the ER, looking down at the dark blood that stained the gauze pads they'd used to clean Sampson's head.

"You can't stay in here, Detective," one of the nurses said sympathetically. "We need the space. Traffic accidents all over the city with this storm."

I nodded, turned, and wandered away, wondering where to go, what to do.

I went out in the ER waiting area and saw twenty people in the seats. They stared at my pistol, at the blood on my shirt, and at the black hole where Soneji's bullet had hit me. I didn't care what they thought. I didn't—

I heard the automatic doors *whoosh* open behind me. A fearful voice cried out, "Alex?"

I swung around. Billie Sampson was standing there in pink hospital scrub pants and a down coat, shaking from head to toe from the cold and the threat of something far more bitter. "How bad is it?"

Billie's a surgical nurse, so there was no point in being vague. I described the wound. Her hand flew to her mouth at first, but then she shook her head. "It's bad. He's lucky to be alive."

I hugged her and said, "He's a strong man. But he's going to need your prayers. He's going to need all our prayers."

Billie's strength gave way. She began to moan and sob into my chest, and I held her tighter. When I raised my head, the people in the waiting room were looking on in concern.

"Let's get out of here," I muttered, and led Billie out into the hallway and to the chapel.

We went inside, and thankfully it was empty. I got Billie calmed down enough to tell her what had happened at the school and afterward.

"They've put him into a chemical coma and are supercooling his body."

"To reduce swelling and bleeding," she said, nodding.

"And the neurosurgeons here are the best. He's in their hands now."

"And God's," Billie said, staring at the cross on the wall in the chapel before pulling away from me to go down on her knees.

I joined her and we held hands and begged our savior for mercy.

CHAPTER
5

HOURS PASSED LIKE DAYS as we waited outside the surgical unit. Bree showed up before noon.

"Anything?" she asked.

I shook my head.

"Billie," Bree said, hugging her. "We're going to find who did this to John. I promise you that."

"You didn't find Soneji?" I asked in disbelief. "How could he have gotten away if you'd cordoned off the area?"

My wife looked over at me, studied me. "Soneji's dead, Alex. You all but killed him yourself."

My mouth hung open, and I blinked several times. "You mean you didn't send his picture out? You didn't look for him?"

"We looked for someone who looked like Soneji," Bree said defensively.

"No," I said. "He was less than thirty feet from me, light shining down on his face. It was him."

"Then explain how a man who all but disintegrated right before your eyes can surface more than a decade later," Bree said.

"I can't explain it," I said. "I...maybe I need some coffee. Want some?"

They shook their heads, and I got up, heading toward the hospital cafeteria, seeing flashbacks from long ago.

I put Gary Soneji in prison after he went on a kidnapping and murder spree that threatened my family. Soneji escaped several years later, and turned to bomb building. He detonated several, killing multiple people before we spotted him in New York City. We chased Soneji into Grand Central Station, where we feared he'd explode another bomb. Instead he grabbed a baby.

At one point, Soneji held the baby up and screamed at me, "This doesn't end here, Cross. I'm coming for you, even from the grave if I have to."

Then he threw the infant at us. Someone caught her, but Soneji escaped into the vast abandoned tunnel system below Manhattan. We tracked him in there. Soneji attacked me in the darkness, and knocked me down and almost killed me before I was able to shoot him. The bullet shattered his jaw, ripped apart his tongue, and blew out the side of one cheek.

Soneji staggered away from me, was swallowed by the darkness. He must have pitched forward then and sprawled on the rocky tunnel floor. The impact set off a small bomb in his pocket. The tunnel exploded into white-hot flames.

When I got to him, Soneji was engulfed, curled up, and screaming. It lasted several seconds before he stopped. I stood there and watched Soneji burn. I saw him shrivel up and turn coal black.

But as sure as I was of that memory, I was also sure I'd seen Gary Soneji that morning, a split second before he tried to shoot me in the heart and blow Sampson's head off.

I'm coming for you, even from the grave if I have to.

Soneji's taunt echoed back to me after I'd gotten my coffee.

After several sips, I decided I had to assume Soneji was still dead. So I'd seen, what, a double? An impostor?

I supposed it was possible with plastic surgery, but the likeness had been so dead-on, from the thin reddish mustache to the wispy hair to the crazed, amused expression.

It was him, I thought. *But how?*

This doesn't end here, Cross.

I saw Soneji so clearly then that I feared for my sanity.

This doesn't end here, Cross.

I'm coming for you, even from the grave if I have to.

CHAPTER
6

"ALEX?"

I startled, almost dropped my coffee, and saw Bree trotting down the hall toward me with a wary expression.

"He made it through the operation," she said. "He's in intensive care, and the doctor's going to talk to Billie in a few moments."

We both held Billie's hands when Dr. Kalhorn finally emerged. He looked drained.

"How is he?" Billie asked, after introducing herself.

"Your husband's a remarkable fighter," Kalhorn said. "He died once on the table, but rallied. Besides the trauma of the bullet, there were bone and bullet fragments we had to deal with. Three quarters of an inch left and one of those fragments would have caught a major artery, and we'd be having a different conversation."

"So he's going to live?" Billie asked.

"I can't promise you that," Kalhorn said. "The next forty-eight to seventy-two hours will be the most critical time for him. He's sustained a massive head injury, severe trauma to his upper-left temporal lobe. For now, we're keeping him in a medically induced coma, and we will keep him that way until we see a significant drop in brain swelling."

"If he comes out, what's the prognosis, given the extent of the injury you saw?" I asked.

"I can't tell you who he'll be if and when he wakes up," the neurosurgeon said. "That's up to God."

"Can we see him?" Bree asked.

"Give it a half hour," Kalhorn said. "There's a whirlwind around him at the moment. Lots of good people supporting him."

"Thank you, Doctor," Billie said, trying not to cry again. "For saving him."

"It was an honor," Kalhorn said, patted her on the arm, and smiled at Bree and me before returning to the ICU.

"Damage to his upper-left temporal lobe," Billie said.

"He's alive," I said. "Let's keep focused on that. Anything else, we'll deal with down the road."

Bree held her hand and said, "Alex is right. We've prayed him through surgery, and now we'll pray he wakes up."

But Billie still appeared uncertain forty minutes later when we donned surgical masks, gloves, and smocks and entered the room where Sampson lay.

You could barely see the slits of his eyes for the swelling. His head was wrapped in a turban of gauze, and there were so many tubes going into him, and so many monitors and devices beeping and clicking around him, that from the waist up he looked more machine than man.

"Oh, Jesus, John," Billie said when she got to his side. "What have they done to you?"

Bree rubbed Billie's back as tears wracked her again. I stayed only a few minutes, until I couldn't take seeing Sampson like that anymore.

"I'll be back," I told them. "Tonight before I go home to sleep."

"Where are you going?" Bree asked.

"To hunt Soneji," I said. "It's what John would want."

"There's a blizzard outside," Bree said. "And Internal Affairs is going to want to hear your report on the shooting."

"I don't give a damn about IA right now," I said, walking toward the door. "And a blizzard's exactly the kind of chaotic situation that Gary Soneji lives for."

Bree wasn't happy, but sighed and gestured to a shopping bag she'd brought with her. "You'll need your coat, hat, and gloves if you're going Soneji-hunting."

CHAPTER
7

OUTSIDE A BLIZZARD WAILED, a classic nor'easter with driving wet snow that was already eight inches deep. It takes only four inches to snarl Washington, DC, so completely that there's talk of bringing in the National Guard.

Georgetown was a parking lot. I trudged to the Foggy Bottom Metro station, ignoring my freezing-cold feet, and reliving old times with big John Sampson. I met him within days of moving up to DC with my brothers after my mother died and my father, her killer, disappeared, presumed dead.

John lived with his mother and sister. His father had died in Vietnam. We were in the same fifth-grade class. He was ten years old and big, even then. But so was I.

It made for a natural rivalry, and we didn't much care for each other at first. I was faster than him, which he did not like. He was stronger than me, which I did not like. The inevitable fight we had was a draw.

We were suspended for three days for fighting. Nana Mama marched me down to Sampson's house to apologize to him and to his mother for throwing the first punch.

I went unhappily. When Sampson came to the door equally annoyed, I saw the split lip and bruising around his right cheek and smiled. He saw the swelling around both of my eyes and smiled back.

We'd both inflicted damage. We both had won. And that was that. End of the war, and start of the longest friendship of my life.

I took the Metro across town, and walked back to St. Anthony's in the snow, trying to will myself not to remember Sampson in the ICU, more machine than man. But the image kept returning, and every time it did, I felt weaker, as if a part of me were dying.

There were still Metro police cars parked in front of the school, and two television trucks. I pulled the wool hat down and turned up the collar of my jacket. I didn't want to talk to any reporters about this case. Ever.

I showed my badge to the patrolman standing inside the front door, and started back toward the cafeteria and kitchen.

Father Close appeared at his office door. He recognized me.

"Your partner?"

"There's brain damage, but he's alive," I said.

"Another miracle, then," Father Close said. "Sister Mary Elliott and Theresa Ball, the cook, they're still alive as well. You saved them, Dr. Cross. If you hadn't been there, I fear all three of them would be dead."

"I don't think that's true," I said. "But thank you for saying so."

"Any idea when I can have my cafeteria and kitchen back?"

"I'll ask the crime-scene specialists, but figure tomorrow your students bring a bag lunch and eat in their homerooms. When it's a cop-involved shooting, the forensics folks are sticklers for detail."

"As they should be," Father Close said, thanked me again, and returned to his office.

I returned to the cafeteria and stood there a moment in the empty space, hearing voices in the kitchen, but recalling the first shots and how I'd reacted.

I went to the swinging industrial doors and did the same. We'd done it by the book, I decided, and pushed through them again.

I glanced at where the cook and nun had lain wounded, and then over where Sampson had lain dying before turning my attention to the pantry. This was where the book had been thrown out. In retrospect, we should have cleared the rest of the building before tending to the wounded. But it looked like femoral blood and...

Three crime-scene techs were still at work in the kitchen. Barbara Hatfield, an old friend, was in the pantry. She spotted me and came right over.

"How's John, Alex?"

"Hanging on," I said.

"Everyone's shaken up," Hatfield said. "And there's something you should see, something I was going to call you about later."

She led me into the pantry, floor-to-ceiling shelves loaded with foodstuffs and kitchen supplies, and a big shiny commercial freezer at the far end.

The words spray-painted in two lines across the face of the fridge stopped me dead in my tracks.

"Right?" Hatfield said. "I did the same thing."

CHAPTER
8

I WAS UP AT four o'clock the following morning, snuck out of bed without waking Bree, and on three hours of sleep went back to doing what I'd been doing. I got a cup of coffee and went up to the third floor, to my home office, where I had been going through my files on Gary Soneji.

I keep files on all the bad ones, but Soneji had the thickest file, six of them, in fact, all bulging. I'd left off at one in the morning with notes taken midway through the kidnapping of the US secretary of the treasury's son, and the daughter of a famous actress.

I tried to focus, tried to re-master the details. But I yawned after two paragraphs, drank coffee, and thought of John Sampson.

But only briefly. I decided that sitting by his side helped him little. I was better off looking for the man who put a bullet through John's head. So I read and reread, and noted dangling threads, abandoned lines of inquiry that Sampson and I had followed over the years but which had led nowhere.

After an hour, I found an old genealogy chart we and the US marshals put together on Soneji's family after he escaped prison. Scanning it, I realized we'd let the marshals handle the pure fugitive hunt. I saw several names and relations I'd never talked to before, and wrote them down.

I ran their names through Google, and saw that two of them were still living at the addresses noted on the chart. How long had it been? Thirteen, fourteen years?

Then again, Nana Mama and I had lived in our house on 5th for more than thirty years. Americans do put down roots once in a while.

I glanced at my watch, saw it was past five, and wondered when I could try to make a few calls. No, I thought then, this kind of thing is best done in person. But the storm. I went to the window in the dormer of the office, pushed it up, and looked outside.

To my surprise, it was pouring rain and considerably warmer. Most of the snow was gone. That sealed it. I was going for a drive as soon as it was light enough to see.

Returning to my desk, I thought about going back downstairs to take a shower, but feared waking Bree. Her job as Metro's chief of detectives was stressful enough without dealing with the additional pressure of a cop shooting.

I tried to go back to the Soneji files, but instead called up a picture on my computer. I'd taken it the afternoon before. It showed the fridge and the spray-painted words the shooter had left behind.

CROSS KILL
Long Live Soneji!

I had obviously been the target. And why not? Soneji hated me as much as I hated him.

Had Soneji expected Sampson to be with me? The two pistols he'd fired said yes. I closed my eyes and saw him there in the doorway, arms crossed, left gun aimed at me, right gun at Sampson.

Something bothered me. I turned back to the file,

rummaged around until I confirmed my memory. Soneji was left-handed, which explained why he'd crossed his arms to shoot. He was aiming at me with his better hand. He'd wanted me dead no matter what happened to John.

It was why Soneji shot for center of mass, I decided, and wondered whether his shot at Sampson was misaimed, if he'd clipped John's head in error.

Left-handed. It had to be Soneji. But it couldn't be Soneji.

In frustration, I shut the computer off, grabbed my notes, and snuck back into the bedroom. I shut the bathroom door without making a peep. After showering and dressing, I tried to get out light-footed, but made a floorboard squeak.

"I'm up, quiet as a mouse," Bree said.

"I'm going to New Jersey," I said.

"What?" she said, sitting up in bed and turning on the light. "Why?"

"To talk to some of Soneji's relatives, see if he's been in touch."

Bree shook her head. "He's dead, Alex."

"But what if the explosion I saw in the tunnel was *caused* by Soneji as he went by some bum living down there?" I said. "What if I didn't see Soneji burn?"

"You never did DNA on the remains?"

"There was no need. I saw him die. I identified him, so no one checked."

"Jesus, Alex," Bree said. "Is that possible? What did the shooter's face look like?"

"Like Soneji's," I said, frustrated.

"Well, did his jaw look like Soneji's? His tongue? Did he say anything?"

"He didn't say a word, but his face?" I frowned and thought about that. "I don't know."

"You said the light was good. You said you saw him clearly."

Was the light that good? Feeling a little wobbly, I nevertheless closed my eyes, trying to bring more of the memory back and into sharper focus.

I saw Soneji standing there in the pantry doorway, arms crossed, chin tucked, and...looking directly at me. He shot at Sampson without even aiming. It *was* me he'd wanted to kill.

What about his jaw? I replayed memory again and again before I saw it.

"There was something there," I said, running my fingers along my left jawline.

"A shadow?" Bree said.

I shook my head. "More like a scar."

CHAPTER
9

THREE HOURS LATER, I'D left I-95 for Route 29, which parallels the Delaware River. Heading upstream, I soon realized that I was not far from East Amwell Township, where the aviator Charles Lindbergh's baby was kidnapped in 1932.

Gary Soneji had been obsessed with the Lindbergh case. He'd studied it in preparing for the kidnappings of the treasury secretary's son, the late Michael Goldberg, and Maggie Rose Dunne, the daughter of a famous actress.

I'd noticed before on a map the proximity of East Amwell to Rosemont, where Soneji grew up. But it wasn't until I pulled through the tiny unincorporated settlement that I realized Soneji had spent his early life less than five miles from the Lindbergh kidnapping site.

Rosemont itself was quaint and leafy, with rock walls giving way to sopping green fields.

I tried to imagine Soneji as a boy in this rural setting, tried to see him discovering the crime of the century. He wouldn't have cared much for the police detectives who'd worked the Lindbergh case. No, Soneji would have obsessed on the information surrounding Bruno Hauptmann, the career criminal convicted and executed for taking the toddler and caving in his skull.

My mind was flooded with memories of going into Soneji's apartment for the first time, seeing what was essentially a shrine to Hauptmann and the Lindbergh case. In writings we found back then, Soneji had fantasized about being Hauptmann in the days just before the killer was caught, when the whole world was fixated and speculating on the mystery he'd set in motion.

"Audacious criminals change history," Soneji wrote. "Audacious criminals are remembered long after they're gone, which is more than can be said of the detectives who chase them."

I found the address on the Rosemont Ringoes Road, and pulled over on the shoulder beyond the drive. The storm had ebbed to sprinkles when I climbed out in front of a gray-and-white clapboard cottage set back in pines.

The yard was sparse and littered with wet pine needles. The front stoop was cracked and listed to one side, so I had to hold on to the iron railing in order to ring the bell.

A few moments later, one of the curtains fluttered. A few moments after that, the door swung open, revealing a bald man in his seventies. He leaned over a walker and had an oxygen line running into his nose.

"Peter Soneji?"

"What do you want?"

"I'm Alex Cross. I'm a—"

"I know who you are," Gary Soneji's father snapped icily. "My son's killer."

"He blew himself up."

"So you've said."

"Can I talk to you, sir?"

"Sir?" Peter Soneji said and laughed caustically. "Now it's 'sir'?"

"Far as I know, you never had anything to do with your son's criminal career," I said.

"Tell that to the reporters who've shown up at my door over the years," Soneji's father said. "The things they've accused me of. Father to a monster."

"I'm not accusing you of anything, *Mr. Soneji,*" I said. "I'm simply looking for your take on a few loose ends."

"With everything on the internet about Gary, you'd think there'd be no loose ends."

"These are questions from my personal files," I said.

Soneji's father gave me a long, considered look before saying, "Leave it alone, Detective. Gary's long dead. Far as I'm concerned, good riddance."

He tried to shut the door in my face, but I stopped him.

"I can call the sheriff," Peter Soneji protested.

"Just one question and then I'll leave," I said. "How did Gary become obsessed with the Lindbergh kidnapping?"

CHAPTER
10

TWO HOURS LATER AS I drove through the outskirts of Crumpton, Maryland, I was still wrestling with the answer Soneji's father had given me. It seemed to offer new insight into his son, but I still couldn't explain how or why yet.

I found the second address. The farmhouse had once been a cheery yellow, but the paint was peeling and streaked with dark mold. Every window was encased in the kind of iron barring you see in big cities.

As I walked across the front yard toward the porch, I stirred up several pigeons, flushing them from the dead weeds. I heard a weird voice talking somewhere behind the house.

The porch was dominated by several old machine tools, lathes and such, that I had to step around in order to knock at a steel door with triple dead bolts.

I knocked a second time, and was thinking I should go around the house where I'd heard the odd voice. But then the dead bolts were thrown one by one.

The door opened, revealing a dark-haired woman in her forties, with a sharp nose and dull brown eyes. She wore a grease-stained one-piece Carhartt canvas coverall, and carried at port arms an AR-style rifle with a big banana clip.

"Salesman, you are standing on my property uninvited," she said. "I have ample cause to shoot you where you stand."

I showed her my badge and ID, said, "I'm not a salesman. I'm a cop. I should have called ahead, but I didn't have a number."

Instead of calming her down, that only got her more agitated. "What are the police doing at sweet Ginny Winslow's door? Looking to persecute a gun lover?"

"I just want to ask you a few questions, Mrs. Soneji," I said.

Soneji's widow flinched at the name, and turned spitting mad. "My name's been legally changed to Virginia Winslow going on seven years now, and I still can't get the stench of Gary off my skin. What's your name? Who are you with?"

"Alex Cross," I said. "With DC…"

She hardened, said, "I know you now. I remember you from TV."

"Yes, ma'am."

"You never came to talk with me. Just them US marshals. Like I didn't even exist."

"I'm here to talk now," I said.

"Ten years too late. Get the hell off my property before I embrace my Second Amendment rights and—"

"I saw Gary's father this morning," I said. "He told me how Gary's obsession with the Lindbergh kidnapping began."

She knitted her brows. "How's that?"

"Gary's dad said when Gary was eight they were in a used book store, and while his father was wandering in the stacks, his son found a tattered copy of *True Detective Mysteries,* a crime magazine from the 1930s, and sat down to read it."

Finger still on the trigger of her semiautomatic rifle, Virginia Winslow shrugged. "So what?"

"When Mr. Soneji found Gary, his son was sitting on the floor in the bookstore, the magazine in his lap, and staring in fascination at a picture from the Lindbergh baby's autopsy that showed the head wound in lurid detail."

She stared at me with her jaw slack, as if remembering something that frightened and appalled her.

"What is it?" I asked.

Soneji's widow hardened again. "Nothing. Doesn't surprise me. I used to catch him looking at autopsy pictures. He was always saying he was going to write a book and needed to look at them for research."

"You didn't believe him?"

"I believed him until my brother Charles noticed that Gary was always volunteering to gut deer they killed," she said. "Charles told me Gary liked to put his hands in the warm innards, said he liked the feeling, and told me how Gary'd get all bright and glowing when he was doing it."

CHAPTER
11

"I DIDN'T KNOW THAT about Gary, either," I said.

"What's this all about?" Virginia Winslow asked, studying me now.

"There was a cop shooting in DC," I said. "A man who fit Gary's description was the shooter."

I expected Soneji's widow to respond with total skepticism. But instead she looked frightened and appalled again.

"Gary's dead," she said. "*You* killed him, didn't you?"

"He killed himself," I said. "Detonated the bomb he was carrying."

Her attention flitted to the boards. "That's not what the internet is saying."

"What's the internet saying?"

"That Gary's alive," she said. "Our son, Dylan, said he's seen it online. Gary's dead, isn't he? Please tell me that."

The way she clenched the rifle told me she needed to hear it, so I said, "As far as I know, Gary Soneji's dead and has been dead for more than ten years. But someone who looked an awful lot like him shot my partner yesterday."

"What?" she said. "No."

"It's not him," I said. "I'm almost certain."

"Almost?" she said before a phone started ringing back in the house.

"I...I have to get that," she said. "Work."

"What kind of work?"

"I'm a machinist and gunsmith," she said. "My father taught me the trade."

She shut the door before I could comment. The bolts were thrown one by one.

I almost left, but then, remembering that voice I'd heard on my way in, I went around the farmhouse, seeing a small, neglected barn around which dozens of pigeons were flying.

I heard someone talking in the barn, and walked over.

Click-a-t-clack. Click-a-t-clack.

Pigeons started and whirled out the barn door.

There was a grimy window. I went to it, and peeked inside, seeing through the dirt sixteen-year-old Dylan Winslow standing there by a large pigeon coop, gazing off into space.

Dylan looked nothing like his father. He had his mother's naturally dark hair, sharp nose, and the same dull brown eyes. He was borderline obese, with hardly a chin, more a draping of his cheeks that joined a wattle above his Adam's apple.

"You need to learn your place," he said to no one. "You need to learn to be quiet. Emotional control. It's the key to a happy life."

Then he turned and walked by the pigeon coop, running a hoop of keys across the metal mesh.

Click-a-t-clack. Click-a-t-clack.

The sound rattled the pigeons and they battered themselves against their cages.

"Be quiet now," Dylan said firmly. "You got to learn some control."

Then he pivoted and started toward me, raking the cages again.

Click-a-t-clack. Click-a-t-clack.

A disturbing little smile showed on the teen's face, and there was even more upsetting delight in his eyes. I have a PhD in criminal psychology and have studied serial killers in depth. Many of them grew up torturing animals for sport.

Had Dylan's father?

I stepped inside the barn. Gary Soneji's son had his back to me again, walking away while raking the front of the cages.

Click-a-t-clack. Click-a-t-clack.

I took another two steps and noticed a large piece of cardboard nailed to one of the barn's support posts.

There was a well-used paper target taped to the cardboard and six darts sticking out of it. The target featured a bull's-eye superimposed over a man's face. It had been used so many times that at first I didn't know who the man was.

Then I did.

"Who the hell are you?" Dylan said, and then gaped when I faced him.

"From the looks of it," I said, "I'm your dartboard."

CHAPTER
12

DYLAN WINSLOW PURSED HIS lips in long-simmering anger, said, "If Mama would let me, I'd use one of her shotguns on it instead of darts."

What do you say to the disturbed son of the disturbed criminal you shot in the face and watched burn?

"I can understand your feelings," I said.

"No, you can't," he said, sneering. "This an official visit, Detective Alex Cross?"

"As a matter of fact," I said. "A man fitting your dead father's description shot my partner in the head last night."

Dylan's sneer disappeared, replaced by widening eyes and that disturbing, delighted grin I'd seen earlier. "It's true, then, what they're saying."

"What are they saying?"

"That you didn't get my dad," Dylan said. "That he escaped the tunnels, badly wounded, but alive, and is still alive. Is that what you're telling me, too?"

There seemed so much hope in his face that, whether he was in need of psychological help or not, I didn't want to destroy it.

"If it wasn't your father who shot my partner, it was his twin."

Dylan started to laugh. He laughed so hard there were tears in his eyes.

Thumping his chest, he said, "I knew it! I felt it right here."

When he stopped, I said, "What do you think is going to happen? That he's going to suddenly appear to rescue you?"

Dylan acted as if I'd read his thoughts, but then shot back, "He will. You watch. And there's nothing you can do about it. It's like they say—Dad was always smarter than you. More patient and cunning than you."

Rather than defend myself, I said, "You're right. Your father was smarter than me, and more patient, and more cunning."

"He still is. They say so on the internet."

"What site?" I asked.

Dylan gave me that disturbing smile again before saying, "One you can't get at in a million years, Cross." He laughed. "Never in a million years."

"Really?" I said. "How about I march back up to your mother and tell her I'm coming back with a search warrant for every computer in your house?"

Dylan's grin stretched wider. "Go ahead. We don't have one."

"How about every computer in your school, in the local library, in every place your mother says you get online?"

I thought that would rock him, but it didn't.

"Knock yourself out," he said. "But unless I have a lawyer present, I am done answering your questions, and I have pigeons to feed."

Or torture, I almost said.

But I bit back the urge, and turned to leave, calling over my shoulder, "Nice to meet you, Dylan. Wonderful getting to know the son of an old enemy."

CHAPTER
13

IT WAS PAST SIX when I finally reached the ICU at GW Medical Center. The nurse at the station said Sampson's vitals had been irregular most of the day, and there'd been little if any reduction in brain swelling.

"You sick in any way?" the nurse asked.

"Not that I'm aware of. Why?"

"Protocol. The shunt draining the wound is an open track straight to the inside of your friend's healing skull. Any kind of infection could be catastrophic."

"I feel fine," I said, and put on the gown, mask, and gloves.

When I pushed open the door, Billie stirred awake in her reclining chair.

"Alex? That you?"

"The man behind the mask."

"Tell me about it," she said, getting up to hug me. "I've been wearing one the past forty hours and I'm getting rubbed raw."

"His vitals?"

Billie scanned the monitors attached to her husband and said, "Not bad at the moment, but his blood pressure took a short, scary dive about four hours ago. I was thinking stroke until he just kind of came up out of it."

"They say talking to people in comas helps," I said.

"Stimulates the brain," she said, nodding. "But that's usually with a non-induced coma, when there aren't drugs involved."

"All the same," I said, and went to Sampson's side.

"I'll be a few minutes," Billie said.

"Be right here until you get back," I said.

When she'd gone out, I held Sampson's giant hand and gave him an account of the day's investigation, sparing him no detail. It felt good and familiar, and right, to talk it out with him, as if Sampson were not drugged down to the reptilian part of his brain, but acute and thoughtful and funny as hell.

"That's it," I said. "And, yes, I want another crack at Soneji's widow and kid before long."

The door opened. Billie stepped back inside, and then several of the monitors around Sampson began to squawk in alarm.

A team burst in. I was pushed to the corner with Billie.

"It's his blood pressure again," Billie said in a wavering voice. "Jesus, I don't know if his heart can take this much longer."

Ninety seconds later, the crisis passed and his vitals improved.

"I don't know what happened," I said, bewildered. "I was telling him about the investigation and…"

"What?" Billie said. "Why did you do that?"

"Because he'd want to know."

"No," she said, shaking her head. "That's done. That's over, Alex."

"What's over?"

"His career as a cop," Billie said. "No matter how he recovers, that part of John's life is over if he wants to continue to be my husband."

"John loves being a cop," I said.

"I know he does...did...but that's over," Billie said sharply. "I will care for him, and defend John until the day one of us dies, but between now and then, his days carrying a gun and a badge are behind him."

CHAPTER
14

"SHE'S GOT THE RIGHT to demand that," Bree said later in the hospital cafeteria. "John took a bullet to the head, Alex."

"I know," I said, frustrated and heartsick.

It felt like part of John had died and was never coming back. And it would never be the same between us, as partners anyway. That was dead, too.

I explained this to Bree, and she put her hands on mine and said, "You'll never have a better friend than John Sampson. That friendship, that fierce bond you two have, will never be broken, even if he's no longer a cop, even if he's no longer your partner. Okay?"

"No," I said, pushing my plate away. "But I'll have to learn to live with it."

"You haven't eaten three bites," Bree said, gesturing at the plate.

"No appetite," I said.

"Then force yourself," Bree said. "Especially the protein. Your brain has to be tip-top if you're going to find Soneji."

I laughed softly. "You're always looking out for me."

"Every moment I can, baby."

I ate quite a bit more, and washed it down with three full glasses of water.

"Not quite Nana Mama's cooking," I said.

"I'm sure there'll be leftovers," Bree said.

"You trying to get me fat?" I said.

"I like a little cushion."

I didn't know what to say to that, and we both burst out laughing. Then I looked over and saw Billie standing in the doorway, watching us with bitterness and longing in her expression. She turned and left.

"Should I go after her?" I asked.

"No," Bree said. "I'll talk to her tomorrow."

"Home?"

"Home."

We left the hospital and were crossing a triangular plaza to the Foggy Bottom Metro station when the first shot rang out.

I heard the flat crack of the muzzle blast. I felt the bullet rip past my left ear, grabbed Bree, and yanked her to the ground by two newspaper boxes. People were screaming and scattering.

"Where is he?" Bree said.

"I don't know," I said, before the second and third shots shattered the glass of one newspaper rack and *ping*ed off another.

Then I heard squealing tires, and jumped up in time to see a white panel van roar north on 23rd Street, Northwest, heading toward Washington Circle, and a dozen different escape routes. As the van flashed past us, I caught a glimpse of the driver.

Gary Soneji was looking my way as if posing for a mental picture, grinning like a lunatic and holding his right-hand thumb up, index finger extended, like a gun he was aiming right at me.

I was so shocked that another instant passed before I started running across the plaza to 23rd, trying to get a look at his license plates. But his plate lights were dark, and the van soon disappeared into evening traffic, headed in the direction of whatever hellhole Gary Soneji was calling home these days.

"Did you see him?" I asked Bree, who was shaken, but calling in the shots to dispatch.

She shook her head after she'd finished. "You did?"

"It was him, Bree. Gary Soneji in the flesh. As if he hadn't been blown up and burned, as if he hadn't spent the past decade in a box under six feet of dirt."

CHAPTER
15

THE NEXT MORNING, I called GW to check on Sampson. His vitals had destabilized again.

Part of me said, *Go to the hospital,* but instead I drove out to Quantico, Virginia, and the FBI Lab.

For almost seven years, I worked for the Bureau in the behavioral science department as a full-time consultant and left on good terms. I have many friends who still work at Quantico, including my old partner, Ned Mahoney.

I called ahead, and he met me at the gate, made sure I got the VIP treatment clearing security.

"What are friends in high places for?" Mahoney asked when I thanked him. "How's John?"

I gave him a brief update on Sampson and my investigation.

"How could Soneji be alive?" Mahoney said. "I was there, remember? I saw him burning, too. It was him."

"Then who was the guy who shot Sampson and tried to shoot me last night?" I said. "Because both times I've seen him, my brain has screamed *Soneji!* Both times."

"Hey, hey, Alex," Mahoney said, patting me on the shoulder out of concern. "Take a big breath. If it's him, we'll help you find him."

I took several deep, long breaths, trying to keep my

thoughts from whirling, and said, "Let's start with the cybercrime unit."

Ten minutes later, we went through an unmarked door into a large space filled with low-walled cubicles that were in a soft blue light Mahoney said was supposed to increase productivity. There were three, sometimes four computer screens at every workstation.

"The only thing that separates the IT brainpower in this room from a company like Google is the dress code," Mahoney said.

"No Ping-Pong, either," I said.

"There's agitation in that direction," Mahoney said, weaving through the cubicles.

"Any chance it happens?"

"When the Bureau starts admitting J. Edgar preferred panties," he said, and then stopped in front of a workstation in the middle of the room.

"Agent Batra?" Mahoney said. "I want to introduce you to Alex Cross."

A petite Indian woman in her late twenties in a conservative blue suit and black pumps spun around from one of four screens at her station. She stood quickly and put out her hand, so small it felt like a doll's.

"Special Agent Henna Batra," she said. "An honor to meet you, Dr. Cross."

"And you as well."

"Agent Batra is said to be at one with the internet," Mahoney said. "If anyone can help you, she can. Stop by the office on your way out, Alex."

"Will do," I said.

"So," Agent Batra said, sitting again. "What are you looking for?"

"A website where there are active conversations going on concerning Gary Soneji."

"I know that case," Batra said. "We studied it at the academy. He's dead."

"Evidently his admirers don't think so, and I'd like to see what they're saying about Soneji. I was warned we'd never find the site in a million years."

With Special Agent Batra navigating the web via a link to a supercomputer, the search took all of fourteen minutes.

"Quite a few that mention Soneji," Batra said, gesturing at the screen, and then scrolling down before tapping on a link. "But I'm betting this is the one you're looking for."

I squinted to read the link. "ZRXQT?"

"Anonymous, or at least attempting anonymity," Batra said. "And it's locked and encrypted. But I ran a filter that picked up traces of commands going into and out of that website. The density of Soneji mentions in those traces is through the roof compared to every other site that talks about him."

"You can't get in?"

"I didn't say that," Batra said, as if I'd insulted her. "You drink tea?"

"Coffee," I said.

She gestured across the room. "There's a break room over there. If you'd be so kind as to bring me some hot tea, Dr. Cross. I should be able to get inside by the time you come back."

I thought it was kind of funny that Batra had started the conversation as my subordinate and was now ordering me around. Then again, I hadn't a clue about how she was doing what she was doing. Then again, she was at one with the internet.

"Oolong?" I asked.

"Fine," Batra said, already engrossed in her work.

I found the coffee and the tea, but when I returned, she was still typing.

"Got it?"

"Not yet," she said, irritated. "It's sophisticated, mul-tilevel, and..."

Lines of code began to fill the page. Batra seemed to speed-read the code as it rolled by, because, after twenty seconds of this, she said, "Oh, of course."

She gave the computer another command, and a homepage appeared, featuring a cement wall in some abandoned building. Across the wall in dripping black graffiti letters, it read *Long Live The Soneji!*

CHAPTER
16

I WON'T BORE YOU with a page-by-page description of the www.thesoneji.net website. There may be archives of it still up on the internet for those interested.

For those of you less inclined to explore the dark side of the web, it's enough to know that Gary Soneji had developed a cult of personality in the decade since I'd seen him burn, hundreds of digital devotees who worshipped him with the kind of fervor I'd previously assigned to Appalachian snake handlers and the Hare Krishnas.

They called themselves The Soneji, and they seemed to know almost every nuance of the life of the kidnapper and mass murderer. In addition to an extensive biography, there were hundreds of lurid photos, links to articles, and an online chat forum where members hotly debated all things Soneji.

The hottest topics?

Number one that day was *the John Sampson shooting*.

The Soneji were generally ecstatic that my partner had been shot and barely clung to life, but a few posts stood out.

Napper2 wrote, Gary fuckin' got Sampson!

Gary's so back, The Waste Man agreed.

Only thing better would be Cross on a Cross, wrote Black Hole.

That day's coming sooner than later, said Gary's Girl. Gary's missed Cross twice. He won't miss a third time.

Aside from being the subject of homicidal speculation, something bothered me about that last post, the one from Gary's Girl. I studied it and the others, trying to figure out what was different.

"They think he's alive," Agent Batra offered.

"Yeah, that's hot thread number two," I said. "Let's take a look there, and come back."

She clicked on the "Resurrection Man" thread.

Cross saw him, came face to face with Gary, wrote Sapper9. Shit his pants, is what I heard.

Cross was hit in first attack, wrote Chosen One. Soneji's aim is true. Cross is just lucky.

Beemer answered, My respect for Gary is profound, but he is not alive. That is impossible.

The believers among The Soneji went berserk on Beemer for having the gall to challenge the consensus. Beemer was attacked from all sides. To his credit, Beemer fought back.

Call me Doubting Thomas, but show me the evidence. Can I put my finger through Soneji's hand? Can I see where the lance pierced his side?

You could if he trusted you the way he trusts me, wrote Gary's Girl.

Beemer wrote, So you've seen him, GG?

After a long pause, Gary's Girl wrote, I have. With my own two eyes.

Pic? Beemer said.

A minute passed, and then two. Five minutes after his demand, Beemer wrote, Funny how illusions can seem so real.

A second later the screen blinked and a picture appeared.

Taken at night, it was a selfie of a big, muscular

woman gone goth, heavy on the black on black right down to the lipstick. She was grinning raunchily and sitting in the lap of a man with wispy red hair. His hands held her across her deep, leather-clad cleavage, and he had buried three quarters of his face into the side of her neck.

The other quarter, however, including his right eye, was clearly visible.

He was staring right into the camera with an amused and lecherous expression that seemed designed to taunt the lens and me. He knew I'd see the picture someday and be infuriated.

I was sure of that. It was the kind of thing Soneji would do.

"That him?" Batra asked. "Gary Soneji?"

"Close enough. Can you track down Gary's Girl?"

The FBI cyber agent thought about that, and then said, "Give me twenty minutes, maybe less."

CHAPTER
17

AT FIVE O'CLOCK THAT afternoon, Bree and I drove through the tiny rural community of Flintstone, Maryland, past the Flintstone Post Office, the Stone Age Café, and Carl's Gas and Grub.

We found a side street off Route 144, and drove down a wooded lane to a freshly painted green ranch house set off all by itself in a meticulously tended yard. A shiny new Audi Q5 sat in the driveway.

"I thought you said she's on welfare," Bree said.

"Food stamps, too," I said.

We parked behind the Audi and got out. AC/DC was blasting from inside the house. We went to the front door and found it ajar.

I tried the bell. It was broken.

Bree knocked and called out, "Delilah Pinder?"

We heard nothing in response but the howling of an electric guitar against a thundering baseline.

"Door's open," I said. "We're checking on her well-being."

"Be my guest," Bree said.

I pushed open the door and found myself in a room decorated with brand-new leather furniture and a big curved HD television. The music throbbed on from somewhere deeper inside the house.

We checked the kitchen, saw boxes of appliances

that hadn't even been opened, and then headed down the hallway toward the source of the music. The first door on the left was a home gym with Olympic weight-lifting equipment. The music came from the room at the end of the hall.

There was a lull in the song, just enough that I heard a woman's voice cry, "That's it!" before the throbbing, wailing song drowned her out.

The door to that room at the end of the hall was cracked open two inches. A brilliant light shone through.

"Delilah Pinder?" I called out.

No answer.

I stepped forward and pushed the door open enough to get a comprehensive view of a very muscular and ar-tificially busty woman up on all fours on a four-poster bed. Gyrating her hips in time with the beat, she was naked, and looking over her shoulder at a GoPro cam-era mounted on a tripod.

I just stood there, stunned for a moment, long enough for Bree to nudge me, and long enough for Delilah Pinder to look around and spot me.

"Christ!" she screamed and flung herself forward on the bed.

I thought she was diving for modesty, but she hit some kind of panic button and the door slammed shut in my face and locked.

"What the hell just happened?" Bree demanded.

"I think she was doing a live sex show on the inter-net," I said.

"No."

"I swear," I said.

The music shut off and a woman shouted, "God-damnit, whoever you are, I'm calling the sheriff. They are going to hunt you down!"

"We are the police, Miss Pinder," Bree yelled back.

"What the hell are you doing in my house, then?" she screamed. "I've got rights, and you had no right to come into my house or place of business!"

"You're correct," I said. "But we knocked and called out, and we felt we were doing a safety check on you."

"What I do here is perfectly legal," she said. "So please leave."

"We aren't here about your, uh, business," Bree said.

"Who are you, then? What do you want?"

"My name is Alex Cross. I'm a detective with the DC Metro Police, and I'm here concerning Gary's Girl."

There was a long silence, and then the music cranked up. But over it I heard the sound of a door slamming loudly.

"She's running," Bree said, spun around, and took off.

CHAPTER
18

I CAN HOLD MY own in the weight room, but I am no match for Bree in a footrace. She exploded back through the house and barreled out the front door.

Delilah Pinder, who was now dressed in a blue warm-up suit and running shoes, had already sprinted around the end of the house and was charging across the front lawn, heading for the road. I came out the front door in time to see Bree try to tackle the big woman.

Delilah saw her coming and stuck out her hand like a seasoned running back, hitting Bree in the chest. Bree stumbled. The internet sex star raced out onto the road and headed toward the highway.

I cut diagonally through the yard, trying to close in on her from the side. But when I broke through the trees and jumped the stone wall onto the road, Bree was right back behind Pinder.

She jumped on the much bigger woman's back, threw an arm bar around her neck, and choked her. Delilah tried to buck her off, and to pry her hold apart. But Bree held on tight.

Finally, the big woman stopped running. Her massive thighs wobbled, and she sat down hard at Bree's feet.

"Oh, my God," Bree gasped when I ran up. "That was like 'Meet the Amazon.'"

"More like 'Ride the Amazon,'" I said, as she put zip ties on Delilah's wrists.

The woman was regaining her strength. She struggled against the restraints.

"No," she said. "Let me go."

"Not for a while yet," I said, picking her up.

Delilah twisted her head around in a rage, and spit in my face.

"Knock that off!" Bree shouted, and wrenched up hard on Delilah's bound wrists. "That kind of bullshit gets you in trouble, and you're already in a world of trouble. Got it?"

Delilah was obviously in pain, and finally nodded.

Bree eased up on the pressure while I used a tissue to wipe my face.

"I don't know what this is about," Delilah said. "I told you, I have a legitimate business, registered with the state and everything. Delilah Entertainment. Check it out."

"You know exactly what this is about," I said, grabbing one of her formidable biceps and marching her back toward her house. "You're a member of The Soneji. You're Gary's Girl. You like to take selfies of you and Gary together. Isn't that true?"

Delilah looked at me smugly and said, "Every single word of it, Cross. Every single word."

"Where is Gary Soneji?" Bree asked.

"I have no idea," Delilah said. "Gary comes and goes as he pleases. Our relationship is strong enough for that."

"Yeah, I'm sure it is," I said, rolling my eyes. "But you understand you've abetted a man who shot a police officer in cold blood?"

"How's that?"

"You housed him," Bree said. "You fed him. You

dressed up goth and had sex with him, maybe even did one of your kinky shows for him."

"Every night, darling," Delilah said. "He loved it. So did I. And that's where yours truly will shut up. I have the right to remain silent. And I have a right to an attorney. I'm taking both those rights, right here and right now."

CHAPTER
19

PALE MORNING FOG SHROUDED much of the cemetery from my view. The fog swirled on the wet grass, the melting snow that remained, and the gravestones. It left droplets on the pile of wilted flower bouquets and empty liquor bottles and remembrances that had to be moved before the backhoe could begin its work.

The last item was a baby doll, naked, with lipstick smeared on the lips.

Shivering against the dank March air, I zipped my police slicker higher and pulled on the hood. I stood off to one side of the grave with Bill Worden, the cemetery superintendent, alternately looking at the baby doll and watching the backhoe claw deeper into the soil. A baby doll, I thought, recalling a real baby tossed through the air with total indifference, if not cruelty.

Someone brought that doll here, I thought. In celebration. In reverence.

That's just sick. How could you worship that?

I glanced at the headstone Worden dug from the ground after I'd brought him an order from a federal judge in Trenton. The grave marker was simple. Rectangular black polished granite.

"*G. Soneji*" was etched in the face, along with the date of his birth. The date of his death, however, had been chiseled away. That was it. No mention of his brutal crimes or his disturbing life.

The man six feet under the headstone was all but anonymous.

And yet they'd come. The Soneji. They'd chipped away at the gravestone. Spray-painted the grass to read *"Soneji Lives."* I took pictures before the backhoe destroyed it.

"How many visit?" I asked over the sound of the digging machine.

Worden, the cemetery superintendent, tugged his hood over his head and said, "Hard to say. It's not like we keep it under surveillance. But a fair number every month."

"Enough to leave that pile of flowers," I said, eyeing the baby doll again.

Worden nodded. "For some it seems almost like a pilgrimage."

"Yeah, except Mr. Soneji was no saint," I said.

Drizzle began to fall, forcing me deeper into the collar of my jacket. A few moments later, the backhoe turned off.

"There's the straps, Bill," the equipment operator said. "I'll hand-dig the last of it."

"No need," Worden said. "Just hook up and lift, brush the dirt off later."

The backhoe operator shrugged and got out cables, which he attached to the bucket. Then he got down into the grave and clipped the cables to the rings of stout straps that had been left after the casket was lowered.

"They're not weakened by being in the dirt ten years?" I asked.

Worden shook his head. "Not unless something chewed through them."

The superintendent was right. When the backhoe

arm rose, the straps easily lifted the casket of a man I helped kill.

Wet dirt slid and cascaded off the top of the casket as it came free of the grave and dangled four feet above the hole. The wind picked up. The casket swayed.

"Put it down there," Worden said, gesturing to one side.

I was fixated on the casket, wondering what was inside, beyond the charred remains I'd seen placed in a body bag beneath Grand Central Station a decade before. He was in there, wasn't he?

Every instinct said yes. But…

As the casket swung and lowered, I happened to look beyond it and between two far monuments. The wind had blown a narrow vent in the fog. I could see a slice of the graveyard between those monuments that ran all the way to the pine barrens that surrounded the cemetery.

Standing at the edge of the woods, perhaps eighty yards from me, was a man in a green rain slicker. He was turning away. When his back was to me, he pulled off his hood, revealing a head of thinning red hair. Then he raised his right hand, and pointed his middle finger at the sky.

And me.

CHAPTER
20

I STOOD THERE, TOO stunned to move for the moment it took for the wind to ebb and the fog to creep back, obscuring the figure, who stepped into the pine barrens and disappeared.

Then my shock evaporated, and I took off, drawing my pistol as I sprinted between the gravestones. Peering through the fog gathering again in the cemetery, I tried to figure out exactly where I'd seen him go into the pines.

There it was, those two monuments. He'd been framed between them. I ran to the spot and looked back toward the fog-obscured backhoe and the exhumed casket. When I thought I had the correct bearings, I turned and headed in a straight line toward the edge of the forest.

"Dr. Cross?" the superintendent called after me. "Where are you going?"

I ignored him and charged to the edge of the dripping pines, scanning the ground and seeing a scuff mark that looked fresh, not yet beaten down by the rain. I pushed my way into the trees.

The forest was thick there, crowded with young saplings with wet branches that bent away and wet needles that slid past my clothes. I stopped, unsure where to go, but then noticed a broken branch on the ground.

The inner wood looked bright and new. So did the

broken branch to my left at ten o'clock. I went that way for fifty, maybe seventy-five yards, and then broke into an expanse of older trees, more than ten feet high, and growing in long straight rows, a pine plantation.

Despite the fog, I soon spotted dark, discolored spots on the mat of dead needles that covered the forest floor. I went to them, and saw where he'd kicked up the duff as he'd run down one of those lanes through the trees.

I ran after him, wondering if I could catch up, and numerous times whether I'd lost the way. But then I'd find some disturbance in the pine needles and push on one hundred, two hundred, three hundred yards deeper into the barrens.

What direction was I going? I had no idea, and it didn't matter. As long as Soneji was leaving signs, I was staying with him. I thought I'd cross a logging road or trail at some point, but didn't. There was just the monotony of the plantation pines and the swirling fog.

Then the way began to climb up a hill. I could clearly see where he'd had to dig in the edges of his shoes to keep his footing, and more broken branches.

When I hit the top of the knoll, there was a clearing of sorts with a jumble of tree trunks to one side, as if a windstorm had blown them over. I skirted the jumble, crossed the hilltop, and found myself looking down into a long, broad valley of mature pines.

The forest had been thinned there, as if some of the trees had already been harvested. Despite the fog, I could see down a dozen lanes and deeper into the woods than at any other time since I'd entered it. Nothing moved below me.

Nothing at—

A rifle cracked. The bark of a tree next to me exploded and I dove for the ground behind one of those downed tree trunks.

Where was he?

The shot came from the valley. I was sure of it. But where down there?

"Cross?" he called. "I'm coming for you, even from the grave if I have to."

If it wasn't him, he'd studied Soneji's voice, right down to the inflection.

When I didn't answer, he shouted, "Hear me, Cross?"

He sounded to my right and below me, no more than seventy yards. Raising my head as high as I dared, I scanned the valley there. The fog was in and out, but I thought I'd see him move or adjust his angle if he wanted another shot at me.

But I couldn't make him out.

"I know I didn't hit you," he called, his voice cracking weirdly. "I did, you would have gone down like the shit bag you are."

I decided not to engage, to let him think he'd gotten lucky, taken me out with one bullet. And it was odd the way his voice had cracked, wasn't it? Gone to a higher pitch?

Tense moments passed, a minute and then two, while my eyes darted back and forth, trying to spot him, hoping he'd come in to make sure of the kill.

"How's your partner?" he called, and I heard him chuckle hoarsely. "He took a hit, didn't he? What I hear, best-case scenario, he'll be a veg."

It took every fiber of my being, but I did not engage with him, even then. I just lay there and waited, scanning and scanning and scanning.

I never saw him go, or heard anything like a distant twig breaking to suggest he was on the move again. He never said another word, and nothing told me he'd left but the time that kept ticking away.

I lowered my head after ten minutes and dug out my phone. No service.

The rain started in earnest then, drumming, beating down the fog and revealing the plantation. Nothing moved but a doe a hundred yards out.

I wanted to get up and go down there, look for him. But if he was waiting, I'd be exposed again. After fifteen more minutes of watching, I crawled back in the direction I'd come until I was well down the backside of the hill.

There was a bitter taste in my mouth when I got to my feet and started back toward the cemetery.

I hadn't gotten halfway there when my cell phone buzzed in my pocket.

A text from Billie.

"Alex, wherever you are, come. John's taken a bad turn. We're on deathwatch here."

CHAPTER
21

BY THE TIME I reached the cemetery, the superintendent had already loaded the casket into the FBI van that would take it to Quantico for examination. I explained the urgency of my situation, and left.

I called ahead to New Jersey, Delaware, and Maryland state police dispatchers, asking for help. When I reached I-95, there were two Jersey state trooper cruisers waiting. One in front, the other behind, they escorted me to the border, where two Delaware cruisers met me. Two more waited when I reached the Maryland line. At times we were going more than a hundred.

Less than two hours after I'd read the text, I got off the elevator to the ICU at GW Medical Center, still in damp clothes and chilled as I ran down the all-too-familiar halls to the waiting area. Billie sat at the back, her feet drawn up under her. Her elbows rested across her knees and she had a skeptical, faraway look in her eye, as if she couldn't believe that God was doing this to her.

Bree sat at her left, Nana Mama on her right.

"What happened?" I asked.

"They decided to bring him up out of the chemical coma," Billie said, tears streaming down her cheeks.

"He flatlined. They had to paddle him," Bree said. "He came back, but his vitals are turning against him."

"Billie's called in the priest," Nana Mama said. "He's giving John the last rites."

Whatever control I'd maintained until that point evaporated and I began to grieve in gasps of disbelief and an explosion of sorrow and tears. It was real. My best friend, the indestructible one, Big John Sampson, was going to die.

I sank into a chair and sobbed. Bree came over and hugged me. I leaned into her and cried some more.

The priest came in. "He's in God's hands now," he said, consoling us. "The doctor says there's nothing more they can do for him."

"Can we go in?" Billie asked.

"Of course," he said.

Nana Mama, Billie, and Bree got up. I looked at them, feeling numb.

"I can't do it," I said, feeling helpless. "I just can't watch this. Can you forgive me?"

"I don't want to either, Alex," Billie said. "But I want him to hear my voice one last time before he goes."

Nana Mama patted me on the shoulders as she followed Billie into the ICU. Bree asked if I wanted her to stay, and I shook my head.

"Going in there scares me more than anything has in my entire life," I said. "I need to take a walk, get my courage up."

"And pray," she said, kissed me on the head, and went inside.

I got up and felt like a coward walking toward the men's room. I went inside and washed my face, trying to think of anything but John and all the good times we'd had over the years, playing football and basketball, attending the police academy, and finding our way through the ranks to detective and partners against crime.

That would never happen again. John and me would never happen again.

I left the restroom and wandered off through the medical complex, sure that any minute now I'd get a text that he was gone. Guilt built up in me at the thought that after all we'd been through, I wouldn't be there at Sampson's side when he passed.

I stopped and almost turned around. Then noticed I was standing outside the plastic surgery offices. A beautiful Ethiopian-looking woman in a white jacket came out the door.

She smiled at me. Her teeth gleamed and her facial skin was so taut and smooth she could have been thirty. Then again, she could have been sixty and often under the knife.

"Dr. Coleman?" I said, reading her badge.

She stopped and said, "Yes?"

I showed her my badge, said, "I could use your help."

"Yes?" she said, looking worried. "How so?"

"I'm investigating the shooting of a police officer," I said. "We want to know, how difficult would it be to make one person look almost exactly like another?"

She squinted. "You mean, good enough to be an imposter?"

"Yes," I said. "Is it possible?"

"That depends," Dr. Coleman said, glancing at her watch. "Can you walk with me? I have to give a lecture about twenty minutes from here."

"Yes," I said, glad for the diversion.

We walked through the medical center and out the other side, ending up on the George Washington University campus. Along the way, the plastic surgeon said that similar facial structure would be key to surgically altering a person to look like someone else.

"The closer the subject was to looking like the original to begin with, the better the results," she said. "After that it would all be in the skill of the surgeon."

"So, even the similar bone structure wouldn't guarantee success for your everyday surgeon?"

Dr. Coleman smiled. "If the end product is as close to the original as you say it is, then there is no way an average boob-job surgeon did it. You're looking for a scalpel artist, Detective."

"What kind of money are we talking?"

"Depends on the extent of surgical alteration required," she said. "But I'm thinking this is a hundred-thousand-dollar job, maybe less in Brazil."

A hundred thousand dollars? Who would spend that much to look like Gary Soneji? Or go to Brazil to get it done?

I felt my phone buzz in my pocket, and sickened.

"Here I am," Dr. Coleman said, stopping outside one of the university's many buildings. "Any more questions, Detective?"

"No," I said, handing her a card. "But if I do, can I call?"

"Absolutely," she said, and hurried inside.

I swallowed hard and then got out my phone.

The text was from Bree: "Come now or you'll regret it the rest of your life."

I started to run.

Ten minutes later, I went through the door of the ICU, trying to keep my emotions from ruining me all over again.

When I reached the doorway to John's room, Billie, Bree, and Nana Mama were all sobbing.

I thought I'd come too late, that I'd done my best friend and brother the ultimate disservice, and not been there when he took his last breath.

Then I realized they were all sobbing for joy.

"It's a miracle, Alex," Bree said, tears streaming down her cheeks. "Look."

I stepped inside the crowded room. A nurse and a doctor were working feverishly on John. He was still on his back in bed, still on the ventilator, still hitched up to a dozen different monitors.

But his eyes were open and roving lazily.

CHAPTER
22

WE SAT WITH JOHN for hours as more of the drugs wore off. They removed his breathing tube, and he came more and more to consciousness.

John did not acknowledge his name when Billie called it softly, trying to get him to turn his head to her. At first Sampson seemed not even to know where he was, as if he were lost in some dream.

But then, after the first nap, he did hear his wife, and his face lolled toward her. Then he moved his fingers and toes on command, and lifted both arms.

When I sat beside him and held his hand, his lips kept opening as if he wanted to talk. No sound came out, and he appeared frustrated.

"It's okay, buddy," I said, holding tight. "We know you love us."

Sampson relaxed and slept again. When he awoke, Elizabeth Navilus, a top speech-language pathologist, was waiting. She was part of a team of specialists rotating through the room, performing the various exams on the JFK Coma Recovery Scale, a method of diagnosing the extent of brain damage.

Navilus ran Sampson through a brief battery of tests. She found that John's cognitive awareness as expressed through his language comprehension was growing by the moment. But he was having trouble speaking. The best he could do was chew at the air and hum.

It crushed me.

Out in the waiting area, Navilus told us to take hope from the fact that head trauma patients often exhibit understanding before being able to respond.

Later, when Nana Mama had left for home to cook dinner, and Bree to the office, and Billie to the cafeteria, I sat by John's side.

"I was there when you were shot," I told him. "It was Soneji. Or someone who looked just like him."

Sampson blinked, and then nodded.

"I came close to catching him this morning," I said. "He was watching when we dug up Soneji's body."

He looked away and closed his eyes.

"I'm going to get him, John," I said. "I promise you."

He barely nodded before sagging off to sleep.

Sitting there, watching him, I felt better, stronger, and more humbled and in debt to my Lord and savior than ever before. The idea of Sampson dying must have been as much of an abomination to God as I thought it was.

If that wasn't a miracle, I don't know what is.

CHAPTER
23

I STAYED AT THE hospital until nine, promised Billie I'd be back in the morning, and headed home. Given what had happened the last time I'd exited GW Medical Center and looked for a cab, my head was turning three-sixty.

I saw no threat, however, and stepped to the curb. As I did, Soneji's voice from earlier in the day echoed back to me.

I'm coming for you, even from the grave if I have to.

It sounded so much like Gary, it was scary. I'd had multiple conversations with him over the years, and Soneji's tone and delivery were unmistakable.

After I'd gotten into the cab and given the driver my home address, I almost pushed these thoughts aside. But then I blinked, remembering how his voice had cracked weirdly and turned hoarse when he said, "I know I didn't hit you. I did, you would have gone down like the shit bag you are."

It sounded like he had something wrong in his throat. Cancer? Polyps? Or were his vocal cords just straining under the tensions wound up inside him?

I tried to remember every nuance of our encounter in the pine barrens, the way he'd swaggered into the trees, finger held high. Where was the gun then? Had he been trying to lure me in for a shot?

In retrospect, it felt like he had, and I'd fallen for it. Where was all the training I'd done? The protocol? I'd reacted on emotion, charging into the pines after him. Just the way Soneji had wanted me to.

That bothered me because it made me realize that Soneji understood me, could predict my impulses the way I could predict his a dozen years before. I mean, how else would he have known to be at the cemetery when I was there to exhume his body? What or who had tipped him?

I had no answers for that other than the possibility Soneji or The Soneji had us bugged. Or had it just seemed the rational thing to do at some point, given the fact that I'd seen someone who looked just like him at least three times now?

These unanswerable questions weighed on me the entire ride home. I felt depressed climbing from the taxi and waiting for the receipt. Soneji, or whoever, was thinking ahead of me, plotting, hatching, and acting before I could respond.

Climbing the porch stairs, I was beginning to feel like I was a fish on a hook with some angler toying with me, messing with my lip.

But the second I stepped inside the house, smelled something savory coming from Nana Mama's kitchen, and heard my son, Ali, laughing, I let it go. I let everything about the sonofabitch go.

"Dad?" Jannie said, coming down the stairs. "How's John?"

"He's got a fight and a half ahead of him, but he's alive."

"Nana Mama said it's, like, a miracle."

"I'd have to agree," I said, and hugged her tight.

"Dad, look at this," Ali called. "You can't believe how good this looks."

"The new TV," Jannie said. "It's pretty amazing."

"What new TV?"

"Nana Mama and Ali ordered it off the internet. They just installed it."

I stepped into our once cozy television room to see it had been transformed into a home theater, with new leather chairs, and a huge, curved 4K resolution HD screen on the far wall. Ali had on a repeat of *The Walking Dead,* one of his favorites, and the zombies looked like they were right there in the room with us.

"You should see when we switch it to 3D, Dad!" Ali said. "It's crazy!"

"I can see that," I said. "Does it do basketball?"

Ali took his eyes off the screen. "They're right in the room with you."

I smiled. "You'll have to show me after dinner."

"I can do that," Ali said. "Show you how to run it from your laptop."

I gave him the thumbs up, and then wandered through the dining room to the kitchen upgrade and great room addition we'd put on two years before.

Nana Mama was bustling at her command-center stove.

"Roast chicken, sweet potato fries, broccoli with almonds, and a nice salad," she said. "How's John?"

"Sleeping when I left," I said. "And dinner sounds great. Nice TV."

She made a deep inhaling sound, and said, "Isn't it? I can't wait to see *Masterpiece Theatre* on there. That *Downton Abbey* show."

"I was thinking the same thing," I said.

Nana Mama looked over her shoulder, gave me a sour, threatening look, and said, "Don't you be mocking me, now."

"I wouldn't dream of it, Nana," I said, trying to hide

the smile that wanted to creep onto my face. "Oh, I thought you said you weren't going to let the lottery money change our lives."

"I said I didn't want some big mansion to get lost in," she snapped. "Or tooling around in some ridiculous car. But that doesn't mean we can't have some nice things in this house, and still do some good for people. Which reminds me, when is my hot-breakfast program going to be able to start up again?"

I held up my hands. "I'll find out tonight."

"I'm not getting any younger, and I want to see that ongoing," she said. "Endowed. And that reading program for kids."

"Yes, ma'am, and you're sure you're not getting younger? Isn't there a painting of you in some attic that shows your real age?"

She tried to fight it, but that brought on a smile. "Aren't you just the smoothest talker in—?"

"Dad?" Ali cried, running into the kitchen.

He looked petrified, on the verge of crying.

"What's the matter?"

"Someone's taken over my computer," he said.

"What?" Nana Mama said.

"There's this crazy man on the screen now, not *The Walking Dead,* and he won't turn off. He's holding a baby and saying, like, over and over that he's going to come for you, Dad, even from the grave."

CHAPTER
24

IN THE VIDEO CLIP, Gary Soneji was just as I remembered him: out on one of Grand Central Station's train platforms, holding the infant, and taunting me.

I'd never seen the video. Never knew it existed, but it was definitely legitimate. After viewing the clip six or seven times, I could see my own shadow stretched in the space between me and Gary Soneji. The camera operator all those years ago had to have been right off my left shoulder.

Was the cameraman a fluke? A random passerby? Or someone working with Soneji?

The clip started again. It appeared on endless loop.

"Dad, this is giving me the creeps," Jannie said. "Turn it off."

"Gimme the remote and the computer, Ali," I said.

"I've got homework on this computer," he said.

"I'll transfer your homework to the one in the kitchen," I said, and gave him a gimme motion.

He groaned and handed it to me.

Bree came in the front door. I hit the Power button on the remote, but the screen did not turn off. Instead, it broke from that endless loop to Kelly green.

I tried to turn the screen off again, but it jumped to black, slashed diagonally with a golden beam of light.

The camera zoomed closer to that light and you could see a silhouette of a person there.

Closer, it was a man.

Closer still, and it was Soneji.

He was giving the lens the same quarter profile we'd seen in the still image that Gary's Girl posted on the website forum, the one where his eye and the corner of his mouth conspired to leer right at me.

But this time Soneji spoke.

In that cracking, hoarse voice I'd heard earlier that day in the pine barrens, Soneji said, "You're not safe in the trees, Cross. You're not safe in your own home. The Soneji are everywhere!"

Then he threw his head back, and barked and brayed his laughter before the screen froze. A title appeared below: www.thesoneji.net.

"What's that, Dad?" Ali asked, upset.

I stormed to the screen, followed the cord to its power source, and tore it violently out of the wall.

"Alex?" Bree said. "What's going on?"

I looked at Ali. "Was that *Walking Dead* episode streaming from Netflix?"

"Yes."

Yanking out my cell phone, I looked to Bree and said, "Soneji hacked into our internet feed."

"I'll shut the router down," Bree said.

"No, don't," I said. I scrolled through my recent calls and hit Call. "I have a feeling it will be better if the link's still active."

The phone picked up. "Yes?"

"This is Alex Cross," I said. "How fast can you get to my house?"

Forty minutes later, as we were finishing up Nana Mama's roast chicken masterpiece, and fighting over who was going to get the last wing and who the last sweet potato fries, there was a sharp knock at our side door.

"I'll get it," I said, put my napkin down, and went out into the great room and unlocked the door that led to the side yard and the alley behind our place.

I did not turn on the light, just opened it quickly and let our visitors inside. The first was Ned Mahoney, my former partner at the FBI. The second was Special Agent Henna Batra of the Bureau's cybercrime unit.

"Who's making sure you're safe in your own home?" Mahoney asked once I'd closed the door.

"Metro in unmarked cars, both ends of the block," I said.

"Soneji's still the type to try."

"I know," I said. "But I think we're good."

"I'm still unclear why you wanted me here, Dr. Cross," Agent Batra said.

"I think Soneji or The Soneji may have made a mistake," I said. "If I'm right, they left a digital trail inside my house, or on our network, anyway."

CHAPTER
25

I GOT TO GW Medical Center early the following morning with my children's howls ringing in my head. Special Agent Batra had taken every computer and phone in the house to Quantico. She'd promised to work as fast as she could, but it was like they'd lost their right hands when the phones were taken away.

I kind of felt the same way walking to Sampson's room, and decided to buy a cheap phone afterward. I was happy to find John sitting up and drinking through a straw.

Billie hadn't arrived yet, so I'd gotten to sit with him awhile, and brought him up to date on all that had occurred the prior day. Though his eyes tended to drift off me, he seemed to understand much of what I was saying.

"If anyone can find this guy, it's Batra," I said. "I've never seen anyone like her before."

John's eyes softened and he smiled. He tried to say something and couldn't. You could see how frustrating it was.

I put my hand on his shoulder and said, "You're in for a long haul, buddy, recovering from this. But if there's any man alive who can do it, you can."

Sampson's lazy, sad gaze came and dwelled around me for several seconds. Then he started struggling, as he got more and more upset.

"Hey," I said. "It's okay. We'll—"

Garbled sounds came out of his mouth.

He tried again. And again.

The sixth time, I thought he said, "Evan-widda."

"Evan-widda?" I said.

"Evan-widda…b…bag," he said, and then smiled and lifted his right hand to point to the surgical bandage. "Ho-ho…n…ed."

I frowned, but got it then, and smiled. "Even with a big hole in your head?"

Sampson smiled, dropped his hand, and winked at me before nodding off to sleep again, as if that had taken every bit of his strength.

But he'd spoken! Sort of. Definitely communicated. And the doctors had said his sense of humor could be gone with a wound to that part of his brain, but here he was making a joke about his situation.

If that wasn't a miracle, I don't know what is.

Billie arrived shortly before eight and beamed when I told her what had happened.

She kissed John, and said, "You spoke?"

He shook his head. "Alack vent…r…wrist…crist."

"What?"

"He said, 'Alex is a ventriloquist.' I think."

John grinned again and said, "Whips do no move."

Billie had tears in her eyes. "Lips don't move."

Sampson made a wheezing sound of delight that stayed with me on the way to work and buying a burner phone.

I went to Bree's office, and I knocked on her doorjamb.

"Long time no see," I said.

Bree glanced at the clock, said, "Are you getting obsessive about me?"

"I've always been obsessive about you, from the very first," I said.

"Liar," Bree said, but she was pleased.

"The truth," I said. "You had me the first time you glanced my way."

That pleased her even more. "Why are you buttering me up?"

"I'm not buttering you up," I said. "I was just flirting with my wife before I told her that Sampson spoke this morning."

"No?" she gasped. "He did?"

"It took a little interpretation, but he was telling jokes."

Bree got tears in her eyes, stood up, came around the desk, and hugged me. I got tears, too.

"Thanks," she said. "What a perfect thing to hear."

"I know," I said, before the cheap phone I'd bought on the way to work buzzed. Who knew the number? I'd just gotten the damn thing. Just activated it.

"Hello?" I said.

"It's Special Agent Batra."

"How'd you get this number?"

"By being good at my job," Agent Batra said, sounding annoyed. "I thought you'd be happy to hear from me so soon."

"I'm sorry," I said, though I was beginning to think there wasn't a box in the virtual universe that Henna Batra couldn't find and unlock if she set her mind to it. "You found something?"

"You were compromised in a troubling fashion."

I wanted to say that I could have told her that, but asked, "How so?"

"They got a bug into your son's computer operating system, piggybacked to a game app he downloaded at school."

"At his school?" I said, feeling queasy.

Soneji or The Soneji were not only threatening me in my house, they were targeting my youngest child.

"What else?" I demanded.

"Your daughter, Jannie, had the same bug in her system," Batra said. "It was uploaded to her computer without her knowledge when she was using her phone as a mobile hotspot at a coffee shop not far from your house."

This was worse. Both my children were being targeted.

"What about my phone? My wife's?" I asked, and turned on the speaker on the burner phone so Bree could hear.

"Clean," Batra said. "I'll have them messengered over in the next hour."

"Thank you," I said. "Is that it?"

"No, as a matter of fact," the FBI cyber expert said. "There was a similarity in the signature of the bug coder and the coder who created www.thesoneji.net."

I looked at Bree, who shrugged in confusion.

"You want to run that by us again?" I said.

The cybercrimes expert sounded irritated when she said, "Coders are artists in their own way, Detective. Just as classical painters had recognizable brushstrokes, great computer coders have a recognizable way of writing. Their signature, if you will."

"Makes sense," I said. "So who coded the website?"

Batra said, "It took me much, much longer than I expected to break through the firewalls that surrounded the identity of the creator and curator, but I did just a few minutes ago."

"Have you been up all night?" I asked.

"You said it was important."

Bree leaned forward, said, "Thank you, Agent Batra. It's Chief Stone here. Do you know who he is? The website creator?"

"She, and I've learned quite a bit about her in the

past hour or so, thanks to a friend of mine at the NSA," Agent Batra said. "Especially the boyfriend she's fronting for. In fact, I know about him going right back to what his first-grade teacher said about him the day she recommended he be expelled from school."

I felt fear in the pit of my stomach. "And what was that?"

"She said she thought he was kind of a monster, Dr. Cross. Even then."

CHAPTER
26

AN HOUR LATER, I set in to wait on a bench in a hallway by the door to a loft space on the fourth floor of an older building off Dupont Circle.

I'd gotten into the building by showing my badge to a woman entering with groceries. I told her who I was looking for.

"Out running, that one," she'd replied. "Every lunch hour. Quite a sight."

I'd knocked on the door just in case, but there was no answer. I had a search warrant. I could have called for patrol to break the door down, but I hoped I could get more information by going patient and gentle.

Twenty minutes later, a fit Asian American woman in her late twenties came huffing up the staircase. Her black hair was cut short and her exposed arms were buff and sleeved in brilliantly colored tattoos.

Sweat poured down her face when she reached the landing and saw me getting off the bench. She didn't startle or try to escape as I'd expected.

Instead she hardened, said, "Took you a while, Dr. Cross. The intrusion was almost six hours ago. But here you are. At last. In the flesh."

"Kimiko Binx?" I said, holding up my badge and ID.

"Correct," Binx replied, walking toward me, palms held open at her sides, and studying me with great interest.

The closer she got, I noticed a device of some sort, orange, and strapped to her upper right arm. When I saw it blink, I thought *bomb,* and went for my gun.

"What's that on your arm?" I demanded, the pistol out, pointed her way.

Binx threw her hands up, said, "Whoa, whoa, Detective. It's a SPOT."

"What?"

"A GPS transmitter. It sends my position every thirty seconds to a satellite and to a website," she said. "I use it to track my running routes."

She turned sideways and held up her arm so I could examine the device. It was smaller than a smartphone, commercially made, heavy-duty plastic, with the SPOT logo emblazoned across the front of it and buttons with various icons. One said SOS and another was a shoe tread. The light blinked beside the shoe.

"So it tracks you?" I said.

"Correct," Binx said. "What do you want, Dr. Cross?"

I held the search warrant up and said, "If you could open the door."

Binx read the warrant without comment, fished out a key, and opened the loft. It was an airy work-and-living space with a view of an alley, a hodgepodge of used furniture, and a computer workstation that featured four large screens.

She moved toward the station.

"Do not go near your computer, Ms. Binx. Do not go near anything."

Binx got aggravated and took off the SPOT device. "You want this, too?"

"Please. Turn it off. Put it on the table there, and your phone if you've got it. I'd like to ask you some questions before I call for my evidence team."

"What do you want to know?" she asked, using her thumbs to play at the buttons on the transmitter.

"Why do you worship Gary Soneji?"

Binx didn't answer, hit one last button, and looked up at me before setting the SPOT on the table with the light no longer blinking.

"I don't worship Gary Soneji," she said finally. "I find Gary Soneji interesting. I find you interesting, for that matter."

"That why you built a high-security website about Soneji and me?"

"Yes," she said, sitting down calmly. "Other people find you two interesting also. Lots of them. It was a safe way to handle our common passion."

"Your members cheered when they found out my partner, John Sampson, was shot," I said.

"It's a private forum of free expression. I didn't approve of that."

"Didn't you?" I said angrily. "You provided space for sickos to plot terror in the name of a man who committed utterly heinous acts and died ten years ago."

"He's not dead," Binx said flatly. "Gary Soneji will never die."

I remembered the coffin coming up out of the ground in New Jersey, wondered how much longer the FBI's DNA testing would take, but said nothing of the exhumation of her idol.

Instead I said, "I don't get this, smart woman like you. Virginia Tech graduate. Write code for a living. Paid handsomely. Yet you get involved in something like this."

"Different strokes," she replied. "And it's my personal business."

"Not when it involves the shooting of a police officer. Nothing's personal."

"I had nothing to do with that, either," Binx said evenly. "Nothing. I'll take a lie detector."

"Who did, then?" I asked.

"Gary Soneji."

"Maybe," I said. "Or maybe Claude Watkins?"

Binx shifted her eyes ever so slightly to look just over my right shoulder before shaking her head.

I said, "Watkins's name is on your company's incorporation documents."

"Claude's a limited partner. He lent me some start-up money."

"Uh-huh," I said. "You know his background?"

"He had problems when he was younger," she said.

"He is a sadist, Ms. Binx. He was convicted of carving the skin off a little girl's fingers."

"He was chemically imbalanced back then," she said defiantly. "That was the diagnosis of both the state and his personal psychiatrists. He took the drugs they recommended, paid his dues, and moved on. Claude's a painter and performance artist now. He's brilliant."

"I'm sure he is," I said.

"No," Binx insisted. "He really is. I can take you to his studio. Show you. We've got nothing to hide. It's not far. He rents space in an old factory down by the Anacostia River, west bank."

"Address?"

She shrugged. "I just know how to get there."

I thought for a moment, said, "After my team gets here, you'll take me?"

She nodded. "Be glad to. Can I take a shower in the meantime? You can search the bathroom if you need to. I assure you it's nothing but the usual."

I stared at her for several beats, and then said, "Make it quick."

CHAPTER
27

THE CRIMINALISTS ARRIVED TEN minutes later. I was giving them instructions to call if they turned up anything when Kimiko Binx emerged from her bedroom in jeans, Nike running shoes, and a short-sleeved green blouse.

"Ready, Dr. Cross?" she said, coming toward me and then stumbling over a loose cord and losing her balance.

I reached out before she could fall. Binx grabbed onto my left hand and right forearm and got her balance.

She turned from me, looking back, puzzled. "What was that?"

"You should put your cords under rugs," I said. "Let's go."

We went downstairs to my car.

Binx got in the front seat, said, "Where's the siren?"

"It's not like that," I said. "Where am I going?"

"Toward the Anacostia Bridge. It's an old tool and die factory by the river."

I drove in silence until I realized she was studying me again.

"What are you looking at?"

"The object of Gary's obsession," she said.

"Soneji's sole obsession?" I asked.

"Well," Binx said, and turned to look out the windshield. "One of them."

She was so blithe and relaxed in her manner that I wondered if she was on some kind of medication. And yet, she made me feel strange, scrutinized by a cultist.

"How did you meet Claude Watkins?" I asked.

"At a party in Baltimore," she said. "Have you met him?"

"Haven't had the pleasure."

Binx smiled. "It is, you know. A pleasure to see his paintings and his performances."

"A real Picasso, then."

She caught the sarcasm, turned cooler, and said, "You'll see, Dr. Cross."

Binx navigated me toward a derelict light industrial area north of the bridge, and an abandoned brick-faced factory with a FOR SALE sign on the gate, which was unlocked.

"This is where the great painter and performance artist works?" I said.

"Correct," Binx said. "Claude moves around, takes month-to-month leases on abandoned buildings, where he's free to do his art without worrying about making a mess. When the building and the art's sold, he moves on. It's a win-win for everyone involved. He learned the tactic in Detroit."

It made sense, actually. I parked the car outside the gate, and felt odd, a little woozy, the way you do if you haven't eaten enough or stayed well hydrated. And my tongue felt thick, and my throat dry.

I heard Binx release her seat belt. It sounded louder than it should have. So did the key in the ignition beeping when I opened the door. I took the key out, stood up, felt the warm spring breeze, and felt almost immediately better.

I called up Google Maps on my phone, pinned my location, and texted the pin to Bree along with a message that said, "Send patrol for backup when you get the chance."

Then I drew my service weapon.

"Sorry to do this, Ms. Binx," I said. "But I need you in handcuffs."

"What? Why?"

"You're technically under arrest. I've just been a nice guy until now."

The computer coder didn't look happy as she came over. I got out my cuffs and buckled down her wrists, arms forward. She'd been cooperative for the most part and didn't seem much of a threat.

"What am I under arrest for?" Binx demanded. "Free speech?"

"How about fomenting and abetting attempted murder of a cop?"

"I did not!"

"You did," I said, pushing her in front of me.

We passed through the gate, crossed fifteen yards of scrub ground where purple crocuses poked out of weeds by a metal double door. Binx seemed on the verge of tears, opening one of the doors and saying, "I would never hurt a cop. My dad was a cop in Philly."

That surprised me. "Was?"

"He's retired," she said. "With a gold shield."

I looked at her differently now, the daughter of a good cop. Why would she get involved in something like this?

"You said you wanted to meet Claude," Binx said, trying to wipe her tears with her sleeves. "Let's go."

At first a voice in my head said not to enter the abandoned factory, to wait for backup, but then the voice was gone, replaced by a surge of clarity and confidence.

Keeping Binx squarely in front of me, I went inside.

Whenever you leave a sunny day for a darker quarter, there's always a fleeting moment when you're all but blind before your eyes adjust. It's also a time when you tend to be silhouetted in the doorway and are therefore an easy target.

But I heard no shot, and my vision refocused on a large, airy space, ten, maybe fifteen thousand square feet, with a ceiling that was warehouse-high and crisscrossed with rusted overhead tracks for heavy industrial lifts and booms.

Ten-foot-tall partitions carved the space up like a broad maze. The cement floor right in front of us was cracked, broken in places, and bare but for stacks of pipe and sheet metal, as if a reclaiming operation was under way. Thick dust hung in the air. Waves of it danced and swirled in the weak sunlight streaming through a bank of filthy windows high on the walls.

"I'm not seeing any paintings or studio," I said. "Where's Watkins?"

"He and the studio are in the back," Binx said, gesturing into the gloom. "I'll show you the way."

For the second time that day, that internal voice of mine, born of years of training and experience, raised doubts about following her until I had someone watching my back. And for the second time that day, I felt my heart beat faster, sensed more sharply my surroundings, and surged with another rush of complete confidence in my abilities.

"Lead on," I said, smiling at her, and feeling good, real good, like I was perfectly fine-tuned and ready for anything that might come my way.

Binx took me down one dim hallway, and then another, passing empty workroom after empty workroom before I smelled marijuana, fresh paint, and turpentine. The smells got stronger as we walked a short third hallway that dog-legged left and opened into a large, largely empty assembly-line room with dark alcoves off it on all four sides.

The only lights in the room were strong portable spots trained on one of several large paintings hanging on the far wall about fifty feet away. The painting showed a crane lifting a coffin from the ground. The headstone above the grave read "G. Soneji." Two men stood by the grave. A Caucasian in a dark suit. And an African American in a blue police slicker. Me.

I almost smiled. Someone who'd been at the ex-humation, probably Soneji or one of his followers, Watkins, had painted this, and yet I had to fight to keep from grinning at all the goodwill I felt inside.

The furthest of the three spotlights went dark then, re-vealing a man I couldn't see before because of the glare. He wore paint-speckled jeans, work boots, and a long-sleeved shirt, but his face was lost in shadows.

Then he took a step forward into a weak, dusty beam of sunlight coming through the grimy windows, revealing the wispy red hair and distinctive facial fea-tures of Gary Soneji.

"Dr. Cross," he said in a cracking, hoarse voice. "I thought you'd never catch up."

CHAPTER
28

SONEJI MOVED HIS ARM then, and I saw the gun he held at his side, a nickel-plated pistol, just like the ones he used to shoot Sampson and me.

Take him!

The voice screamed in my head, ending all of those strange good feelings that had been inexplicably surging through me.

I raised my service pistol fast, pushed Binx out of the way, aimed at Soneji, and shouted, "Drop your weapon now or I'll shoot!"

To my surprise, Soneji let go the gun. It fell to the floor with a clatter. He raised his hands, studying me calmly and with great interest.

"Facedown on the floor!" I shouted. "Hands behind your back!"

Soneji started to follow my orders before Binx hit my gun hand with both her fists. The blow knocked me off balance, and my gun discharged just as a spotlight went on from above the paintings, blinding me.

There was a shot.

Then all the lights died, leaving me disoriented, and blinking at dazzling blue spots that danced before my eyes. Knowing I was vulnerable, I threw myself to the floor, expecting another shot at any moment.

It was a trap. The whole thing was a trap, and I'd just walked into…

The spots cleared.

Soneji was gone. So was Binx. And Soneji's nickel-plated pistol.

I held my position, and peered around, noticing for the first time a metal table covered in cans of paint and paintbrushes. And then those alcoves all around the room. They were low-roofed and dark with shadows.

Soneji and Binx could easily have slid into one of them. And what? Escaped? Or were they just waiting for me to make a move?

I had no answers, and stayed where I was, listening, looking.

Nothing moved. And there was zero sound.

But I could feel him there. Soneji. Listening for me. Looking for me.

I felt severely agitated at those ideas, almost wired before an irrational, all-consuming rage erupted inside me. Standard protocol was gone, burned up. All my training was gone, too, consumed by the flames of wanting to take Gary Soneji down. Now and for good.

I lurched to my feet and ran hard at the nearest alcove on the opposite wall. Every nerve expected a shot, but there was none. I got to the protection of the alcove, gasping, gun up, seeing the remnants of machine tools.

But no Soneji.

"I've got backup, Gary," I shouted. "They're surrounding the place!"

No response. Were they gone?

I dodged out of the alcove and moved fast along the wall to the next anteroom, the one directly beneath the painting of the exhumation. At first I saw only large rolls of canvas laid on sawhorses and tables made of plywood.

Then, in the deepest shadows of the alcove, and in my peripheral vision, I caught a flash of movement. I spun left to see Soneji stooping forward on the balls of his feet as he took two halting steps, and straightened up.

His mouth opened as if in anticipation of some long-awaited pleasure. His gun hand started to rise.

I shot him twice, the deafening reports making my ears buzz and ring like they'd been boxed hard. Gary Soneji jerked twice, and screamed like a woman before staggering and falling from sight.

CHAPTER
29

MY HEART BOOMED IN my chest, but my brain sighed with relief.

Soneji was hit hard. He was crying, dying there on the canvas-room floor where I couldn't see him.

My pistol still up, I took an uncertain step toward Soneji, and another. A third and fourth step and I saw him lying there, no gun in his hand or around him, looking at me with a piteous expression.

In a high, whimpering voice, he said, "Why did you shoot me? Why me?"

Before I could answer, Soneji went into a coughing fit that turned wet and choking. Then blood streamed from his lips, his eyes started to dull, and the life went out of him with a last hard breath.

"Oh, my God!" Binx screamed behind me. "What have you done?"

"Soncji's gone," I said, feeling intense, irrational pleasure course through me. "He's finally gone."

Binx was crying. I started to turn toward her. She saw the gun in my hand, turned terrified, and leaped out of sight.

Binx had led me into a trap, I thought. Binx had led me here to die.

I ran after her into the main room, saw her running

crazily back the way we'd come in, and heard her making these petrified whining sounds.

"Stop, Ms. Binx!" I yelled after her.

As I did, I caught a shift in the shadows of an alcove at the far end of the room. I looked toward it, shocked to see that beyond two fifty-five-gallon drums, Gary Soneji stood there in the mouth of the alcove, same clothes, same hair, same face, same nickel-plated pistol in hand.

How was that…?

Before I could shake off the shock of there being two Sonejis, he fired at me. His bullet pinged off the post of one of those spotlights trained on the paintings. On instinct, I threw myself toward him, gun up and firing.

My first shot was wide, but my next one spun the second Soneji around just before I landed hard on the cement floor. Doubled over, he went down too, gasping, groaning, and trying to crawl back into the alcove.

I scrambled to my feet, and charged his position. A spotlight went on above the alcove, trying to strike me in the eyes again. But I got my free hand up before it could blind me.

From high and to my right, a gun went off. The bullet blew a chunk of cement out of the floor at my feet.

I dove behind the fifty-five-gallon drums, glanced at the second Soneji, who was still crawling, and leaving a trail of dark blood behind him.

The voice in my head screamed at me to use my phone and call it in. I needed sirens coming now.

Then I heard the sirens, distant but distinct, before another gunshot sounded from up high and to my right again. It smacked the near barrel, the slug making a clanging noise as it ricocheted inside.

I winced, rolled over, and peered up through the narrow gap between the barrels, seeing a third Gary

Soneji standing on the roof of the alcove above the ex-humation painting. He was trying to aim at me with a nickel-plated pistol.

Before he could fire, I did.

The third Soneji screamed, dropped his gun, and grabbed at his thigh before toppling off the roof. He fell a solid ten feet, hit the cement floor hard enough to make cracking sounds. He screamed feebly, then lay there moaning.

I stood up then, shaking with adrenaline, and feeling that beautiful rage explode through me all over again, searing-hot and vengeful.

"Who's next?" I roared, feeling almost giddy. "C'mon, you bastards! I'll kill every single Soneji before I'm done!"

I swung all around, my pistol aiming high and low, finger twitching on the trigger, anticipating another Soneji to appear on the roof of the alcove or from the darkness of the three remaining anterooms.

But nothing moved, and there was no sound except for the moans of the wounded and of Kimiko Binx, who sat in the far corner of the main room, curled up in a fetal position, and sobbing.

CHAPTER
30

KIMIKO BINX WAS STILL crying and refusing to talk to me or to the patrol officers who arrived first on the scene, or to the detectives who came soon after.

Not even Bree could get Binx to make any kind of statement, other than to say sullenly, "Cross didn't have to shoot. He didn't have to kill them all."

The fact was, I had not killed them all. Two of the Sonejis were alive, and there were EMTs working feverishly on them.

"Three Sonejis?" Bree said. "Makes it easy for them to cover ground."

I nodded, seeing how one of them could have shot Sampson, while another staked out Soneji's grave, and the third could have driven by Bree and me outside GW Medical Center.

"You okay, Alex?" Bree asked.

"No," I said, feeling incredibly tired all of a sudden. "Not really."

"Tell me what happened," Bree said.

I did to the best of my abilities, finishing with "But all you really need to know is they set up an ambush, lured me, and I walked right into it."

Bree thought about that, and then said, "There'll be an investigation, but from what you said, it's cut-and-dry. Self-defense, and justified."

I didn't say anything because somehow it didn't seem quite right to me. Justified, yes, but cut-and-dry? They'd tried to kill Sampson, and me, twice. But some of the threads of what had happened just didn't—

"By the way," Bree said, interrupting my thoughts. "The labs came back on the exhumation."

I looked at her, revealing nothing. "And?"

"It was him in the coffin," she said. "Soneji. They compared DNA to samples taken when he was in federal custody the first time. He's dead, Alex. He's been dead more than ten years."

One of the EMTs called out to us before I could express my relief. We went to the Soneji in the far alcove, then the one who'd been crawling away, leaving blood like a snail's track. They'd shot him up with morphine and he was out of it. They'd also cut off his shirt and found the raised latex edge of a mask that could have been crafted by one of Hollywood's finest.

After photographing the mask, we sliced and peeled it off, revealing the ashen face of Claude Watkins, painter, performance artist, and wounded idolizer of Gary Soneji.

The second Soneji was up on a gurney and headed for an ambulance when we caught up to him.

We tore open his shirt, found the latex edge of an identical mask, photographed it, and then had the EMTs slice it off him. The man behind the mask was in his late twenties and unfamiliar to us. But as they wheeled him out, I had no doubt that, whoever he was, he'd been worshipping Gary Soneji for a long, long time.

We waited for the medical examiner to arrive and take custody of the dead Soneji before we cut off the third mask.

"It's a woman," Bree said, her hands going to her mouth.

"Not just any woman," I said, stunned and confused. "That's Virginia Winslow."

"Who?"

"Gary Soneji's widow."

"Wait. What?" Bree said, staring at the dead woman closely. "I thought you said she hated Soneji."

"That's what she told me."

Bree shook her head. "What in God's name possessed her to impersonate her dead husband and then try to kill you? Did she shoot John? Or did Watkins? Or that other guy?"

"One of them did," I said. "I'll put money one of the pistols matches."

"But why?" she said, still confused.

"Binx and Watkins and, evidently, Virginia Winslow made Soneji into a cult, with me being the enemy of the cult," I said, and thought about Winslow's son, Dylan, and the picture of me on his dartboard.

Where was the kid in all of this? Seeing Binx being led out, I thought that if we leaned on her hard enough, she'd eventually want to cut a deal and tell all.

"You look like hell, you know," Bree said, breaking my thoughts again.

"Appreciate the compliment."

"I'm serious. Let's go, let the crime-scene guys do their work."

"No formal statement?"

"You've made enough of a statement to satisfy me for the time being."

"Chief of detectives and wife," I said. "That's a conflict of interest any way you look at it."

"I don't care, Alex," Bree said. "I'm taking you home. You can make a formal statement after you've had a good night's sleep."

I almost agreed, but then said, "Okay, I'll leave. But can we stop by Sampson's room before we go home? He deserves to know."

"Of course," she said, softening. "Of course we can."

I stayed quiet during the ride away from the ambush and shooting scene. Bree seemed to understand I needed space, and didn't ask any more questions on the way to GW Medical Center.

But my mind kept jumping to different aspects of the case. Where had Watkins and Soneji's widow met? Through Kimiko Binx? And who was the other wounded guy? How had he come to be part of a conspiracy to kill me and Sampson?

Riding the elevator to the ICU, I promised myself I'd answer the questions, clean up the case, even though it was all but over.

As the door opened, I felt something sharp on my right arm and jerked back to look at it.

"Sorry," Bree said. "You had a little piece of Scotch tape there."

She showed me the tape, no more than a half inch long, before rolling it between her thumb and index finger and flicking it into a trash can.

I twisted my forearm, to see a little reddish patch, and wondered where I'd picked that up. Probably off Nana Mama's counter earlier in the morning, left over from one of Ali's latest school projects.

It didn't matter because when we reached the ICU, the nurse gave us good news. Sampson was gone, transferred to the rehab floor.

When we finally tracked him down, he was paying his first visit to the physical therapist's room. We went in and found Billie with her palms pressed to her beaming cheeks, and her eyes welling over with tears.

I had to fight back tears, too.

Sampson was not only out of bed, he was out of a wheelchair, up on his feet, with his back to us, using a set of parallel gymnastics bars for balance. His massive arm and neck muscles were straining so hard they were trembling, and sweat gushed off him as he moved one foot and then the other, a drag more than a step with his right leg. But it was incredible.

"Can you believe it?" Billie cried, jumped to her feet, and hugged Bree.

I wiped at my tears, kissed Billie, and broke into a huge grin before clapping and coming around in front of Sampson.

Big John had a hundred-watt smile going.

He saw me, stopped, and said, "'Ow bout that?"

"Amazing," I said, fighting back more emotion. "Just amazing, brother."

He smiled broader, and then cocked his head at me, as if he felt something.

"Wha?" Sampson said.

"I got him," I said. "The one who shot you."

Sampson sobered, and paused to take that in. The therapist offered him the wheelchair, but he shook his head slowly, still staring at me intently, as if seeing all sorts of things in my face.

"F-get him f-now, Alex," John said finally, with barely a slur and his face twisting into a triumphant smile. "Can't yah see I got dance less. . .sons ta do?"

I stood there in shock for a moment. Bree and Billie started laughing. So did Sampson and the therapist.

I did, too, then, from deep in my gut, a belly laughter that soon mixed with deep and profound gratitude, and a great deal of awe.

Our prayers had been answered. A true miracle had occurred.

My partner and best friend had been shot in the head, but Big John Sampson was not defeated and definitely on his way back.

EPILOGUE

TWO DAYS LATER, I awoke feeling strangely out of it, as if I were nursing the last dregs of the worst hangover of my life.

Department protocol dictated I sit on the sidelines on paid administrative leave while the shootings were investigated. After what I'd been through, and because I was feeling so run-down, I should have taken the time to stay home and recover with my family for at least a week.

But I forced myself out of bed and headed downtown to talk with my union representative, a sharp attorney named Carrie Nan. I walked her through the events in the factory. Like Bree, she felt comfortable with me talking to Internal Affairs, which I did.

The two detectives, Alice Walker and Gary Pan, were polite, thorough, and, I thought, fair. They took me through the scenario six or seven times in an interrogation room I'd used often on the job.

I stuck with the facts, and not the swinging emotions of elation and rage that I'd felt during the entire event. I kept it clean and to the point.

The scene was an ambush. In all three shootings, I'd seen a pistol. I'd made a warning. When the pistol was turned on me, I shot to save my life.

Detective Pan scratched his head. "You sound kind of detached when you describe what happened."

"Do I?" I said. "I'm just trying to talk about it objectively."

"Always said you were the sharpest tack around, Dr. Cross," Detective Walker said, and then paused. "After you shot the third Soneji, did you scream something like 'I'll kill every single Soneji before I'm through?'"

I remembered, and it sounded bad, and I knew it.

"They had me surrounded," I said at last. "I was caught in an ambush, and had already engaged with three of them. Did I lose my cool at that point? I might have. But it was over by then. If there were others, they were long gone."

Pan said, "Kimiko Binx was there."

"Yes. What's she saying?"

Walker said, "We're not at liberty to say, Dr. Cross, you know that."

"Sure," I said. "Just being nosy."

Pan said, "There *were* others there, by the way. In the factory."

Before I could say anything, Pan's cell buzzed. Then Walker's.

"What others?" I asked. "I didn't see anyone else."

The detectives read their texts, and didn't answer me.

"Sit tight," Pan said, getting up.

"You need anything?" Walker asked. "Coffee? Coke?"

"Just water," I said, and watched them leave.

There were others there, by the way. In the factory.

I hadn't seen a soul. But was that true? Different spotlights had been aimed at me from different places and angles. There had to have been a fifth person at the least. There had to—

Two men in suits entered the room along with Chief Michaels and Bree. The first three were stone-faced. Bree looked like she was on the edge of a breakdown.

"I'm sorry, Alex, but…," she said, barely getting the words out before she looked to Chief Michaels. "I can't."

"Can't what?" I asked, feeling as if I were suddenly standing with my back to the rim of a deep canyon I hadn't even realized was there.

"Alex," Michaels said. "The third Soneji, the one you shot off the roof of the alcove, died two hours ago. And some very damning information has come forward that directly contradicts your account of the shooting."

"What evidence?" I said. "Who are these guys?"

One of the suits said, "Mr. Cross, I am Special Agent Carlos Ramon with the US Justice Department."

Coming around the table, the other suit said, "Special Agent Jon Christopher, Justice. You are under arrest for the premeditated murder of Virginia Winslow and John Doe. You have the right to remain silent. Anything you say can and—"

I didn't hear the rest. I didn't need to. I'd recited the Miranda warnings a thousand times. As they handcuffed me, I kept looking at Bree, who was crushed, and wouldn't return my gaze.

"You don't believe them, do you?" I said, as Pan started to urge me toward the door and booking. "Bree?"

Bree looked my way finally with devastated, teary eyes. "Don't say another word, Alex. Everything can and will be used against you now."